Let Us Not Talk Falsely Now

Let Us Not Talk Falsely Now

T. Patrick Graves

To order additional copies of this book, contact:
Xlibris
844-714-8691
www.Xlibris.com
Orders@Xlibris.com
842521

For Karen, Kelly & Daniel

Prologue

I KIND OF WANTED to get up front to see and hear Trump, but Peter told us to stay back. We had some clubs, of course, and I kind of figured he was trying to keep us out of trouble. But Trump told us that we were all walking to the Capitol, and that he was coming with us, and that's when Peter told us that we were going to start off to the Capitol right then. There were some others who were headed that way already, maybe 200 or so then.

Lots a people had red hats, carried Trump flags or American flags, even a few Confederate flags which I liked. Lots of people had some other stuff too, I saw plenty of guns.

*Lots of 'em wore shirts that said **Proud Boys** or had some pictures, a bunch of guys wore ones with big green shamrocks with swatsikas in the middle of the shamrocks. Another group of guys was wearing Hawaiian shirts over military fatigue pants. Some of them had flak jackets over their Hawaiian shirts and a couple had assault rifles hanging from their necks. Some guys had shirts with big yellow words, Oath Keepers. A few people wore masks, but it was to keep themselves from being known, I think, not to protect them from the China virus. Everybody I saw was white, although there was an Oriental or two. One guy I recognized was from Des Moines. He was wearing a blue T-shirt with a big Qannon sign right in the middle of it. I liked that. Just lately I've been reading some Q stuff, and it makes so much sense. Some of them were yelling. It wasn't like Charlottesville. They weren't yelling about Jews. They were yelling that*

Biden stole the election, which, I'm pretty sure he did. And something about Pence and Pelosi. Trump. Told us to get them and we were going to try.

When we got to the Capitol there were a few police behind some steel barricades. Wasn't much and I was pretty sure we could get past those guys. I was close to the front and more and more people were coming up behind us. A few people were yelling at the cops. There were only four or five or so and they just kept yelling at us to stand back. I saw one of the Proud Boys grabbing on to the barricade. I didn't do nothin', just watched. All four of us stood together, our clubs down by our sides, our guns and knives hidden by the jackets Peter had told us to wear. Then a couple of other guys were grabbing the barricades. One of the cops hit one of 'em with his big black baton. That pissed us all off and we surged forward. Peter was saying something but damned if I knew what. There was a lot of noise. There was some kind of chant, "Stop the steal" I think it was. Also, "hang Pence."

The barricades came down and the four or five cops started running up the steps toward the building. We followed. By then there had to be four or five hundred of us. Mostly, but not all, men. Quite a few women, in fact. Lots of Trump flags and American flags. A few confederate flags. A few flags had Nazi symbols. By now, I could see quite a few firearms.

When we got up the steps there was another group of guards, Capitol Police, I guess. There were ten or twelve and our numbers were surging. We were within thirty feet or so of the building. We walked up alongside this tall aluminum structure that I didn't know what it was. Someone told me it was for the swearing in. "Let's take it down!" I said, but Peter was right behind me. He told me they'd use it to put Trump into office and never mind. Behind me, they were passing up some timber. We helped pass it up and some rope and I didn't know what it was for. When I left the building later, I saw it was a scaffold and it looked pretty good. 'Course, no one was hanging there, but there was a sign that said it was for Pence.

The Pence stuff all kind of surprised us. I thought he was one of our friends and had stood by the Prez pretty well. But there was lots of shouts of, "Kill Mike Pence," and "we want Mike Pence" and "find the VP." I had heard Trump say something about how Pence wasn't doing the right thing, but I figured, if we got *in there and he was with us, he would do right. He would overturn the election in a heartbeat. It had been stolen. Somebody needed to.*

The police ran back to the building, went in the doors and we followed. I wasn't sure where we were exactly…I'd never been in the building before…but it was locked and there were riot cops on the other side of the door. I looked around, backed up and went down the side of the building 'cause I could see someone tryin' to smash something with a flagpole. Another guy was using a riot shield…didn't know if he'd brought it or taken it from a policeman. Then I heard glass breaking. They kept hammering at it, it broke some more. Then someone went through it. And then the doors to the Capitol opened from the other side.

Guess I should of hesitated. Would it be a crime to go in? I was just finishing probation and couldn't afford…but goddamn it anyway, the President of the United States told us to do it. Which meant, I figured, them cops there were the ones committing a crime.

I followed a few people into the doors. More were coming behind me. I heard later about some skirmishes between us guys tryin' to do the right thing and the cops…but I didn't see anything much like that. Right as we entered into the building there were a few cops tellin' us to back out and leave but we just walked right by them. A few of the cops talked to us, I guess they were admitting we were in the right.

"Hang Mike Pence!" I heard. "Trump won," I heard. "Fraud" I heard. "The President is with us," I heard. And, "Where is Nancy Pelosi?"

We were in this big hallway. Part of the sides were marked off with red cones and we just followed the path it had set out. Didn't see anybody cross those cones. We entered this great big room with a really tall, round ceiling. Parts of it were colored glass. There were some big statues and some big paintings on the wall, most of it was pretty old. You see Washington, Lincoln and some others. Knew they'd be proud of us. Lots of flags were flying. Saw a couple of guys waving theirs, American, one, but with something else in place of the stars. One was a Confederate flag. Thought that was cool. If the guys who carried that flag during the Civil War had been in this building, we might not have had any of these current problems.

Just ahead was the guy in the blue shirt, the guy from Des Moines. We followed him up a flight of stairs. Things kind of stopped for a moment, so I moved up and then I saw this Afro policeman. He was saying something and pushing out with his hands. He shoved the guy from Des Moines and then backed away. He had a baton, I think. We followed him. Figured he was going where we wanted to go. We wanted to go where the votes were being "counted," where the election was being stolen. We followed the black cop up another stairway, then we were outside some great big room. There were a bunch a doors. I heard some guys trying to break in their windows, so I went to the one to my left, extended my baton and then hammered a window. I don't know if I was the first one in the place, seems like a bunch of us went through doors about the same time. It was a mezzanine, like you find in old-time move theaters, I guess. We looked down and there was a big room with a bunch of desks.

Peter came up behind me. "I think this is the Senate chambers," he said. "Cool," I said.

"Ya," he said, "'cept I think the votes are being counted in the other chamber. The House." He turned and walked back through the door I'd walked through. I looked down on the Senate floor. There were a few people by the big desk but nobody by any of the smaller desks. A few people were still going out the doors in back of the room, away from us. I didn't see nobody with a gun and nobody trying to stop us. A few feet from me I saw a guy pull himself over the ledge and drop to the floor of the room. He seemed okay. I thought about going back out, then thought, hell why not? I grabbed the railing and pulled myself over, holding the railing with both hands. Then I let go. Damned if I didn't land on a desk.

A cop walked over to me. "You okay?"

I stood. I was all right. I realized then at least some of the cops were with us.

"Ya," I told him. I sat down by the desk and opened it. There was a newspaper in it and somebody had been working on the crossword puzzle. My ma used to do that. I woulda taken it home to her, if she was still with us. Several Proud Boys entered from the back of the room. "Come on," one of 'em said, "search the desks. We'll find some of the things we need."

Underneath the crossword was a map of Texas and an iPad. I slipped the iPad in my back pack. Then there were some papers, something about the election results in Michigan and Pennsylvania. Thought that was part of what we needed, I didn't know for sure. I walked 'em up to the front where a couple of Proud Boys was looking through papers.

"Good!" one of 'em said, taking my papers, "Look through another desk."

Looked through another couple of desks and took them the papers then I walked out the back door of the place. Walked down a corridor that was pretty jammed with people. A few were trying to open some doors, but they were jammed good. Kept walking until we got to another hallway. Turned left and walked and then got to another big hallway that went down. A few of us started down the stairs and when we did we saw about four older guys in suits, walking toward us. There were a couple of other guys there who I was pretty sure were guards, looked like former Marine guys to me. One of the guys in the suit I recognized. Some kind of Mormon guy and Peter has told me that guy is doing wrong. They all turned around in a hurry and kind of hurried back down the stairs. I never saw them again. We kept walking down the stairs… no hurry now, after all, the place was ours.

I ran into another hallway and turned left again, walked down with about five more people then down another long hallway, up some steps and found the other big room. Peter was in front and he was looking through this huge desk in front. "What's up?" I asked.

He lifted his head. "Oh, Nick," he said, "we were hoping to find the ballots. But I think they got 'em out. Maybe that's why they shot that young lady."

"They shot somebody? Who?"

Peter looked up. "Not sure, shot by a cop I guess." He looked back down but kept talking to me. "Seen Ricky or Harry?"

"Nah."

"I think we should go while we can."

So the two of us walked back out of the room and around another great big room with paintings. Someone had spray painted signs on some of them, swatiskas and red plus signs. We saw an exit door and headed out. We were on a big patio, then, and had to walk down steps and away from the building.

We walked over to the street and then in front of another building and waited for Ricky and Henry. We were headed home. We hadn't found the ballots, nor Mike Pence nor that Pelosi dame, but I was pretty sure we changed things. People would know better.

I missed Johnny of course, he was always the best when we got into it with somebody, but that's another story. Just wish he'd been with us. "Jews will not replace us." "The election's been stolen." Trump said so.

BOOK ONE

there must be some way out of here

There must be some way out of here
Said the joker to the thief
There's too much confusion, I can't get no relief
Businessmen, they drink my wine
Plowmen dig my earth
None of them along the line know what any of it is worth

No reason to get excited, the thief he kindly spoke
There are many here among us who feel that life is but a joke
But you and I, we've been through that, and this is not our fate
So let us not talk falsely now, the hour is getting late

Bob Dylan, "All Along the Watchtower"

One

NICK SAYS, "LET'S go to the Starbucks," but I say no and we go for coffee at a local shop, Grounds for Appeal, or some such bullshit. He wants to know why, but I don't say anything 'cause he doesn't need to know why. The Starbucks the last time I was there in the morning had a black guy making the coffee, being the barista. As if you could teach that monkey how to prepare a good cup of American coffee. And I don't want no Afro making my latte. It's too bad, 'cause I do like a Starbucks; still, they're anti-gun, so this is strike two.

You're going to think I hate all Afroes. That's just not true. I know some that I like just fine. I have worked with some that I kind of like. I've spent time in jail with some I could tolerate, although most got that smell. Jail smell is bad anyway. Afro jail smell is just overwhelming. So it just ain't true that I hate Afroes. There's some that's fine. They know what's what. They know we don't need to mix the races. They want as little to do with white people as I want to do with them. But there's lots of 'em I can't stand. There's some that think this is their country too, that they're as good as us, and I just can't stand that bullshit. I just want them and you and Nick and everyone to understand that this country is white, it was made by whites and made for whites, and it's going to hell in a handbasket. And it will so long as the white race does not stand up for itself. It's just pitiful to see white people who want to be a part of the coon culture. Sad.

We sit at Grounds for Punishment—that ain't its fruity-tooti name either—and we talk Trump. Jesus, nothing has given me hope like this. I should know better. I mean I've been sorely disappointed before, but by God, we have to make sure that bitch Hillary is not our next president. It's been shameful enough with Barry Hussein Somalia acting like he's all white and belongs in the White House, him and his Afro family. And Trump is the guy who can stop her, I can feel that. But mostly, mostly, I know he's the man 'cause of how the media hates him. Have you ever seen the girls at CNN get their panties in a bunch like when they're talking about the Donald?

A skinny little white girl brings our coffees to the table. She hasn't got much of a behind and I can't tell that there's any chest at all, but she has a cute smile and I like how she pushes her hair out of her eyes when she asks us if we need anything else.

Mainly though, it's her Southern accent that gets me going. I may have to live here in Des Moines now, but by God, I'm a Southern boy through and through and I live or die by the Crimson Tide and NASCAR nation and I listen to Eric Church and Tim McGraw and Brooks and Dunn. I carry a Glock in my purse (the Germans know how to make shit), and I've got a Thompson rifle with a gorgeous sight and a twelve-gauge pump-action in the back of my pickup. And I'm trying to identify her by her accent.

"Well, thanks, darling," Nick says, but I stop him. I know just what he'll say. *What I want ain't on the menu.* She might giggle at that, or she might sigh in disgust and walk away. I don't let either of those things happen.

"Hush," I say, "just hush. I think I hear South Carolina . . . not the seashore but up in them lush Appalachia mountains. Is that what I hear, darling?" I turn to her.

She laughs. "How'd you know?"

"We children of the Confederacy have got to stick together," I tell her.

"Maybe, maybe not," she says, "but I'm from right near Charleston, practically on the seashore."

She winks at me but then turns around and leaves to serve somebody else and then Nick and I get down to business. Nick works with me on construction. He does framing and I do siding, which pays a little better. Ain't enough. Ain't enough when you got child support and you got to pay the government more than half so the Afros in this country can get food stamps and other kinds of welfare and sit home on their asses and people get to not pay their mortgages but stay in their houses. We work Friday and Saturday nights at Quality Point Security, usually working bars, but sometimes music festivals. It's part-time. We work for Howard, a big hulking man that Nick served with in Iraq. Between the two gigs, we get by.

Except, Nick has another idea: a quicker return on our investment. He knows I've been in jail. He knows I know my way around. He says he's been thinking about this for a while and he's looked at more than one opportunity, but now, he thinks he found one. One that's surefire. Surefire as long as the men know what they're doing, ain't scared, and are ready to act.

Nick thinks he's ready for this shit because he was in the shit. He served in the 402nd National Guard unit, infantry, out of Boone and they got deployed to Iraq. He's seen some nasty shit, I'm sure. But this is different. This ain't about killing or being killed and it ain't about technology and it ain't about following orders from some straight-laced cocksure little first lieutenant who don't know shit that don't come out of a book.

"Nick," I say, "you just shut up now. We'll talk about this after we have our coffee."

"But see," he says, all excited.

"Jenny don't get off for another hour," I tell him. "So let's drink our lattes and then we'll get in my truck, where nobody can hear us, and then we'll do the talking."

So we talk Trump. Hell yes, he'll build that wall. And hell yes, Mexico will pay for it. And the best part will be when he puts Hillary in jail. Goddamn Clintons. A disgrace to Arkansas, although she ain't really from there.

Nick is still thinking about the wall. "But how, Johnny" he asks. "How we going to make Mexico pay for it?"

"Well, don't you think Trump can figure that out?" I ask. "How you think he built all those towers and casinos and golf courses? Don't you think he can figure out how to build a wall and how to make those beaners pay for it?"

And Nick has to agree.

He starts to tell me. I stop him. "No," I say, "no, you won't be wearing camouflage and carrying an assault rifle, and you won't just be able to shoot anybody who speaks Farsi."

He nods.

"I'm the one who's going to run this little operation. So we'll follow your guy. And we'll do it like you say, but, but this is important. It don't matter how long we take. If we gotta follow him day after day, night after night for weeks, we're going to do it when the moment's right, not a moment before and not a moment after. Capisce?"

"What the fuck's that mean—capisce?" he asks. "Is that Jew talk?"

"Think it might be camel jockey," I say, laughing now.

Jenny is pregnant and showing. I'm not sure how many months, 'cause it's none of my business, but it seems like she shouldn't be standing on her feet anymore. I park right by the front door, even though I'm not supposed to, and she hustles out of the Walmart just a couple of minutes after her time to check out.

She opens the passenger door, crawls in, shuts it, lights a cigarette she's had cupped in her hand, and I take off slowly, because there are always lots of people walking out of Walmart. Beaners. Niggers. Foreigners of all kinds, some of them wearing their Muslim crap. I ain't yet seen a woman in a full burka at Walmart, but some of them African women with their robes come mighty close.

"How you doing?" she asks. "And thanks for picking me up."

"Glad to."

"Oh," she says, "I know you do it as duty to my dad, but it's still nice of you."

Her dad is Peter, as in Peter Thurgood. Ya, that Peter Thurgood. Leader of the Posse Comitatus. Communications director of the White Aryan Brotherhood, Midwest. Editor of the best goddamn website this side of Breitbart—well, frankly, more sound ideologically than Breitbart. It's called The Right Way. He started it as The Aryan Way, as a pamphlet. After a few years, he got on the Internet and decided that it sounded better not to include Aryan in the title. I know that was controversial in some circles, and at first I hated it. I am proud to be Aryan and I think we should all be. But Peter convinced me that we are looking for a wider tent, that we need new recruits all the time, that our movement is growing and calling it Right instead of Aryan would comfort some of the people who might eventually like to join us or, at least, help us.

Same thing goes with tattoos. All my running mates have them, of course, but now we're convincing people not to make them obvious. I can't get rid of the swastika on my forearm, of course, but a long-sleeved shirt covers it. My three new tattoos, Nazi-based all of them, are places most people wouldn't normally see.

Peter is a giant. But I met him at Aryan camp at Jester State Park when I was just a kid. He seemed like the fatherly type. He didn't speak at the general rally but had a little tent for the kids. When the kids had their education meetings, it was Peter who spoke, telling them they should be proud of their heritage, proud of their race. It was Peter who told us about Western civilization, asked how many popes were white. How many kings? Emperors? How many presidents were white? How many prime ministers of England were white?

Asked us who the greatest scientists were, who the greatest astronomers were, who the greatest explorers were. Made it clear to us that white people created civilization and moved it forward. White people. While the Indians were still in tepees and living off buffalo hunts, while the blacks were still in African tribes, killing each other with spears, we were exploring the world. I am one of

Peter's lieus now, one of his lieutenants, and I couldn't be prouder. Jenny's husband is in jail again, as usual, for driving while revoked, and so I try to help with Jenny. It's not a long drive to Peter's house, but it would take two buses and Jenny's in no shape for that kind of shit.

I walk her to the door. Usually, Peter would invite me in, give me a beer, show me his latest blog. Tonight, he's got instructions for me. So I take the paper and go back to my truck and drive toward Drake University.

Drake is a private *liberal arts* school, with lots of students from Chicago and Minneapolis, but it's located in the city's largest ghetto. Cheap, decrepit old houses and apartments surround the campus, but the campus itself is all fine new concrete-and-glass buildings with sandwich and coffee shops on the first floor of the dorm buildings.

I'm looking for a kike professor. I've heard a little about him. He's always preaching the Holocaust . . . Holocaust this, Holocaust that, like it justifies the economic slavery we are all experiencing at the hands of the rich Jews in this country. But lately, he's been on local television all the damn time talking about Trump's Muslim ban. I can't make up my mind whether Trump is right about the Muslims or, like he says, he's just trying to keep them out so they don't blow up any more buildings. But honest to God, unless we go back to being a Christian nation, we're fucking doomed.

I pick up Corey on the way. Corey is good to have with in a fight, not that I expect that little Hebe to put up much of a fight. Somehow, Peter knows that this little Hebe professor is going to be walking out of his office building—he teaches at Meredith Hall—and going over to Woody's on Forest Avenue. I don't know why he's walking. It's only about four blocks and the schizo liberal probably drives a Prius—but never mind. Peter finds out shit like this, and plans. He's taught me this. Planning is everything.

From Meredith, he probably walks on campus to Thirtieth, then crosses, walks behind that new dorm and across the parking lot, which is not well lighted, to Woody's. If he doesn't do that, we'll miss him, because Corey and I pull into the student parking lot, turn off the lights, and walk over to a grassy spot between two lots. We stand idling, smoking cigarettes and don't really seem out of the ordinary. It's close to nine now, and dark, and I see someone coming our way. It's two people, which isn't really much of a problem, a man and a woman, but the man is tall and overweight and he ain't that little Hebe we're looking for.

They walk by—usual Iowans. "Good evening."

"Yes," I say, "nice out tonight."

A couple of students walk by and they are still in hailing distance when I see a small man in a rumpled suit with a goatee, walking our way but looking down, not paying much attention.

As he nears me, I call out, "Professor? Professor Lowenthal?"

He stands straighter, lifts his head, looks at me. Not a worry in the world. Just like he was a white man walking.

"Yes," he says.

"I saw you on the news," I say, "and I just wanted to shake your hand."

"Well," he says, "well," and he walks up to me and puts out his right hand.

My baton is behind my back. I release it at the same time that I punch him, just at the bottom of his rib cage. I hear *oof*, and the man is down on his hands and knees just like that.

"You fucking Jew asshole," I say, as I blast the top of his head with the baton. Now he's on the ground, and I think he might be crying. Corey kicks him in the side, once, twice, again. I reach down, searching for a cell phone. It's a new Apple and I enjoy stepping on it, especially when I hear the glass breaking. I think 'bout finding his wallet, but Peter's instructions are always clear on this point. We do not want anyone to think we are stealing. We are at war. We are soldiers in the war for a white, Christian nation.

"You're a sick homo Jew cunt," I tell him, stepping on his left hand and grinding down with my boot. "Go back to Israel."

He looks up but I am turning and Corey and I go to our car and squeal out of the parking lot, headed east toward downtown, just in case. By the time we hit the freeway and turn west, the police, if they've been called, are searching the Drake area.

Two

I T WAS DARK. But we weren't wearing ski masks because, well, that would have been kind of obvious to anyone who'd see us. So I assumed the Drake Hebe could try to identify us. This was not my first rodeo. Even before I hooked up with Peter's crew, I ran with some talented Aryan commandos. Mainly, we messed up gays. I never knew why those guys were so into the gays, when there are lots of white gays and they may be messed up, of course, but they aren't the real problem.

I went to jail for one of those raids, and it was one of the most famous and one of the biggest disasters for us too. We pulled it off down at Pullman Place, near Methodist hospital, where they built about a hundred little cottages and gave 'em to poor black people to live in. 'Course, it quickly became a haven for drugs and for women raising their babies without their men, most of whom were in jail or prison, or in some other baby momma's bed. My commandant at the time, Tony, wanted us to go down to the playground and bust up some drug deals. There was a debate about what to do with the drugs: destroy them or sell them.

There was no debate about what to do with the money, or the guys we caught there selling and buying drugs. Even if the guys were white, they were going to take it from us that night. We drove three cars down there, parked behind the massage parlor, where they wouldn't be noticed, brought out our baseball bats, and hiked up the hill in the dark. We ran across a wino drinking cheap gut vino on the hill and a woman walking down the hill toward the Kwik Trip. You'd think one of them would have been bothered by us, but they didn't seem to be. They ignored us.

When we got up the hill, we walked down a narrow path to just below the playground. We were crouched down on the ground, looking out at the activity in the playground. There were three different guys there in hoodies. Young men and women, and even a couple of kids, would walk out onto the playground, then we'd see them touch hands with one guy, then go over to another guy and do the same. The first was payment, the second delivery. Of what drugs, we weren't sure.

It was cold that night and I was a little scared and I was shaking just a bit. Tony put his arm on my shoulder and told me something about how I'd do great once I got in it. *I'd do great?* I was a brawler from way back, and Tony might have skills, but I could put him down easily any time I felt like it. I was bigger, stronger, and meaner.

Finally, we got up and walked toward the playground. This demonstrates the need for reconnaissance. None of us knew that there was a fence on our side of the playground. Oh, it wasn't much of a fence, just a steel rod at about thirty inches, but we all had to climb over it. By that time, they could see us coming. Two of three people took off running for the parking lot. I was surprised that none of the gangbangers did. They all stood there, waiting. Four guys, two of whom had been selling drugs and two more who, apparently, were part of the deal.

"Get the fuck out, crackers," one of them yelled at us.

"Us?" Tony asked, "You talking to us?"

I didn't worry about talk. I still don't usually worry about talk. It's overrated. Action counts for a lot more. I was walking with the bat by my side, unlike most of the crew, who were holding them out in front of them. I just walked up to the first guy and used my bat on his lower leg.

He yelled, "Motherfucker," and went down on one knee. Before anyone could do anything else, I beaned him and he was out.

"Fucking assholes!" somebody yelled, but then, as the other ten or so guys in our crew went to work, one of those Afroes drew a revolver. If you've ever seen gangbangers shoot, you'll know what I mean. He could have killed me easily. But he pulled out his gun, extended his arm, pointed his gun parallel to the ground—do they all do this because of what they've seen in the movies?—and blasted away. Nothing came close to me and by the time he'd let out three shots, I had pushed my bat hard into his belly and he'd released his revolver.

Unfortunately, from behind, I heard someone shout and then I heard someone say, "Barnes is hit."

From the corner, one of the guys who had just seemed to be standing there had pulled out his own piece though, and shooting just like his buddy (arm extended but gun turned sideways), he was firing off rounds.

Which was when it struck me, *Tony is an idiot.* He'd figured out everything but that drug dealers at a Afro housing project might be armed.

Somebody hit the guy with the second revolver and then two of them were on him, wailing on him with their bats. But behind me I heard our crew leaving. "Get out, get out now," Tony was yelling. I turned and got to the fence, but there I saw one of our crew on the ground.

"Don't leave me," I heard him crying.

I dropped my bat, kneeled down, and dragged him up, but he could barely move. He'd been hit by a bullet in the thigh and was bleeding pretty good. It was really hard to get him over the fence. I heard a couple more of our crew running by me. Then I practically dragged him down the hill. Ahead of me, I heard sirens and then cars leaving. I just kept working my way down the hill, dragging my compatriot, a younger white guy whom I didn't even know.

When we got to the parking lot, there were three police cars waiting for us.

"Stop right there," one of them yelled. "You're under arrest."

"Thank God you're here," I said. "He needs help. He's bleeding."

I was in jail for almost three months. My public defender kept bringing me offers: "Tell who did it, tell who planned the raid, who was with you, and the State of Iowa will cut you a sweetheart deal." But in the end, as I expected, the gangbangers couldn't be located to be witnesses and nobody had actually seen me do anything but drag the shooting victim down the hill.

While I was sitting in jail, Peter visited me. Visitors at the Polk County Jail are on a kind of Skype system. But Peter had come into the regular part of the jail to meet with me in private in one of the professional rooms. This usually required an attorney or counselor and sometimes a minister. I didn't ask him how he did it. I had heard him in camp before, at our rallies, but I didn't really know him. He asked me why no one had bailed me out.

"No one all that interested in seeing me out," I told him.

"Family?"

I told him how I never had a dad. And I told him how my mother left Mississippi because her boyfriend was beating us, her kids. When I turned sixteen, I left home. Sometime later, my mother moved and I'm not sure where.

"Hmmm," Peter said, "what about a girlfriend?"

"Guess she's not that interested," I told him. "She calls me in here sometimes, but when I asked about bail, she said she didn't think she could raise it."

He asked me about jail conditions, then asked me about who was in the jail. "Mainly jigaboos?" he asked me.

"Maybe half and half," I said.

"Which says a lot," Peter said, "since Des Moines is less than a tenth black. How about beaners?"

"Ya, there's quite a few of them too," I said. "They hang by themselves."

"Any Aryan movement?"

"Not that I've seen. A guy here and there, but most people are in and out of here pretty quick. The ones, like me, who are in for a while, tend to try to stay out of trouble."

"Understood," he said.

Peter sat back. "I hear," he said, "you really shined the other night over at coonville."

"The whole thing was a goddamn disaster," I said, "one big fuckup."

Peter smiled. Then he laughed, lightly.

"Ya," he said, "I heard that too. But I heard you were righteous, brought a fallen comrade down the hill to safety."

"Is he all right? My lawyer told me he got out of the hospital, but that's all I've heard."

"He's going to be fine," Peter told me, "thanks to you. That was pretty impressive, man."

"I don't know."

"Why'd you do it?"

"You don't leave your comrade behind."

"OK," he said, standing, "when you get out, come see me."

Peter is a little on the thin side, but he has broad shoulders and a thick neck. You might call him wiry. Then I didn't know—today I do—that he's well-muscled. He has been at this for a while, I knew that.

"Can you talk to me for a minute?" I asked.

He sat back down.

"How'd you get back here?"

Peter laughed, just a little. "I'm the pastor of the First Reorganized Church of the American Baptists. Ha! Made the whole thing up, but we have it recognized by the state."

"I want to talk to you about something," I said.

"OK," he said, sitting back in his green plastic chair.

"There are some black guys in here—"

"Some Afroes."

"Ya, some Afroes. There's some in here that ain't so bad."

"See," he said, becoming animated, "this is what I tell people. Being a fighter is all well and good, but it don't help nothing if you don't understand. Ideology is destiny. We don't hate Afroes. No. We hate fags maybe, a little. The point is, Afroes and whites should live apart. And this, this is our country. That's the point. You can like a

Afro, an individual one. You can be nice to one. But you can't agree that they have equal rights."

"I get that."

"So don't sweat being nice to a Afro now and then, especially ones that know their place. What we need, see, is a new country, a country just for Afroes."

He smiled. I didn't know if he was joking or what.

"They had one of those once, you know. Monrovia. In Africa. It was settled by American slaves."

"You're shitting me," I said.

"No, son, you got a lot to learn. You got a place to live when you get out of here?"

"Nah," I admitted, "pretty sure I lost my apartment 'cause I been in here too long."

"That you did," he told me, "but we got your stuff out and loaded it into the little place I got above my garage. When you get out, you can stay there until you can afford to pay rent."

"I appreciate that. Any particular reason you're being so nice to me?"

"You may have a lot to learn," Peter told me, "but it's easier to teach somebody than to find a cold-blooded fighter. They're damned hard to come by. Can't teach somebody courage."

He left me two books by Ayn Rand. He told me there were some other good books, but it wouldn't be safe to have me walking around the jail with them. I'd get them on the outside. I wasn't much for reading, and these were seriously big books, but Peter was, well, Peter. He was the closest thing in Iowa we had to Tom Metzger. I picked up *The Fountainhead*—big book. *Howard Roark laughed. He stood naked at the edge of a cliff. The lake lay far below him.* And I never looked back.

We went to trial on a Wednesday morning. The prosecutor kept trying to put things off, but Adrian, my public defender, told me we weren't going to waive speedy trial and they'd only have ninety days.

I got to the courthouse, and Peter had brought me some of my clothes. I put on gray slacks (they barely fit, the food in the jail is so carb-intense that I'd put on pounds), a black shirt, and a pair of black sneakers. I didn't look all that good, but when the deputy took me to the courtroom, it was all over but the shouting.

"He's making you a really good offer," Adrian told me. "In fact, it's absurd. He's going to let you plead to simple assault and go, time served."

"Ya, why is that?" I asked.

None of the state's witnesses had shown up, and my case was dismissed. I was free to go. Peter was in the back of the courtroom, smiling.

Three

WE LAY LOW after that hit at Drake. That's always smart. If you strike again too soon, some cop might put two and two together and then you're facing charges. So after a good hit like that fag Jew professor, you stay low, keep your head down, go about your life. I stayed away from the Drake campus, of course, and away from the Des Moines police.

I live now in the flat above Peter's garage. It's OK. It's one big bedroom, a bathroom with a shower, and a small kitchen area that includes a small folding table I found at Walmart. I probably wouldn't shop there, but that's where I pick up Jenny. When I bring a girl to the place, they don't seem too impressed, and they're usually looking for a little weed. I enjoy grass myself, don't get me wrong, but as Peter says, it's the easiest way to get locked up. So I keep a couple of bottles of Jack and several cold bottles of Blue Moon in the fridge. The fridge is about ready to give out, and I'm not sure what I'm going to do 'bout it because the space it's in just isn't big enough for the units they make today. I looked all over Menards, and they didn't have nothing that would fit in that space, so like I said, I'm worried.

I don't have much free time. The best work right now is out west of the city, Waukee, which is growing leaps and bounds. There's a good reason for that, Peter explained to me. It's in Dallas County, unlike Des Moines, and so taxpayers out there don't have to pay taxes to keep the Afroes on welfare like we do in the city. But I kind of like the city, especially downtown. They're building a lot of apartments downtown now, and I could probably find work there if I wasn't busy pretty full-time in Waukee.

Downtown Des Moines is now full of bars and restaurants and theaters and comedy clubs and a nice little jazz and blues music bar called the Wabash Club. It's kind of a dive. I don't know why the owner won't put any money into the building, guess he's waiting for some big builder to come along and put up a tower and then buy him out at top dollar. The bands are usually Afro bands, of course. But this is an example of how the uneducated don't understand the movement. I love jazz. It's true, I like Brubeck and Stan Getz better than Charlie Parker or those boys, but I think that's just 'cause I'm white. You get it, I hope. Whoever sounds the sweetest is who I go to listen to, even Afro bands.

It's also full of gay bars. We even got a gay state senator in this town. And shit, is he coiffed and good-looking. Should have been a girl, I guess. See, and this is the thing, I'm not all that worried about this gay shit until they want to stick it in our faces. Leave us alone, fag, and we'll do the same.

Nick tells me the guy is ready to be hit but I tell him I have to lie a little low in Des Moines, per Peter's orders.

"Why should we take his orders?" Nick asks me.

I just looked at him. I mean I just stare at him, right there, looking through him.

"Ya," he says.

"You know why," I say.

"Ya."

"Does this drug dealer ever work out in the burbs?" I ask.

"Ya, maybe," Nick says. "But how we going to know?"

"Look," I say, "I told you we need some reconnaissance, didn't I? Trail the boy—that's all. Trail him for a little while."

None of the Des Moines Afro drug dealers are really big-time, see. Most of them are penny-ante, really penny-ante. The drugs mostly come in here from Mexico. The beaners make it down there because no one cares especially if they're sending it up here. We're on the Matamoras route, straight up from The Valley, then Dallas, then through Kansas City to here. Mules usually, guys who barely speak English but know where they're supposed to deliver the product.

Nick does what I say, but it doesn't go well. He stands out like a turd in a punch bowl, and the boys figure he's a cop or something and move on. He doesn't find out where.

I talk to Peter. He gives me the blessing to go for it. What we're doing, he says, doesn't really impress him as the same kind of thing as the hit on the fag and he doesn't think police will put two and two together. But he tells me to be careful. "You're needed for bigger things."

Two nights later, we're wearing our dark stocking caps. We had smeared a little greasepaint on our cheekbones and kept the light off in the car. We got the car there early—that's usually the key—about a block and half away and pointed away from him. Then I used my LL Bean binoculars to watch him. He's operating in the parking lot of a barber shop about a black and half east of Drake. This was almost always a two-man operation. You paid one person, you got the drugs from another. But according to Nick, this was a little different. Blacky we called him, not knowing his name. Blacky would stand on the corner wherever he'd set up, and his guys would bring him money. After a couple of twilight hours, he'd leave again, having been greeted by six to eight of his people. Sometimes, Nick told me, there'd be some muscle there with him, a hulking huge-bellied and huge-shouldered six-foot-five-inch behemoth of a Afro. Bald too—that always looks more formidable for some damn reason. Sometimes, there weren't, hence our surveillance. Nick just wanted to hit him about an hour and half in one night when he didn't have muscle with him.

"No," I told him. "No, we wait. We follow the pattern. We see what's going down."

About five thirty, just before the sun was going to set, he got into his black SUV and turned west down University Avenue. He kept going then and pulled into a house on Forty-fourth. The house was fairly nondescript, hardly anything at all noticeable, except that there were three other black SUVs in the driveway and on the streets in front. Plus, when I looked at the place as we drove by, I could see that the basement windows had bars. This wasn't exactly downtown, and it wasn't one of the high-crime areas either. It was kind of the middle-class area of the city, not quite as nice as the suburbs, but somewhere people moved to before they moved to the burbs. It was a brown stucco house with a one-car garage. Our man drove into the driveway, walked into the house without knocking, and then we waited. A little over two hours later, he walked back out, and so did three other goons. One of them was actually white, one a beaner, and one was a fellow homeboy. I figured they were all a little lighter in the pocketbook too.

"You see," I told Nick, punching him lightly on the shoulder. "You see, we found ourselves a much bigger kill."

We watched that Afro for two more weeks. While his times varied, his location varied, and the muscle men varied, in fact, even the runners who paid him varied, the house on Forty-fourth was solid. Always there, always where the man took the cash—or so we assumed. And I began to formulate a plan.

I picked up Jenny from Walmart again. I took her home. She said her stomach hurt and her feet hurt. "You shouldn't be workin'," I told her. "You're just gonna have to quit that job. It's not good for you or the baby."

She laughed. "Come in," she said. "Daddy's gone. I got some beer, and I'd love to have some company."

Here's the thing about Jenny. I know she's pregnant now and I know she don't have the perfect face, but she's got a killer bod, or will again, if and when she trims back the weight she'd gained having this baby. Plus, she has a really sweet smile and a really sweet disposition. I don't know whether she's as smart as Peter, but I know she's got a great heart.

Strangely enough, she's barely even a part of the movement. I'm not sure she even really believes.

She brings out two Blue Moons. I myself like a Corona, but I think that Peter bans any Mexican beers. She cuts an orange in slices, and because we're drinking from bottles, we squeeze a little orange juice into our drinks.

She pulls off her shoes and socks and stretches her legs out on the sofa. She's wearing slacks and a light cotton blouse.

"Shit, my dogs hurt," she says.

"I'll bet," I tell her.

I'm wearing a green T-shirt and jeans and work boots. I just stay sitting in my chair, sipping a beer.

"So," she says, "what's up?"

Here's where I get tongue-tied. I mean I can talk to my pro-Aryan comrades, I can talk to people at work, and I can talk to women generally when we're out. But with Jenny, I just never know what to say. She's cute. She's also got a guy and pregnant. Worse, she's Peter's daughter.

"Nothin' really," I say.

She smiles, then chuckles just a little. She extends her legs again, this time onto the chair next to me.

"Oooh," she says, "they are really sore."

Finally, after hesitating, I take her right foot, lift it onto my leg, put my beer on the table, then start massaging the ball of her foot.

"Oh man," she said, "that feels good. This is something Antonio would never do."

"His loss," I say, "his loss."

Gently, as I've been taught, but firmly, I massage her right foot. Jenny closes her eyes and leans back. "Oh God, Johnny," she says. "Oh God, that feels good."

When I finish, I lower the right foot and bring the left one up, holding it in my hands, and I knead and push and rub her sore, swollen foot.

To my surprise, she doesn't say anything more. To my surprise, I see her swollen belly rise and fall, and I hear a light, soft snore.

Four

WHEN I WAS seven years old, I spent three months in a foster home. One morning I was lying in my bed, when I felt someone touching me through the sheet. I expected to see my mother, but another woman was there, a very large, ebony-colored woman with hair all drawn up in a beehive. I must have reacted physically, moving backward and away from her, because she reached out, clutched my legs, and told me, "Now, now, honey, you got nothing to worry about."

"The check's in the mail" was still one of the big lies, but the biggest lie I now know is "I'm from social services and we are here to help you." Honest to God, the only people who don't know that social services is only there so they can fuck up families are people so well off that they never have to deal with social services. In Iowa, they're called the DHS. When this woman showed up in my bedroom, my mother was outside on the couch with two police officers, hands cuffed, under arrest, because my father—the man who fathered me, at least—was never in our lives. It didn't used to matter too bad when we lived in Mississippi, because my grandma and my poppa were only a town away. They'd come see us regularly, and when they didn't, we'd go see them. Grandma would make pancakes or French toast for me. She'd make roasts and stews and fried chicken. They didn't have much—now I see that. They just had a little house right outside Oxford, but they never seemed to mind giving things to me.

I had a teddy bear the whole time I was growing up. My mama told me that Grandpa gave it to me on my first birthday. I had a little radio above my bed. My grandma gave it to me one Christmas. I had a tricycle, although we didn't have any sidewalks to use it on. My grandpa brought it over for my fifth birthday. We lived in a little shack, a duplex, I now know, with an older couple on the other side of the house. Trouble was, they didn't appreciate noise and I was a kid. My life consisted of making noise. The old man yelled at me all the time. I think the old woman liked me all right, because she was sweet to me when the old man wasn't around, but not otherwise.

We didn't have much for furniture, and what we had was old and seemed broken. To me it was normal. The only other house I knew was my grandparents', and their furniture was even older.

We had an old green couch that Momma kept a sheet over, because there were big tears in the cushions and on the back. We had one chair, an old recliner in a brown leather, and we called it Grandpa's, because any time he came to see us, he sat in it. No one else tried to use it. At night, though, Momma would sit there, reading, usually books that came from the library. We had a TV, an old boxy one (this was before the days of the flat screen) that stood out in the middle of the living room. Well, it was a living room and a dining room and a kitchen, I guess. We did have a bathroom and two bedrooms, so that was something. I had a box spring, which was on the floor and a mattress on that. It was getting a little small for me by the time we moved to Iowa.

We moved to Iowa within a few months of my grandpa dying. No one ever told me what he died of, but I saw him at the funeral home. He was in the coffin. He had on a white shirt and a tie. I never saw my grandpa even one time wear a tie while he was alive. His hands were clasped together and his eyes were closed. But his face didn't look right. The color was out of it, and his mouth was bigger, swollen, I now understand. And he had a rosary in his hands.

"But we ain't Catholic," I remember my momma saying. "It's Catholics that have rosaries."

"Never mind," my grandma told her. "You never mind. I think it looks nice."

The next day, we watched them put Grandpa in the ground. I remember that Momma and I were there, and Uncle Edward and another old man I'd never met before. They explained to me he was Grandpa's brother from Tennessee. I'd never met him before. Funny thing—he cried. He cried through the funeral and at the grave. I never remember my mama crying, and I'm pretty damn sure my grandma didn't cry either, tough old bird.

When it was done, my mama went to the car—she had an old substitute car, copper in color with a silver fins sticking out—and brought out a paper bag. She placed the bag in the back of Uncle Earl's pickup truck.

"Now, Johnny," she said, "Grandma needs you right now."

"Tsk," was all Grandma said.

"Tsk, yourself," Momma said. She leaned down and kissed my forehead. "You're going to Grandma's for a while so she's not alone."

"But, Momma," I said, "I got school."

"Shh," she said, "most boys'd be happy to skip school."

"He ain't skipping school," Grandma said. "I already got him registered in Hattiesburg."

I didn't see my mama again for six months. I never knew why. When she drove up to the house one morning in August, she had a different car. It was a newer Ford, a little one; it was green, and she had several bags of stuff in the back seat. She also had a swollen left eye and a nasty-looking cut on her right cheek.

"What happened?" Grandma asked, but I just ran to her, put my arms around her waist, and started to cry. "Momma," I said, "Momma."

"Now you be quiet, Johnny," she told me. "Go get the stuff out of the back seat and bring it into the house."

"No, Johnny, don't do that," my grandma said.

"Momma . . ." my momma said, and I thought she was going to cry.

"Don't momma me," I heard Grandma say. "Where you been? I lost my husband of some forty-four years, and you never even come by to see if I'm all right. And you leave that . . . that bastard boy of yours with me . . . well, he and me is doin' all right. You can come in for iced tea and leftover chicken potpie if you want, but be gone by his bedtime."

"He ain't got no bedtime—" Momma started.

"He does now," Grandma insisted.

Momma turned to me. She looked me over. I was wearing a nice pair of shorts and a T-shirt, my hair was cut, and I wore white socks in my sneakers. In short, she probably wondered what had come over me.

"Johnny," Momma said, "get your things."

"Don't do this," my grandma said, "don't do this to the boy. Please, Sandy, don't do this to the boy."

"Momma," my own mama said, "I got no place to go. Isn't home the one place you can always come back to?"

"One night," my grandma said, putting her hands on my shoulders, turning me toward the house, "one night. You can sleep in your dad's room. Johnny's in our old bedroom."

The next morning, when I got up, Grandma had the griddle fired up and she was making hot cakes. Momma's door was still closed. Grandma was whistling while she was flipping those cakes, and I sat there, expectantly waiting for the fine odor of real butter melting on the top of my flapjack.

As I started in on my first two, my grandma poured me a glass of orange juice and then sat down across from me. "Your mama and me had a little talk after you went to bed last night," she told me. "Everything's going to be all right."

"Are we staying here?" I asked, just as a forkful of pancake stopped at the entrance to my mouth. I shoved the hot cakes in and looked at my grandma.

"You are, sweetheart," she told me, "you are."

It was a splendid life. It was the best six months of my life. In the fall, I started school. Most of the kids had been in kindergarten and were ahead of me, but Grandma had read with me and I was ahead of most of them in reading. We also started studying arithmetic. It came to me easily. Where I was deficient was things like geography and history and civics. But that's not exactly a big part of the curriculum in first grade in Mississippi.

The class was all white. I never even gave that a thought. Although there were colored folks all around us (some even worked at the school), I never saw a colored kid, not one at our school. There was a kid from India, and he was pretty dark, especially when compared with the rest of us, but the teacher explained that he was a foreigner and not to be treated as colored. She said it exactly like that: "Now don't you treat Bhuno as if he was a colored boy." So we didn't.

I really expected Grandma to be sad. After all, Grandpa was gone. But something held up her spirits, and it never occurred to me then that it might have been me. It was really just the two of us in that little ranch house. Of course, I didn't think it was little then, since it had much more room than my and Momma's place. Grandma drank coffees with a couple of neighbor women and played cards sometimes during the day when I was in school. Otherwise, we'd just stay home together. I'd play in the front yard, watching who was coming down the gravel road in front of the house or in the back, where there were woods that beckoned with all kinds of mysteries.

Edward, who turned out to be her son, although I'd never met him before Poppa's funeral, came around every couple of weeks and he would bring his wife and their kids once a month or so for dinner. The kids were both teenagers, two girls, and they often wanted to have nothing to do with me, which was fine. I had friends of my own, in the neighborhood and in the school. When they'd come, they'd go to my room and lie on the twin beds and talk, gossip mainly. Occasionally, because it was my room, they'd let me sit there on the floor between them. I did love to listen if they'd let me. They talked about boys and they talked about makeup and movie and rock 'n' roll stars. Becky, the oldest, said some of her friends were *doing it*. It was another ten years until I figured out what they meant.

School was exactly four blocks away. It was two blocks down the road in front of our house, then you turned left (I think that was south but I don't remember for sure), and then walked almost two blocks that way. Grandma would get me breakfast, usually just corn flakes on a school morning, and then the two of us would walk down the street. When we got to the street where I turned, she'd stand on the corner and watch me go the rest of the way. I wondered sometimes whether she was still watching me, but almost always when I looked back, I could see her there and she'd wave at me. At the end of the day, which was just early afternoon, I walked back alone, although I quickly fell in with all the other children who lived nearby my grandma's place.

Grandma was not a large woman, but she was pudgy. She was short too, I know now, but at the time, I failed to recognize it because I was so little myself. Her hair was ginger, and she wore it all coiffed up. She went to the hairdresser every Friday morning the whole time I was with her, and on any occasion that I didn't have school, I went with her. She had a little white purse that appeared to me to be plastic, although I now realize might have been faux leather. It went with her everywhere; otherwise, it was sitting on the kitchen table.

One afternoon I sat bored, as a teacher droned on about something or other, I've forgotten what, when we heard a commotion in the hallway. We were all keen to listen to that and conversations soon ensued between students, although the teacher shushed us. Then the door to our classroom burst open, and my momma appeared in the doorway, still holding on to the door handle.

"Johnny," she called out.

I hid behind the student in front of me.

"Johnny," she said, "where are you?"

The principal appeared right behind her. "Ma'am," we heard him say, "ma'am, please don't interrupt class."

"Johnny," she said again, and I stood.

"There you are," my mama said, but she didn't move. "C'mon, we're leaving."

"Now you wait right there, son," the principal said. But as afraid as I was of that man, I was much more scared of my mother. After all, the principal had never put his cigarette out on my thigh.

I walked to my mama. She took ahold of my collar and dragged me into the hallway. To my surprise, my grandma came walking at her fastest gait up the hallway.

"Lisa," she said, "Lisa, please. Don't do this."

"This is my son," I heard Momma yell. "It's my son, not yours. My son. I got rights, don't I, Mr. Principal?"

The man proposed that the four of us go to his office. When we got there, I was directed to a bench in the hallway, where I sat. I could hear voices from the man's office, but mainly Momma and Grandma. His voice, when I noticed it, was just a low murmur. Then I heard my mama's voice grow louder and louder. I also heard my grandma's voice, and I could tell it was the sound of a woman begging, pleading. A few minutes later, the two women, mother and daughter, came out of the principal's office and stood toe to toe.

"At least take his stuff. He's got clothes and books."

"OK," Momma said, "we'll take his clothes. I ain't got room for lots more than that."

The three of us walked outside. On the curb, there was a long beige station wagon with the radio playing country music. A heavyset young bald man sat in the driver's seat, smoking a cigarette.

Momma walked to the passenger side. "We'll only be a minute," she said. "We got to get his clothes."

The man murmured something—something about a long drive. "I know," Momma answered, "but the boy needs his clothes."

The three of us walked toward the house. About a block down, I heard the station wagon crank, then start, then stop again. Then it did start and we heard it driving up the street behind us.

"That's Hank," Momma told me. "He's taking us on a big adventure. We're going to drive north. Now doesn't that sound like fun?"

"I'd rather stay with Grandma," I told her, and waited for a slap I expected. It didn't come.

"You don't mean that," Momma said. "You belong with your mama, and that's that."

While Momma pulled my clothes off their hangers and out of the chest of drawers, Grandma made ham sandwiches. She put them in a bag, threw in some Fritos (my favorite) and three Cokes. All pop in Mississippi was called Coke, but these were actual Coca-Colas. At the car, Grandma bent down and kissed my forehead.

I wanted to say something. But there was too much to say, and I knew that if I said the wrong thing, I'd pay for that. I knew my mama, and payback was only a question of time. I climbed in the backseat. Momma threw the bag of my stuff in the trunk, got in the car, and we pulled away. I waved at Grandma, who stood at the curb the whole time we were driving off, as long as I could see anyway.

I never saw her again.

Five

W E PULLED NICK off his regular work and had him watch the house. I showed him where he could park that didn't seem suspicious and told him to use my binoculars, but we both knew that we couldn't see the back of the house. For two days, it was just a waste, although both days, he saw our Mr. Right and three or four other guys come to the house in the evening, for what we assumed was payment to someone.

Finally, on the third morning, he saw someone leave the house. To my surprise, it was neither a black guy nor a Mexican, but a blond white guy, young, driving a newer Acura. Nick followed him, but it was pretty useless. He went to the Hy-Vee, came out with a small bag of groceries and a cup of Starbucks. Then Nick followed him while the man bought gas, stopped at the US Cellular store and drove back home.

"Where's the cash going, if he's really getting in?" I asked.

"Wouldn't we both like to know?"

Peter summoned me the next morning. "I need you for a couple of days."

"Fine. When?"

"Thursday and Friday. If it runs over to Saturday, well, I guess you're stuck then too."

"OK." I do not turn Peter down. There are wheels within wheels, and Peter runs things.

"So how's that car of yours?"

"Gets me around."

"For a long haul?" Peter asks.

"Not too long. I'd be kind of worried—"

"What I thought," Peter interrupts. He brings cash out of his front shirt pocket, counts off four one-hundred dollar bills. "You got a credit card?"

"Ya," I say, "I think I still got a Discover card. Don't use it."

"Rent yourself a car from Enterprise. Nothing flashy. A Camry. Or a Hyundai. But get a V-6. You may have to run. I don't think so, but just in case, we want some power. We just don't want to look like we got any. Get it tomorrow, go pick it up, and then come back here. After I look it over, if you done OK, you'll be headed out early Friday morning."

"OK."

Peter turned away, then turned back. "Your license is current?"

"Ya," I say, "it is."

"Good boy." And Peter is gone.

Thursday night, when I bring the Ford Taurus into the driveway, Peter is outside, talking to a couple of guys. I turn the car off, step out, and lean against it. It is one of those modern metallic colors. I think they call it copper. I wait for at least ten minutes, and then the two men walk away from Peter, get in a pickup, and are off. Peter puts up his hand as if to say *wait* and then pulls a cell phone out of his pocket, presses some keys, and puts it to his ear. The conversation is quick. It is a conversation because I hear him say, "Ya, it's me."

A minute later, he comes over.

"This a six?"

"Ya," I tell him, "it's got some power."

"Looks like a car your grandmother would drive."

"Kinda thought that was the point," I answer.

Peter smiles. "Good boy. You don't know how many shitkickers would've come back with some muscle car. C'mon in. I'll tell you what we're doing."

This makes me think that Peter might be coming with me, but no. I am instructed to drive south, through Kansas City and down to Joplin or Springfield, whichever way I want to go and then into Pea Ridge National Military Park in northern Arkansas.

"You know it?"

"Union victory in the War of Northern Aggression," I tell him.

He laughs. He hands me a burner. "OK, they're gonna have this cell number, and they'll tell you where to meet them. It'll be Saturday morning. They're going to be easy to spot. Two guys. Middle-aged. One's gonna be wearing a Make America Great Again red hat."

"And the other?"

"Teachers for Hillary, of course," he says, and he laughs.

The burner phone is standard procedure for delicate outings; it means I leave mine home. Peter tells me to be at the park by 7:00 a.m. Saturday.

"And," he says, "I hope you don't get picked up driving down. But for God's sake, do not get picked up coming back."

"OK. You know you can trust me."

"I trust you, Johnny," he says, "but coming back, well, there might be heat. If there is, do your best. Your package is important. Got it?"

I nod. I understand.

Driving down was boring. Iowa 35 south is bad enough, but the Missouri part is nothing until you get close to KC. I hit the Hardee's at Kearney, but all that grease gives me indigestion. Then I fight my way through town, past the ballparks, past the warehouse caves and turn toward Kansas, but not quite to the state line. I head back south on Missouri 71, which is a four-lane highway but barely. It's a long drive to Joplin, where I get off to buy gas and then find a Panera Bread, where I drink three coffees so I'll stay awake. I keep going, not stopping until Bentonville, Arkansas, where I get a room at a Sleep Inn.

It's just about six and I'm not hungry yet and I am too tired to sleep. I lie down on my motel bed and watch the news. The news—they have only one purpose in life: to take down the Donald and make sure that Mrs. Wide Ass gets elected. But see, he's on the TV all the time. So their plan ain't gonna work, not unless I miss my guess.

Minutes later, I am dozing off. When I awake, I have left the curtains open on the second-floor hotel room and it is growing dark outside and I am finally hungry. But none of that matters. I flip open my laptop, use the hotel Wi-Fi to go on Backpage, and check out what there is for activity around here. There are a couple of girls, one who'll visit me in my room. I know what Peter would say. *You can't afford to get arrested.*

The girl doesn't exactly look like her photo. *What else is new?* She's a bit older, her bottom is too wide, but she does have a big chest and I can see through the shirt that her nipples are nice and pronounced. I play it cagy. She's a pro too, doesn't ask me what I want or about money. She kisses me first, long and hard and then I feel her tongue against my own. "Want to get comfortable?" she asks.

I strip down to my tighty-whities and wait until she takes off her blouse and bra. Then I get on the bed, she joins me and while I begin to lick her breasts, we agree on a price. She's like most of the girls. She doesn't mind giving a bareback blow job but wants me to wear a condom for anything else and anal is extra. But her blouse is off, and I am no longer able to negotiate with my brain. It's my small head that's doing the thinking.

I showered as soon as she left and this particular physical activity, as usual, gives me a good night's sleep. My alarm wakes me at six, and I'm at Pea Ridge before seven, clutching a bag of doughnuts from QuikTrip and a tall, steaming cup of black coffee. Naturally, I just sit and wait, sipping on my coffee, waking up. I'm at a picnic table in a deserted national military park, and I start to worry. What if my phone doesn't work here? This was a Peter project and Peter always plans well. Problem is, a lot can happen in the meantime.

Two policemen—county Mounties—pull up to my area just before ten. They get out of their car, and one walks the other way, toward the woods. I hear him rustling with his cop pants and then he unzips, leans back, and takes a long, satisfying piss in the grass. The other comes over to me.

"Morning," he says in a slight drawl.

"Good morning," I say, pulling a sprinkled donut out of my bag and biting a third of it off. Eating is always a good delay tactic when the cops are talking to you. The situation is tense for me, but if my instincts are right, the cop is there by coincidence and I don't want his con radar to go off. People wonder sometimes how it is that cops know when someone is an ex-con, but it's not that complicated. The guys give it away, either with their tattoos or their attitude, or both. I tried to be Mr. Regular Guy, and it usually works for me. The cop plants his behind on the other end of the table.

"From Minnesota, huh?"

Of course I wanted to lie and say I was. My Taurus had Minnesota plates. But if his next step was to ask for my ID, well, that wouldn't be a good idea since I was carrying an Iowa license.

"Nah," I said, "rental car." I figured he knew that anyway. There was a green E decal in the back window.

He smiled, lowered his sunglasses down on his eyes, looked across the way at his partner. "Man's got a bladder the size of a *T. rex*. Doesn't have to piss for hours, but once he does, he does."

I laughed.

"Your accent ain't from Iowa."

"No, sir," I say. Taking umbrage right here and now was a bad idea, and I knew it. "Iowa by way of Mississippi."

"Huh," he said.

Then he finally got down to business.

"Seen anyone around?"

"No, sir."

"Whatcha doing here, anyway?"

"Oh," I said, "I got some time before I'm meeting my folks in Branson, so I thought I'd look around a little. This place is on the map."

"I suppose," he said, "but you have to wonder why. Missouri regulars beat the Missouri irregulars here. Not so much a battle as a rout . . . Confederate Army didn't show up, of course."

"Doesn't surprise me."

"What's that mean?" he asked.

"Well, sir," I tell him, "my daddy always said that the South might have won the war if Jefferson Davis had put the capitol in Mobile instead of Richmond."

"Hmmm. Anyway, looking for two men. Actually just one man, but he seems to be traveling with somebody else. Short man. Thin hair. A little past middle-aged. Looks a little, well, I don't know, he looks like a Jew."

"If I see anything," I tell him, but my statement drifts off.

The other officer comes over. "C'mon, Hugh," he says, "let's go. This ain't our boy, obviously."

"Obviously," the first cop says, flipping his cigarette in the gravel and walking toward his car.

Twenty minutes later, my phone rings.

"What'd they want?" whoever is on the other end of the line asks.

"Who am I speaking to?" I ask.

"Never mind," he says. "You're John?"

"Ya."

"Who sent you?"

"Peter Wingert."

"OK," he says, "wait there."

I am still sitting on the picnic table when a red minivan, old, rusted, loud, pulls up by the table. Three young men get out, and all of them rush toward me. I can barely stand when the first has his arm across my throat and is pushing me down on the table. I didn't wrestle in Iowa for nothing. I turn his arm, come close to breaking it, push him back into one of his friends, then bend the arm back. He goes down on one knee, moaning.

The third man laughs. "Serves you right, asshole," he says. "Now, John," he continues, "let him go."

I do so and sit back on the table.

"So you work for Peter Wingert," he says. "Got the sign?"

I show him the tiny kelly-green swastika on the bottom of my rib cage; it's offset by a black shamrock.

"Christ," he said, "I didn't believe it when they told us. It's like a St. Patrick's Day swastika."

I just smiled.

"OK," he says, pulls out a cell phone, calls a number, lets it ring twice, and hangs up again.

Minutes later, two more cars pull up, one black SUV and one old red pickup. Both carry Missouri plates.

The three men get back in the van and pull away. The SUV backs out of its parking place and pulls away too.

Two men climb out of the pickup. One has the red Trump hat, the other a Hillary hat. I almost laugh.

The man in the Trump hat approaches me. "You got the package?" he asks.

Now I am not only befuddled but worried. Had I screwed things up?

"Package?" I say. "What are you talking about? I'm here to pick something up, not to deliver something."

The other man walks up. He is quite short, older, and when he takes off the Teachers for Hillary hat I can see that his hair has mostly receded, but he combs it forward in long swaths so he almost appears to have hair. "What did the police want, John?" he says.

"I don't believe we've been introduced," I say, but I can see the man is unhappy with that.

He clenches his teeth and hisses at me, "What did the police want?"

"You, I guess," I said.

"I thought so." His voice is thin, high, and lyrical-sounding. It's almost as if he were singing.

He turns to the man in the red hat. "Thank you, Hubert," he says. "I think Peter, and my young friend John, have this from here."

"But," he starts, "I'd be fine going along. I don't know if John here can handle things."

The little man just nods to him. He walks to the back of the pickup, pulls out a soft mid-sized duffel bag, and takes it over to my rental. He pulls open the driver's door, pushes down on a latch, and my trunk opens. Then he walks to the trunk, throws his duffel bag in but bends into the trunk as if he's looking for something.

I walk back there. He has pulled up the carpet and exposed the spare tire. He unbolts the jack, then reaches in and comes out with a pack of cigarettes, or at least what appears to be a pack of cigarettes. He hands it to *Hubert*, if that is his name.

"OK," he says, "now, go home. Be careful. Be safe."

He closes the trunk, walks around the car, and gets in the passenger side.

"John," he says, "your burner."

"What about it?"

"Get rid of it."

I take it out of my pocket, put it on the gravel, raise my right foot, and smash it. I reach down, find the SIM card, and put it in my pocket. The phone I throw in a trash barrel.

"The card?" he asks.

"Next garbage can," I answer. "Can't have them found together." We both buckle up and I back up the Taurus and head out of the park. "Where to?" I ask.

"Home, take me home," he says.

"And that is?"

"Wherever Peter is, my friend."

Six

I HEADED EAST a bit, wanting to go back through Springfield instead of Joplin, just in case someone was looking for us. I asked the man who sat in the passenger seat for more information on that, but he simply smiled. He had one of those simple, long, closed-mouth smiles that never look genuine, and he said, "We can't worry about that."

I didn't respond. He went on, "I think you can assume they're looking for us."

A few miles north, as I drove carefully, about two miles above the speed limit, he told me just a bit more. "I'm pretty sure," he said, "that they expect us to be heading into Kansas. They'll be watching for my friends there."

"And . . ."

"Yes, at least one of those cars will be going to Wichita. But once they apprehend him, it won't take long to figure out they've caught the wrong guy. Even if he stays mum, which is what he is supposed to do, my friend."

I knew that I didn't need to know any more operational details and I was pretty sure everything was hush-hush, but I still asked another question. "How do you know Peter?"

"I don't," he said, "not personally. But Peter is—well, Peter is important to the Nordic cause."

I said nothing. I had the cruise control on, the radio off, my sunglasses on, and I looked forward down the highway.

"How do you know him?"

"That's complicated," I say.

"He recruited you?"

"You could say that."

"And you live in a flat by his house?"

"How do you know that?"

"I did not get in your car," he said, "without knowing who you are. You are the man who wouldn't leave a comrade behind. You are a son of the Confederacy who now lives in Iowa. You are . . . well, that's enough, don't you think?"

I nodded.

There is silence. We are driving north on a Missouri two-lane, and we watch as a Missouri trooper passes us, heading south.

"Make no moves," the man said, "even if he turns around."

Ten minutes later, the trooper is behind me. The little man next to me just keeps looking forward, even after I tell him.

"What do I do?"

"It is what it is," he says. "You are armed?"

"'Course."

"And where is your firearm?"

"Center console."

"Leave it there, please. You won't need it, even if they take me into custody."

I feel relieved, but I am also worried about that. I got my permit to carry in Iowa, but is it any good in Missouri? Also, I didn't have no instructions from Peter about whether I'm supposed to try to fight it out with a trooper, and I can't really call and ask him now.

The trooper seems to be following us, matching our speed and staying back three car lengths. Then just as I pull past another little county road, he pulls off.

"He's gone," I say.

"Good. It means those local Arkansas boys did not report your plates to anyone. We should be safe now."

That, however, was one prediction the little man had wrong.

North of Springfield, we are on a four-lane road heading west toward Kansas City. The little man still isn't talking much, even when he's awake. And he has slept for more than an hour now, which I can tell from his snoring. Then his cell phone rings.

I think he won't get the call answered, but on the fourth ring, he does.

He listens for a while, then puts the phone down. "So," he says, "it appears they're running some kind of a law enforcement interdiction on I-35 north of KC."

"Interdiction?"

"They've got several different departments looking for us, and they may set up a traffic stop somewhere. Although . . . that would be difficult to do on an interstate highway."

"So," I said, "if I can avoid them until we get on I-35, we might be OK?"

"That's my thought, exactly," he said.

I turn off on the next county road, head north, and then east until I find Highway 13, a little two-lane road headed north. It's the best I can do. It's easier for police to barricade a road like this than an interstate or four-lane, but if they don't think we know, they may not be looking for us. Of course, the whole thing was a bit of a mystery to me. I didn't know who I had in the car. I didn't know if he'd been charged with a crime, and if so, what crime? Was he Aryan Nation? He said Nordic Nation, but I wasn't familiar with that term. Was he involved in or planning some big attack on the government?

It was a nice boring drive north, and he was no longer sleepy, so finally he talked to me.

"What's Des Moines like?"

"OK," I said, "it's about the only town I know. In Mississippi, I lived in small towns."

"Ya, so? Tell me more about Des Moines."

"Keeps growing, especially west. Lots of nice tall buildings downtown, then a kind of a bleak area of ghetto housing. Nice river. Huge pretty reservoir north of town for recreation."

"That the one that flooded the town so you didn't have drinking water?"

"Before my time," I told him, honestly. I had hardly ever heard anyone talk about that. It was in 1993, the year I was born at a hospital in Oxford.

"I suppose," he said, now staring at the side mirror of the Taurus.

"You see something?" I asked.

"No, not yet. So, good people there?"

"Hmm," I said, "not as good as they think they are. Iowans think they're God's gift to America, the only friendly decent people in the country."

"Ya," he said, chuckling. "I see that a lot. Pretty white town?"

"The state's almost exclusively white," I tell him, "especially the farms. But Des Moines has a pretty big population of Afroes—"

"I don't like that," he broke in. "Don't use terms like that."

"What? *Nigger*?"

"Ya," he tells me, still absorbed by the passenger-side mirror, "African Americans is what they want to be called."

"I assumed—" I said.

"You assumed I was a believer in the Aryan Nation. The white supremacy? That white people started civilization? That without white people we'd all still be carrying spears and shields and living in tepees or grass huts?"

"Something like that."

"You'd be right too. I am a theorist for the Aryan Nation. Specifically, I am trying to demonstrate to the country and the world that white and black people should live apart. It's the only way to peace and sanity."

"So why?"

"Why do I not want you to not call them Afroes?"

"Ya, why not?" I asked.

"Because calling them names doesn't help our cause, and it will harm it in some quarters. Smart African Americans know too that they are a nation apart, that they are a religion apart, and that they should not live with us. We want to encourage them, not denigrate them."

I gave that a little thought.

"Now, calling them Afroes makes you feel better, right?"

"I guess."

"But it really pisses them off, you understand that?"

"Ya," I admit.

"We will only get what we want and need accomplished with their acquiescence," he says, "their—"

"I know what acquiescence means," I tell him, sounding perturbed. I was, at least a little.

He reached over with his left hand and touched my shoulder. "Fine," he says. "I knew you weren't some kind of goon. So do you vote?"

"Honestly," I said, "I never have before."

"Voted?"

"Ya."

What passed for farms in southern Missouri went by us. There was some traffic, but I hadn't seen a single police car.

"You said you hadn't voted before. Are you going to this year?"

"Ya," I said, "I just registered."

"So that you can vote for Trump?"

"Right."

He paused. I thought he was trying not to say something.

"So," he said, "have you heard Trump's message to black people?"

"That they should give him a try because them Democrat programs haven't really helped them."

"Yes," he said, "that's it in a nutshell, I guess. But Democrat isn't an adjective. The Republicans just say it that way to insult the Democrats."

I said nothing.

"Anyway," he continued, "blacks in America live in abject poverty. Yet their leaders continue to preach integration, in schools, in society, in government. It isn't working. It will be some time before a majority of them decides that segregation is what they really need. They need their own country, their own rules, their own way of life without us. And then, and only then, can we accomplish a better world for all of us."

"Hmmm. Never thought of it that way."

"So since they gotta figure things out, calling them Afroes just doesn't help."

"What about Jews?" I ask. "What—"

"They should be gassed," he said softly, without emotion. "Hitler had the right idea. You exterminate vermin."

I said nothing. I didn't like kikes either, but God almighty, I'd never heard anyone express that exact thought before.

"Don't get me wrong, son," he said.

I said nothing.

"You know why Hitler started with the Jews?" he asked.

"No, sir."

"Because there weren't any African Germans. If he'd had a nice big population of Negros, he would have started with them. They ain't our struggle. We got so many Negroes in this nation, and we got them completely dependent on government handouts or drugs or both. And there ain't any solution but to let them be on their own."

Again, I waited. I felt, just a little bit, like I was out of my league.

"Anyway," he said, "I was asking what Des Moines was like. They have a ghetto area for our colored friends, huh?"

"Ya, between downtown and Drake University, mainly."

"OK," he said, "is it a big population?"

"Less than a tenth," I said, "but they make up half the jail population."

"Ever so," he said, "ever so."

"There's even more bean . . . there's even more Latinos," I said.

"It's that way everywhere. Not that I believe we can build a wall, but the Donald is right about one thing: you don't have a country if you can't protect its borders."

"I agree," I said.

"Do you believe Mexico will pay for it?"

"I believe it would be worth paying for, unlike so many things my tax dollars go for."

"So why does he say Mexico will pay for it?"

I thought about this for a moment. Finally, I told him what I thought was the truth. "You know how them Hare Krishnas are like at the airport?"

"Of course."

"Hare Krishna. Krishna. Hare hare. It don't mean shit. It literally don't mean nothing. But they like the sound and the repetition. And so does Donald and so do the people who come to his rallies."

"My boy," he said, "you should go to college."

Traffic was getting congested and slowing down as we neared a little Missouri town called Chattesville. It was just a few miles ahead of us, and it wasn't like there was any way on this highway to avoid it.

"Must be something going on in town," I said.

"What?" he said, then he spun around and noticed the slowing lanes of traffic. "No," he said, "they've got a blockade up somewhere on this road. Stop if you can."

"I see a green highway sign ahead," I told him. "Probably a county road, might not even be paved. I'm going to take that."

We turned right onto County M-26, headed due east, the wrong direction to get us to Iowa. It was paved for the first mile, then turned into a rather rough gravel road. I didn't give a shit what it was doing to Enterprise's Taurus, so I kept it going at a pretty good clip, at least fifty, and as we drove on by farmhouse after farmhouse and saw no other road that cut north, I asked myself the best way to get out of this mess, if indeed we were in one.

I pulled into a farmstead, which, while not abandoned, seemed unoccupied on this given day. I just parked and reached for the

Missouri road map I'd picked up the day before at the first rest stop entering the state. I unfurled it and looked again.

"What's up, Dr. Watson?" the man asked.

"Well," I said, "if you were Sherlock Holmes, I'd know to ask you how we should do this. I was kind of thinking about trying to hole up somewhere and then go ridin' tonight, after dark."

"Might be smart," he said. "Law enforcement grows tired of these kinds of deals, and it's hard to blockade a highway at night."

I figure a bird in the hand. I walk to the front door of the farmhouse—the whole place feels deserted—and knock on the front door. Nothing. I walk around back. Again, I see no one. No one answers my knock there either. There's no sign of a dog, unusual in a Midwestern farmstead. The back door has several small glass panes. I put on leather gloves and smash one, then reach in and unlock the door from inside. I have brought my gun, which I now remove from my pocket and place at my side, just in case. Carrying a gun inside the house makes it burglary (for what else is it?), increases the risk, but I'm trying to ensure my safety too.

The back door leads to a mud room, which then leads to the kitchen. The kitchen looks like it has had recent use; there are dirty dishes in the sink, but no one seems home. From the kitchen, I walk through the living room and to the front door, which I open and let my passenger in.

"Deserted?" he asks me.

"For the moment," I tell him. "Not sure they're just not in town this morning. And I still have to check the upstairs. If you hear a siren, leave the car and walk toward that field. Try to hide if you can, and if I get out of this mess, I'll meet you on the road east of here."

"OK," he says, and sits down on a sofa.

I got up the stairs and find that only one room seems to be currently occupied, and that by just one person. So an old farmer, or an old farmer's wife, probably lives here. From the decorating, it's not anyone young. In for a dime, in for a dollar, I figure.

We make sandwiches in the kitchen, go back into the living room, and watch TV. They have Direct TV, something I've never used, but my passenger seems adept at it and he finds video on demand and orders a movie. It's a Will Ferrell movie. I had expected something ideological, but what the hell. We watch it, eat, and wait.

After a while, my passenger goes to the computer that's on a table in one corner of the room, turns it on, and waits. There is no password, but the Internet is slow, unbelievably slow. He complains.

"It's a farm," I say. "They probably don't have a line to give them decent speed."

"True," he says, "and I can't log in to anything either—that might give us away." But he stays at the desk, slowly going through Internet pages.

The farmer is tall, thin and at least in his latter seventies, if not early eighties. He's wearing a corn seed hat, a long tan coat over dark slacks. He also has a double-barreled shotgun pointed at me. I don't know when I fell asleep, but I did and this is how my mistake has been repaid.

"Good afternoon," I tell him.

"Don't do nothin'," he says. "I already called the cops."

"Oh," I say, sitting up, "do you have a cell, old-timer?"

"Don't call me that."

"OK," I say quietly, wanting to make sure I show him I am neither afraid nor that surprised and that having a gun pointed at me does not intimidate me.

"Why you asking about my cell phone?" he asks.

"I wonder if you'd mind showing it to me."

"I would mind," he says, now prodding me with the gun barrel. "Just what in the hell are you doing in my house?"

"The reason I want to know about a cell, sir," I tell him, "is that I cut your phone line."

The farmer chuckles.

My passenger walks out of the kitchen. The farmer is surprised and moves his gun to point it in that direction.

"Daryl," my passenger says, "may I call you Daryl?"

The farmer seems unfazed by being addressed by his name. I suppose someone who's broken into his house can easily figure out his name.

"Get over here," he says, moving the shotgun so it points at the seat next to me on the couch, which creates my opportunity. With both hands, I grab the barrel and pull the shotgun down and away from the farmer. Moments later, I am standing with the gun pointed at him.

"Never mind that thing," the farmer says, "I haven't got it loaded."

I laugh at this. And why not? Some things are just funny.

"Daryl," my passenger says again, "I am sorry for any inconvenience and we want to pay for the window in back…"

The farmer looks at him again, intently. "Are you who I think you are?"

"I know you like to read our website," my passenger says.

"So you are Benjamin Petticourt?"

The name surprises me. Of course I recognize the name. I've just never seen a picture of the man, so I didn't recognize him, if indeed this is my passenger.

"Pleased to meet you, Daryl," my passenger says, reaching out to shake hands. "It's always nice to meet one of the people who believes in our cause."

After our chicken dinner and lots of fresh coffee, it has finally turned good and dark. We thank our guest and leave his place shortly after. I cut east just a few miles, pick up a county road headed north, and take my course of two-lane roads, driving carefully, headed for Bethany, Missouri, where I will then join I-35 and we'll be less than three hours from Peter's house in Des Moines.

Seven

I T WAS ALMOST midnight when I saw that a car was trailing behind me on the highway. He seemed to be holding a mile back and matching my speed, just like a trooper. 'Course, I was only driving fifty-seven miles an hour, so . . .

"What do you want me to do?"

"Are you sure it's a cop?" Petticourt asked me.

"No," I said, looking again in the rearview mirror. "But I want to know what to do if it is."

"How close are we to Bethany?"

"Seven, eight miles," I estimated.

"I'm thinking," he said.

The car continued to follow me, matching my speed perfectly. I know this 'cause I had taken off the cruise and varied it down and up, just a few miles an hour. The trailing car kept to our speed, best as he could.

"Is there any way for me to get out of the car without him seeing?"

"I don't see how," I answered. I gave this a thought but still couldn't figure out a way.

"Can you outrun him?"

I laughed. "A trooper?"

"Any other ideas?"

"Can you talk your way out of it?" I asked.

"That depends, doesn't it?" he answered.

"On just what?" I said, and then I could see the lights of Bethany ahead of me.

"On whether he's just looking for two men and one of them looks like me, or if he's got my photo."

I probably had five miles more to go. I thought about gunning the car. I thought about turning off onto the next gravel road, turning off my lights. I thought about reaching into the center console for my revolver.

Whoever was behind me started to speed up, coming up behind me.

We watched the blue light flash on the top of his car.

"Out of time," I told Mr. Petticourt.

"Don't do anything stupid."

"That really doesn't help much," I said, and I started to pull onto the shoulder.

The car pulled up behind me. He pulled in a bit closer than they usually do, probably because the gravel shoulder had just begun to widen where I pulled off.

We waited. I saw that there were two of them and they both got out and were approaching us on different sides.

"I could probably kill one of them before they knew there was trouble," I said.

"Jesus," Petticourt said. "Don't be ridiculous, none of that. I've put Peter's package in your bag already. I'm hoping they'll release you, if nothing else."

We sat. The man finally came up to my door. He had a flashlight in his left hand, looking in at us. I couldn't see his right hand, which I assumed was placed on his sidearm. He signaled that I should roll down the window.

"Evening, gentlemen," he said, "where you headed?"

"Right now," I said, "trying to get into the McDonald's at Bethany before it closes."

"Well," he said, "sorry to tell you but I think you missed it. Still, you from the Twin Cities?"

"No, sir," I tell him, "Des Moines, sir."

I don't know if that sir bit ever works, but I always figure it's worth a try. He is a middle-aged man, a deputy sheriff, I figure, and there's really no reason not to try to see if a little niceness will work.

As he moves the flashlight to look at Petticourt, I finally realize that something is different. While the exchange so far has been very police-like, when the flashlight moved, I could see him. He's not in uniform. I look at my rearview mirror, and the other man is standing at the corner of our vehicle—smart move—and he's not in uniform either.

"And you, buddy?" the man asks, as the light settles on Petticourt's face.

"Just catching a ride with my nephew here," he says, all the time looking straight forward and down a little.

"Well," the man says, "you boys is out kinda late. I'm looking for someone, a Jacob Petticourt. Wouldn't know anything about that, would you?"

"No, sir," I say, "I surely wouldn't."

"License and registration, please."

I pull out my driver's license and hand it over. Then I tell him, "It's a rental, so I guess the registration would be, where, in the..."

"Hold on," the cop says.

He walks behind the car, lights up the back window.

That's when I get out of the car.

"Please stay in your vehicle," he says loudly.

"No," I say, standing up, "I think you should show me your badge."

He raises his gun now, no longer at his side but in his right hand.

"Look," he says, "you son of a bitch—"

I know there's a chance he'll shoot me. I figure it's probably one in three, but I also figure that since he may not have that much training, I might just pull this off.

I walk a step toward him, then move sideways, onto the road bed, then ask him, "Could I see your badge?" He raises the gun another two inches, like he's taking sight on me.

"Ralph!" It's the other man.

You have gotta make that first shot count. If he'd been lookin' down at all, I woulda missed him. But now, see, my fist comes in short, hard, and sweet, and I connect with his Adam's apple. A moment later, I hear an intake of breath, then he's down on the ground and gasping for air.

His buddy's flashlight turns to me, and I don't hesitate but move onto the paved roadway, crouching down, just hoping he doesn't have his gun out. He's attempting to get it out of his holster when I tackle him, both arms out, hitting him solid and knocking us both into the ditch. Seconds later, we are both flailing. He's a big man and I can feel his softness, but he gets the upper hand by landing on me. I grab for anything I can and find one of his arms and start to bend it back. Then with a flat hand, I strike him just below the chin.

His hands flail and grab at my face. We roll over and he's off me. I'm still worried about him having a gun and I see his flashlight in the ditch, but not him. Then he's on me again, knocking me down and himself in the process. We roll and I'm on top. I punch his head once, then get scratched in the face in return. Ineffective, I know, to scratch someone in a fight like this. It hurts but doesn't do anything to immobilize your opponent. My hand-to-hand training comes in handy sometimes, but I think grit is more important. I hit him again in the face, this time hearing his nose crunch, and blood spurts out all over both of us. "Shit," he says, "shit," and lies down in the ditch.

I scramble up. Luckily, the first man is still on the ground and hasn't recovered enough to reach for his firearm. I pick it up, grab him by the shoulder, and direct him into the ditch with his buddy.

"Sir," I call out to Petticourt.

He has gotten out of the car.

"There's some long plastic ties in my center console."

He hands them to me quickly. "Would you like to hold the gun or tie them up?" I ask Petticourt.

When we've got them secured, I tell them to lie down in the ditch. I get the clip out of the gun, then put it in my belt. I find the second man's gun, take it out of his holster, and do the same. I tell them to lie down and they do.

In the car again, I tell Petticourt we're looking for the first body of water we see for these pistols.

I drive off, leaving their car just like it was, blue light flashing and all.

"What now?" Petticourt asks.

"Don't think they was real cops," I said.

"That I gathered. How'd you know?"

"Weren't in uniform but," I said, "he didn't call us in either. Once I saw the car, I was pretty sure. Local magistrates or somethin' . . ."

"That all?"

"Talked like me," I admitted. "That made me think too."

"What now?"

"So let's get on I-35 and see what happens."

"Son," he answers, "I think Peter sent the right man."

An hour later, we were comin' into Iowa. We headed into Des Moines without further trouble.

Peter had me pull the car into his garage and then we went into his house.

"Good work," Peter told me.

"Thanks. Kind of waiting for the next shoe to fall."

"From what we hear, you're clear. They're sure as hell after our passenger though."

Eight

HANK WASN'T THAT bad of a guy. He wasn't all that interested in me, but later, from some of the others, I learned that disinterest wasn't all that bad of a thing. He never beat me, never even slapped me. When he wanted control of me, he'd put me in the kids' bedroom—every other weekend, a couple of his kids came to stay with us—and tell me to sit tight. We didn't have a computer and no TV in the kid's room, just a desk and two bunk beds, but I always had library books. From my grandma, I'd learned that a book could take you someplace else when you needed it to.

One time I nearly peed my pants staying in that room till he called me again. I finally cracked opened the door and crept quietly, my back against the wall, to the bathroom.

"Whatcha doin?" he asked me from the living room.

"Have to pee."

"Well, go on, then," he said, "if you make a mess in that room, it's you who's gonna clean it up."

It was a little house, two bedrooms, a living room, kitchen, and bathroom, but it was nicer than the one we had in Mississippi, and for whatever reason, Mom left it cleaner too. There was a one-car garage, which was for Hank's truck, and Momma's car sat on the road in front. Hank had a cat, which was not great for me, because I got me one good cat allergy. When Momma told him, Hank said he wasn't getting rid of ol' Lucifer (it was the only time I heard the cat's name), so what did she suggest?

We lived like that for six months. One night, dinner had passed, and I was still alone at home after school. I'd made a couple of peanut butter sandwiches and was sitting in front of the set with a glass of milk. I was careful. Although Hank didn't hit me, making a mess in the living room would have resulted in lots of time in the bedroom, and you never knew what Momma would do. Sometimes I thought she was harsher to me when her boyfriend wouldn't hit me.

I watched some police show on TV. That got over, and during the break, I took my plates and glass to the kitchen. I lay down on the floor to watch the next show—we only had five channels—but then Lucifer wanted to lie by me, so I got on the couch.

Not sure of the time, it was either eight or nine, I suppose. Hank came in from the garage.

"Where's your mama?" he asked.

I looked up, terrified as usual, and said nothing.

"'Course you don't know," he said, and then he slammed down the box he was carrying, which landed on the floor with a crash and then the sound of breaking glass.

"Goddamn it," he bellowed.

He walked to the kitchen, came back with a beer in his hands, and motioned me to get off the couch. I went to my bedroom.

I don't know how long it took before I heard the yelling. I had been asleep on my bed, on top, still in my clothes.

I heard Momma yelling first, then Hank, but I noticed she was doing the shrieking while his voice seemed steady, in control. *This ain't gonna be good*, I told myself.

Moments later, I heard a slap, then a loud shriek. What is it that makes a boy want to protect his mama? Oh, I understand if you got one of them mamas who's always there for you, tryin' to protect you, takin' care of you. But that wasn't my mama. Still, I stood, opened the door, and bolted into the living room.

Hank had her by the back of her hair, pulling her toward their bedroom.

"Stop that!" I yelled.

"You go back in your room, now!" Hank yelled.

"Stop!" I yelled again. I started crying. He held up.

Momma looked down at me. "Now, honey," she said, "you do what Hank says."

When she came to me an hour, maybe two, later, she was just wearing her housecoat and one eye was shut. Her face was red in color and one cheekbone had been cut.

She came in and sat on my bed. "You all right?" she asked.

What I wondered then, and since, is why she never asked me that after she had punished me in ways just as severe. But we sat together awhile, then she lay down on the bed next to me. It creaked but didn't cave in. Then she fell asleep. I stayed awake awhile but must have slept too, because at some point, I heard Hank at the door ask for her, and she got up and went to him.

The third time this happened, she called the police. Not sure why that time was any different—she had a cut mouth and was bleeding, but she did. Hank had driven off, and when the police came, she tried to make light of it. But they found him drinking at Christopher's, and he spent the night in jail. He didn't come home then and I wondered why, but Momma never explained it to me. Didn't matter. It was just the two of us for a couple of months, then one morning, she got dressed up and said she had to go to court. When I got home from school that afternoon, the two of them were in the living room, watching TV and drinking pink frozen margaritas from the blender. I didn't think much of it.

A couple of weeks later, I was home alone after school till it was time to go to bed. I did. When I woke up, I heard them yelling again. Then a slap, but this time, she must have hit him, 'cause he yowled then I heard someone hit the floor. My mama, I thought. I ran to the hallway and to the living room, and I saw her on the ground, whimpering.

"Come look," Hank yelled. "Come on in and look at your mother. See the whore drunk I brought back from Mississippi. What a sorry sight it is!"

My mother was crying, and I could see that her nose was bleeding. I walked over to the phone and started to dial 911, but Hank grabbed it from me and slammed the receiver down.

He left us then, walked into their bedroom, and I heard the sound of rustling. He came out with her clothes, some of them at least, and threw them at her.

"Get out!" he yelled.

She said nothing. She was sobbing.

"Did you hear me?" he said. "Get the hell out of my house."

She got up then, took my hand, and walked the two of us into my bedroom, closing the door behind us.

We moved into a one-bedroom apartment in a brick building just northwest of downtown in Sherman Hills, right near Methodist Hospital. It was three flights up. I slept on an old couch. I don't know where it came from—that, or Momma's bed either.

I'll be damned if I can remember all the men who came home with my mama. We moved in with three or four of 'em. The rest usually spent their time with us.

I do remember Charlie, a big hulking man who'd been in Desert Storm, or so he told us. When he took off his shirt, I was taken with his tattoos, as surprised and mesmerized by them as by his big beer belly. I remember him because of his particular brand of meanness. We moved into his apartment on the north side of Urbandale, a sprawling complex of some three or four hundred units. At first I was confused about how to find his apartment. The school bus (I had changed schools for the second time that year) dropped us off in the parking lot, and there were three buildings one could go to and three doors for each building. It took me more than a week to remember the right door. "He's touched," I remember Charlie telling my mama."

"Nah," she said, but nothin' more. I don't think she had any idea whether I was smart or stupid or anything else. I don't ever remember her going to a school conference or interacting with a teacher in any way. If the whole school had to bring something or fill out paperwork or get permission, I figured out early on to take care of it myself. When I got a report card, I'd just leave it in my pack. I don't think she ever saw one. We never had a book in the house unless I brought it home from the school library. I watched *Sesame Street* when I could have the TV alone, but I don't ever remember a kids' movie coming in the house either.

Charlie had three bar stools set up to a counter in the kitchen and no table. I was only to sit there when at a meal or when I was being disciplined, which was surprisingly often. Charlie would make me sit on the barstool, close my eyes, and say nothing. My hands were to be down, my arms and legs hanging down, my feet didn't touch the floor, and I was to hold my head up, eyes closed, seeing nothing, saying nothing. Occasionally he'd cuff me on the back of the head during that time, but the only real discipline was sitting there for a whole hour.

I could not go to the bathroom—that might have been the hardest part. I held on for dear life. Once, I couldn't and the deluge followed. He beat me with a leather belt on my back and buttocks. "Baby," he hissed at me, "baby needs a diaper, huh?" I was warned when I went to school the next day to neither say anything nor show anyone. "Not if you want to find your mama here when you come home," he said. I have had dreams of revenge, of course. Oh, God, I would love to run into Charlie now. He would go home that day, if at all, bruised and battered. But this is life, and life ain't like the romance books Jenny reads. No, life never allows for that sort of thing. I've never run into Charlie. One day, Momma picked me up from school and had her makeshift luggage in the back seat.

We lived at Billy's for about three months, the usual amount of time. As with the other men, they adored my momma at first, which sometimes meant they'd try hard to make me happy so she'd be happy. It usually didn't take long before they figured out pleasing me wasn't really necessary: I was part of the package, but it didn't matter much to her how I was treated. They also figured out who my mama was, what she'd do and what she wouldn't. So like I say, we usually lasted three to four months, and that was that.

Billy had two daughters who stayed with him every other week. On the weeks they weren't there, I had their bedroom. When they were, I had the couch. Didn't mind it, although the couch was often unavailable to me until late, after everyone quit watching TV. I remember going to bed several times after watching the conclusion of the Letterman show.

The girls were three or four years older than me and didn't like me—that was clear. What was crazy was that they kept accusing me of things: stealing things, hitting them, trying to see them in the bathroom. None of it was true. I was still young enough to be walking on eggshells. It was then I realized that you could just make stuff up and people would believe you.

Billy had one and only one means of discipline, at least for me. When he got mad enough, he'd simply grab me by the neck and drag me to the bathroom and force my face in the toilet. Then he'd flush. It wasn't the worst thing I ever faced as a kid, not by any means, and it left no marks.

Bobby was a special terror. He really didn't get mad at me and he never really complained to my mama about my behavior. I was his little project, meaning he looked for ways to torture me. He tried putting out cigarettes on my feet, but that wasn't really all that interesting, so he moved on. It worked better on the back of my butt; it hurt like hell and made quite a mark. He did it as low on my buttocks as he could, for some reason. Then he inserted a plug in my rectum and insisted that I couldn't take a shit for three days. By the third day, I was in absolute fuckin' agony. I can't remember if my ma knew about it, but I don't see how she woulda had a complaint anyway.

He liked to take out my pecker, that little thing barely hanging down, and paw at it like a cat with a ball of string. He'd punch my nuts to see how much it hurt. He would go in my backpack at night, find my homework, and rip it up. He tied a rope on my midsection and lowered me off the back deck. We were on the third floor. This one got him in trouble. The cops were called. I heard him tell them at the door that no kid lived in his apartment.

Where was my mom? By this time, she was on meth. I never knew who introduced that shit to her. It's the worst stuff in the world, and I mean that. I know people who took it once and chased that first high the rest of their pitiful lives. I know people who lost houses, jobs, wives, and kids chasing the meth high. I knew women who would do anything you asked for a hit.

It was Eric that got Momma arrested. I never knew what he saw in her. By this time, she was really skinny, she often smelled bad, and her teeth were growing increasingly stained dark. I was in third grade and had spent numerous hours at Just Say No meetings. So I figured I knew what was wrong with Momma. But Eric didn't seem to care. He seemed really into her.

It was years before I realized he was pimping her.

One evening, Eric and Momma lit up one of their little pipes and smoked. Momma told me to go to bed. I closed my door, got in bed, and tried to read. But I fell asleep soon enough.

I heard the front door chime more than once. I heard some people come and some people go. I heard my mama making those sounds she made in her bedroom. *Oh baby. Oh honey. Oh, that feels so good.*

I heard the chimes again and a deep voice in the living room talking to Eric. Then he went into the bedroom. I heard Momma say something. Then I heard my mother squeal and I heard someone run into the bedroom. Pretty sure it was Eric. Then I heard him yell and her cry and plead. Eric said something, something like *trapment* or something. I turned and went back to sleep.

It was early in the morning when the DHS lady woke me up, got me dressed, and took me outside. There was a cop in the living room but no sign of Momma or Eric. "We're going to find you a nice family," the fat lady said.

Like I said, you know how to tell when a social worker is lying? Her lips are movin'.

Nine

I DON'T KNOW where they put Petticourt. It wasn't at Peter's, 'cause I was told to take the back bedroom and get some rest. We had come in about 4:00 a.m. and I was pretty trashed. I don't know how long I slept, but when I came out and sat down in the living room, Peter was there with two guys I knew and one older lady I didn't. I sat down, and Jenny brought me coffee, which was nice. She asked if I was hungry and I was, so she went to get me something. I looked at the clock, and it said two.

"Here's what we know," Peter said. "We know they're looking for your passenger—"

"Petticourt."

"He tell you?"

I sipped my coffee. Jenny didn't know I took cream, and it tasted weird without. "Three different people used that name," I said, "so he finally dropped the pretense. Heard more than one first name, though."

No one said anything. Peter continued, "They're looking for Ben, but to the best of our knowledge, they're not looking for you.

"The boys you roughed up in Missouri—and that was a big chance. I surely admire your balls, if not your judgment . . . Anyway, they appear to have been local reserve officers of some kind. They didn't call anything in to the best of our knowledge.

"They were discovered by a deputy sheriff sometime during the night and they're both OK. About all they reported was that you're from Minnesota. So we hope they're looking for our friend there."

"Tell me to shut up if I'm supposed to," I said, "but how do you know all this?"

One man coughed. Peter started, "Maybe you—"

The woman interrupted him. "Peter," she said, then stopped and sipped her coffee. I realized she had a porcelain cup, while the rest of us were drinking from Styrofoam. "I believe this young man has earned our trust. You've been telling us about him for some time, and I like what I've heard. I think we should no longer worry about what this young man knows. Anyone disagree?"

Peter started, "No, I've been telling you that Johnny was the right man for some time."

The second man, a small, thin man with a gray comb-over, said, "I agree."

The third man, a huge middle-aged man with a gray beard, said, "I'm not so sure, but I think it's pretty clear that I'm in the minority."

"As usual," the woman said. "John," she continued, "there is more than one organization in this effort. Parts of it are public and parts are private, secret. We have many people on the ground, almost everywhere, and we have police contacts in Missouri and Kansas who help us. Someday, we won't have to be secret, we'll come out of the background, and America will be renewed. Do you believe that?"

I nodded.

"So," she said, "we've got this from a Missouri state trooper who works to assist us. He's important to us, as you might guess, so we didn't have him intervene yesterday. We just used him for reporting."

I didn't know what to say.

"What now?" the big man asked.

Peter now took over the meeting. "We've got our friend in a good place. He has delivered the package. But our next question is where he should go from here. John, I want you to wait one more day then take that car back. We'll have someone go with you in case you get arrested. My guess is that you won't. But if one of those reserve officers has an accurate plate, they know it came from Enterprise and the company is waiting to get it back. We've been watching your place in case cops show up, hasn't happened yet.

"Tomorrow night," he continued, "we'll have a meeting at the usual place. John, you need to come. Our guest will talk. He'll take questions too. Figure about two hours.

"Then we have to figure out how to get him out of here and where we're going to take him. I'd just use Johnny again, but that seems too risky."

"You got somebody else you trust?" I asked.

The thin man snickered. "Don't confuse being the latest with being the greatest."

Peter said, "Ya, don't worry about that. Although I gotta say again, we all admire your willingness to take action. That is sometimes lacking these days."

I stayed at Peter's that day, got some rest. The next day, I had a gig from Howard. We were security at an office building. Boring gig and siding would have paid better. But Howard needed somebody, and if I want to get work from him, I gotta take it sometimes just 'cause he needs it. I got off at five, went to my own place, showered, dressed in my nicest shirt over black jeans, and went over to Peter's for the meetin'.

Ten

I'M NOT SURE I got all this right. I did my best.

I go down to Peter's place, and he drives me. We go to a downtown coffee shop that has closed for the day. It has an adjacent area that's used for small concerts. I've been there before for the Drunk Book Club. I've seen a folk group there and a jazz combo. The place fills up quickly. By the time we are supposed to start, there are at least thirty people sitting at tables, waiting. Peter has disappeared.

Shortly after seven, Peter and Petticourt walk onto the stage. They take chairs. Peter stands and tells the audience that first, Petticourt is going to lecture, then there will be questions and answers. But first, he says, "We need to pass the hat." We use someone's Cubs hat, and everybody throws in some dollars.

"Now," Peter says, "reach in again. Our guest needs cash. He needs cash for lots of reasons, but primarily because our treasury is low and we need to get him transported to safety. Some of you may have heard that we had trouble when we brought him up here. They're after him, people, and we need to get him north of the border. Now give."

More money gets thrown in the hat, for sure, then Petticourt stands, approaches a lectern, coughs, takes a sip of water, and begins. I took notes. And I've done some reading since. I still may not have got all this right, but I tried:

You know that they call us white supremacists. We are not white supremacists. That is a term the African American advocate, the secular humanist quasi-scientist uses as a means to defeat us. Using a term that is debilitating to the other side is one of the classic tools of the propagandist. It has been effectively used by many dictators, including Stalin and Castro.

We are not white supremacists. We are white nationalists. We are white separatists. The distinction is important. Since the days of Charles Darwin, since the days of Samuel T. Francis, since we heard the views of Jared Taylor, serious students of human biology, of evolution, of civilization, of history, of sociology and politics, we have known that the white race is not only the preeminent mover of civilization, of history, of economy, the creator of those things which matter, of technology, or medical advancements, of agriculture, of, in short, society. All of that is threatened by miscegenation.

He was losing me a little. I didn't know what miscegenation meant, but I've learned it since—mixing the races.

Our responsibility now, our duty, is the protection of the white race. The history and the future of the human species are at risk. It is at risk because culturally and politically we are allowing the subservience of the white race. What this is, ladies and gentlemen, is white genocide. If the white race is destroyed, either by evolution or revolution, civilization itself will fail.

The audience exploded in applause. People stood. I stood. People clapped. I clapped. There were a few yelled comments, things like "That's right." He waited for us to sit down again.

"Please," he said, "we don't have enough time. Please, please listen to me."

What is the primary, nay, the sole weapon the other side uses in the battle to destroy the white race? It is the notion of equality. The idea of equality is the single greatest canard in the history of humanity. People are not equal. Am I equal to this young man here? No, I am older, I am more educated, but he is stronger. Am I equal to this young woman? No, I cannot give birth, I cannot nurture another human being in a womb. In some ways, I am stronger physically. In another, vital way, she is the stronger one.

Our forefathers did not promise equality in fact. They promised equality in opportunity. In a race, the fast will seize the opportunity. In the marketplace of ideas, the better idea will rise. In a political battle, the better politician, the one with more money, the one with better ideas, the one with a better image, will rise to the top.

I lost the thread then, but he said some other really interesting things about life and our country's current plight. They asked him about Trump.

I think he's going to win. I hope he doesn't. He will further our ideas some, if he does. He will expose the graft and the chicanery of the African-American politician and the sheer ideology of their welfare culture. But it will not be enough. Now if Billary wins, if we get another Eva Peron with a husband pulling the strings behind the puppet wife, we will get another eight years to further the mediocrity of the welfare state. Then, perhaps, then, we will be ready for a true revolution. If on the other hand, as seems likely, Trump is elected, the vigor of the right-wing movement will be sorely tested and the left's resistance will rise. The pro-Muslim, pro-Mexican, pro-welfare, pro-African-American elite will resist, loudly, and after four or eight years, we'll return to Democratic socialist rule.

On Obama:

We should daily thank Hussein Obama, for being Hussein Obama. He has shown us again what we already knew, that individual blacks can rise, that they can take advantage of affirmative action and people who bend over backward for black people, to rise to power. In his first two years, Hussein did great things, reordered the universe. By that, ladies and gentlemen, I mean that he was doing horrible things, such horrible things that if he had been able to continue, we would have gotten to the point of revolution. What hurt us were the Republican victories of 2010 and 2012, which pulled back on power by seizing one branch of the American government. If only the Democrats had kept power, today, the people would know about the charlatan that is Obama. Maybe they'd be coming to realize that the American way is being subverted, maybe they'd be ready to return to the American Christian way of life.

On religion:

The point of separation of church and state was not to protect us from religion. It was to protect religion from the awful power of the state. But remember, we didn't begin as a country of various religions. We began as a Christian nation. There was some question about allowing Catholics or Quakers full membership, but Christians all were our founders and Christians all were the people who brought the ideas, fought the wars, and created this nation. Christians.

White Christians. Not Jews, not Muslims, not atheists or agnostics. You will not find me a Jew who died at Lexington or Concord, not on our side anyway.

Our allies:

> Our natural allies are the people who stand for states' rights, the persons for limited government, the persons who would willingly enforce the Twelfth Amendment and prevent the big bad autocratic government from doing everything, being everything, and stifling the free-enterprise system that made this country great. They are the believers of personal rights over those of the rights of the central government.

I took the car back to Enterprise the next day. I was ready to be arrested, but nothing happened. I got dunned for a little damage, probably from running on a gravel road, but Peter had paid for everything anyway.

I never heard what happened to Petticourt next. Peter told me he got out of the country. That he would continue to write. That he would help lead. That we would rise up. And I knew that Peter was right. He was always right.

Eleven

I WORKED THE next day. I needed the cash. And it was good to get back to siding. We were just doing a reframe of a house in West Des Moines, and as usual, I had to supervise a couple of beaners. Nick and I worked the west side of the house, where the tricky spots were, while I sent the beaners round to the east to cover that whole large side with nice, even, painted siding. They had their crap Mexican music on the radio the whole time. Luckily, in an expensive suburban neighborhood like that, everyone was at work during the day anyway.

Nick seemed standoffish, so instead of talkin', we worked steadily and fast. By eleven, the only thing left to do on the west was the flashing around the chimney then the short pieces of siding to cover it. I told him to get our lunches.

We drank coffee from a thermos and ate the sandwiches his wife had made us.

"Look," I said, "I couldn't tell you what I was up to. It was a secret."

"I thought we ran together," he said. "Did you make a score?"

"It was for Peter," I told him. "I sure as hell didn't score, just lucky to get out in one piece."

"Ya," he said, "I seen your face is scratched, and I don't think your left shoulder is working right."

"I'll be OK, doctor."

"Ya, it weren't a score?"

"I told you no."

"OK," he said, now seeming excited, "I think I may have hit on a score."

"Ya?"

"Ya," he says, "I found the guy. The guy they all take their cash to. I'm not sure who he's working for, but I got him pegged."

"How's that?"

"So," he tells me, "he sits in that house, even has the groceries delivered. And from time to time, he calls in a hooker. But on Monday mornings, only Monday mornings, muscle comes to the house, and the three of them drive away."

"To?" I ask him, worried that he doesn't know.

"Nowhere else but Iowa Choice Credit Union."

"A deposit?"

"No, sir, no deposit."

"Oh?"

"He just goes to the safe-deposit boxes. They got them a big one. He takes in his suitcase, the banker gets him his safe-deposit box, then he leaves again. And I'm pretty sure his briefcase is lighter."

"You are damned right it's lighter," I say. "I just wish . . ." I take a bite.

"Wish what?"

"Wish I knew who picked up the cash later."

"Should I case the bank?"

"Wouldn't help. Couldn't be sure when our boy came, and besides, we know what we gotta know. We know when we gotta act. It's just a question of getting up a plan."

Nick eats now, lookin' straight ahead. Thinking? Maybe. That's what I'm doin', all I'm doin'. This is gonna be a killing. I just don't want us to be the ones killed.

Jenny gets off at ten again. She's holdin' her belly and her back, and her purse is on her shoulder as she walks slowly, ever so slowly, out of the Walmart. I'm parked right where I always am, where I'm not supposed to be. She grabs the car handle and fights to get her eight-month bulk into the car.

"Time to quit," I tell her.

"Jesus," she says, lightin' up, "not again. You after me. My father after me. C'mon, I want to go home and have a beer."

"You can't drink," I say seriously.

"I know that, dumbbell," she says, cracking a smile. "And ain't supposed to smoke either, but I do get to go home and go to bed now, so will you please take me?"

When we get home, Peter is there. He shakes my hand at the door, but I can tell I'm excused. I walk over to the garage, walk up the outside wood stairs, and . . . someone has been in my place. The door stands open. It's trashed inside, my few belongings thrown out of the chest of drawers. My clothes torn off from where they hung. My television set is thrown on the ground, and the screen is cracked. Luckily, I had my Glock with me, but my .22 squirrel gun is missing.

I walk back downstairs to the garage, grab the tool chest, and start up the stairs to see if I can fix my door. I'll sleep easier if . . . then I change my mind and walk to Peter's.

"Ya, Johnny," he says, "what's up?"

I tell him. He frees two bottles from the fridge and walks me over. He looks over the damage. "Amateurs," he proclaims.

"What I thought," I said. "So can I call it in?"

He leans back, takes a long swig of Sam Adams. "Nah," he says, "we better live with this . . . for now. I just hope we catch whoever is pulling this shit."

"What, somebody else get hit?"

"Ya, Mrs. Cready," he says, "three doors down. While you was playing games in Missouri."

"At night or during the day?"

"During the night," Peter tells me.

"We should do something about that," I say. Peter nods. I go fix my door and finally, just after midnight, go to bed. I am siding a new house the next morning, beginning at seven.

It is Thursday. We're going to see what we can do Monday morning. But I expect there will be a couple of big back guys serving as muscle, so I'll just check them out and then see what idea I can come up with for the next Monday. In the meantime, I am thinking we should see what we can do about the neighborhood and I ask Nick if he's in. He says ya, and that evening, we sit in my car, dressed in as much dark shit as we could find, everything turned off in the car. Watching. Nothing happens. We quit just before midnight.

The next night, we're there again and the next. It's Saturday night, and tomorrow night, we're not going to be here, because we are going to be busy Monday morning. Just after eleven, I see an old rusty pickup pull down our block. We both lie back, trying to be invisible, but I don't think these three stoners are paying any attention. They are young, Afroes all—sorry, African Americans—and I can't tell if they're carrying. That's my only worry.

They drive the whole block, turn the corner, and I watch for their headlights down the next block. They stop somewhere on that block, and we hear a car door.

"OK," I say, "we can walk through on the west side of Peter's house." We pulled down our stocking caps to cover our faces, our revolvers in our belts, and carrying flashlights and our police batons. It's dark, but I know where we're going. As we go by Peter's house on the west, we watch behind a tree. They've parked in front of a one-story stucco with no lights on. I can't remember who lives there, but it does look deserted. One man, a kid really, goes to the front door and rings the doorbell. If someone comes to the door, they'll probably leave. But no one does. The kid then walks around the house, to the back, scoping it out. A moment later, he comes back to the car, and I watch as all three of them walk around the back.

"Going in the back door," Nick says.

"Ya," I say, "gonna be surprised what they find."

Once they're out of sight, we walk up, plug their tailpipe with a potato rammed in as far as we can, then hurriedly go to the front door. With my key wrench set, I have the front door unlocked in a jiffy. These houses in this neighborhood are old, so they don't all have the same pattern but they all tend to be small, so I figure I know where the door to the basement is. And I'm right. Nick and I are standing there. When the first one walks in, I place the barrel of my Glock on his forehead. God, that'd make a mess in here. Anyway, I signal him to be quiet and that he should get down, on his knees. Nick moves past me. The next kid comes out and Nick points his own gun at the kid, but he ain't that smart, I guess, because he tries to hit Nick with his baseball bat. A second later, Nick has fired a shot into the kid's leg, and he's down on the ground, bleeding. I hit the man on the ground with my baton and he crumples, but I can tell he's not out. I hit him with the barrel of my gun. I know that's dangerous, it can really hurt somebody, but I gotta keep him down. We can hear the third man running in the basement, going to leave, I expect, out the back door.

As we walk to the front door, I spy the telephone. It's hanging on the wall in the kitchen. I dial 911 and let the receiver drop to the floor. "Better tell 'em to come quick," I tell the kid writhing on the floor, "or you might bleed out."

We go out the front door, allowing it to hang open. We see the third kid running to the van. He starts it, and it backfires, goes only a few feet before it breaks down.

The kid's out of the car quick and running hard. Ain't no way Nick and me, at our age, are gonna catch him. Nick squares to fire at him, but I say, "No, we better get the hell out of here." As we reach Peter's house, we hear sirens.

"In here," Jenny says. We cut east and go in the basement back door. She's holding on to it.

"Have fun?" she asks.

I just grin at her. While Nick and I are drinking Blue Moons, there's cops all over the neighborhood. Peter tells the two that come to his door, "No, officer, didn't hear or see anything. What's going on?"

"Couple of burglars one street over," he tells him. "Think one of 'em must have shot the other, and they called 911."

An ambulance arrives, and they rush one of the kids toward the county hospital, Broadlawns. The other one's sitting in the back seat of a cruiser. I'm a happy man.

Peter calls for a day of action. Saturday. It kind of interferes with our plans, but you gotta do what the man says. We start with flyers on the windshields at the temple on Grand Avenue. *Hitler was Right.* We paint some graffiti near one of the ghetto neighborhoods. We put up signs at one of the Mexican grocery stores about how they should get out of our country. We break windows at some church on the south side, spraying swastikas on the side of the building. That night, we burn crosses. We pick houses where Africans live in otherwise white neighborhoods. The Des Moines PD says it's a hate crime. What the fuck does that even mean? I don't hate anybody. I just agree with Petticourt. We should be apart, then we'd all get along.

It's a neat trick. Sunday morning, 'course, the TV has got some Holocaust survivor talking and some black guy saying how his kids got frightened. But they also got Peter. Peter is saying, and this is the part I really love—shows how goddamned smart he is and why he's able to twist the media in their own knots. Peter himself is on TV saying that burning crosses and flyers about Hitler are wrong, wrong, wrong. But he goes on. It shows again that there is a majority that understands that the races should be separate. People are taking action now, he explains. Some of it is wrong, but they're taking action.

We don't work Monday, not siding anyway. I find the best spot I can, use my binoculars, and watch a dark SUV drive up to the little house on the west side that Nick has identified. A huge African gets out of the car. He's wearing one of them colored loose-fitting Muslim fake suits and a Muslim hat—don't know what they're called. He walks to the front door, and moments later, he's escorting a short little white guy—I swear he looks like a Jew—to the SUV. They roll. I can see as they drive by me that there is another muscle man in the back seat—all I know about him.

At the credit union, the muscle in back gets out with Jew boy. He's tall, dark but American-lookin', and the weird part is, I recognize him.

"See who that is?" I ask.

"Nah," he says, "I saw him last week, but I don't recognize him."

"That's Howard's buddy," I say. "I think his name might be Bart."

"Ya," he goes, "you're right. Short for Bartholomew."

He's hard to forget. He's about six foot seven, and his face is completely scarred with them scars that turn some Afroes' faces a kind of rusty color. But what's most memorable is we've been in a fight with the man. Howard sent us over to a new hip-hop club on Ingersoll. I think the place used to be a dinner theater. Trouble was, it was a street full of Africans, and most of 'em were carrying. Once they figured out we were checking the armament at the door, they were taking it back out, probably lockin' the guns in their cars, which means they were damn dangerous, 'cause they could easily go get those guns if they wanted to.

Somebody did somethin' or said somethin' to somebody's else's girl, I think, and moments later, there was a brawl on the dance floor. I didn't jump in. I couldn't see why we'd care if they were hurting each other, especially since we didn't let 'em bring in their guns. But Bart jumped right in. He was throwing home boys right and left, and pretty soon, he was holding two of 'em apart. At that point, one of the friends of one of 'em got in the way, comin' up to Bart and drawing on him. Don't know where he had that short little .22 pistol, but we'd missed it.

I couldn't let that stand. I came up behind him and brought my blackjack down on the back of his hand. He goes down, 'course, but hell ensues and in the fight, I can't figure out where that .22 has gone. It's Bart who's saving my ass now, pulling guys away. I gave 'em good, of course, but there were too many Africans there who were willing to beat up a white boy. After a few minutes, Bart has got 'em on the run, and we clear the place. Owner ain't happy though and bitches at Howard for the lost business. You can't win with some people.

"Well," I tell Nick, "we sure as hell don't want to fight him."

"That's what I was thinkin'," Nick said, and of course, he leaves it to me to come up with a plan, which is gonna have to wait at least a week.

On Tuesday, we're back sidin'. I need some cash. During lunch, I sit in my truck with Nick as we eat tacos he brought back from a red Taco Truck. The Mexicans laugh when they see this.

"Look," I say, "we started this out to take down one Afro sellin' drugs. Now we moved on to the bag man. And that's OK, but maybe we should just take down the Afro, get what we get, and leave it at that."

"They are going to be just as pissed at that as if we do the bigger deal, right?" Nick said.

Nick ain't no strategic thinker, but he's right on that.

"In for a penny, in for a pound," I tell him.

He looks at me. He don't know what that means. I'm still thinkin'. There's got to be a way.

Twelve

I AIN'T SURE how many foster homes I was in. The first was a group home on the east side. They had eight or nine kids there, all ages, and one raggedy ol' woman running the show. She was in it for the money.

We get there about three in the morning, this immense black woman and me. The new foster mom got woke up but she's all smiles and sugar. "Oh, Ms. Jones," she says, "how lovely to see you."

"Hello, Mindy," the social services lady says. "This is the little boy I told you about."

"Oh, isn't he a sweetheart," she tells the social service lady. "Just a darling. We're going to get along just fine."

The social services lady has a brown paper bag she hands over, with my school clothes in it. "Don't worry about tomorrow," she says, "but enroll him at Mann for Monday." Mann turns out to be an elementary school within the shadow of the state capitol, and it's pure chaos for the three days I'm there. I am also one of the very few white kids there. At recess, the black kids pick on us few honkies.

As soon as Jones is out the door, Mindy says, "Now look, this is my house. You follow the rules here. If you don't, you'll be sorry. Your bed is in the middle bedroom. You have the upper bunk because it's the only one open. C'mon, I'll boost you up. Try not to wake anyone."

I'm afraid but I am about to pee my pants, so I tell her. She points at the hall bathroom. "This one," she says, "don't even think about using my bathroom." She points the other way. "That's my bathroom!" I pee, quickly, and she hoists me to the top bunk. I get in, stay quiet, try to sleep.

From below me, a girl's voice: "Hey, shit for brains," she says, "what'd you do to get jailed?"

Two other kids laugh, but quietly. They're probably afraid too, I figure.

"Nothin'," I say quietly.

"Jesus," one of the other kids, a boy, says, "I think he's just a little kid. Fuckin' A man, poor little bastard."

Grandma is all I can think. *Grandma. She'll come for me.*

The next day, she sits me in front of the TV set. We have cereal for breakfast and it's not even a regular brand, comes out of a big sack, but it looks and tastes like Froot Loops. When I finish my bowl, I am told to wash it in the sink and put it and my spoon in the dishwasher. Then I get dressed in the clothes the lady brought for me, and Mindy sets me in front of the TV set. She puts on a channel and then she goes into the kitchen, where she downs three cups of coffee, smokes several cigarettes, and gets on the phone. She doesn't change channels until after lunch when she wants to watch a soap opera.

At first she's talking about cards and such, and I don't pay no attention. Then I hear her say somethin' about how she'll keep me. "Little bastard'll bring in six hundred a month," she says. "I like it when I get a full house. They're in school all day, but God how I detest the weekends."

The next day, I'm once again wearing the same clothes, which weren't actually clean when the social services lady put 'em in a sack, and we wait while the other seven kids get on a school bus. I am by far the youngest. Then, Mindy and I walk down a block, over another, and across the street to a dark brick building that turns out to be Horace Mann School. In front of the school is a four-lane busy road, but we don't have to cross it. I can see a whole bunch of big concrete buildings from here, and the golden dome that I eventually learn is the State Capitol Building.

We sit in the principal's office and Mindy makes out paperwork.

"Where's he been going?" the principal asks and they both look at me.

"Well?" Mindy asks, and I finally catch on that they're askin' me.

"Rolling Green," I says.

"Urbandale?" he asks Mindy, who just rolls her eyes. She never asked.

A few minutes later, he takes me into the second grade room. The teacher sits me in back. She's nice, but she's supposed to take care of just about thirty little jigaboos, beaners, and a couple of Asians, whom I notice are right up front.

She asks my name and tells the class to welcome me. They probably lose a student every week and gain another, if not more often. I get a free lunch. I didn't think it was that bad. I sit alone, on the end of one table. I don't know nobody. At recess, I stood against the school building while the other kids played. Didn't care. I figured it was only a day or so 'fore my grandma would show up.

On the second day at the school, the teacher calls on me. The work they were doin' was easy, so I answered. Everybody looked at me like I was from Mars. I didn't give any more answers. At lunch, I sit alone again but then this scrawny tall black kid comes over. He says, "Can I have your lunch?"

I give it to him. What did I care? Tomorrow at the latest, I'd be eatin' my grandma's cooking.

On the third day, Mindy let we walk to school alone. I could see that the school was on a busy street and the street was going north and south. And I knew Grandma was south. I walked past the school, took the sidewalk, and walked against traffic. Soon there was this giant bridge that went over some river, and when I passed it, the way got really steep. It was one of the longest hills I ever saw. It walked on and on but I was in good shape and I'd had Froot Loops and I figured sooner or later somebody would give me a ride.

The cop picked me up about an hour later. He was all cheery and nice and asked me where home was. So I told him about Grandma's. But he figured that wasn't where I actually escaped from, and I finally gave him Momma's address. When we got there, 'course, the place was closed up 'cause Momma was probably still in jail. I didn't know. He asked me if I had anyone else and I said, "Just Grandma." This was when I met the next social worker, who, 'course, lied to me too.

"We're gonna find you a nice home," she told me. Fuckin' liars. I asked her about my grandma, and she never answered.

I stayed somewhere for a couple of nights, then Ms. Jones showed up again and said she had found me just the right home in someplace called A-dell. She got me in the back seat, put on a seatbelt, and we drove for a long time. We ended up in this little town with a town square and what appeared to me to be a big old Baptist church. It was the courthouse. On the west side of downtown, I met Mrs. Abernathy. She told me to call her Wilma, so I did.

I wasn't good then, 'course, at telling how old people were. She seemed really old, and I always kinda thought she might fall over dead at any moment. She had two other foster kids but they were both girls, so I had a bedroom to myself. In that bedroom, there were two twin beds, a desk, and a chest of drawers. Ms. Jones had found the rest of my clothes from Momma's house, and it took up one single drawer of the chest.

"Gonna have to buy him a few things," I heard her say.

"Well, certainly," Wilma answered, "soon as you get me a voucher for the general store."

Wilma had a husband, Chet, who drove a truck over the road, meaning he was usually gone for five or six days a week. One time, he got a little drunk on beer and told us about his trips west, told us about Yosemite and Yellowstone and Dinosaur National Park. I was so into dinosaurs then that I wanted to go along with him.

"Kid," he said, "if I ever find you in my rig, I'll just drop you off wherever I am, and let's see how good you are at getting home."

Usually, Chet just ignored us. There was three of us, like I said, a girl who was a couple of years older than me, named, well, I ain't sure anymore, it was either Addie or Abbie, and then a girl younger than me. Her name was Olivia, but for some reason, she was always called Lassie. She had long, shiny black hair that Wilma always complained about her not washin'. She had long thin legs too, and she cocked her head to the left all the time, like she was tryin' to listen to somethin' on that side. Her eyes were deep blue, and I didn't think they went right in her head.

It was Addie or Abbie, though, who was interested in me. She was just a little bit chubby. She had curly golden hair and perfect white teeth, unlike every other kid I knew in foster care. Her cheeks were round and pink, and she just barely seemed to be growing boobs, which interested me.

She talked your head off. She'd talk about her family, telling you stuff she had told you just the day before; she'd talk about school, telling you everything every kid in her class did that day, although never about school work or what was taught. And she loved to talk about what she'd seen on television; even if you sat there and watched it with her, she'd recount the show from beginning to end, and if she didn't always get it right, her version was more interesting anyway.

The house was small. It was near downtown, not that there was much downtown, and the yard, though fenced, gave little privacy. So it was when Wilma was gone that Abbie first asked me to come into the house. We were supposed to stay outside, that was clear, but we did go in to use the john. Anyway, Abbie asked me to come in with her and then she took my hand and took me into her room. She said, "Now we're going to play doctor. You ever played doctor before?"

I shook my head no. I had no idea what she was talkin' about.

"Just stand there," she said, in her best imitation of a teacher's voice. "I'll show you." She was wearing a dress, and I watched as she reached down, pulled down her underpants, and then stepped out of them. "Now you," she said.

I had on shorts. They came down easily. "Now your undies," she said.

I did as she had. I didn't quite see the point. I knew that my soft little dick had something to do with sex, but I really wasn't sure what.

She came over to me, got on her knees and proceeded to touch me, look me over, and then fondle my balls, which were small, tight and didn't have any more feeling in them than any other part of me. After a couple of minutes, she said, "Your turn."

She lay down on the bed now and pulled her dress up. I could see her naked pud.

I'd seen naked girls before, so it didn't surprise me, but then she took my hand and put it on her slit. "Rub that," she said. I did as I was told. She opened her legs further and guided my hand into her twat.

"This is what doctors do?" I finally asked.

"This is what people do for fun," she said.

It was many years before I understood. But to this day, I wonder why would Abbie wanta do that anyway?

Wilma was OK. She didn't like, hug or kiss us or anything, but she did cook and she did make us take baths, do our homework, brush our teeth, and go to bed at night. It was, honestly, more attention than I'd gotten since I left Grandma's.

School was weird. The schools, all three, were up on the highway. Wilma drove us every morning and picked us up after school. All the kids were white. A lot of 'em got the free lunches, and the ones that didn't carried paper bags. Most of them had a peanut butter sandwich and something like a Twinkie. That was better than the school lunch, but I didn't mind.

Funny thing was, the class was ahead of Horace Mann school, but still behind my regular class. So school was easy but also boring.

One day a lawyer came to see me. She was young but she had a huge butt and she moved slowly. She said all this stuff 'bout how was I, did I like where I was livin', and what did I know about Momma? And also, was there a daddy? This all happened with me sitting in the livin' room with Wilma, so I was careful about what I said. I knew better.

Last I saw her. I stayed with Wilma for two, three months, and I don't know why I got pulled out. I had a birthday, but nobody knew it. I didn't tell. Couple of weeks later, a different social worker came, told me to pack my stuff, which we put in a grocery bag, and she drove me to Des Moines.

It gets hard to remember now what happened after that.

For a while, I lived in a big white house just off Beaver Avenue. It was close to an elementary school in Beaverdale, so I and two other kids walked to it. They were OK people. I can kind of remember her being a little plump and havin' a sing-song voice, but I can't recall him at all. I stayed with them from one winter to the next fall, most of a year, and then that lawyer and a social worker came to see me and told me that my mother was doin' good now, she was living at House of Mercy, and did I want to go back to her? I said yes, of course, yes, right away. God knows why, I had a bedroom, a bed, three meals a day, and clothes that fit me. There must be somethin', I don't know, biological, that says if you ask a kid whether he wants to go with his ma, he'll always say yes.

Didn't matter. House of Mercy was a hellhole. Momma and I had a little room with two beds. The place was full of women and quite a few kids. It was an old high school, I know now, and while we got food and medical care and they made sure Momma wasn't on drugs, that was about the extent of it.

School was about three blocks away. We all walked to it, rain, sun, snow, or anything else, including the day it was minus ten below. It was an African school, right on Martin Luther King Parkway, and I kind of liked it because I was in my grade but they were learning stuff I'd learned the year before. One day I came back from school, went to our room, and found Momma lying out on the bed dead. Or so I thought. She was just stoned. Another woman walked in to see why I was crying, and she slapped Momma, who groaned and then she went and found Momma's counselor. What followed was hours of talk between Momma and several different counselors, then Goddamn it, that huge Afro woman, Jones, showed up and she said, "We'll find you a nice place to live." Fuckin' liar.

I had a nice place to live, I wanted to say, but I was just going on nine years old and nobody listened to me. Just as she's pushing me outta the front door, I speak up.

"What about my grandma?" I ask.

"Don't know nothin' 'bout that," is all she says.

Believe it or not, I was back with Mindy again that night. There was only one other kid there now, a boy who was younger than me, a little blond boy with white teeth that stuck out of his mouth who never talked.

"Jeremy," Mindy said, "say hello to Johnny."

Jeremy stood there, first nodding his head, then shaking it, then nodding again, but never said nothing. So I had a peaceful sleep that night, the first one in a while.

But it was only one night. The next day they hauled me off to another foster home. This was a very nice older couple. They had a great big backyard, where they had three dogs that ran free. I could spend time out there too if I wanted, which was OK except that there was dog shit all over the backyard. I don't remember their names. She seemed sweet, but she told me first day, "You won't be here long. We're too old to adopt."

The next couple did want to adopt. I know this because ten minutes after that old Mrs. Jones dropped me off, the two of them was sittin' in the livin' room with me, a huge Bible with a leather cover on the table, and we was all three holdin' hands and prayin'.

"Dear Lord," the man said, "Jonathan has joined this family—"

"It's Johnny," I says.

His voice rose. "We do not interrupt someone in prayer, Jonathan," he said. "Lord, Jonathan has joined this family. May he renounce his former sin, may he come to know you, the Lord God Jehovah, may he . . ." Bla bla bla, he went on for twenty minutes. I was hungry. I was thirsty. I had to pee. I figured telling him any of these things while we all had our eyes closed and he was praying up a storm was a bad idea.

Finally, he finished. I was thankful, not for the prayer, but for the fact he'd finished. Turns out we prayed all the time. We prayed at morning table before we had breakfast. We prayed at lunch, when I was home for lunch. We prayed before supper and we prayed before bed. Seems like they were the holiest people I ever knew.

Otherwise, they were nice enough. I was the only child in the house. He went to work every morning at seven and woke me up just before that. She would be in a bathrobe and she'd watch me as I cleaned up, brushed my teeth and changed clothes. They bought me clothes. I ate cereal and headed off for school.

I don't know what changed. One night, I was in bed and I heard some kind of commotion in their room, then he stormed into my room.

"On your knees," he commanded. "Get out of that bed and on your knees." We both knelt next to my bed. He had his Bible. He started praying, head down but watching me, then raising the Bible as he looked up and talked directly to Jehovah.

"Dear God Jehovah," he said, "smite the infirmity that this boy has brought into this house. Cleanse us, make us innocent again."

I'm not sure how long this lasted. Seemed like forever to me. I kept falling asleep but he would poke my shoulder and then he'd go at it again.

When he finished, I went back to bed. He went to his room. I heard them, although she tried to whisper.

"It ain't his fault," I heard her say. I wondered what they were talkin' about.

"Never happened before he came here," the man said.

"Look to yourself," she told him. "You get right with God. It ain't about the boy."

A couple of nights later, I was awoken again with them shoutin' at each other. I made out the word *perversion*, although I wasn't sure what that meant. And I heard her say, "It ain't the boy's fault." But he was in my room a minute later. He didn't drag me out of bed this time, just knelt and prayed. I could hear it all but I pretended to sleep. I remember him prayin' that I be forgiven for my perfidy.

I guess I wasn't. Just a couple of days later, a social services worker picked me up from school, and I was off to another house where they warehoused foster kids who hadn't found a real home.

Thirteen

I FIGURED THEIR weakest point was when two of them went into the bank. The bag man wasn't a fighter; indeed, that's why he had muscle with him. It was only in the bank that he was with only one guy. One guy Nick and me might be able to handle. But of course, we wanted to do it without them knowing it was us and with as little harm to anybody as we could get away with. That didn't seem likely in the bank. We thought about getting our own box so we could be in the room when they came in. 'Cept we'd have to give our names to get a safe-deposit box.

So I figured it had to be done before he dropped off the money. It had to be done when he was with just one guy. And if Bart is one of the guys, we gotta make sure he doesn't see us. If he sees me, I know we're toast. I assume he might remember too. So this deal just ain't easy.

We need the money. We install siding in the western suburbs every day, even Saturday. By Saturday night, I'm dead tired. I'm sitting right outside the Walmart and I catch myself falling asleep.

Jenny finally comes out.

"It's time," she says.

"Ya," I say, "I know. I was here on time."

"No, you dummy," she says, a big grin on her face. "It's time."

On the way to the hospital, we call Peter. He doesn't answer the landline or his cell. It's like that sometimes with Peter…well, it's like that sometimes with me when I'm doing something for Peter. It's like that even more with Peter. When you're doing somethin' for the movement, you're off the grid.

It's Jenny's first baby, so the nurse at the hospital maternity ward tells us there's probably no hurry.

"Dad?" the nurse asks me. "Do you have Mom's bag?"

I don't know what she's talkin' about. I start to say somethin' but Jenny jumps in and she doesn't correct the nurse about who I am. "He picked me up at work and I was feeling contractions," she says. "Does he have time to go home and get it?"

She tells me where it is, and I'm headed out the door. I'm hoping when I get there, I'll find Peter.

A half hour later, I'm back in her room. I brought her bag but Peter was a no-show. Nobody's in the room with her when I get back, so I sit down next to be bed. She don't look too good.

"How you feelin'?" I ask.

"Take my hand." I do. She squeezes it, hard. Really hard. Harder than I think she should be able to.

A nurse walks in. "Dad," she says, "let's talk." She makes a motion like I should stand up and go to the hall with her.

"I ain't—" I start.

"Quit kiddin'," Jenny says, so I catch her drift and I go outside to talk to the nurse.

"Who's Peter?" the nurse asks.

"Her dad."

"The grandpa?" the nurse asks and I nod. "They're real close."

"Well," the nurse tells me, "she's been asking about Peter. Now, Mr. Thurgood, we are a little concerned tonight."

I ignore the mistake. If Jenny wants them to think I'm the dad instead of the jerk who is still in fuckin' prison when he could be with his fiancé and baby, then I'll let the hospital think so. At least until Peter gets here.

"What?" I ask. "What's wrong?"

So she tells me. And I don't get it all, but I figure this much: they are needin' to get that baby out. If not, one of 'em, and maybe both of 'em, are going to be in trouble. So where the fuck is Peter?

I go to the little coffee area, get myself a hot cup, and try to think. The coffee is real hot but tastes like shit, so I throw it away, not giving it a chance to help me figure things out. Besides, Jenny is way smarter'n me anyway, so I go sit next to her bed.

"You OK?" she asks. "Need anything else? A snack maybe?"

"Shove it," I say.

"She told you?"

"Ya."

"What do you think?" Jenny asks.

"Damn it, Jenny," I say. "I ain't any good at this . . . just . . ."

"Just? Just what?"

"Just tell 'em to take care of you and not worry about the baby."

"Shut your mouth," she says.

"OK."

"We're both gonna be OK."

"Right," I say, "that's the spirit."

She laughs, then doubles over in pain.

There's a doctor in the doorway now. He's in green scrubs and he's got a stethoscope draped on one shoulder. He seems pretty young to me, not much older than me, if any, but his voice is reassuring.

"How's our girl?" he asks.

"Which one?" I ask. "'Cause I'm worried about this one and the one in the oven."

The doctor looks at me like I'm an idiot. He's not far wrong.

"Well, folks," he says, but Jenny's wincing in pain again. He puts a hand on her belly then asks her how bad it hurts.

"Out of ten?" she asks.

"Yes," the doctor says.

"Eleven."

"They're prepping a room right now," the doctor says. "The nurses will be coming in to set up an IV and get you ready. Dad, one of them is gonna take you to the locker room to get scrubs on too."

"What? What? What do I need scrubs for?" I ask.

"You sound a little hyper, Dad," he says. "Just breathe and maybe you can calm down."

"But—"

Jenny has my hand. "You're coming in the operating room," she tells me. And she looks in my eyes and there is no way I'm telling her no. Not Peter's daughter. And come to think of it, not Jenny, even if she weren't Peter's daughter. And for the first time ever, I have this thought: *I wish Jenny was having my daughter.*

It takes me maybe three minutes to get into scrubs, a green shirt and green slacks that I cinch at the waist and paper covers for my shoes. But when I get back, Jenny is wearing only a hospital gown and socks and I'm kind of embarrassed for her. The gown barely hides her crotch and I try not to look. I look at her lower legs and see that her ankles are huge.

"How long your ankles been swollen?" I asked.

"Couple of weeks," she answered.

"Tell the doctor?"

"Ya," she says, "he knows."

They've got something on Jenny's waist, it's hooked up to a machine and it's giving us the baby's heartbeat, or so they tell me. There's a nurse there, a really big African woman with a red afro and she's putting a needle in Jenny's arm. I am ready to say something when I get this look from Jenny, a look that I better know better, so I bite my tongue.

"OK," the nurse says, "it won't be long now."

But it was. We just stayed there and Jenny tried to breathe but nothin' cut the pain. She moaned and sighed, and when I tried to talk to her, she told me to shut up. A moment later she asked me to talk to her. A nurse came in, looked at the monitor, hurried out again. The Afro nurse came in, stood on the other side of the bed, next to

Jenny and stayed with us, helping Jenny breathe, watching things, and waiting like we did.

Then a couple of people came in with a gurney and acted like they were gonna move her, but then they left. Another nurse came in and told us, "We had to move one in ahead of you." She took the gurney.

"What?" I asked. "Why?"

"I presume," she said, "that their baby is in distress."

I stood and shouted, "And how about this baby!"

Jenny took my hand again, squeezed it hard, and I gasped. We waited. And waited. The black nurse left, then, came back and told us somebody else had been moved in ahead of us again.

I whisper to Jenny, "Want me to start making a fuss?"

She shook her head no. We waited again.

Finally, they loaded her on the gurney. The nurse gave me a little paper hat and a mask, and I walked next to Jenny, holding her hand. We get in a great big elevator, go up a couple of flights, and they whisk us into an operating room. I'm kinda shoved aside, and Jenny's moved off the gurney and onto the operating table and they attach her to a bunch more tubes and they put some sheets or towels across her to cover her up, push up her gown, and a nurse is putting some red crap all over her belly. There's three doctors there and nurses and I'm not sure who's who. Up by Jenny's head, there's a black guy sitting on a stool with a big mask. He's got a heavy accent like he just came over from the Congo. "Once we give you the anesthesia," he says, at least that's what I think he says, "they need to work fast. So I'm going to start you out with something that'll just make you a little drowsy, then when they're ready, we'll hit you with the good stuff."

Jenny nods.

He lowers the mask on her and I want to scream, to get a different gas passer there, but Jesus H. Christ, what right do I have to step in?

The doctor down by Jenny's baby nods, and then the black doctor starts counting Jenny down from ten. She only gets to three.

I can barely see anything, but the doctor is doing something to her, then he's tugging at something, then he says, "Christ. Code blue, code blue."

An alarm goes off. A nurse grabs my arm, starts to try to get me out of the room.

"Fuck that," I say, and I am too strong for her. I stand my ground.

They're still workin' on Jenny and no signs of the baby yet that I can see when three people come chargin' into the room, not in masks or anything.

"What's going on?" one of them asks, and the doctor gives 'em all kinds of medical jargon, but I get the gist of it. This baby ain't breathin'. I'm in the corner. They put Jenny completely out. Three or four people are workin' on that baby, and it looks like they got her breathin', or else they're breathin' for her. They seem to be satisfied with what's happening. One of 'em says somethin' like "I think we got her."

"What's that mean?" I say, and I'm frantic. I admit it.

"She's breathing on her own, Dad," that doctor says, in a kind voice.

Then they're still workin' on Jenny, but they're done with that little girl. Another doctor finally comes over and talks to me. "Mr. Thurgood," he says, "we're taking your daughter to the NICU. Want to join me?"

Jenny's out like a stone. Good for her. I walk with him, up a couple of sets of stairs and into this area with lots of little rooms. Jenny's baby is in an incubator, and she has only a diaper on but plenty of tubes and lines going in and out of her.

"Is she . . . is she breathing?"

"Yes," he says, "she's breathing on her own. The only problem is we don't know how long she was without oxygen."

There's a nurse in the room, working on the baby, putting her in a blanket. And the doctor's talking to me about cooling the baby—I have no idea what the hell that means. And then the nurse asks me for the baby's name. I'm pretty sure I know what Jenny wanted to call it, but I say, "Not until Mom is here."

The doctor says, "Let's talk about what we're facing."

I don't know what to say, but then there's an agitation behind me and I see Peter stick his head into the room. A security guard is trying to hold him back.

"This is?" the doctor asks.

"Grandpa," I answer. "Let him in."

Peter walks right up to me, mad I see, and gets an inch from my face. "What are you playing at?"

I whisper, "This is what Jenny wanted. You weren't around."

He steps back. Takes it in. Decides that's OK. Turns to the doctor.

"Now," Peter asks, "just what's going on?"

Fourteen

IT'S A WEEK later, and Jenny's out of the hospital but the baby ain't. Peter has heard the whole story, and he's happy with me again, proud of me, kind of, it feels like. The baby had *cooling* for several days, which was kind of bizarre; they kept her intentionally cold, and she looked downright blue. But the good news is she moves everything on her own, her legs and arms and toes, and it just may be that she'll be OK. I heard what this one PA said. She said, "You can know a baby is OK just by looking at her."

Her name is Marie Petra Thurgood. I like it. She's gonna be in the hospital for a while, and I get some hospital duty with the baby and with Jenny and she can't drive herself, so I ain't workin' much. But I do tell Peter I gotta have next Sunday and Monday off. And that's all I tell Peter.

Nick went ahead and watched 'em the Monday I was at the hospital, and to his surprise, our friend Bart was not one of the two guys acting as muscle.

"Too goddamn bad we didn't strike that day," he says.

"Ya," I say, "that ain't really gonna matter."

"What?" he says.

"Well," I tell him, "I think we missed the obvious play that's gonna be the easiest way to pull this off." And that happens to be true. It was sitting in the NICU, watching that little blue girl struggle for life. I had time to think things over and figured out the best way to take all that drug money.

I told Nick they were most vulnerable between the time the cash was delivered on Sunday and when they went to the bank on Monday. I was surprised; in fact, I wasn't even sure that the little Jew would be home alone that night. I assumed they would have the money in a safe. And we could be sure that the little Jew would have a cell phone.

"To call the cops?"

"Nah," I said, "that's one thing he won't do. But by the time he knows we're in the house, he'll call somebody for backup, probably those big muscle guys."

"So we take 'em all out?" Nick asked.

"Nobody's gonna get killed," I tell him. "If we can rip off the cash without anybody dying, the cops will never hear about it."

Sunday night, we parked behind the house, in the cemetery parking lot. When night came, we walked down the hill through the prairie grass and cut through the chain link fence to create an opening we could slip easily and quickly through. From the bottom of the hill, we could see through the open lots to his driveway. So we could see when the cash deliveries came and went. All five deliveries were made—we counted, then we saw one of the big muscle guys leave too. But we still didn't know for sure who was in the house.

It was approaching nine, but I told Nick we needed to wait even longer.

After midnight, when the last light went out in the house, we went to the back of the house and looked for lines. We were all dressed in dark clothes, with our ski masks pulled down over our faces. We knew that was suspicious if a neighbor saw us, but protectin' our identities was damned important too.

Nick found a line and cut it. Probably the telephone line, which might or might not be active. He found what he thought was a security line too, and cut it. Then we retreated, to the neighbors' backyard, standing by a large fir tree and waited. Thought we might hear the security system go off. Thought some of the muscle might show up. Nothing happened.

"Whaddya think?" Nick asked.

"Five minutes," I said, looking at my watch.

After ten minutes, we approached the back door. I got out my Allen set and started tinkering with the lock. It opened easily.

We found ourselves in an unfinished basement, with wooden steps up to the next level. That door was also locked and the Allen set did its job again. We were trying to be quiet, but you can't be perfect.

Upstairs, the house was quiet. There wasn't a light on. But it was lighter than the basement, and we could see that we'd entered a kitchen. The linoleum creaked as we walked toward the next room, a long living room. That room appeared to have a wooden floor. The front door entered there and there was an opening to a hallway, which probably had the bathroom and a couple of bedrooms.

We hadn't heard anything, but I still thought we had to figure he'd heard us and called it in. We were in a hurry. I waved one hand out in the hallway. Nothing. Now, I put the gun out in the hallway, and before I could even turn it, I heard the sound of a pump action on a shotgun. That is a sound you know and never can forget. It came from the south room. I waved at Nick to move that direction in the living room and set up. He did it, slowly, quietly.

I grabbed a candy dish off a table and dropped it in the hallway. It made a nice crash. And the shotgun blast coming down the hallway south to north was damned loud.

Nick then raked the wall with four shots, beginning high and moving down, where he thought the firing had come from. There was no ricochet, luckily. It can be dangerous shootin' into a wall, especially if you hit a nail.

I heard something in the south room fall down, probably a person. I wasn't sure he didn't still have his gun ready to go again—I entered the hallway and ran that way. He was lyin' on the ground, the shotgun next to him, his hands covering his ears.

"Don't shoot," he said, "don't shoot. We ain't got nothin'."

I kicked the shotgun aside. Then I reached down, pulled his hands back and tied them in long plastic ties. Then I lifted him up, sitting him against the rumpled bed. What I saw surprised me. It was a king bed and I thought both sides had been slept in.

"Where's your cell?" I asked.

"Don't got one."

Nick joined us. I clipped the man's ear with my revolver, more a nick than anything else.

"Don't lie. Your cell?"

The closet door opened and out walked a skinny white girl dressed only in panties, maybe half the man's age. I couldn't help starin' at her.

"Take a picture, it'll last longer," she said, handing me a cell phone. "He told me to call but I was too scared."

I turned it on, got his password from her, and looked at the phone. "Says no recent activity," I said.

"I've called the police," the man said.

I reached down and slapped his face. "Bullshit," I said, "that's the one thing you wouldn't do."

Nick directed the woman to lie on the bed, on her stomach, and we secured her hands behind her.

I put the gun barrel on the man's temple and asked the one question we cared about: "Where's the money?"

"We ain't got much—" he started, and I clipped him harder with my gun.

"I'm looking for your sack of drug money," I said, "the one you're takin' to the credit union tomorrow morning."

He looked at me.

"They're going to kill you," he said, finally.

"Get in line," I said, "you should worry about me killing you."

"Nah," he said, "they'd kill me if I told you."

"Buddy," I said to Nick, "shoot the girl."

He looked at me. We were in our ski masks, so I couldn't give him the hint I wanted to with a look. I reached over and pointed the gun at the back of the woman's head.

"We'll do it," I said. "Now where's the money?"

"She's a whore," he said. "Kill her."

Well, I could tell she was no whore. And I could see that she didn't like what he said, but I thought a little more persuasion could help. I cocked the gun.

"Stop, stop," she said. "He's got a safe. In the other bedroom."

We left her and dragged him down the hallway, pretty rough too, until we got to the bedroom on the north. It had a desk and a gun case and a safe.

"Now," I said, "the combination."

"No way, they'll kill me," he said.

"Think what I'll do," I say. I pull out my knife, reach down, and scrape the blade roughly across his neck.

"You won't get the combination if I'm dead," he says. But that's the wrong thing to say. If he'd said he didn't have the combination, well, I knew that was possible. But now, I was pretty sure he actually knows it.

This is getting us nowhere. I take the knife and put it behind his ear.

"In ten seconds," I say, "I'm going to slice your ear off. If you still don't tell me, I'll take the other ear, then your nose. Now what's the fuckin' combination?"

He says nothing. I start cutting on the back of his ear, just a nick really, but enough to draw blood.

He wobbles around, shaken, I can see.

"Stop it," he says, "stop it."

The money bag is empty, and the safe has cash nicely counted and grouped on the shelves. We hurry putting it in the bag, then we run out of the hallway.

"Cut me loose," he says.

"It'll be better for you come mornin'," I say, but I'm being too optimistic. I hear tires squealing outside, and I figure, shit, somehow he got a hold of his people.

We go down to the basement. It's dark and I'm worried someone's there, but that ain't the real problem. Thank God, it's empty. When we open the back door, there are two of them. At least. The fire comes from two separate places anyway. Handguns.

We get back inside, and the fire against the door continues. Glass breaks. I hear slugs hit the outside of the house and just hope it holds. Not all of it does, a couple of slugs come through.

"What now?" Nick asks.

"Wait for it," I say.

"Wait for—" More gunfire from outside, closer now. I have my gun ready. "Wait for the sirens," I tell him. "If they want to come in the door, we kill them. Otherwise, we let the sirens chase them off."

I hear the men outside talking. I hear yelling. They're yelling to someone at the front of the house. There is a second round of gunfire at the back of the house.

Finally, I hear sirens. We hear someone running. Nick bolts. Too soon, 'cause he runs right into one of the muscle boys and the two of them fall down. I arrive a moment later, to see Bart and Nick on the ground, both trying to get up. My blackjack is out and so is Bart in a moment. We run west, get through the fence, and into my van. I don't look back.

When we get to the van, we throw the money bag in, Nick gets in back, closes it, and I remove my cap and start the van. But I don't move, waiting to see where and when the sirens arrive. As two cops zip past the entrance to the cemetery on University, I roll the van out of the parking lot, down the street, pulling the lights on as I turn west. And we drive away.

It hadn't occurred to me that Nick might be hit. He said nothin', which takes lots of guts. It's not a bad wound, the bullet has nicked his shoulder, but we got to get it treated. I drop him at my place, then park the van three blocks away and walk back. I put the money in the trunk of my old car, stop at Peter's for the medical bag—he ain't home, probably at the hospital—and walk up the stairs to sew up Nick's shoulder.

I poured alcohol over the wound, and Christ, did Nick howl. But when I put on gloves and poked in the wound to ensure the bullet was gone, he was a soldier. It has plainly gone through and didn't hit anything major either, since he was walking and talking. I sewed it up and then poured alcohol on it again.

I gave him $200, out of my wallet. "We're going to have to clean the money we got tonight," I said. "Maybe next week."

I have Nick lie down on my bed. He's not going to die because I let him go home alone, and then I walk downstairs, across the lot to the garden shed, walk in, and hide the take from tonight.

Fifteen

NOT SURE I remember all the foster homes. But there never was another family that wanted to adopt me. I really had no idea what had happened to my mother and had no idea how to reach out to my grandma either. I kept thinking she'd just show up some day, take me in her arms, and we'd drive away. I asked the social worker more than once, but she didn't seem interested.

I liked school but I became a holy terror there. At some of the schools, I was one of the very few white kids. I hung with the others and we fought the African kids when we had to. In some of the schools, minority kids were rare. I still usually found a way to fight with the ones there were. I stole kids' food, got in fights at recess, bullied the slow kids, and talked back to teachers. One teacher I loathed. He was older, about to retire, I was told, and he went out of his way to humiliate me in class when I hadn't done my homework, which was often. After class one day, I reentered his courtroom, went to his desk, found his grade book, and put it in my backpack. On the way home, I threw it in a dumpster. More than once after that, I saw him conferring with the principal and talking about the lost grade book, but no one ever asked me about it, so I ignored the whole deal.

Usually, I became a holy terror at my homes too. I stole money, stole food, beat up the other kids in the house, or got beaten up by them, and it became kind of routine to only be in a house for two or three months. A few times, there was a girl about my age. I'd initiate her into the doctor game, and when we were found out, which we usually were, there'd be hell to pay.

Every time I moved, I changed schools.

Then they placed me with Edna and Earl. I don't remember their last names.

Edna was a lively, short, chubby woman with teased blonde hair and a weird accent. Turns out she came from Germany. Earl had served in the army there, and I'm guessing to his chagrin, had returned with Edna as his bride after he was done being deployed. Earl drove a truck around the Des Moines area, delivering stuff. He left every morning before seven, got home in the afternoons about four, and started to drink beer. He drank Coors from a can. There was a long wooden porch on the front of the house. It ran thirty feet in length, was six feet wide, and there was a fence on the front of it. In nice weather, he'd sit there, downing one Coors after another and throwing the empties to the other end of the porch. Edna would come out and gather the cans after a while. Usually she said nothin'. On occasion, she'd bitch at Earl in her broken English and on occasion, he'd cuff her too.

I didn't get in trouble with Earl for at least a month. Then, one night, I felt like a peanut butter sandwich during the middle of the night. I might not have got in trouble if I'd been careful. But I was a kid. I made the sandwich and left the butter, the peanut butter, and the open bread sack on the counter. In the morning, Earl came upstairs into my room and dragged me by the neck of my pajamas down to the kitchen.

"Put that shit away," he said then he slapped the back of my head, kinda hard.

I did what he wanted. I thought that was the end of it. Earl was at the table, drinking coffee and eating a bowl of cereal. I started to leave the kitchen.

"Stop," he said.

I did. He told me to kneel down. I did. He told me to bend down and put my forehead on the linoleum. I did.

The first strike didn't catch me cleanly. It hurt, but it was nothin' special. I'd had worse by my own mother. The next was better, and by the third, I knew he was hittin' me with somethin' other than just his hand.

I started cryin'. "Now," he says, "every time you cry you get an extra pop. See?"

"Ya," I said.

Then down it came again, whatever it was, a belt, a switch, somethin' with a pretty good sting. When he was done, I looked up and he had a long metal spatula in his hand.

It was hard to sit in school that day, but I never showed nobody. I knew better than that. *Social workers are there to help kids.* Jesus. Lies, lies, and more lies.

But I think Earl had found somethin' he liked. The beatings happened more and more often, and he seemed to want to beat me so bad, he began makin' up things to blame me for. And he changed things up so they hurt more. Using my bare bottom. Using some kind of a whip. Playin' games with the punishment, but always endin' up with the same thing: a bruised and scarred buttocks for me. Edna said nothin'. When it was punishment time, she disappeared. Afterward, she'd put some salve on my butt.

The one time I was really safe was when Earl was good and drunk on Coors. Oh, I know, there's plenty of mean drunks, but Earl usually put himself to sleep. Then, after a short nap, he'd come in and we'd eat one of Edna's German meals.

He got off early on Friday. Didn't work Saturday. So on Friday afternoon, he wouldn't stop at six beers, or eight. He'd down a few on the porch and keep drinking through supper. After supper, wherever, in the living room watching TV, on the porch, or just at the kitchen table, he'd keep drinking. Maybe twelve, maybe fourteen.

And on those nights, he'd end up passed out wherever he was drinkin'.

So one Friday afternoon in May, he started in as usual, then had dinner then went back to the porch, and by seven, he was clearly out, snorin' away.

I started by easing his belt. I figured he'd wake and I'd be done, but no, he slept on. Then I unsnapped his pants. I pulled down the zipper. Nothin' from him. As I started to pull down his pants, he kind of snorted and shook a little, but he didn't wake. I had a hard time getting them pulled off his butt, but I did. I pulled down his pants to his ankles.

For a moment, I figured that was good enough. Then I thought, "Heck, why not?" and I took hold of the elastic on his tighty-whities and started them down. He seemed like he would wake, his hand flew up, but his head slumped and he slept on. Soon, his whities were around his ankle. I tried not to look at his dick, but it was clearly visible now as he sat there, his pants and underpants around his ankles on the front porch of his house, on a nice evening in May, snoring away but exposing himself.

Guess I was young enough to think they wouldn't figure it out, but somehow they knew it was me. I got beaten, then grounded, told to stay in my room. But of course, when they went to bed, I headed out. I got in a neighbor's car and found four dollars. I got a Coke and a candy bar at the Casey's. Then I sat in front of the Walgreen's on Douglas with some older boys, and smoked my first cigarette. When the cops brought me back to Earl's place early that morning, I knew social services would be there soon. *We'll have you in a nice home soon.* Liars.

I didn't go to another foster home for a while. I went to a shelter on the east side. It was kind of a lockdown, except that you could get out if you wanted. Others couldn't get in. I was younger than most of the kids. We had bunk beds in a large room with eleven other boys. There was always staff around and counselors. Once a week, I met with the counselor. She was easy to figure out. Tell her how you're feeling sad, that you feel upset about not havin' parents and a home and you just want to be loved. They eat that shit up.

Buses took us to school, although I had changed schools again. I kind of gave up in school. I didn't pay attention, didn't study, didn't worry about homework. We had study time at the shelter, but I found books to read. I finished Mark Twain's books about Huck and Tom, as well as *Connecticut Yankee* and *The Prince and the Pauper*. I found some other adventure books, about Tarzan and Dr. Strange and another guy, I can't remember his name, who was kind of a superhero. I also liked readin' about science and dinosaurs.

I stayed there several months, then one day, a lawyer came to see me. Told me she was my lawyer now. Wanted to know what I wanted. A week later, a new DHS worker came to get me. Said I was movin' to a farm in Madison County. It was a decrepit old farmhouse, white clapboard that needed to be scraped and painted. It was a little two-story with a steep stairway up to the three bedrooms on the second floor. The roof had several holes in it, and so pans were set up in various parts of the three bedrooms to catch rainwater. There were no curtains on any windows, something I'd not seen before, but I hadn't lived in rural Iowa before either.

The house was set on luscious, green, rolling farmland that was sporting the beginning of a crop of green corn. The first floor was a kitchen, a living room with an old-fashioned wooden TV set, a ratty old sofa, and a chair that looked like they got it from the dump. There was also a wooden horse barn, which, I realized, was in better shape than the house. Later, I learned that they only owned the house, barn, and one adjacent acre or so; the farmland belonged to a neighbor.

The woman was old; she wore thin, flowery dresses, had her hair up in a severe bun, and walked slowly, with a limp in her left leg. She didn't talk much, but when she did, you could see that she had lost two of her upper front teeth which caused a whistle when she did say something. That first day, she had me sit at the kitchen table and she warmed up some food. It was a pasta dish, noodles, tomatoes, and hamburger and it tasted wonderful. Although Edna could cook, this woman really knew how to make food flavorful. About an hour later, her husband came in. I think his name was Brian, or Byron, or something. He looked like he was ten years younger than her.

"Ever work a day of your life?" he asked me.

"No, sir," I said.

"Well," he said, "you're on a farm now. You're gonna learn how to work."

He was a mean old shit, and it was clear that he just wanted me as a slave. I was thirteen years old, and I learned to groom and feed the horses, weed his one-acre field, run the machinery needed to do so, and grade the long gravel driveway from the highway to the house. In my spare time, Brian showed me how to scrape paint. I started scraping the front of the house, and when I seemed to know what I was doin', Brian brought out a ladder so I could scrape above my head as well.

"Soon as you get this side scraped," he said, "you and me'll start painting."

I never got to ride the horses, but I fell in love with this one, a gray, spotted mare whose soft body I brushed as often as I could. She had a sweet demeanor and would purr when I brought her a carrot or an apple. Those huge teeth would stick out from her gums, and she'd chew on my offerings with a kind of guilty pleasure. It wasn't really much of a farm. Brian worked in town, in West Des Moines, at a manufacturing plant. But he tried to keep that acre producing sweet corn, and he expected me to do the work. In the late summer, we took our sweet corn and set up a stand in West Des Moines. He gave me a sign, told me the prices and left me there to sell to housewives who stopped by. I skimmed some of the money but it wasn't bad work, and I got to miss school.

Farming was not all that bad. And the old lady's cooking never got any worse. And I guess, although I knew they didn't care about me, whether I lived or died, I liked the old coots and I liked the old farmhouse. I bussed into Winterset to school, and I quickly set my sights on learnin' somethin'. I tried to stay out of trouble, although that wasn't always possible. I read lots of books, I worked hard because I liked it, and I decided that I had found a home at last.

We had a wonderful math teacher who realized that I was at least two years behind. Instead of setting me back, he started meeting me during lunch—I always brought a sack lunch that the old lady made me—and working through the concepts I'd missed.

In gym, we tried wrestling. I had become stronger, more powerful, from the work at the farmstead. But kids who knew wrestling moves beat me easily, so I started to learn those moves. Within three weeks, I started to win matches.

I also finally had a couple of friends. Matthew and David were both kids from Winterset, and they just kinda hung out with me. Both of 'em played baseball and basketball, and David was on the junior varsity football team. I wasn't allowed to be in a sport after school, because I was needed to work at the farm. But we did have time after school, especially if I skipped the bus and caught a ride from David, who had an old Ford. That, of course, was how I got into trouble. After school one day, we skipped the bus and went to the park. It was a lousy little park, just a patch of green, one basketball court, a few tables, and a kids' swing set and jungle gym. We sat on the swings and talked and then David said he had some weed. I had never tried it before, and when I inhaled, it surprised me. They laughed when I coughed. But I got it in and it tasted sweet and then I felt my first buzz. I liked how it made me feel.

Trouble was, from then on, I needed some money if I was going to get grass. It was that simple. David had a limited supply but it was his brother Doug who dealt. Doug was a senior in the Winterset high school. A baggie went for twenty. As much as I should be paid for the farm work, I never saw a cent. I literally never got a dime from Brian or his wife. I took to lookin' around the place for cash, and I found a little. I stole a ten from a teacher's purse and found a few bucks in school lockers, which turned out to be easy to break into, if no one else was around and if you was patient and quiet when you turned the combinations numbers and waited to see where they stuck. But week to week, it was hard to come up with twenty and I really wanted that weed. Plus, I was smoking ciggies too, and even though I could sneak a pack a week or so from the old lady, I was still a little short all the time to pay for dope.

So I got a better idea. I tagged along with David after school, even though I should have headed back to the farm for work, and when David was busy looking at a *Playboy*, I went into Doug's room and rifled his drawer. Nada. Tried the closet. I found several small plastic sandwich bags of pot, in a coat pocket. I took three.

Might have gotten away with it. But I decided to sell one of the baggies, figuring I could make a profit. Word soon got around school that I was dealin'. Noon, two days later, Doug and a friend found me on the playground.

"You sellin'?" he asked.

"Nah," I said.

"How come we hear you are?"

"Just had a little extra."

"How you'd come upon extra?" his friend asked.

"From the old man at my place," I said. "Didn't figure he'd miss a baggie."

"Stuff any good?" Doug asked. "Maybe I could buy it."

"Don't have any on me," I told him.

"That's right," he said, "because you ain't selling in this school." He cuffed me on the back of the head.

"Huh?"

"This is my territory. You ain't sellin' here," he says.

"Well—" All I said, 'cause he hit me on the back of the head again, harder.

The other guy came at me from the other side, pushed me down. I went down on my hands and knees on the gravel. When I got up, I went right for Doug's friend, surprised him, and knocked him down with a tackle. I went down on top of him, and I tried to slug him. But then, Doug was grabbing me by the neck of my shirt and pulling me off.

"Little asshole," he says, and then, standing me up, he hits me a good one in the stomach. I bend over, but here's the secret I have they don't know. I'm used to getting hit, burned, stuck and slapped.

Nothin' they can do scares me, nothin' they can do really hurts that bad. And I'd been taught, in shelter and at various homes, how to hurt somebody. Plus, I now know wrestling moves.

When I come up, I strike as fast and hard as I can. I kind of leap at Doug, who in his surprise, looks up. I hit him right in the Adam's apple. He drops his hands, bends over just a bit, and tries to breathe. I leave him, approach his friend, who has his hands on the ground as he tries to get up. I hit him square on the nose, and it starts to bleed. He lies down. I kick him in the ribs, as hard as I can. He rolls over, uses his hands to protect them. I'm on him, taking a hold of his head and mashing it into the ground. I hear Doug still gasping. I walk to him. He turns, stands up a little, and I kick for his nuts. I miss and he grabs my leg. This is awkward. He kind of turns me around and throws me off. So I rush him again, knock him down, and now he's on the ground, legs sprawled, and I use my knee and connect right in the groin.

"Oh," he goes, gasping, sounding miserable.

The other kid is trying to stand. I grab Doug's book bag, sling it over my shoulder and then down on Doug's friend. He lies down again, in a ball, and tries to cover. I grab his book bag too, walk over to the creek, and throw them both in.

I stand there, looking at those two pussies, and then laugh. "Tough guys," I say, "really tough."

Math has just begun when a secretary from the principal's office comes to the door asking for me. We walked the long halls to the office, and there was a cop sittin' there and a tall, older man in a cowboy outfit—at least that's how I thought of it. He wore cowboy boots and a bolo tie, but he had on a sport coat too, light blue.

We all went in the principal's office and she told them, "I just can't understand this. Johnny is no trouble . . . he's been in no trouble and he's a pretty good student."

The cop looked at her like she was crazy. The other guy told me his name was Pat and said they wanted to talk to me about an incident at John Wayne Park.

"Huh?" I asked.

"Did you beat up two kids over at the park yesterday?" the cop asked.

"Now you hold on," the principal said. "Iowa code says if you're investigating this young man for a crime, you have to have a parent present."

"That ain't it," the cop says. "We're thinking Johnny here will be a witness, right, Pat?"

The cowboy put up his hand. "Johnny," he said, "I'm Pat Coughlin, the juvenile court officer for this county. You've been accused of assault and of theft and of possession of marijuana with intent to distribute. You wanna tell us what happened and see if that makes it go easier on you?"

"Who is he supposed to have assaulted?" the principal asked.

She was a frumpy woman but not old, and for the first time in my life, I felt like somebody was on my side.

"Douglas Becvar and Randy Hull," Pat said.

'Two high school kids?" she asked.

"That's right," the cop answered.

"They've got to be two or three years older than Johnny."

"Irregardless," the cop said, "they're hurt pretty good and one of 'em's in the hospital."

"And Doug is a known drug dealer," the principal went on. I was likin' her better and better.

"So?" Pat said. Then he turned to me, "Johnny, you wanna tell us what happened?"

"Doug was accusin' me of stealing his drugs," I said, figurin' if I was gonna lie, somethin' close to the truth might work best. "He pushed me down. He started the fight. I finished it."

They both looked at me, surprised. So did the principal. I was surprised. I wanted to take it back, but I couldn't. Didn't it matter than they attacked me first?

"Look," the cop said, "I just wanna know one thing. Where'd you learn to fight like that?"

But they didn't wait for me to answer. Pat answered for me: "The Des Moines shelter," he said.

They cuffed me, in front, and I rode in the back of the Winterset police car to Des Moines. They didn't have a juvenile jail in Madison County, and I couldn't be with adults. This time I wasn't in a shelter; I was in detention. Lockdown. A jail, except only for juveniles.

Two days later, I'm back in Winterset, in the courthouse. This old-fart-lookin' guy—gray hair, jowly—tells me he's my judge. He says he wants to let me out of detention, except there's no place for me to go. He talks about schools, but he ain't talkin' about Winterset or Des Moines schools; he's talking about places where you are put away with other delinquents.

My lawyer is a young guy. I don't know if he knows anything, but he is tryin' to help me, I see that. He says somethin' about how I can go back home. Brian is in the back of the courtroom and the judge asks him. "He's a good worker," is all Brian says. And he nods.

"OK," the judge says, "but, Mr. Desmond, we'll have no further problems with you, is that right?"

The lawyer nudged me.

"Ya," I say.

"Yes, Judge," the lawyer whispers.

"Yes, Judge," I say.

"We'll see."

So I'm out. Two days later I'm back in school. I'm behind, of course, and the teachers give me the back assignments. When I get back to the farm, walking up the gravel road to the farm from the bus, Brian greets me.

"Here, give me your shit," he says, "and get to them horses. And when you're done with that, get in that field and start weeding. We'll call you for supper."

That night, after the first decent meal I had in days, I sit up in my room tryin' to get some of my schoolwork done. There's a table that passes for a desk, with a lamp, and I'm young so I try to stay up 'till about two or so, when I'm finally too gassed to keep studying.

The next morning, Brian gets me up just after six so I can feed and groom the horses a little. Breakfast is scrambled eggs with ham and a glass of milk, then I'm back on the school bus. Doug and his buddy and I have a no-contact order against each other, both of them being back in the juvenile system again, but his friends don't. Between first and second periods, a couple of them are waiting at my locker.

One of 'em shoves me a little and I kind of shuffle sideways. Then they both laugh. *Big fuckin' deal*, I think, and go back to my locker. I figure more is coming.

The next day, I arrive at school with my homemade brass knuckles in my pocket. It's really just dimes, lopped together with rubber bands so they won't come out of my hand when I use them. They can really hurt—this I know from shelter. Nothin' happens that morning though, and David and I walk over to the park during lunch, takin' our brown bags with us. He tokes up, and I'm too stupid to resist. A little dope sounds good.

It's the last break of the day and I need my science book and when I get to the locker, there's not one or two or three, but four older guys standin' there. They might not have done much, of course, but I don't wait to find out. My dimes are ready, and as I am walkin' around the first guy (a tall blond kid with a wide grin), I turn and punch him in the nose as hard as I can. I hear a very satisfying crunch and then he's bleedin' all over everything.

Most of the other guys just stand there, but one hefty kid goes after me and gets his arms around my waist and drives me into the wall. There ain't much I can do until he slacks his hold, and when he does, I drive my fist into his jaw. It doesn't hit him squarely, and he doesn't seem affected by it. But he does bring down his fist on the top of my head and I'm on my knees. I reach up and try to hit him again but then they're on me, at least four of 'em. I'm on the ground and trying to protect myself. I squirm, kind of crawl down the floor, run into the wall again, and then I hear yellin'. As most of 'em run, a teacher approaches and finds me lyin' against the wall and the tall blond kid holdin' on to his nose and bleedin'.

"You just can't stop fucking up, can you?" Coughlin says about a half hour later in his office. "You know I hate this shit. It's after four and I'd like to go home and have a beer, but I got to deal with you."

My lawyer is there too. "As I understand it," he says, "they jumped him."

"What about this?" Coughlin asks, throwing my homemade brass knuckles on his table. "Was that yours, Johnny?"

Ain't no point in lyin'. "There were five or six of 'em," I say, "so I thought I needed some protection."

"Andy Weir's got a broken nose," Coughlin said.

"Well," my lawyer says, "I just talked to Brian, and he'll allow him back again. But," he turns to me, "Johnny, you got stay out of trouble."

"All right," Coughlin says, "but first, we're going to have him pee in a cup. You clean, Johnny?"

Maybe he wouldn't have had me take the test. I'll never know, 'cause I told him I'd smoked weed that day and then they cuffed me again and Coughlin drove me to Des Moines. More lockup.

Sixteen

I WAS SIDING a house on the east side of Urbandale the next morning when two guys in a big car get out and walk up. Detectives—clear as glass.

"John Desmond?" the big one asks.

I get down from the ladder and walk over to him. "Ya," I say.

"Wonder if you could help us?"

"Depends," I say. "Who are you?" As if I don't know.

He shows me his badge: Des Moines PD.

"What's it about?"

"Well, to be honest," the detective says, "we're not sure. We've had some gunplay at a house near the cemetery. We've got someone in custody. We want to figure out what's going on."

"I've got nothin' to do with any of that."

"Ya? Good to hear. So why does your name come up?"

"Jesus," I say, "I don't know how to answer that. From who?"

"Whom," the other detective, a tall, lean man, said.

"Whom said it?" I ask, jokin' now.

The big man answers, "We aren't going to tell you that."

"Well then," I say, "how would I know why my name comes up? Got nothin' to do with it." I turn to go back to the house.

"Would you come downtown with us?"

I turn back. "Why? Am I under arrest?"

"No," the tall man answers. "But I think you know what's happening here. If you don't want to go with us, we'll get a material witness warrant issued, and then you'll sit in the jail until we get this figured out."

I wonder if they're bluffin'. I also wonder whether I'm better to make 'em go through the hassle of that material witness bullshit. They might not. But I also know, from the movement, that sometimes guys sit in jail a long time on a material witness warrant.

"Hold on while I talk to my boss," I tell 'em. They stand there.

'Course I'm the lead dog on this crew. I get on the cell, tell Jeb what's up, ask him if I can leave the Mexicans in charge. He says no, but he could be there about two to cover.

"Listen," I tell the detectives, "could you do me a favor? My boss will take over here at two. Could we do it then?"

The minute they're out of sight, I call Nick. He's holed up in my apartment. No, he hasn't heard from cops. We talk about what to do. I say lie low. 'Course, he doesn't take my advice any better than anybody else. He decides to walk down to the QuikTrip for a Coke, and that's when they pick him up. When I get to the police station just before two thirty, the tall cop comes to reception, gets me, and when we go upstairs, Nick is sitting there. Thank God he's wearing a long-sleeved shirt so it doesn't show where I stitched him up.

They make it simple. They know we're involved. They know we were in the house. They want to know who shot at whom, and they want to what the hell was going on. Otherwise, they'll arrest us both.

"Look," I say, "we don't know nothin'."

"Stop right there," the big guy says, then reads us our Miranda rights. Just like on TV. "Now," he says, "we're going to bring someone in. He's going to tell us whether you are involved. If so, you're going to be arrested. If not, fine, we'll see you another day. Got it?"

I nod. Don't know what Nick, sitting next to me, thinks, but he don't say nothin'.

The tall guy leaves, comes back into the room a moment later with Bartholomew, in street clothes, but cuffed.

"All right, sir," the tall man says, both of 'em still standing there while Nick and I sweat bullets and don't know where to look, "were either of these men there that night?"

Bart looks at Nick, then looks at me. He winks.

"These guys work with us at the security company," he says.

"All right," the detective says, "but were they there that night?"

"Not these guys," Bart says, "nah, I'd know if it was either one of these guys."

I'm relieved, but in shock too. Why the hell did this big African protect us?

Jenny's baby finally came home from the hospital. While we waited, Peter picked out some paint and I painted the room in a nice soft pink. Jenny put up some new white curtains and Peter brought up Jenny's old crib from the basement and he and I put it together. The mattress was in pretty rough shape though, so I went out to Target and bought her a new one.

She and the baby were home about three weeks when she heard that Antonio had come up for parole. She got word he'd been granted parole but he had to live at the Fort, an old army barracks now used by corrections as a kind of a halfway house for people coming out of prison. Still, he was able to be there when we had Maria's three-month birthday party. I was surprised when I met him. He was a small man, but when he stood, he kind of hunched over so he appeared to be smaller still. I woulda guessed he was Jewish but knew he was Italian. I guess wop was OK with Peter, although from what I now knew of Jenny, she didn't always worry about the advice her old man gave her.

After we all had a little cake and soda, Antonio walked into the baby's room. Jenny was holding Maria, and handed her to me. Jenny walked to the nursery. I could hear them talking in there, and from years of experience, I could tell the tone was not friendly. I just walked around with Maria, enjoying having her. I held her in my arms like a football and she didn't move much. Her eyes were open, but I couldn't tell whether she was taking anything in.

Jenny walked out first, took the baby, and walked to Peter. I saw the two of them talking quietly. Then Peter signaled me, and the two of us walked to the nursery.

Antonio was holding the mattress. "Where'd this come from?" he asked.

"What difference is that to you?" Peter said. "We took care of things because you couldn't."

"Well, that's my daughter, and I want to take care of her. Who painted this room? Looks like shit."

Peter walked over, took the mattress from him, put it back in the bed, and then announced, "You're leaving now, Antonio."

"Says who?" But immediately Peter had one arm bent behind the man's back.

Antonio tried to hit him with his other hand, but I caught his fist, without any harm coming to either of us. "Stop that shit, man," I said.

And then he spit on me. I wanted to lay him low, I really did. But I was thinkin', see, that if I did so, Jenny might never forgive me. I just took hold of his free arm, bent it back, and we escorted him out of the front door.

It wasn't the end of Antonio, as I didn't think it would be. A couple of nights later, when I took somethin' back to Peter, the three of them were in the kitchen, eatin' dinner together like a family.

"Oh, Johnny," Jenny said, "Antonio wanted to tell you something."

He stood, looked just a little down, and said, "John, I'm sorry for how I behaved. Thanks for what you did for Jenny."

I wasn't sure how to take it, this apology. To tell you the truth, I didn't believe it. I muttered somethin' and was getting ready to leave, but Peter asked me to wait on the front step. I did, and a minute or so later, he came out.

He brought out two beers. We popped 'em and each took a swig. "Got a little something for you to do," he said. And then he told me. It was just about the first time I wanted to tell him no. But it was Peter. Peter. In a way, he was the movement to me. How could I tell him no?

There are three Jew temples in Des Moines that I know of, two up on Grand and one near Roosevelt High School on Polk Boulevard. All of 'em are on the near west side. There are now a couple of Islamic centers also. We never had bothered them before, always havin' hit the Jew cemeteries, the temples, and just harassing the Hebes. But 'course, we knew it was the Muslims who were the real threat these days.

They've built a kind of temple. They call it an Islamic center, on the west side of Des Moines, nearly to Windsor Heights, one of the smaller suburbs. It's an old elementary school. 'Course, they pay no taxes on the property. Old darkies in full African garb walk to and from the place, and they have a playground but it's in really awful shape. They also built an Islamic learning center up on Douglas, near Merle Hay Mall. That place is not so regularly occupied, and Peter figured it'd be easier to hit. But this wasn't just leaflets or spray paint. Peter had a bolder idea.

He wanted to act fast, but I told him we needed to spend at least a couple of nights casing the joint. Peter didn't seem happy; he told me I was getting too careful, but he went along.

Nick and I parked at the IHOP one evening, then at the cigarette store on Douglas the next. Both were weekdays, and on both occasions, the last person left about nine. So I figured if we waited until after that, we could hit he place, and no one would be there.

I don't do bombs. I don't like 'em. They sometimes go off before you want 'em to. Also, they don't always go off when you want 'em to. And I don't like settin' 'em. I told Peter, and he told me he had the man for me. His name was Donnie and he was one of us. That's important to me, 'cause a guy just workin' for the money will turn on you easily. I asked Peter to just use a Molotov cocktail, but he said no, and thank God he did.

Donnie brought us the box. It was a square box, about the size a cake would come in. I thought it was a little too big. When you lifted off the top, you could see what looked like two sticks of dynamite. There was also a clock. It was set to ten minutes. Donnie showed me how to turn it on. Once I do, he said, it'll go. No backing up, no foolin' around.

The U-Haul place next to the Islamic center closes at nine. At five minutes after, we pull in the parking lot, drive as far south as you can, turn behind the building, turn around, and park. Nothin', nada. We wait a half hour. Nothin'. I get out, walk around and Nick hands me the box he's been holdin'. I hand it back to Nick once he gets out. We walk around the back of the U-Haul building, cross the lot to the south side of the Islamic center, then along the wall to the front door. Nick holds the box and I work the door. At first it resists, and I think about breakin' in. Then at the last second, I feel the lock give in to my Allen wrench, and the front door opens. I figure there might be an alarm, but I really don't worry about it. We walk in. I put the bomb down in the reception area, take off the box, and set the clock. Then we're out. It's that fast.

We walk to our car, drive out across the street, and wait at the IHOP. I know, I know. Standard operating procedure is to leave. But I had to see what was going to happen.

One minute. Two. Three. Then goddamn it, a light goes on at the south end of the Islamic center.

"Fuck," I say.

"Let's go," Nick says.

"What?"

"Let's get out here. Let's not wait——"

"I ain't killin' anybody," I answer. The clarity of my feelings on this surprised me. It is an Islamic center. It's likely to be an African in there, and either way, a Muslim. What do I care? But something in me is stinkin' apparent: *I ain't killin' nobody.*

So I drive back to the U-Haul. This time, I park so the car is blocked by the U-Haul building. If that thing blows, Nick ain't goin' with it. I run around the building, across the parking lot, and into the back door of the Islamic center, which is not locked. I see no one.

I yell, "Hey, anybody here?"

I hear nothin'. I think about grabbin' the box, but what am I gonna do with it? Where could I put it so it wouldn't hurt nobody?

I enter a hallway. At the end, there's an office with a light on. I hurry down to it, open the door, and there's a little old, man, wringing out a mop in a janitor's sink.

He looks surprised.

"Yes," he says, in some kind of accent. He's fairly dark, more Afro than Arab.

"C'mon," I say, "we gotta get out."

He doesn't move. I grab his shoulder. He doesn't move. I implore him, try to make him move. Nothin' happens. I have no idea how much time has passed, but I don't think I can argue with him. I slug him, he goes down, and I grab him and use the fireman's hoist and we're back in the hallway. I use the back door. I get outside and hustle as fast as I can west. We get to the U-Haul building, and he's flailing now. He falls off me. I grab his arm, dragging him west still. He's trying to fight me. We get around the corner so that the U-Haul building is between us and the other building.

It blows. It shakes us, rattles the windows of the U-Haul building. It's a huge fireball that I can see over the top of the U-Haul building. The man holds his ears and stays on the ground. I'm in the car, and we're out of the parking lot as fast as I can. But I figure I'm in trouble.

BOOK TWO

shelter from the storm

'Twas in another lifetime, one of toil and blood
When blackness was a virtue, the road was full of mud
I came in from the wilderness, a creature void of form
Come in, she said
I'll give ya shelter from the storm

Bob Dylan, "Shelter from the Storm"

One

TEN O'CLOCK CAME, and I hadn't been called, so I said, *screw it*, and opened a beer. Barb had picked up a six-pack of Blue Moon; usually she bought whatever was on sale, and the Blue Moon was speaking to me. It said, *You're going to have to drink me. No one else is going to.* I sat in the recliner, lights out, and turned on the local news. Mainly I watch the weather and the sports. With a presidential election less than a month away, the news was mostly annoying. I sat back, enjoyed my bottle, and almost dozed off. But a second Blue Moon called me. They're relentless.

Barb came down in her pajamas. "Coming to bed?" she asked. She's pushing fifty, about four years younger than me, but when I see the outline of her breasts against her pink nightgown, I'm still attracted. So I took a good pull on the second bottle I'd opened, started shutting off all the lights, checked that the garage door was closed, and started upstairs. Halfway up, I hear the phone. *Christ*, I think and start hurrying up the stairs. Barbie picks up.

"Yup," she says.

"Yup," I hear her say again.

"Hold."

I get to the bedroom. She's lying there in our warm, cozy queen-sized bed, her reading glasses on, her book in her lap, handing me the phone. "It's work," she says.

The fire is almost out, but the building is a goddamn mess. It's going to end up being torn down, that much I can tell. The south side is badly burnt, with black streaks coming out of the windows. The north end, though, has been blown apart, with plaster, wood and glass having been propelled outward, turning it into shrapnel that flew into the adjacent U-Haul building and Douglas Avenue. And I also see that it's an Islamic educational center. *Christ,* I think, *a goddamned hate crime and I draw it. The mayor will be all over it, as will the* Register *and TV news. There'll be reporters here soon. In fact, if it wasn't so early in the morning, they would have beat me here.*

There are five of our patrol cars parked nearby, blocking the street as officers mill around. There are three patrol cars from Urbandale. For a second, I have hope. I tell myself, *Please, please, please let it be in Urbandale.* But it's not. That suburb's line is just west of the U-Haul building, which is west of the Islamic center. It's a Des Moines crime.

Dominic Annina was there. Sergeant, patrol. Good guy. He's on night duty right now, in charge of the patrol officers in the western part of the city.

"What the fuck, Dom?" I ask.

"Get you out of bed, Bobby?" he asks.

"You know it. Aren't I lucky?"

"Well," he says, "it's an interesting one, that's for sure. See over there?"

I look where he's pointing. Two cops, but three other men, in loose-fitting, free-flowing, colorful Muslim garb, all with those caps that I think of as Shriners'. "Is that Ali?" I ask.

"Yes, sir, the one and only," he says.

Abdul Samad Ali. Onetime Bobby Carpenter. Onetime gang member, drug dealer. We never got him on anything more serious than drug possession, and he went to prison for eight or nine months. While he was there, some of his gang members got in a shootout near downtown and killed an innocent woman in a nearby car. But he was in prison and couldn't be tied to any of it. When he came out, he was changed, different. He ended up going to the University of Iowa, becoming an imam, a preacher, and school board member, and he runs a drug treatment and community center on the east side. All in all, he's beneficial to our community. What was he doing all the way over here?

"Anybody hurt?" I asked.

"Matter of fact," Dom tells me, "ambulance just left with a janitor."

I look at the building again. "He survived?"

"Well, yes," Dom said, "since we found him clear on the other side of the U-Haul building. Lying down. A little banged up but not even singed."

"Wait a second, wait a second," I said. "What the hell?"

"Ya, makes you wonder. Wouldn't we be lucky if he just put together some chemicals the wrong way? Jerry Levinthal talked to him. He's over there with the Urbandale cops. They brought coffee."

We've got the road blocked. The assistant state fire marshal is here and he and I walk in the front door, where there's little left, but he tells me there's not much doubt that it was an explosion and that it occurred here in the lobby.

"Could it be gas line or the furnace or something?" I ask.

"In the lobby?" he says.

"Seems like I have to ask," I said. "You're thinking incendiary device?"

"I am."

Levinthal gives me the information about the janitor. Our technicians have arrived; they're taking photographs and measurements. The fire marshal owns the scene, but I've got maybe twenty cops on scene and he has three people, so we work together. His people are looking for pieces of a device. I leave Tommy to watch the scene, throw on my blue lights, and speed toward Broadlawns Hospital, the county hospital, where indigents and anybody without insurance gets medical care. I show my badge to get in the ER and find Dr. Patel there. I don't remember his first name. He's from Pakistan or India. I get that mixed up sometimes.

"You have a guy here from the fire?"

"Firebomb is what I hear," Patel says. "Ya, he's in room 3. But I think he may have lost his hearing."

"Wouldn't surprise me."

He did have a hard time hearing me. His wife, a short, overweight brown woman with a thin, reddish Afro, huge loops earrings, and a wonderful smile, sat next to him and helped the two of us communicate.

"What happened?" I asked.

"I don't know."

"Tell me what you do know?"

"I was just filling the sink."

"He's the janitor," his wife said, "but it's a part-time gig. He doesn't really get paid for doing it."

"Oh," I asked, "how often do you work?"

"One, two nights a week," she tells me. "I told him not to go in last night. It was too late. He has to work at seven in the morning, but he hadn't cleaned up the center for a couple of days, so he left me and the children."

"You have kids at home?" I was sorry I'd asked. I could see they were too old.

"Grandkids. You know," she said.

"Huh?" he asked. "What are you saying?"

I raised my voice. "Can you tell me what happened?"

"Like I said," he said, "I was just filling the sink. I didn't see nothing, I didn't hear nothing. I walk in the back door, on the south side, you know, and I go in, put some soap in my mop tank and I start filling the sink."

"OK," I say, nodding at him, hoping he'll continue.

"Ya," she said, "he'll go on about that sink forever. Lester may just be a janitor, but he does it just as good as you can do it. When he cleans a place, it's clean. He's dedicated."

"I can see that," I tell her.

"What are you saying?" Lester asked, in a voice too loud for the room.

"We're just chatting," his wife answered.

"Then?" I ask, almost yelling. "What happened then?"

"Like I say, I was filing the sink and then this guy comes in the room."

'What guy?" his wife asks.

"Ya, what guy?" I ask.

"Didn't know him."

I use my hands to motion that he should continue.

"Young white guy," Lester says. "Never seen him before."

"Go on," Lester's wife yells at him.

"Young guy wearing a dark coverall, white, young, as I said that."

"And?" I yell.

"He says, 'We got to get out of here.' But I don't know what he's talking about. I say something like 'Huh? And he grabs me by the arm and I am filling my sink, so I don't move. Then, I don't know, he hits me or something and then he's dragging me out the back door. We walk toward the next building. He's helping me. And then he's kind a dragging me. I don't know."

We both wait. Lester starts again.

"Last thing I remember is a hell of an explosion. Then that boy gets in his car and drives off. Good Samaritan, I guess."

Not what I was thinking. Not at all.

I got back to the scene but the fire marshal's people are busy and Dominic has the scene barricaded off. Having Douglas closed is a bitch; it's a main thoroughfare. But what are you going to do. So I go home, slip into the sheets.

"What time is it?" Barbie asks.

"Four, four thirty," I tell her, looking at the big red clock she has on her table next to the bed. She's going blind, a fact which has precipitated three surgeries to no avail and which keeps me working because we're too young for Medicare. I have enough years in for my pension, but not to pay health premiums without an employer.

"OK," she says. "Get some sleep."

"Unless you want to play?" I ask her. Her slap is playful but meaningful and I tell her I can't sleep, then my head hits the pillow and I am out.

Two

I'M LATE BUT everyone knows how late we were on the scene; in fact, some of our people are still there. The chief wants to see me. She's got the morning news show from the NBC affiliate on in her office when I arrive.

"Hell of a deal," she says.

"No shit, Judy," I tell her. I've known Judy since she was a new recruit, in the class just after mine, and while I think she's all right in the job, I don't exactly treat her with reverence.

"So?"

"Fire marshal is handling the investigation right now," I tell her. "We won't have results for a day or so. But it looks like an incendiary device."

"A bomb?"

"Sure, a bomb."

"Any leads? Is it a hate crime? Do we need help?"

"Christ, Judy," I say, "one question at a time. But the answers are maybe, maybe and maybe."

"Well," she says, "you and I are walking across the bridge there to see the mayor in ten minutes. We need to tell Frank something. And what should I have Bobby say? Should we have a press conference?"

"First of all," I say, "the good news is no one died. There was a janitor in the building, but somebody got him out of range before the thing went off."

"Somebody?"

"Certainly our perp or one of our perps," I told her.

"So why?"

"There's a 64,000-dollar question," I say. "Speculation, he didn't mind firebombing an Islamic center, but didn't want anyone to die."

"Still," Judy says, "risky."

"Very."

"Hate crime?"

"Maybe."

"Can we say that that's how we're treating it for now?" she asks.

"That's our theory for now?" I propose. "How's Frank going to take that?"

"The mayor is not too bad about staying the hell out of these things generally, but a hate crime at this moment, well, he's going to want to put his two cents in."

"I see that. But we need to be clear we don't have any suspects. And as to the janitor, he and his wife asked that he not be identified."

"That's well and good," she says, "but Abdul isn't going to listen to us. He's called a press conference for this afternoon."

"Where?" I ask.

"At the center."

"Well," I answer, "we're going to have to keep him away from the crime scene."

"So," Judy says finally, "any ideas?"

"I think we have got to look to Peter Thurgood and his people. The campaign has kind of stirred them up, and you know about that we had Petticourt in the city for a day or two. We looked for him but didn't find him. That had to be Thurgood as well."

"You don't think he did it?"

"If he had a hand in it, it was to order it. But no, he wouldn't have done it."

"Why do you say that?"

"Because he wouldn't have saved the janitor."

Mayor Carney wants to go on the air before Abdul. Judy and I stand behind him and the fire marshal—the fire marshal, not his assistant who has been working the scene since early morning—and the county attorney stands to his right.

"This kind of hate crime has no place in Des Moines," the mayor says, and he probably means it. He just doesn't know what he's talking about. Even if it is a hate crime, and I suspect it is, it's nothing new here or anywhere else in the country. Just last month, we had Nazi slogans painted on the walls of a temple, leaflets passed out during service calling for *ovens for Jews*, and crosses burned at African American homes. I'm not liberal, I'm a solid Republican voter, and I am particularly for gun rights, but this shameless racism should have no place here or anywhere in our country. But don't be naive. It does have a central place in this country's culture, beginning with slavery before the actual nation was born.

Carney, Judy, the county attorney and the fire marshal all commit any and all resources necessary to catch the culprit and "bring them to justice," a phrase used to redundancy. But I get the questions about the actual event and the investigation. I praise the fire marshal's office, "They're the true professionals in a fire investigation," I say, and then take questions.

No, we don't have a suspect. We believe two men in an old sedan were responsible.

Yes, we think it was an incendiary device, but we'll know when we get the fire marshal's report.

Hate crime? When we catch the persons responsible, that will probably become clear. But it was an Islamic center. There's been a lot of Islamophobia in the news, and some people have taken it this way.

Finally, I ask for help. "Someone out there saw something, maybe not something they thought of as important at the time. Someone saw our perpetrator, either at the Islamic Institute or somewhere else on the block. Please call the Des Moines police department with the information. We need your help."

This kind of request is risky. Usually, it turns out to be call after call that are totally bogus. But every once in a while, someone saw something that's meaningful. In this case, I think we're going to need information from the public.

I'm at Abdul's press conference. He asks me to allow him into the crime scene. I say no, but he does get a nice television shot of the three of them standing so that you can see the burned-out front of the Islamic center.

It is a hate crime, he tells the viewers. It is aimed at Muslims. He decries Trump and the hate that the Republican Party is spewing. The people who use this center are mostly Iowans, long-ago citizens of the United States who came here from refugee countries or who converted to Islam. The people who use this center are peace-loving; they are your brothers and sisters. They don't want to harm anyone. They simply want to be able to live in peace. This tactic of making Muslims into the scary guys is growing old. They will not accept that their way of life has to be one of fear. Peace. Peace. Peace.

It's the next day before I see Lester again. He can almost hear now, and the doctors don't think there will be any long-term effects from the blast. I bring along another detective, Dick Thill, who brings along a binder of photos of folks we know have been active in the white supremacy movement. Hard to believe that there's this many from central Iowa, but as I said, racism lives on.

"I don't know that I'll be able to recognize anyone," he says.

"Well, Lester," I tell him, "just try, would you?"

"Here's the thing, detective," his wife says.

"Yes?"

"If we identify this man, you're going to pursue him as if he's the one who blew up the center, right?"

"We just want to talk to him."

"He's a goddamn hero is who he is," Lester says emphatically. "I'd like to know who he is so I could give him a hug and a kiss on the cheek."

"Same here," says his wife.

"He may have saved you," I tell Lester, "but if he's the man who put that bomb in there, he's the person who put your life at risk. I don't think he deserves your protection."

Lester seems to be thinking. "You could be right," he said. "It may be he brought this all on, but when he came back to get me, he risked his life. His damned life. Risked it. Understand?"

"Would you look at the books?" the other detective said.

So Lester did. I just didn't think he was trying very hard. I watched him, as intently as I could, to see if he picked up a clue on anything. There were a couple of times I thought he might have recognized someone. I just wasn't sure. He denied it.

The fire marshal's office invited me over late in the day. They had not quite completed their investigation, but one thing was for sure, someone had bombed the center. They had recovered several pieces of the bomb and pieces of the timer, which happened to be a pretty standard ten-dollar watch.

"If that guy did go back in to get the janitor," Paul Bishop told me, "he was really taking a chance. These watches are pretty iffy on timing."

"But you don't have a whole watch?"

"No," Bishop said, "you rarely get that in a bombing. We have pieces, little pieces of plastic and at least one shard that's from the face of the watch."

"Where were they found?"

"Just outside the front door, in the parking lot."

"So could they have been in the parking lot to begin with and you now just think they were part of a bomb?" I ask.

"Yes, Mr. Defense Attorney," Bishop says, and laughs, "that's possible. But we can tell you that it's the right plastic in the right shade for the Timex RX-L sports watch, which is favored by bomb makers because of its large face."

"Good," I say, "how do you distinguish the glass from the face with the glass from the front door?"

"They are not at all alike. The real problem was there's so much door glass, finding a single piece of face was really hard. That's where we're a bit weak, but I think we'll find some more."

"Other than that," I asked, "what do we have of the bomb?"

"Well, you don't get much combustible material, for obvious reasons," Paul said, "and we haven't actually found anything. But the explosion pattern and the black marks on the inside wall suggest TNT. Plus, you know, if these guys are amateurs, which seems pretty certain, TNT is much safer than sending them with one of the liquid explosives."

"Like nitro?"

"Unusual these days," Paul said, "but there are several better liquids. The problem is all the same, they so often blow up in the vehicle on the way to the scene."

There was no other evidence of combustible materials, and the bomb had either been placed in the foyer or thrown in. But the glass in the front door seemed to have blown outward, at least that was their best guess. Not broken in, like something had been thrown through it. This would take further testing.

"Any chance of foreign DNA?" I ask.

"Sure," Paul told me, "we've got a lot of it, from several different donors. So who the hell knows which one we're looking for?"

There is no video surveillance. Abdul tells me they have cameras at the mosque, but hadn't thought to do it at the educational center. And the front door lock was not broken, so we probably are looking for someone who burgled the place first.

The U-Haul people are no help. They closed up at nine—that's all they know. They want to know who's going to pay for damages. I tell them to call their insurance agent.

I have officers talk to everyone at every business around the area. The IHOP was open twenty-four hours, but I can't find the two girls on the shift late that night. The cook was in back and saw nothing. I have to wait until the next day to talk to Melinda and Jerri, who were the waitresses at the time.

The Mexican restaurant about a block down had shut down already. The owner said he and his wife were still there, cleaning up the kitchen, when they heard the explosion and then sirens. They saw nothing.

The Casey's a couple of blocks up was open too. But we hadn't been able to find the old guy on duty at the time. We had to wait until he worked again, when another cop could go interview him.

Other than that, what we had was a mainly empty mall parking lot where to the best of our knowledge, no one was parked at the time of the explosion. On the other hand, the brew-pub movie theater was still in its last showing of the new Jason Bourne movie, so we might find someone who saw something when they left. The movie theater was able to give us the names of the people who bought through Fandango or the IMDB, but anyone who walked in and paid cash was never going to be identified.

There was something else I found intriguing. The fire marshal believes the door was blown out, meaning someone came in the door, someone, most likely, who knew how to come indoors. So I tell Thill that we might be looking for someone who knows how to burgle a business or conduct a home invasion. Ask around to the other detectives and patrol officers, I say, and see who might have been involved in a home invasion lately.

Three

I SLEEP IN the next morning and Barbie surprises me. When I come down about ten, she is griddling French toast, my favorite. I put in a k-cup, start brewing, and then sit at the kitchen counter.

"What's the occasion?"

"Your retirement."

"Jesus, Barb," I say, "what are we going to do with ourselves?" This is not a new argument. We've been going around and around about it for some time.

"How's your mom?"

"Don't change the subject."

"I'm not," she says. "How is your mom?"

"Christ," I say, "I don't know."

"When's her birthday—"

"Fuck," is my only response.

"I told her you were busy on a bombing. She seemed to understand. I just don't know how many birthdays she's got left."

"I know," I said sheepishly.

"And how's Yellowstone?"

This time I get the drift. I stand, get my coffee, and sit back down in the exact same place. I am facing her; she is at the griddle. There's a plastic green plate in front of me, silverware, and a bottle of buttery syrup.

"And Great Teton?"

I say nothing.

"Arches National Monument?"

"That's actually a national park," I tell her.

"Sequoia? Is that a national park?"

"It is."

"And what's the volcanic park?"

"Lassen," I tell her. "It's straight north of Sac, and just another couple of hours further north is Crater Lake."

"A national park?"

"Right."

"And your grandchildren?"

"We saw Emma last week."

"Emma and her parents live in West Des Moines. How about Carter and Eliza?"

"You were out just two months ago, with your mother."

"Don't remind me," Barbie says.

"So?" I ask.

"Their mother seems to think her father should visit too. And besides, once we're in Monterey, we can turn a rental car north and see Crater Lake and Lassen and any other goddamned natural world you'd like." She takes two pieces of French toast off the griddle and plops them on a plate, hands it over to me.

"Now," she says, "when are you retiring?"

"I'll think about it."

I can't believe how fast she is. I have one piece of the French toast on my fork but the rest of the plate is taken from me, tossed in the sink and she turns on me, heading toward the garage.

"Call me when you're ready," she says.

"OK, OK," I say, "talk to me."

She turns. She gives me that *I'm listening* look.

"I want to finish this bombing case. And then I'll have to turn in my pension application. You have to do that six weeks in advance."

"How long to get these bombers?" she asks.

"Give me six months."

"Six," she says, "one hundred eighty days. April 15. No more. Get your application in six weeks before that date. OK?"

Unsaid, of course, was what else lay between now and April. Her next MRI is in February, to determine whether the chemotherapy and radiation had shrunk the tumor in her cavernous sinus. If not, there would not be enough time for those national parks. I didn't really want to go on without her either. The idea of getting to all those national parks without her is just, well, depressing. On the other hand, if Barbie isn't with me, I don't want to quit working. She and work—that's my life. All my friends are on the force. I liked reading, watching the news, watching movies. Otherwise, I work, and besides my family, it's the most interesting thing in my life.

I want to say something, to argue, to tell her just how I feel, but I'm no good at that. She puts up with it. I'm also too goddamned tired. Plus, I really need to get to Dubuque to see my mother. Soon.

"What about your job?"

She laughs. "I already told them I was retiring the last day of the year. December 31, 2016, my day of freedom."

"That's what you want to do?"

"Yup. I do. You know my pension is fully vested. I won't get social security yet, but I intend to file for it early. And if you are willing to retire on April 15, if you really do it, I'll be here, waiting for you. If. You understand?"

I wanted my French toast back. I wanted to keep working. I wanted to stay married. I wanted Barbie to live and to keep working so I could keep working. You can't have everything.

"I'm not sure I appreciate this emotional blackmail," I said, expecting her to blow up. She is a lovely person, better than I deserve as a spouse, but she can get angry fast and I never deal with it well.

She did not get mad. She kept her easy composure, the composure I've seen this morning. "I guess I'm not being clear," she said. "You should do whatever you want. But I am not going to sit around and wait for you. I'm going to lead my life. And if you're going to keep working for the police, I am going to go see my grandkids and stay awhile. I'm going to take some tours, national parks to start, but later, Europe, Australia, whatever. With or without you."

I said nothing. What could I say?

"So?" she asked.

"I can't put the papers in until March 1. I'll do it that day." It wasn't quite true, but it was true that I wouldn't have to put my papers in until after we'd heard the results of her MRI.

"Good," she said. "More French toast?" I didn't see any point in turning that down now.

I get to headquarters just before one and I meet with Thill and the chief who gets the fullest update we can give her. "You know," she says, "you don't have to keep me informed about everything, just tell me if you need something. I just want an arrest."

Thill goes back to his desk, in the detective's bull room. It is covered with files. Detective work, like everything else, is often just paperwork. I grab my coat and go downstairs. I drive the five blocks to the courthouse where I am the witness in a hearing. A motion to suppress. A legal mechanism for claiming that the police screwed up, did not have a right to procure the evidence they did, and therefore for suppressing that information from the evidence. A legal mechanism, in other words, for protecting the guilty.

Nan Horwatch, a long-time veteran assistant county attorney with more years in service than I do, barely talks to me as we go in. "Find the bombers?" she asks.

"We're one day in," I say.

"Ya, well, most arrests are made by the next day at the latest. After four days, there's a 50 percent failure rate."

"Thanks for your support," I tell her. And I take the stand.

As always, I have my police report in front of me. Police reports aren't necessarily discoverable by defense counsel, and some county attorneys hand them over and some don't. I have just got done reading this one. Judge Ray Pille is on the stand. He covers the mike with his hand and leans over to me. "Anything on the bombing?"

"It would help if I could be doing police work instead of being in court," I tell him, and he laughs.

"Don't get your hopes up," he says and then we're off.

I know this is a game, at least to me and the two lawyers. It might seem like something else to the defendant, who will either go to prison for having the drugs we found in his car or get a Get Out of Jail Free card. I have seen police officers handle testifying so many different ways. Some of them bend over backward to help the prosecutor. Some of them bend too far. I have found that what works best is tell what you remember and don't let the defense attorney put you off.

The problem with this matter is the officer who stopped the defendant, a young officer, an officer who works for patrol, not me, went a little far in suggesting to the defendant that he could get off with a little cooperation. I told him no such thing, of course, because there really wasn't much point. First of all, I can't get him off. That's up to the county attorney, and while they listen to my recommendations, they make their own decision. And because I was the second man to interview the defendant, it didn't much matter what I said. If the first officer had said something about which the defendant relied (*promissory reliance* is what the lawyers call it), there isn't much I can do about it.

Thill is waiting.

"We have had some white supremacist crap going on for sure," he told me, "but this is a whole new level. Makes me wonder if chasing down these particular rabbit holes makes sense."

"Did you check out home invasions?"

"There are so damned many," he tells me. "But I do have an interesting two or three where Allen wrenches are used to pick locks and then the house is burglarized. Remember that case where we think the guys went into the house to steal from the drug dealers?"

"Ya," I say.

"Johnson seems to think that's how they got into that house. Allen wrenches."

"That sounds different though, doesn't it?" I answer. "I mean, that was drug dealers being robbed by other druggies, wasn't it?"

"I guess so."

"Stay on the supremacists angle for now. We're just starting. Let's drive over to the mall and see if we find any of our potential witnesses."

Gary was at Casey's. He saw nothing, remembered nothing. There wasn't much traffic on Douglas and he didn't notice anyone driving fast either way after the explosion. And he did hear the explosion.

"Hard to miss that," he said, "Knew right away something was wrong."

Melissa was coming on at IHOP at six, so we had to wait. I ordered French toast. It wasn't as good as Barbie's. Melissa sat down with us about a quarter to.

"See anything that night?"

"Well," she said, looking earnestly into Thill's eyes, "more like we heard something."

"Ya?" Thill asked.

"Ya," she said, "we heard this car screech. I went to the front door. It was slow, you know, always is that late."

"Anyway," I said after a moment.

"Anyway," she answered, "I looked out. There was this car tearing out of the lot, on the road right next to us, you know?" The entrance to the mall. "Anyway," she said, "he went barreling out of here, through a red light and right into the U-Haul parking lot. He stops at the end of the lot. He gets out of the car door and I see him running."

"Did you see where he went?" Thill asked.

"Some customers wanted coffee, so I walked back to the serving area, got a pot, and went to his table. That's when we heard the explosion."

"See it?"

"Ya, we all walked to the front again, me holding my coffeepot, Mary too and a couple of customers."

"And then?"

"We saw the place burning then I see that car pull back out of the U-Haul lot, backing up fast, and then turn west up Douglas. Funny thing too."

"Yes?" I asked.

"He wasn't even in the right lanes."

"What did the car look like?"

"Shit," she said, "I was afraid you'd ask that. It was old. Tan. A sedan. I'm thinking Dodge, but I could be wrong."

"How old?"

"No idea."

"How many people in the car?"

"I think there were two . . . maybe three. The driver is the guy who got out and we saw him running. That's when I got asked for coffee."

"Right," Thill said. "Listen, anything at all you can remember. License plate?"

"Nah," she said, "he was too far away."

"Was the plate lit?"

"Don't think so."

"Anything you can remember might help."

"Nah."

"Did you see where he was parked before he drove to the U-Haul?"

"Funny," she said, "I think Mary did."

Thill's shift is over. I drop him off at home and drive back to the crime scene. I'm sure if I was a better detective, I'd catch something. I put on my blue shoe covers, just in case, although I'm pretty sure the fire marshal has taken everything they wanted from the scene. I park at the U-Haul and walk around the building to the Islamic center, what would once have been the front door. Then I hoof it back, running. I do it again. This time, crouched down, pretending I'm dragging something. It was arduous and I didn't really have a two-hundred-pound janitor to drag.

One thing is obvious, not that we didn't already know it. The purpose of dragging Lester over here, to this spot, is to protect him from the blast. The man who dragged Lester to safety at least knew there was going to be a blast, probably because he had placed the bomb in the center to begin with.

Mary from IHOP came in the next afternoon. Thill and I interviewed her in the detective's conference room, not an interview room, with coffee. We made sure she knew she was there to help us, not because we suspected any wrongdoing.

"I told Melissa," she said, "I just don't think I remember much."

"Well," I said, "what do you remember?"

"I remember Melissa telling us that it was kind of strange how that car pulled through the intersection, and then a minute later, we heard the explosion."

"Just a minute?" I asked. That really wasn't enough time for him to do what Lester told us the man had done.

"Well, no more than five minutes, ten tops."

Mary wasn't going to be much help. Still, it was nice she came in.

"Did you see the car before the explosion?"

"I think so. A dark-green beater, American, at least ten, maybe fifteen years old."

"Where?"

"You know where the southwest entrance to the mall is?"

"Right next to your shop?" I asked.

"Ya."

"OK."

"Well, he was parked right there . . . just in the parking lot but actually in the way of anyone who wanted to pull in the parking lot. Not that it mattered. Everything but the movie theater and us were closed."

"Seen anyone do that before?"

"Don't think so. I kind of wondered what was going on. Drug deal maybe? Wondered if they were coming in. You know, for pancakes. Late-night pancakes are a specialty for druggies."

"How many in the car?" Thill asked.

"Two. Both men. Couldn't tell much else."

"Could you read the license plate?" I asked.

"Funny," she said, "they didn't have a front plate."

"Of course not," I said, and she looked at me quizzically but I let it pass. She had no other information except to say she was "pretty sure" it was the same car they saw by the U-Haul dealership a few minutes later, after the blast.

Four

W E CALLED KATIE in Salinas.
"I'm going to send Mom out in January. So far, we bought tickets just for her, but I'll come too if I can get away," I told her. Then the kids got on the Skype screen and made funny faces, then their father whisked them away and then Katie and her mom talked about retirement, the tumor, raising two kids, and on and on. They didn't talk often enough, but when they did, they did.

I got assigned a couple of new cases, neither of which had the priority of the bombing of the Islamic center. I closed one the same day, with a long late-night interview with the suspect. By the end of the six hours, he simply confessed. Tiredness, thirst, hunger—these are sometimes great incentives for confession. It was just a week before the election and the mayor and the chief both called to ask what was happening on the Islamic center. The mayor told me Abdul was sitting in his office, wondering why the crime hadn't been solved. No one liked it, but the chief seemed to understand we were waiting on the fire marshal.

On Monday, November 7, the day before the election, the chief, Thill and I went up the hill to a state office building for a briefing by Paul Bishop. We didn't learn anything new, but it was nice to have an official report and an official cause of the fire, which was an incendiary device.

"A bomb?" the chief asked.

"Yes," Paul said, "as we suspected. It was a fairly crude device. There are two parts to a bomb: an explosive charge and a detonator. That's all it really takes. The detonator can be activated with a phone call or a timer or some physical action, such as a lever, like a bomb that goes off when you step on it."

"A mine?" the chief asked.

"That's one example. But as we thought, a timer was used, a cheap watch with a plastic band. We found a part of the watch face and part of the band. Both manufactured by Timex Corporation, but that's about all we know because they use these parts in several different watches."

I asked a question. "And these watches are sold, where?"

"Amazon, eBay, but also Target and Kohl's and K-Mart. Walmart."

"This watch?" I asked.

"Don't think we'll ever know. We did get a partial serial number off a piece of casing. That narrows it down. But do we care? You think somebody walked into Walmart and used a credit card to purchase a Timex to blow up a building?"

"There's a Kohl's right there in that mall, a quarter mile from where these boys were parked," Thill said. "And a Target."

I open my sack. I pour out twenty different cheap Timexes we bought at the Kohl's.

"Any of these fit the bill?" I asked.

"Problem is," Paul said, "they all probably do. But the piece of serial number we did find identified the watch as probably a sports watch."

"Kind of big," Thill said.

"Ya, but what does this guy care?" I answer. "He's walking it into the building."

"Anyway," Paul continued, "the detonator was on a timer. The detonator is a slick little rig, not something your rank amateur puts together."

"How so?" I asked.

"It's just a matter of sophistication. Most detonators are just blasting caps, especially when your rank amateur builds a little bomb."

"We talking about the explosive compound?"

"No, although don't be confused. There's a difference between the charge used by the detonator and the explosive that constitutes the bomb. The charge is detonated and results in the bomb, the primary explosive material, being discharged. The detonator is generally the charge. It goes off because of some other device. An amateur will use a blasting cap or some other ordinary detonator, but this one has an electronic detonator. Now that's interesting."

All of us looked at him as if he was speaking Greek.

"How so?" I finally said.

"Well, electronic detonators are pretty sophisticated and they give you precision on the delay. If you want three minutes and twelve seconds, you can get that from an electronic detonator. Most bombers don't give a shit. But here's the real rub: so if you are going to go with an electronic detonator, that kind of precision, why are you using a ten-dollar Timex to do the timing?"

We all looked at each other. We were assuming that Paul would have a good idea and so I finally asked, "We'll bite, why?"

"Don't ask me," Paul said. "My best guess is that you have a pretty sophisticated bomb builder who likes electronic detonators, but he doesn't have any precise timers and doesn't really need one. So he sticks the Timex on there and hands it off to the actual bomber."

"Not the same guy?" Thill asked.

"Could be, I suppose," Paul said. "It just doesn't feel right. If you're building a sophisticated bomb and you're putting it somewhere for detonation, you put the good timer on it. If you're handing it off, maybe you don't care."

"So how and when does the timing get set?"

"Now that's a good question," Paul said. "Again, we're not sure, but best guess is the bomber drives up, sets the time, goes in the door and leaves the bomb. Setting the timer inside the building is a bit scary. But I think we've got amateurs here and who knows."

"Are you sure?" the chief asked. "It seems like setting the bomb in the car is scarier. What if it goes off in the car?"

"If it goes off with you there, you're up shit creek," Paul said, "regardless of where you are."

"What was the charge?" I asked.

"Best guess . . . and it's a guess because whatever it was, it blew and burned out, best guess is solid-pack explosive. Not too much, but you don't need much."

"And the big explosive?"

"Just TNT," Paul said, "dynamite."

"Does that mean anything in particular?" the chief asked.

"Not really," Paul told her. "It's the easiest thing to get for a small bomb. But what's funny is, we don't have that big of an explosion. It looks like a single stick. Why not two or three and take this whole building down?"

"Maybe," I said, "taking the building down wasn't the point."

Five

THE MORNING BEGINS at the Iowa Clinic, way out west, waiting for a technician to come collect Barb and take her in for an MRI. Because they know where the tumor is, the MRI isn't that long anymore. The first day they had her locked in that tube for more than two hours.

Barbie told me to bring a book, and I usually have one going, but what's the point? I was way too nervous to read. Plus, because she had to fast, I haven't had anything to eat or drink. I walked down a flight and found the vending machines. The coffee was awful, swill worthy of the industrial coffee I've had in numerous police department headquarters all over this country. The only thing edible in the machine is an almond breakfast bar, which I buy greedily.

I turn. It's Joanna Ward. Joanna's husband was a long-time member of the drug and gang task force; he was officially on the Clive police force and I liked him. But we could all see the pressure was getting to him. Once he moved to the task force, he seemed to change. He was not only edgier; he seemed never to be present with you. And the booze got to him too. Just before it was at a point that someone needed to tell him to get counseling or therapy, he got caught taking some drugs out of the city's evidence locker. Not only did he lose his job, he got prosecuted, and even though he didn't do time, what future is there for an ex-cop who has been convicted of a drug offense? Unfortunately, even that fall from grace didn't stop him. He moved on to heroin, the current number-one killer of addicts in America, and his wife and kids were gone as well. She had two little boys, if I remembered correctly. Joanna was at least ten years younger than me. She was tall, had a nice figure, and a pug nose that looked pretty on her face. Even though she'd added a pound or two to her hips, I always found her attractive. Not that I acted on that, Barb was my gal and I never fooled around.

"Hey," she said.

"Hi, Joanna," I said, "what are you doing here?"

"Bradley hurt himself in soccer. They're getting an MRI of his knee today. Thought it would heal but it hasn't really. The test was supposed to be a half hour ago, but they're waiting for something."

I didn't tell her that she was probably waiting for Barb to get off the machine.

"Oh," I said, "hope it comes out all right."

"Have you heard from Jeff?"

"No," I told her, "not in a long time."

"I'm not even sure where he is. I suppose I should be wanting child support, but really, I just wish he would get involved with his kids. It's kind of—"

"Sad," I answer her.

"Damn straight," she said, placing one hand on my arm, leaning on it, "it really is sad. And how's Barb?"

Barbara and I are different. Aren't all couples? We've been married almost twenty-five years, but the differences don't go away. Here's one example: I don't tell people anything private, I have a fierce sense of keeping our private affairs private. Barb is not that way. She tells almost everyone. When I got hurt during a late-night confrontation with a drug addict, I tried to keep the details of my injury and infection private, away from my fellow officers, but what difference did it make? Barb had told all their wives. And so I thought it wasn't that surprising that Joanna knew about Barb's tumor— except she didn't. She was just asking a general question, and I assumed something else. "Well, you know, we'll find out more today."

A look of concern covered her face. "Oh, Bobby," she said, "what's the matter?"

Then of course, I had to sit down with her and tell her all about it. How her eyelid mysteriously drooped six months ago, she'd developed headaches and double vision. How the doctors suspected stroke but had found a tumor in the cavernous sinus, probably benign. How Barb and I had gone into the hospital every morning for a week while they radiated her head for about ninety minutes. And how today, we were finding out how things had gone. For a moment, she seemed concerned then something else went across her face, something I didn't understand, and then she leaned in and hugged me. Don't get me wrong, I don't mind hugs. I just never offer them. I don't want anyone to get the wrong idea—that's all. And Joanna is a good-looking woman.

"I'm sure it will be all right," I tell her.

"Oh, Bobby," she says, pushing her head toward me and giving me a peck, "I'm sure it will be."

When Barb walks out of the MRI room, just a bit unsteady, Joanna puts an arm across my back and rubs my shoulder.

"What was that all about?" Barb asks me.

"Don't ask."

"I just did."

"She wants me," I told my wife. "There's not much I can do about my animal magnetism."

Barb just grunted. "Never lose that sense of humor," she said, "unless you can find a better one somewhere. Maybe you should buy some books of jokes."

"How did it go?" I ask, and Barb admits that it wasn't too bad. She's a little bit claustrophobic and hates being locked down, slid into a machine, and having loud knocking sounds made at you for a half hour, but all in all, it didn't hurt.

"I just hope we get good results," I tell her, placing an arm around her waist.

"Not sure that's what Joanna wants," she said.

I laugh. I have no idea if this is in jest or another example of Barbara's intuition, but Joanna is really the last thing on my mind. Except that when she walked toward the door, I noticed her butt more than I should have.

While in the neurosurgeon's waiting area, I call Thill. "Got anything?"

"Nothing new," he said, "of course, I've been worrying about other cases."

"I know," I said, "but I'm worried about this growing cold. What's your next step?"

"I think we should go back and look at home invasions. See if anything looks odd."

"Good," I said, knowing full well I had steered him away from that previously. "Good, but leave me a pile on our favorite Nazis, will you? I'm going to start knocking on some doors."

Dr. Jonathan Rozenboom is a thin man of about my age who has lost most of his hair. He has the curt and deliberate demeanor of almost every surgeon you've ever met. After the nurse checks Barb's vitals again and gets the MRI imaging up on the doctor's computer, he comes in, says hello barely, sits down by the computer, and starts bringing up the imaging.

He doesn't look at Barb as he asks, "And how are we?"

"I don't know about you," she says, "but I've been feeling just fine."

"Good. Good. Well, let's see what we've got here."

He goes from slide to slide, all of it the grotesque black-and-white imaging of a head, in this case, my one true love's head. I can't tell shit from what I'm seeing, and I doubt Barbie can either, but does it matter? The expert is here.

He leans back.

"We don't have the radiologist report yet," he tells us.

"I understand," Barb says, "but you've got the imaging."

"Indeed I do," he says and lifts his glasses off his nose and onto the bare front of his head. He rubs his nose and then his eyes. Something is wrong. And in that moment of panic, I think of Douglas Adams: *don't panic.*

"Well," he says, still unable to tell us, I guess.

"Doctor," Barb says, "you're scaring me."

"It hasn't performed like we would wish," he says.

It hasn't performed like we would wish. Perhaps the greatest understatement I've heard since my dad telling me the '85 Bears had a pretty good defense.

"What—" I start. Barb puts a hand on my leg. *Hold up, buster.*

"Doctor," she says, "I think you have bad news for us. Would you like to not sugarcoat it? I'd certainly appreciate that."

He looks at her, then at me, and I can see that he does this from time to time, gives people bad news, and still doesn't know how to really pull it off.

"OK," he says, "you'll remember that we treated your tumor with CyberKnife radiation because it is somewhere that we really are not in a position to physically remove."

"Right," she says, "surgery would have been bad. Got that."

"These are almost always benign tumors and they're very hard and so we don't get huge results from radiation, but our goal is to shrink them, and if we can't shrink them, to stop them in their place. For most people, that's good enough."

"Right," she says. She's losing patience. I reach out and squeeze her hand.

"But this tumor is not acting like it's a hard benign meningioma. Not anymore. It's not really much bigger, but well, it's growing and it's changing shape."

"Which means?" I finally ask.

And we get the C term we've been dreading for the better part of a year.

Derek came over to the house that afternoon with Liza, his thirteen-month-old daughter who just lightens our house up, day or night. We get Katie on the phone. She's bawling.

"I'm coming home," she says.

"Good," Barb says, "but wait until we figure out what we're going to do next. I think if we're going to have surgery or some other treatment, it would be nice if you were home then."

"So look, everyone," I tell my family. "I'm retiring. Mom and I have talked about it and I'm fully vested. So I'm quitting, immediately, as soon as the chief will let me."

And then I get a surprise.

"You are not retiring. No, you are not." It's Barb.

"What?" Derek asks. "Why not?"

"Because, honey," she reaches out and puts her hand on Derek's cheek, "once I'm gone, your dad won't have any life at all except being a police officer. If he retires too, what is he going to have to live for?"

"Oh, it's always the same with you," I said. "Always thinking about yourself."

"Dad," Katie squawked on the speakerphone, "you're not funny."

But it kind of was. And we needed a little levity. Mom laughed, just a little. Derek did too and I heard Katie's husband, Rob, do the same from somewhere in their California living room.

"Well," I said, "you're forgetting one thing, Barbie. There are still treatment options and we are going to—"

"Stop it," she said. And I did.

"Now listen, everybody," Barb said, and we all did. "I'm not sure what I am going to do, but I know I will decide what treatment, if any, I undertake. Neither my husband nor my children will decide for me."

There was silence all around at that. Everyone knew better than to argue the point.

"One thing, though," Derek said, "as a practical matter, Dad, you need your health insurance. Des Moines PD has a pretty good policy, right?"

"True that," I said.

"Stop that," Katie said, and we all laughed.

"Derek has a point," Barbie said. "We do need your insurance now. I'm afraid you're just going to have to keep working for now, big shot."

It was what she called me in front of the kids sometimes. It was a derivation of what she called me sometimes in private, something the kids could not be privy to.

Six

EVERY MONDAY MORNING, Walter Brotherson walks into the Des Moines police headquarters with a Caribou coffee cup in his right hand, a *Des Moines Register* under his armpit and his cell phone on his ear. He is always on the cell phone, if rarely on a call. Because he appears to be on a phone, people leave him alone. Walter, nicknamed Pappa, could have retired fifteen years ago, but he likes to be with the department. He likes to come into the office, even if he just sits at the conference table in the detectives' office and reads the newspaper.

Officially, Pappa is a patrol officer but he's with the detective bureau and probably will be until he dies. He comes in every Monday morning but may not come in the rest of the week. If you need him, however, he'll be there, any hour of the day, any day of the week, and forty-eight hours in a row if need be. I am not sure of his age, but he's past sixty and may have arrived at seventy. His wife died years ago, his kids live out of town, and he drives east to see his grandchildren once a year, on no particular schedule. He neither informs Human Resources when he wants a vacation, nor informs them once he's back. He does answer his cell phone when one of us in the bureau calls him.

Years ago, he had an accident on a bicycle, which resulted in a kind of permanent laryngitis. He talks now in a husky, hoarse whisper, which sounds like it hurts for him to talk. He says it does not. There is no one who cannot hear him but all strain to do so, and they tend to listen to him intently.

He says he has no expertise at all. He says he's never been to any particular forensic school, FBI training, or continuing education programs. His résumé is less than a page long. It lists his experience as police officer, 1977 to 2016. When a new year begins, he asks one of our secretaries to update it. She does, by changing the year. I have seen this résumé actually entered as an exhibit at trial. Actually, he graduated from Iowa State University, served two tours in Vietnam, went to the Iowa Police Academy, worked a stint as an officer in Ames, then joined our department, matriculated from our academy, and then five years later while working as a patrol officer, attended and graduated from Drake Law School. He passed the bar and went back to work as a police officer, by then working up to the detective bureau, which he never really left.

He does have at least three skills that the rest of us in the department appreciate. The first is that he remembers everyone and everybody. If we need to know about any long-ago crime, criminal, or often more important, police officer, attorney, or public servant, he will remember them—not only their name but something worth knowing about them. He can and has informed me which women were mistresses to Big John Guidice, owner of the famous Babe's restaurant in downtown Des Moines, including the correct order of when each was his mistress. "Gloria preceded Molly," Pappa said, "but then he went back to Gloria after he was tired of Molly and before Shelley." Or about how Preston Daniels became Des Moines' first black mayor: "Preston becoming mayor was a surprise. He would have lost that first election to Jim Cownie, of course, but US senator Tom Harkin weighed in against Cownie, announced he was supporting Preston. Only time he ever got involved in a local race. Tipped the balance."

Finally, one of us would take the bait. "Why did he do that?"

"Because in 1986, when Tom Tauke ran against Harkin for the Senate, Cownie, who then was president of Heritage Communications—did you know that we used to have one of the nation's big ten cable companies headquartered right here in Des Moines?"

You couldn't let him get off topic like that. One of us would say, "Pappa, c'mon, Pappa, what about the Daniels-Cownie race?"

"Well, in 1986, when Harkin was expecting Cownie and his PAC to support him in his reelection, Cownie called him up and told him he was going to support Tauke. A real bonehead move too."

This could be useful. It could also be a waste of time. But with some regularity, some of us sought him out for information.

His second skill that mattered was that he could walk into the office of the county attorney, the sheriff, the chief presiding judge of the fifth judicial district, the attorney general of Iowa, the governor, the head of the Department of Public Safety, the head of the FBI or the Speaker of the House, for that matter, and they would listen to what he had to say. There was no one else in our department that could say this. Not the chief, well, especially not the chief. In fact, it may have been his unofficial official status that granted him this rite of passage. I had this demonstrated to me on more than one occasion. Once when I was a very young officer, I saw him walk into chambers with the chief of the Des Moines Public Defender's Office, the county attorney himself and the defendant, a young black man who was being held on a material witness warrant. We didn't know who had killed another young black man near the Oak Ridge apartments, but we were pretty sure this man knew.

"Well," Walter said to everyone, "funny group, isn't it? I suppose that Mr. Robinson here isn't asking, and we don't have a right to ask him to talk without his attorney's permission?"

The public defender, a stout, bald elderly man who had lost most of his face and his vision in a fire as a boy, said so out loud.

"Too bad," Walter said, "too bad."

Nobody said anything. The judge stirred, and I thought he was going to end the meeting.

"Too bad for his aunty," Walter said.

"What?" the kid said.

The public defender told him to shut up.

"What about my aunty?"

"She's worried," is all Walter said.

"Why?" the kid asked, and the PD told Walter to shut up.

"Can he tell me to shut up?" Walter asked the county attorney.

"He cannot," the judge answered.

"Didn't think so. Didn't think so. Your aunty, Makayla, she says that boy who killed Michael Hunter, that he's threatening her."

"Shit," the defendant said.

"Shush," the public defender said.

"You got to protect her," the kid said, "put her in witness protection or something."

"Son," Walter said, "this is Des Moines. We ain't got enough money to gas up our patrol cars, much less put up your aunty in a hotel. But don't worry, if he does anything, we'll arrest him."

"Shiiit."

We left. Walter said that's all we needed to do. Turned out he was right. The kid spilled the beans to the prosecutor within minutes.

His third skill was the one I cared about now. Walter had intuition. He could look at someone, talk to them for just a moment or two, hear their story or not hear it, and he would know in his heart who they were. Of course, that can't really be true. He couldn't be right all the time. You just wouldn't say that to Walter, because he was sure. Once he made up his mind, it was made up until you showed him otherwise. And when you did show him otherwise (it happened on occasion), he was impressed and told you so. "Good for you" was a favorite expression.

This made him one hell of an interrogator. We liked interrogating people late at night. We liked putting them in the box, a conference room really, locking them in, leaving them awhile, at least an hour, then coming in, two or three of us and asking them question after question after question. Over the years, I'd become pretty decent at it. But I was no Walter Brotherson and I knew it. He had all the skills.

On this night, I waited for Walter, whom I had called in from home. Peter Thurgood had been waiting in the box for forty minutes, a single glass of water standing on the table in front of him. We'd been watching him on the video camera, and he had barely moved. He'd said nothing, asked for nothing. He knew me. He knew Thill. And he knew Walter. And we were betting that he would not tell us that he wouldn't talk.

I heard Walter coming up the stairs. He did not have the phone to ear, but he did have a steaming Caribou cup in his right hand.

"Sorry," he said, "needed one if we're going to be awhile."

"I don't mind," I said. "I appreciate your coming."

"Peter, huh? Thought he was lying low."

"Not low enough, we don't think," Thill said.

"This sure seems like a Peter Thurgood program," I said.

"OK," he said. "Bring me a file to plop in front of me." I handed him the actual file on this matter.

"Now," he said, "tell me what you know and what you don't know and what you think."

About twenty minutes later, we walked into Peter's room.

"About goddamned time," Peter said.

"Well, hello to you too," Walter said.

We sat down. Peter in the middle, Thill to one side, and I to the other.

Walter opened the file, paged through it.

"OK, Peter," he said. "We know you did this."

Peter remained nonplussed. "Could have brought me a Caribou."

"My monthly bill there is higher than my social security payment," he said. "I don't buy anyone else coffee." That second part, at least, was true. Anytime I met him at the Caribou on Ingersoll, he made it clear that I was buying.

Peter smiled.

"As I said," Walter whispered, "we know this was you."

"You want to tell me what we're talking about?"

"Peter, Peter, Peter," was all Walter said, the exasperation clear in his hoarse voice.

"Look," Thurgood said, "people blame me for lots of things. Lots of things that I don't do." The malice in his eyes was impressive.

"You see that they turned over a bunch of gravestones in a Jewish cemetery in St. Louis? The FBI called me about that. What bullshit. Turned out to be some Hebe kid trying to lay it off on people like me. People blame me for all kinds of shit. That! I! Didn't! Do!"

"Could be," Walter said, "but this has all your markings. Blowing up an Islamic center, just right up your alley. The thing I don't understand . . ." His voice kind of tailed off.

"Is why the bomber went back for the janitor?" Thurgood asked.

"See," Walter said, putting two fingers up toward his eyes, then moving them so they were pointing at Thurgood's. "See, you and me, we think alike."

"What kind of name is Brotherson?"

"So," Walter went on, unfazed by the question. He had allowed things to get personal. "So we know it was one of your boys. Tell us who and you walk out of here. He'll never turn on you. None of your boys has ever turned on you, have they?"

"You know what I think of that bombing?" Thurgood asked.

"You're going to tell us, aren't you? I can't stop you," Walter said.

"I think they should have brought a bigger bomb."

Walter laughed, just a little. He closed the file, stood. "Robert," he asked, "is Mr. Thurgood free to go?"

"Yes, sir," I said, wondering what the hell had just happened. We three walked out and left the door standing open. Thurgood waited a moment, then walked out himself and headed for the stairs. He was familiar with the layout of the Des Moines police headquarters.

"What the hell," Thill began.

I shushed him.

"It was Peter," Brotherson whispered to us. "He ordered it. You just have to find out which of his boys carried it out. Look at everyone associated with him. Look around the movement. One of them did it on his instructions. But don't expect them to implicate him. No matter what you offer, it won't happen."

Seven

THE WORLD-FAMOUS MAYO Clinic. Sounds impressive, doesn't it? And it is. One tall building after another, one floor after another of doctors, PAs, NPs, lab technicians, nurses, and receptionists. All polite, all friendly, all helpful. In Rochester, Minnesota, three hours away by interstate. Three days off for family leave. But world renowned. The doctor takes maybe ten minutes with us. He has reviewed everything, her records, her MRI, both of them. He tells us he doesn't think it was a meningioma to begin with—misdiagnosed. But he agrees with Barb's doctor in Des Moines that the time has come to act. Chemotherapy. Pour poison into her veins. No reason to wait now. Then radiation, the real tumor killer. He says they could use proton therapy, the newest thing. "In fact," he said, "I wish this MRI had been taken a little sooner so we would have gotten into some prophylactic treatment by now."

"You mean chemotherapy?" Barb asks.

"Yes," he says, still looking at the chart, not at Barb or me, "that's right. Then more radiation."

"And surgery?"

He stops looking at the chart. He looks up. Not so much at us as at the room around him. He's thinking, I suppose.

"It might be productive. What have they told you about surgery in the cavernous sinus?"

"That we wouldn't like the side effects," Barb said. I do sometimes talk in these meetings, but mainly if I think Barb and the doctor aren't communicating with each other, just to make sure Barb understands the interaction. But she's smarter than me, and it's her damn head. No need so far today to speak up.

"Yes," the doctor says, "that's an understatement. I think it could be successful, but you would lose feeling on one side of your face. I think you'd lose the use of your left eye, and depending on how well the surgeon does in not getting into any other areas, you could probably avoid paralysis, but it's a risk."

"Oh, goody," I say.

The doctor looks at me like he doesn't understand. But I guess he did get the sarcasm. "Exactly," he said.

"But more importantly," Barb asked, "would it get rid of the tumor?"

"No," he said, "I'm afraid not. We would de-mass the tumor, and that would assist us. The tumor would be diminished certainly. It might give you more time, but no, we can't remove this entirely."

Everyone let that sink in for a minute.

"So?" I asked.

"What my husband wants to know," Barbie asked, "is what good chemotherapy and radiation would do. Are we talking delaying things, curing me, or neither?"

"Its purpose would be to defer the symptoms for some time. How much time is hard to say. But I hope we can give you twenty-four months or more."

"Fuck," I said, which startled both of them, and then I whispered that I was sorry.

"And what if we do nothing?" she asked.

"At this time, we're unsure of the rate of growth of this tumor," he said. "If this growth is new, since the procedure quit working and was delayed somewhat, well, that's an extraordinary rate of growth. If on the other hand, it has been growing this way basically since it first got hit and stunted by the radio surgery, then the rate of growth is not so fast.

"The problem isn't how long you have, but how long you're going to be capable of taking care of yourself, of—"

"Of being able to get myself out of bed to pee?"

It was almost a smile on his lips. "One way to say it," he answered.

"How will we know?" I asked.

"I am not sure I can accurately predict the symptoms. There are many possibilities. But because of the part of the brain this tumor is now pressing on, I believe that your wife will start to lose some of her physical abilities. Ambulation might be affected first. There could be paralysis, a loss of continence perhaps. It could be the speech or auditory capacity that is first affected. This could all happen on one side, so that she loses ability on the left side and not the right."

I think he would have continued, but Barb stopped him. "Thank you, doctor," Barb said.

She stood. I was still sitting. She leaned in, placing a hand on my chest as if to keep me from falling. She pecked the top of my head. "Let's blow this popsicle joint," she said.

"What?"

"You've got another day, right?" she said.

"Right."

"Let's head over to Minneapolis. Manny's steakhouse. See whether there is anything at the Guthrie. Shop at Mall of America. Sleep with me in a hotel room. What do you say?"

So we did.

When I got in that Friday, after spending the week with Barb in Minneapolis, my desk was full of crap: case files, notes, police reports, lab reports. Thill wasn't in yet. I went to the board. I started to write out the names of the people we knew who ran with Peter Thurgood. There were eleven. But I used the red pen to pare the list some more. Ross Martin was dead. Bill Figgenshue was in prison, as was Carl Peters. Mary Ellen and John Yost had moved to Colorado, where they were probably in trouble as well. There were still three names on the board.

Steve Cooper hadn't been in trouble in a while. But he was neo-Nazi all the way, a true believer in white supremacy who certainly was at least passing out flyers or burning crosses at Peter's recent day of rage. Cooper is a thin, short little guy who has a comic book store in Windsor Heights and thinks we don't know of his predilection. He has a Confederate flag prominently displayed there and surrounding his license plate. I couldn't visualize him with a bomb.

Don "Buddy" Chiodo is a fervent right-wing Catholic zealot who started out in the anti-abortion movement and moved on from there, steadily right. He seems to believe that abortion is a Jewish conspiracy. I can't figure that one out. It wouldn't surprise me at all that he would be involved in a bombing, but it would be an abortion clinic, not an Islamic center. Still, worth checking.

Finally, we had Bruce Kragness. Kragness was mean enough and violent enough that we couldn't cross him off the list. He was pure neo-Nazi too, a true believer in the white cause, but he and Peter Thurgood had repeatedly had differences in recent times and like Peter, he would probably want someone else to do the actual bombing and take the risks.

I had two more non-names up there: Unknown 1 and Unknown 2. We knew that Peter had somebody who had helped him bring and protect a national theorist for the Nordic Conspiracy into town this fall, but we didn't know who that was. And I also knew that Peter always was looking for fresh talent and probably had someone else to call on for something like the bombing.

Assuming, that is, that Brotherson is right, and it actually was Peter who brought this all together. That was our operative assumption, but twenty years as a detective had taught me that blind obedience to your assumptions could be foolish.

I ran home at lunch. I hadn't done that in years. Barb was still in her bathrobe, sitting in her rocker, and I couldn't tell that she was doing anything. I thought maybe she was napping.

"Hey," I said.

"Hey, crumbum," she said, "what are you doing home?"

"Brought you half of a Firehouse sub," I told her. She said she wasn't hungry. But she joined me at the table, grabbed the milk out of the fridge for me, and I started in.

"Is this how you're going to eat after?" she asked as I took my third bite.

I looked at her. I spit the bite of my sandwich out on my napkin.

"Jesus," was all I said. I lowered my head and began to sob. For the first time, I broke down and wept openly.

"Oh, come on, big boy," she said. She stood. She came over to me. I bent my head into her lap and she held on, rubbing the top of my head. "It's going to be OK," she said. "It's going to be OK."

It was not going to be OK. Nothing was going to be OK. I wanted to strike out, to hit someone, to destroy something. I wanted to physically react some way besides crying like a little child.

"So," she said, "are you going to give your new wife my clothes?"

I laughed. I was now laughing and crying, something I don't ever remember doing before. It was an old joke, one of our favorites. One I've retold and retold and one I've heard Barb tell friends too.

Through the crying, through the laughing, I said, "Oh, sure."

"Are you going to let your new wife drive my car?"

I laughed again. "Oh sure," I slammed out.

"Are you going to let her go to our favorite spot?"

"Oh sure."

"Are you going to let her use my golf clubs?"

"Stop it," I said, and I started to cry again.

She held me. She held me until I could control myself. She held me. She took care of me. She was dying and she was taking care of me. How was I going to go on without Barbie?

When I finally got back to the detective' room, Thill was there, waiting for me. "I heard you were back," he said.

"Ya," I said, "sorry about that."

"It's fine, it's fine," he said. "How's Barb?"

I gave him a look that meant *I don't want to talk about it*, but what the hell, how could I not? "Didn't help," I said.

"Oh, Bob," he said, "I'm sorry."

"Ya, well. It is what it is."

"Well, anyway, I've got some good news for you," he said.

I look up. "Ya?"

"Ya," he said, "let's go down the hall."

Room 2A. Crimes against property. A whole other set of detectives.

When we walked in, detectives Mark Taylor and Brent Taylor are sitting at the conference table, files out, both drinking cups of our crappy swill coffee. We call them the twins, because they are both named Taylor, but they couldn't be more different. Mark is a huge, burly guy, former Marine, who works out seriously at our gym and could bench press a couple of me. Brent is a little younger, tall and thin, and if it weren't for the twins nomenclature, he'd carry some kind of mad scientist nickname. He's seriously smart.

"Hey," Mark says.

Thill and I sit down by them.

"Tell him," Thill says.

"You remember about a month ago when we had a couple of guys do a home invasion over on University, just by the cemetery?"

"Yup," I say. "Never made any arrests, right?"

"Have not and not going to," Mark says. "Because we know just who did it and we know how they did it. And we know they hit the place to relieve a drug dealer of his cash deposit."

"Wow," I said, "good work. But you're not going to have an arrest?"

"Not of the guys who hit the house. We have got a guy in stir for the fight afterward, one Brett Anderson, a big black guy, former Marine, served in Afghanistan, been working for OnPoint Security. He's going down as a felon in possession of a firearm. But he didn't do the break-in. He was working security for the dealer."

"OK," I say. Has to be something interesting here somewhere. So far, I just don't know what it is.

"The two guys who did rob the dealer—they are Nick Spencer and Jonathan Desmond. We're pretty sure. They've been careful on the money so far, but they have been going to Tama and Osceola."

"Casinos?"

"Ya, good way to clean your cash, if you're careful about it," Brent answered.

"Records?" I ask.

"So," Mark goes on, "Spencer's got a bunch of misdemeanors, nothin' that really matters. Drugs. Driving. Been in a couple of fights down on Court Avenue."

"Ya?" I ask.

"Something else interesting about Spencer. He served in Afghanistan."

"Ya."

"Ya," Mark says, "with Brett Anderson."

"That is interesting," I agree.

"Desmond," Brent says, "has a nice long juvenile record but not much since. He did get arrested in that mix-up at Oakridge neighborhood, what, five years ago or so? Charged with assault and a hate crime."

"Charged? Not convicted?"

"Couldn't produce witnesses, remember, one of those deals?" Mark said.

"Ya," I said, "that sounds right."

No one said anything.

"You think one of these guys is our guy, or both?" I asked finally.

"Wait for it," Thill said.

"Want to guess where our boy Johnny Desmond lives?"

I didn't. What was the point? The twins were going to tell me.

It was Brent who blurted it out, finally: "That's right, Chief Inspector," he said. "He has a flat above Peter Thurgood's garage."

Eight

T HIS INTERVIEW IS being recorded. This is Des Moines
 Police Officer Robert Greiner, along with Des Moines Police
Officer Dick Thill. It is 11:20 p.m., November 9, 2016. We are at Des
Moines police headquarters. We are joined this evening by Jonathan
Desmond.

Q.   Mr. Desmond, I've informed you that this interview is being
     recorded, haven't I?
A.   Ya.
Q.   Mr. Desmond, you have a right to remain silent. Anything you
     do say may be used against you in a court of law. You have a
     right to an attorney to be present at this interview. If you waive
     the use of an attorney, you will forever be barred from claiming
     that you should have had an attorney at this proceeding. Do
     you understand these rights?
A.   Mmm mmm.
Q.   Was that a yes?
A.   Ya.
Q.   Mr. Desmond, are you willing to talk with us today, and are
     you willing to do so without an attorney being present on your
     behalf?
A.   Sure.

Q. Mr. Desmond, as you know, we are wanting to talk to you tonight about an attack on the Eslan Islamic Educational Center, which occurred about two weeks ago now, the night of October 29, 2016.

A. OK.

Q. We are hoping you can help us here, and if you do, you can help yourself. Understand?

A. Not really.

Q. Which part don't you understand?

A. None of it. I had nothin' to do with that.

Q. Noted. Let me ask you this, who's Peter Thurgood?

A. Well, uh, he's my landlord.

Q. Your landlord.

A. Ya, I rent a room from him.

Q. Is that all?

A. Guess we're kind of friends.

Q. Hang around a lot, do you?

A. Wouldn't say a lot.

Q. Do you know about his activities with the Posse Comitatus?

A. Posse what?

Q. Comitatus.

A. Nope, don't know nothin' about that.

Q. His activities regarding white supremacy?

A. Nah.

Q. Know who Jacob Petticourt is?

A. Who?

Q. Jacob Petticourt.

A. Nah.

Q. Ever talk to Peter Thurgood about white supremacy?

A. Not that I can remember.

Q. Not that you can remember, huh? (Laughs) That's a good one. What do you do for a living, Mr. Desmond?

A.   I'm a siding contractor. Well, I work for a siding contractor. But I'm tryin' to get in the business myself.

Q.   You any good at it?

A.   Ya, I know what I'm doing.

Q.   Seems to me everyone in this town who sides is a Mexican. You're not a Mexican, are you?

A.   Nah.

Q.   But you work with some?

A.   Sometimes.

Q.   The evening of October 29, about midnight, where were you?

A.   Pretty sure I was asleep. We start siding by seven most days.

Q.   You weren't in the parking lot of Merle Hay Mall, near the IHOP?

A.   Not that I remember.

Q.   If we have security camera recordings of that, would you believe them or your memory?

A.   If you had pictures like that, you wouldn't ask me, you'd show me. Got 'em?

Q.   That's very interesting, Mr. Desmond. It's not a denial. Are you trying to tell me you were there and you're just wondering if we have pictures?

A.   I'm saying that if you had photos of me in the lot like you're suggestin', you'd show 'em to me.

Q.   Where you get that old Buick? The one you burned afterward? Did you steal it?

A.   Don't know what you're talking about.

Q.   How do you know Nicholas Spencer?

A.   He works on my crew.

Q.   Siding?

A.   Ya.

Q.   What else does he do for you?

A.   Don't know what you're askin'.

Q. He was involved at the hit on University, where you hit the drug dealer, right?

A. So you guys thought, but when you brought that big black guy in, he told you all that it wasn't us, so there.

Q. Ya, good trick that. How'd you pull that off?

A. Don't know what you're talking about.

Q. Remember when you were involved in that fight up by Oak Ridge? Long time now, right? You sat in jail quite a while.

A. They dropped those charges.

Q. Ya, finding witnesses against you is hard. Why is that?

A. Maybe it's 'cause I'm innocent.

Q. Only explanation, right? Occam's razor?

A. Huh?

Q. Anyway, you were charged then, right?

A. Ya.

Q. And they took your fingerprint at the jail, right?

A. So?

Q. And they took your DNA, remember that?

A. What?

Q. Remember they used a swab inside your cheek?

A. Ya, I guess.

Q. They took your DNA. It's still on file with the State of Iowa.

A. OK.

Q. So I'm guessing you were smart enough to wear gloves. In fact, I'm sure you did, when you placed that bomb. We aren't going to find fingerprints from the Islamic center. But DNA, that is something we're going to find.

A. Don't know what you're talkin' about.

Q. Well, here's the thing, Johnny. It's up to you now. Once we get that DNA report, and we will get it, it will show . . . you see, there's some foreign DNA on the bomb that blew up that center that night. Someone else's DNA is on there, see. And once we get the lab results, we're going to know whose it is. But we think it's yours. Now, before that, before we know that it is you, you can help yourself. You can give us some information, and in return for that, we can help you with the county attorney. We probably can't make this thing go away. It was pretty high-profile, bombing a building like that, but we can help you.

A. You know cops love to lie.

Q. Hah. That's good, I know. It doesn't matter whether we're lying though, does it? You and I both know you blew that center up. You put the bomb in. And then you saw that someone was there and you saved him—that janitor. I'm proud of you for that. That matters to us. It tells me you aren't really a bad guy. It tells me that you want to do the right thing. Now do the other good thing here, tell us who sent you into that center to begin with.

A. Don't know what you're talkin' about.

Q. It was Peter Thurgood, wasn't it? Peter told you to bomb that center. Peter gave you the bomb, found you the old Buick, sent you to do it. Isn't that right?

A. He's my landlord.

Q. Ya. He's your landlord. And he directed the bombing of the Islamic center. Now if you could just give us that bit of information, tell us that, we could help you. Should we get a lawyer in and make a deal? I'm not saying you can get away scot-free, but we can make a deal. You can help yourself here. You just have to give us Peter Thurgood.

A. I think I'll go now.

Q. You can, you can leave if you want. As soon as we get that DNA report, we'll send a car over to pick you up. We will arrest you. We'll charge you with arson, with terrorism, with attempt to commit murder, and anything else we can think of, trespassing, for God's sake. We'll get you arrested and we'll get you convicted and you will be in the prison system of this great state for a long time. You'll be an old man when you see the light of day again. Is that what you want?

A. I want to leave.

Q. Of course. Of course. You have that right. You don't have to sit here. Just walk out, Johnny, if you want. But there is something you ought to think about, isn't there, Dick?

Officer Thill: There sure is.

Q. And what's that, Officer Thill?

Officer Thill: It's really quite simple. We've got this guy, this Nicholas Spencer, and he wants out of this. He wants to walk free. And he might be able to do that. He might get a *get out of jail free* card from us. All he's gotta do is turn in your boy Johnny Desmond, right?

Q. That's right, Officer Thill. And that will be just fine with us. We don't care about Nicholas Spencer.

Officer Thill: No, we don't. We care about Johnny Desmond, but not that much about him either. We care more about Peter Thurgood, don't we? We want to see Peter Thurgood in handcuffs, in prison, don't we? And you know who can do that for us?

Q. Who's that, Officer Thill?

Officer Thill: Why Johnny Desmond, of course, and if he's willing to do that for us, well, one hand will wash the other.

Q. That's right. Of course it will. We can get a lawyer in here to represent him—

A. Look.

Q. Now you be quiet, Mr. Desmond. We aren't talking to you. We're talking between the two of us. You said you wanted to leave. If you change your mind and want to talk to us, again, say so. Otherwise, just let us hash this thing out.

Officer Thill: Ya, we can get him about any lawyer he wants. Don't suppose he wants old Alfredo, does he?

A. Now just a second.

Q. You be quiet, Mr. Desmond, we aren't talking to you. I don't think he would want a black lawyer. He's the gold standard, of course, the best defense lawyer in this town. But he's an African American. He wouldn't want that.

Officer Thill: Don't matter. We can walk up a lawyer. Then get the county attorney down here. And we can cut this deal right now. We get Peter Thurgood, but Mr. Desmond here, he gets a good deal.

A. Forget it.

Q. You sure?

A. Not interested. I'm leaving.

Q. OK, Mr. Desmond, but I have one question. This is off the record, OK? But it's really been bugging me and I need to know the answer.

A. Shoot.

Q. Why'd you go back for the janitor? He's a brown fellow, isn't he? If you hate Muslims and you believe like Peter Thurgood does that whites are better, why save that black man's ass?

A. I don't know what you're talking about.

Interview concluded 1:10 a.m., November 10, 2016.

Nine

WE ALL WORK Election Day. Everyone is always worried about what might happen, but at least in Iowa, there really aren't any problems. Voting goes smoothly, without too many lines, few challenges, and no reports of fraudulent voting.

Three people in Des Moines were arrested for voting fraud prior to the election. Two are older people who apparently didn't know they had already voted. Although one of our vigorous officers pursues charges against them, the county attorney, wisely, drops them after we learn that. Another woman is arrested, a committed Trump voter and Fox News watcher, which I find amusing. She admits that she voted at one of our satellite voting places but was convinced that the auditor would change her vote to Hillary, so she voted again.

Everything is routine and I'm home by ten. Barbie is sitting on the couch, talking to Katie on the phone. "No," she says, "I really think Trump is going to win."

News to me. We all expected Clinton to win in a walk. But state after state is falling, albeit closely, to Trump. I remove my gun, secure it with a trigger lock and put it in its usual resting place, a lamp table in our living room. I sit down by Barbie and rub her shoulder lightly.

"Hey," she whispers, giving me a peck. She returns to her call. "Ya, Dad's home. He's fine. He's going to be surprised too." Katie says something. "Ya, it's going to be chaos," her mom answers. "The man has no idea what he's doing." Barbie is much more into politics than

I am, and she tends to vote Democratic. I shop around. I don't think I've ever voted a straight line ticket. This time I voted for Clinton, mainly because I'm convinced that the Republican loosening of gun laws is going to result in us all living in the wild, wild West.

When she gets off the phone, she goes on up to bed. I grab a beer and renew my place on the couch, switching the TV channels, all with the same result. Clinton will probably get more votes, especially when California comes in, but Trump appears to be winning the close Midwestern states and with them, the presidency.

I go through three beers and keep watching. CNN, MSNBC, Fox News . . . it seems possible still that she'll pull out a victory, but Trump continues to eke out wins in the key states. By two thirty, it seems clear. A New York real estate maven who once said that he was so famous he could grab women by their private parts without reprisal was going to be the president. I went to bed.

Barbie was there, snoring lightly. She turned away from me when I got in, but seemed to go right back to sleep. I rearranged myself so I was spooning her. It's like the most comfortable thing in the world. But it was so late my head barely hit the pillow before I was off to dreamland.

When I awake, I hear something I can't place. Is there a machine running? It can't be snoring. It's such a rasping mechanical sound. Then I feel the vibration.

Barbie's arm is shaking up and down. It's so regular and persistent and dramatic. Her teeth are also grinding, and she seems to be gasping for air.

"Barb," I say. No response. "Barb!"

I should be able to recognize a seizure when I see one. I've been in lots of trauma situations, seen seizures and worse, heart attacks, strokes, persons impaled on car parts after an auto accident, for instance; more than once, I have dealt with people suffering from gunshot wounds. But this is my wife. I keep shaking her, trying to get her to wake up. She opens her eyes, but they roll back in her head. Finally, I call 911.

Late the next morning, by the time Derek stops by, Barbie is sitting up in the bed, bored and wants out of the hospital.

"Mom," he says, "you need to rest."

"I can rest at home," she says. "You didn't bring Liza?"

"To a hospital? Mom, would you do that?"

"If my mother was dying and needed a granddaughter fix?"

I gave her the look. I am not as good at it as Barb is. When she gives it to me, I know I've been in the wrong and I feel chagrined. Maybe I just can't deliver it like she does, or maybe she's so sure of herself (when has she ever acknowledged being wrong?) that my signal just doesn't get through that thick skull of hers.

Derek laughed. "Your mom would have called me up in advance and told me I had to bring Liza!" he said. We both laughed. Humor, of any kind, is always welcome in a hospital room.

Thill dropped by and the chief. There were too many cops for an hour or so, and the nurse came by and said everyone had to leave. We finally saw the doctor again about two in the afternoon. Derek had gone to work, Katie and the grandkids had Skyped, and Barb had worked her way through the hospital lunch, augmented by an egg-white delight from the McDonald's in the basement. Never have understood that, shouldn't a hospital try to have a café that makes healthier food? But the egg-white delight is one of those things that Barb always likes, and it makes her happy. She looks on in disgust at my egg-and-sausage biscuit.

"Have a hash brown too?" she asks, maybe not so innocently.

This is where I have to make a judgment call. Did she somehow figure out via some evidence on my breath or elsewhere that I indeed had gotten a hash brown and disposed of it on the way up the elevator, or is it guesswork on her part? I admit it. "Those arteries," she said, "those arteries of yours must be plugged thick somewhere."

This is another refrain that I hear too much. Barbie has always been curvaceous, and I think she's lovely. She weighs maybe twenty pounds more than the day I married her, but carries it well. She, on the other hand, diets constantly. And it doesn't really work. I remain tall, svelte and always in need of an extra five pounds or so, not because of but despite the way I eat. I am constantly snacking, love doughnuts and potato chips, and my exercise is limited to what I get at work. When we went to Mexico last winter, she came back having gained three pounds and I lost five, despite the fact I ate everything under the sun. Today, I weigh a full three pounds more than when I graduated from high school.

I take it as a good sign that this is our discussion. Sometimes, Derek complains about our interaction. "Can't you two just get along?" He doesn't seem to understand that this is the sound of us getting along. I have long ago realized that I give in to my wife on nearly everything and stand my ground on what I believe to be really important. But if I should ever let her know that I let her decide things without me, it would disappoint her greatly.

Another night in the hospital is decreed. Barb shoos me off about nine, although I had intended to spend the night in the Lazy-Boy next to her bed.

"Go home," she says, "put Steph Curry on the bedroom TV set, and you'll fall asleep before the first quarter is over."

Steph and Damont Green and K.D. lead the Clippers by a sizeable amount before I snooze off, and when I awake after midnight, talking heads are engaging on the sports issues of the day. I turn it off, turn over, and stare at the north wall of our bedroom for at least an hour. Finally, I get up, go downstairs, get on my iPad and walk through some case files. A little before six, I drive to the hospital. I find Barbie still sleeping and sit quietly by the bed, sipping my Starbucks and reading the day's *Register*. It's Trump Trump and Trump, and I don't really want her to even see it. For one fleeting moment, I think she won't have to live through this joke of a presidency, and then that thought, so easily speeding its way to the forefront of my consciousness, shocks me. Could it really be that soon?

After Barb has awakened and been tested and got breakfast, I go into the hall. I catch Thill still at home.

"How is she, Bobby?" he asks.

"You know," I answer. "Hey, I had a thought. You know how we told old Johnny Desmond that Nick Spencer was cooperating?"

"Ya," Thill said.

"Why wouldn't he?"

This time the interview goes so differently. First of all, we include Darren Page from the public defender's office. He represented Spencer the last time he was arrested, and agrees to meet with us and one of the assistant county attorneys, Shannon Cox. Shannon has been around the block and can be tough as nails, something I've witnessed firsthand in court.

She generally believes whatever we tell her to believe and sets out to prove it in court. She starts.

"Mr. Spencer," she says, "you have counsel present. Do you agree that Mr. Page can represent you in this matter?"

"Sure," Spencer says. I can't tell yet what his attitude is going to be.

"Mr. Spencer and I had time to talk, and we're ready to hear your offer," Page said.

"Well," Shannon tells them, "I've agreed to make you an offer that I think is just plain ridiculous. I hate doing it. These police officers tell me your statement could be useful to them and that with it, they can bring the men most responsible for this act of terrorism to justice, so I'm willing to make it."

No one says anything. She continues, "In return for your proffer, your truthful proffer, and your assistance in testifying against Mr. Desmond and Mr. Thurgood, I will take a serious look at your charges and ensure that you get a downward movement on your charges."

Page was smiling. Page is a middle-aged black man who has been a public defender in Des Moines for at least twenty years, but I don't know him at all. His smile grew just a little and then he laughed, kind of. I thought it was a bit phony.

"Downward movement?" he asked. "Downward movement? That just isn't going to cut it, Shannon. Not even close."

"You know how this works," she said. "If we give him a specific offer in return for his proffer, they'll use it at trial to completely trash his credibility."

"Big deal," Page said, "you'll either shore up his credibility or you won't. But he's not making you a proffer without a specific offer from you. And it better be a good one."

"Look," I say, "we don't give a damn about jamming up Mr. Spencer here. We have much bigger fish to fry. He'll get a good deal."

"Great," Page said, "great. Then we'll all sing 'Kumbaya.' Is Mr. Spencer free to leave? Because I'm not hearing anything that is going to make me recommend he give you any information."

"I'm going to have to call John," Shannon told him. As in John Carson, the county attorney.

Thill, Shannon, and I leave the room. Page and Spencer are talking while we're gone.

I join Thill in his office. "You know that's a regular interview room, right?" he asks.

"Huh?" Then I get it. "Kind of a cheap move," I say.

"Take off, then," he says, and I see that he's pulling up the live video and turning up the volume. I close the door to his office so that Shannon doesn't see what we're doing, and we sit down.

"I just don't have any idea what to make of all this," Page says to Seymour. "They seem to think they know who did this, but they haven't made any arrests. So have we got something to give them or not?"

Spencer doesn't say anything.

"I'm your lawyer, you know. They can never make me tell what you've said. You have absolute confidentiality."

"So," Spencer says, lifting his face to look at Page, "what am I looking at?"

"Assuming," his lawyer says, "assuming you were involved in this bombing, well, I suppose they can easily charge you with terrorism, we call it intimidation now, same thing, some kind of assault, maybe attempted murder and certainly a burglary because you entered an occupied structure with the intent to commit a felony. Also some form of criminal mischief, a hate crime and arson. Arson first, I guess.

"If you're found guilty of all of that, or even the most serious offenses, we're talking significant prison time."

"What if . . ." Spencer began.

"Go ahead."

"You don't have to tell anyone what I've said?"

"I don't."

"What if I just went along? Driver, maybe. Nothing more?"

"Well, shit, man. I don't think that's going to make much difference. In Iowa, an accomplice is as responsible as the person who commits the crime. Unless you didn't know prior to . . .?"

We think Spencer is shaking his head no. It's hard to see. He says nothing.

"Then this might be the day you get out of going to prison. They seem pretty sure about who did this. They just want someone to say so. We should be able to get a pretty good deal out of them."

"How good?" Spencer asks him.

"Let's find out."

Ten

THE DEAL TAKES hours, actually days to work out. Shannon talks to her boss, who demurs. I talk to the chief, who talks to the mayor. And then we negotiate on the charges.

"If we're guaranteed a proffer. If you can provide at least John Desmond and better yet, Peter Thurgood. If you testify at trial and testify truthfully about that proffer, if you have evidence that shows that this was a Thurgood operation, that John Desmond was the bomber, then and only then, if you do that—"

"C'mon, Shannon," Page interrupts, "what's the deal?"

"OK, OK," she says, "for the right proffer, your client will be charged with criminal mischief in the first degree, a class C felony. After Desmond is tried and Mr. Spencer testifies against him, we'll reduce it down again to the D felony. He agrees to go to prison and he goes but since it's just a class D, he's probably only going to serve nine months or so."

Page closes his file. "Let's go," he tells his client.

Spencer stands.

"What are you doing?" Shannon asks him.

"What's it look like we're doing? Call me if you get realistic."

Shannon puts her hand up. "What is it you need?"

"Hmmm. Misdemeanor, don't see why simple couldn't work."

"Simple?" she says. "Forget it!"

"OK," Page says, "let me know if you change your mind."

There's some more give and take, but they leave.

"What do you think?" Shannon asks me.

"He was there," I say.

"You are so sure?"

Thill tells her, "We know it for a fact, but not one we can prove in court at this point. I guess if you want to wait and see, we can bide our time and hope we can get all three of them put away."

"Ya," she says, "it's not like there's any heat to wrap this one up."

I smile. "True. What if we just arrested the two of them? Put them both in jail, see what happens."

"We need probable cause. You really sure it was them?"

"We're really sure that he and this Desmond character were there that night, but we don't have anybody who will walk into a courtroom and say that."

"What about DNA?"

"Waiting. We've been trying to put some pressure on the state lab, but it's a little bit like pushing a rope."

Thill asks, "Does your office have some pull with public safety?" The lab is run by the DCI, a division of the Iowa Department of Public Safety, honest to god within walking distance of our headquarters building.

"Wrong party," she says. "John's a Democrat."

"I assume you have a CI?" Shannon finally asks. The question we did not want asked. We can't tell her we were listening in on Spencer and his lawyer, so we fudge the answer.

"Not exactly," I say. "We really can't tell you how we're so sure, but look, the reason we got on to this guy was that dust-up over by Glendale Cemetery."

"Ya," she says, "a shootout, wasn't it? In a residential neighborhood? Ever arrest anyone?"

"Not my case," I told her, "or Dick's, but no, we've only charged one of the muscle guys for the drug dealer, neither of the guys who did the home invasion. Lots of reasons to think it was our boys Desmond and Spencer. Which is why when we figured out that whoever got into the Islamic center did so with Allen wrenches, we remembered that that's how they got in that house too."

"So?"

"So we are pretty sure it's Desmond and Spencer. Problem is, the guy that we did nab, the muscle for the drug dealer, he was in the desert with Spencer. Won't rat him out."

"Hmmm. Still don't see the connection."

"And Desmond rents his apartment from Peter Thurgood."

"Ah," she says, "that snake. Wish we could drive him underground or out of town for good."

"Well, there we agree with you," Thill says. "Hate crime would go down drastically. He's behind a lot of it."

Another late night. Barb is peaceful in bed, for which I'm grateful. They have her on anti-seizure medicine, but the side effects aren't great. Meanwhile, she's developed considerably painful leg cramps during the night, in front of her leg, where there's practically no muscle. So you can't walk it off. Plus, her right thumb twitches.

It's midnight but only ten in California. I call Katie. "I'm worried about your mother."

"I'm sure. You two should get out here while you can."

"You're goddamned right," I say.

"Dad!" she goes. She always feigns surprise when I swear, but she's got to have heard me do so a million times when she was a kid.

Before I get in bed, I go to Travelocity and book flights for San Jose. Buying last minute hurts for price, but I don't give a shit any more. I spring for extra legroom. I spring for a two nights at a bed and breakfast in Monterey for Barbie and me and Katie and Ronny and the boys.

I get into bed next to my wife. I hold her as best I can without waking her. Doesn't work. "Work late?" she asks.

"How are you?"

"No new symptoms," she says.

"What do you have next week?"

"Just a doctor visit Tuesday," she says.

"Reschedule in the morning," I say. "We're going to see the grandkids this weekend."

She reaches out and touches my chin. "You think we're in a hurry now?" she asks.

"Nah," I say, whistling past the graveyard. "But I think my case is coming to a close, and I want to see Max and Elsie. Maybe we can go whale watching, think they're old enough now?"

She smiles. She goes back to sleep.

"Now or never," I tell John Carney. "Now or never. Let's strike."

"Can't we wait for the DNA results?" he asks.

"We can," I say, "we can. Don't think anyone will mind the wait, will they? Abdul won't have another cow? The mayor won't go ape shit? We're coming up on a month."

Carney is thinking, but he's exactly swayed by this. He's a careful enough prosecutor that he won't bow to the pressure for an arrest if he thinks we'll get there eventually.

"How sure are we that it's these guys? That's one of the things I don't like about letting this one kid off scot-free. This thing blows up in our faces if these aren't really the guys."

"We're sure," I say.

"Going to tell me why?"

"Not a good idea," I tell him.

"Shannon," he says, turning to her, "give 'em whatever it takes. I don't care if this Spencer guy walks free." But he sees the disgust on her face. "I know you can get something out of him, though."

He leaves. Thill and I are sitting in Shannon's office.

"I'm not letting him get off scot-free," she says. "I don't care."

"Well," Thill says, "I don't think Page expects that either. I'm pretty sure he'll take something where the guy serves time. Maybe just a little Polk County time instead of the pen?"

"On simples, he can only do thirty days top," she says, telling something we already know.

"Ya," I say, "but can we pile up several simples?"

"I thought of that," she said, "I still want to make a run at his getting at least a serious misdemeanor."

And thus a deal is reached. He'll plead to criminal mischief in the fourth degree, a serious misdemeanor. Gets probation. Plus, trespass, simple assault, and disorderly conduct, three simple misdemeanors. Serves the max, thirty days each, consecutive, for ninety days in the stir. It's a hell of a deal all around.

For that, he gives us Desmond.

On the next Monday, the day before Barb and I are scheduled on a Southwest flight to Vegas, then on to San Jose and then a couple hours' drive into Salinas, Spencer and his lawyer appear at the county attorney's office for his proffer. I sit in the back of the room, quietly taking notes that are probably unnecessary, considering we have a court reporter.

Shannon goes into lots of stuff. How he knows Desmond. What he knows about Thurgood, which isn't much, except that Desmond is a true acolyte of Thurgood's. Turns out he's also the father of Thurgood's grandson. Or so Nicholas thinks—that turns out not to be true.

Shannon tries to ask about the dustup near the cemetery, but Page stops her.

"That is not part of our agreement."

"Look," she says, "he has to tell us the whole story."

"The whole story about the Islamic center, sure, everything he knows. You haven't granted him use immunity for any other potential crimes, and I've advised my client to take the Fifth Amendment. Now if we go down that road, this whole thing may be off."

So she moves on. When we get to the Islamic center, he tells us he had agreed to ride with Desmond that night. He knew they were leaving a bomb in the center. Desmond did it all, though. He drove up, set the timer, and while Spencer carried the bomb, he got the front door unlocked. Then, Desmond took the bomb and put it inside. Then the two of them park across the street, near the IHOP.

"And then what happened?"

"We are sitting there. Waiting. To see if it goes, see. I know nothing about bombs. And I don't think Johnny knows much either. He's just stone-cold—that's why they used him. He don't back down or get scared about nothin'."

"OK, do you know whether he built the bomb?"

"Nope."

"Do you know who gave him the bomb?"

"No."

"You don't know for sure?"

"I don't have any idea."

"Who picked up who?"

"Johnny picked up the car from somebody and the bomb was in the backseat when he did. He then came and got me. I ain't never seen that car before, and I ain't never seen the bomb before that night."

"Did you ask him who gave him the bomb?"

"'Course not."

"Did you ask him who gave him the car?"

"'Course not."

"So," Shannon continues, "you're in the parking lot of Merle Hay Mall and what happens?"

"We saw a light go on in the Islamic center."

"Surprise you?"

"Hell yes, 'course it did."

"Why?"

"There wasn't supposed to be anybody in there. You got to believe me. We were supposed to damage the building—that's all. That's why we did it at night."

"Then what happened?"

"What happened, of course, was that Desmond drove the car across the street, racing through the light and running over to get the janitor. I still can't figure that out.

"Were you scared?"

"Of course. That bomb was supposed to go off."

"Did you say anything?"

"I begged him once we saw that light. I told him we had to go back. I wasn't sure he wanted to. He seemed scared, but I said, 'We can't let someone die.'"

For the first time, alarm bells went off in my hand. This testimony just didn't seem right. It was so self-serving, and what we knew, or were pretty sure we knew, was that Nick Spencer had sat in the car while John Desmond risked his own life to save the janitor.

"What happened?" Shannon asked.

"He gunned the car, right across Douglas and into the lot, and ran to the center. Couple of minutes later, he's dragging some brown fellow on the pavement, around the corner, and leaves him there on the ground. Then boom, the bomb goes off, and the car and everything around us shook. He got back in the car and we took off."

"Did you check to see that the other man was all right?"

"Guess not."

"You stayed in the car."

"Yup."

Like I said, it doesn't add up.

Salinas is almost ninety minutes from San Jose in good traffic, and there's no such thing in California. Once we got in and got our rental car and headed out, it was after six. We grabbed an In-N-Out burger and kept driving south. Barb had endured the whole travel day well, and she just lightened up when Katie met us outside her house. She hugged her mother, and I saw, right through her fatigue, that she lit up. Then when we got to the door, even though it was past their bedtime, Max and Elsie were at the door, bouncing off the ceiling, "Grandma! Grandma!" they proclaimed. I could have been the chauffeur.

She slept pretty good too, waking up once with cramps. We walked the floor but the rest of the house slept on and the next day was full of picnics, parks, and tomfoolery. Then the second morning we head down to Monterey, a short drive from Salinas, and the B&B. We've stayed there before but it's always fun. We know better now than to stay in the John Steinbeck room, because its bathroom is in the hallway.

After we checked in, we went to the aquarium, a favorite of the kids. Barbie was tired, so we left her in her room. When we came back, three hours later, she was in the lobby, drinking wine with some of the other guests. The kids had cookies, and we went to our rooms, got cleaned up, and headed out to eat. Monterey has some great expensive eateries; it also has some fine local joints with really fine seafood. We went to one of those, enjoyed the crabs and scallops, and headed back to put the kids down. Katie and Barb and I sat in the home-living-room-like lobby and talked until late.

I was exhausted and would have slept through it all, but Barbie finally woke me. "Robert!" she said. It must not have been the first time she called me because she only calls me Robert when I've done something wrong or she's insistent that I respond. I sat up in bed, trying to figure out where I was, and saw Barbie finally. Her whole body was shaking. She couldn't stop. She was panting too. "Bobby," she said, "Bobby, I think this is it."

I slip on some jeans, run out to the hallway, knock on the door, and wait until our son-in-law answered the door. "Get Katie," I say. Sleepily, he walks back into the room, I hear a low murmur, then Katie, still in her PJs, is standing there.

"You better come," I say.

I go back to the room, sit next to Barb, and hold on to her.

Katie has her stethoscope around her neck when she comes in. I don't know what good that will do, but having a doctor for a daughter has been more than helpful through the whole event and will be again now.

"We need to call an ambulance," Katie says. "We need to go to the ER."

"No." Barb stamped. "No, no, no."

"I don't think she wants to," I tell Katie, who gives me the look of having to deal with that parent, the one who jokes even as the world is coming apart around him. "Would you joke during a nuclear attack?" she once asked me.

"No limit!" I say, quoting my favorite Far Side cartoon. She didn't get it.

"Look, Mom," she says. "I can't take care of you here."

"I want . . . I want . . . I want . . ."

"Tell us," I said, "whatever you want."

"I want . . . to . . . go . . . to the beach."

I get the spare wheelchair out of the lobby entrance, fight its way through the narrow corridor and into the room. I lift Barbie, who has lost weight, into the chair, and we roll her out the side door to the patio and onto the sidewalk. We're only three blocks from the beach. Half a block down, Katie rejoins us, still in her pajamas but also with a raincoat and boots on.

"Kids OK?" I ask.

"Sleeping," she says, but shakes her head. Clearly, she's worried about the impact on the kids if we don't make it through the night. Barb is still shaking. When we get to the beach, I produce the anti-seizure medicine and we put it under Barb's tongue. She sips a bottle of water. "About time," Katie says.

"Maybe," I say. I'd never seen anything like this before.

But the beach, even in the early morning, just as the sun is coming up, does its magic. It's quiet, with the ever generous sound of water running up on sand, and she looks out over the marina and envisions whales. "Oh," she says, "oh, it's . . . heaven."

Katie breaks down. "You stay with us," she says. "Heaven can wait."

"Oh," Barb says, and the shaking is slower, "they should name a movie that."

Katie laughs. "Sure," I say, "whatever Dad says, snooze. Whatever Mom says, funny."

But we're all laughing. Katie and I sit in the sand, our bottoms getting wet, and within minutes, Barb has her head down and is asleep. Heaven can wait.

Eleven

THEY WAITED FOR me. Here's the funny part. We agree that when I get back to work Monday morning, we'll drive over and arrest John Desmond and then see what we can get him to admit. And on my desk is the report from the state lab. They find evidence of DNA from six different persons, none of whom are John Desmond.

Not that it matters anymore. We've got Spencer and we are going to use him. We just want John Desmond to turn on Peter Thurgood. If he'll do that, well, we will have really solved this case once and for all. We don't know who built the bomb yet, but we're guessing Thurgood can tell us that.

It's uneventful. We find out where Desmond and Peters are siding. We go over about four in the afternoon to a house on the far western side of Clive, actually one county over, and with the help of two Clive police cars, we park, lights flashing. Thill and I get out of our car while the two Clive officers join us.

Two Hispanic-looking guys are up on the temporary scaffolding, about two thirds of the way up the house. One of them shimmies down the rope and runs into the backyard, hell-bent on freedom. I want to laugh, but we are here for a serious purpose, so I hold it in. On the ground, there's one white guy who had been cutting pieces of siding and then handing them up to the workers. He watches the Hispanic guy fleeing, and he does laugh.

"Looking for John Desmond," I say.

"Figured as much," the man cutting the siding says, "can I finish this piece?"

He cuts the piece, hands it up the scaffolding to the remaining man, and then turns to us.

"John Desmond," I say, "you're under arrest for an act of terrorism, arson, attempted murder, criminal mischief, and we'll think of a few other things to throw in." He turns, saying nothing, is cuffed by Thill, and then turned back to me. I give him the Miranda warning.

"We're going down to headquarters," I say, "so we can talk. I think that might be beneficial to you."

He looks at me quizzically. I wait until he's in the back of the patrol car, where things are recorded by the in-car camera, and turn to talk to him again.

"Look," I say, "we know you weren't the guy in charge. If you can hand over Peter Thurgood or the bomber or both, you can help yourself."

"I want my lawyer," he says.

"You can ask—" I start.

"I want my lawyer and I don't want to talk to you. Take me to jail, will you?"

"We're going down to the department," I say.

"Ain't no point," Desmond says. "Let's get this over with. I want to go to the jail, unless I ain't really under arrest."

"Oh," I say, "you're really under arrest."

Standing at the parking, looking in mournfully, is Nicholas Spencer, whom I haven't yet told Desmond has ratted him out.

Desmond is true to his word. He refuses to talk. We take him into one of our interview rooms, leave him there alone, with the video and audio running. He puts his head down on the table and waits. After a half hour, Thill and I walk in.

"You can help yourself now," I begin.

"I want a lawyer. I don't want to talk to you. Take me to jail."

"You got that on a card somewhere?" Thill asks.

"I want a lawyer. I don't want to talk to you. Take me to jail."

"Look," I said, "I get it. We just have one thing to say. We were all pretty damn proud of you for saving that janitor and we want to reward that. But you're going to have to help us. We need to know who planned this deal, and we'd like to know who built the bomb."

"I want a lawyer. I don't want to talk to you. Take me to jail."

We leave him. Thill and I drink coffee outside, watching the room. We would listen too, if he said anything. He puts his head back down on the table. After a few minutes, it's obvious he's gone to sleep.

"Pretty cool customer," Thill says.

"I hope he likes prison," I answer.

The next day, I drive Barbie to the office of Dr. Michael Brumaire, oncologist. Barb has changed her mind. She's not looking forward to chemotherapy but she and Katie talked and Katie convinced her that two years, if she could get two years, was worth a lot to her kids, her grandkids, and come to think of it, her husband. Or maybe it was the symptoms and the night by the bay, when she thought it possible that she would expire.

So today is the first of three treatments. They'll be followed by more radiation. I know I should have some hesitation. I know I should respect Barb's wishes. I know she does not want to sit there while they pour poison into her veins. Instead, I am whistling as I push her wheelchair into the chemotherapy room.

"You don't have to be so damn happy about it," Barb says.

"I know, sweetie, but I just can't help it," I answer truthfully. "I just can't help it."

BOOK THREE

They say every man must need protection
They say every man must fall
Yet I swear I see my reflection
Someplace so high above the wall
I see my light come shining
From the west unto the east
Any day now, any day now
I shall be released

Bob Dylan, "I Shall Be Released"

One

I FUCKIN' HATE jail. There's a new jail since the last time I was here. The old one was downtown, right by the courthouse, several stories high. It was hot and it stunk to high heaven. It was awful. The new one has been built out on the east side of the town, and it's one story. It's all cement and it's cool in here. It still stinks to high heaven. And they still lock the doors behind you and you can't go anywhere without permission of the deputies in their red polo shirts. I still hate the place. It looks like I'm gonna be here awhile. They arrest me on a Monday late in the day, when I'm sweaty and tired from siding. They don't let me clean up. They don't let me eat. Then they take me downtown for hours, even though I tell 'em I ain't talkin' to 'em. Cops. Devious bastards.

Then after midnight, they take me to jail. I know why they wait until after midnight. When you go to jail, you get a bond review the next morning. If you go to jail after midnight, you don't get a bond review hearing the next morning, but the morning after. So I won't have it until Wednesday morning. That's the rule. All day Tuesday, I sit in a small cell by myself, in my own sweaty work clothes. They do bring breakfast and lunch, such as they are. After dinner, which they don't offer me, I'm given the standard orange jumpsuit and moved into a big dormitory with bunk beds. There are twelve guys in my pod, and six of 'em are black. Three are Mex.

Wednesday morning, they take me to jail court. Two deputies stay by me and I'm in shackles, like I murdered somebody. The jail court is a small, windowless room dominated by a wooden bench where a judge sits. There's a table for the public defender and another for the county attorney. They've got it on video and if you sit outside in the jail lobby, you can see the judge and the defendant. The judge is an older woman who just seems bored. She sets bond at $100,000 cash only. Might as well be a million. I say nothin'. The public defender stands by me and asks to reduce it to twenty-five grand. Denied.

I sit another two days. I got no idea how long I'm gonna sit till somebody pays some attention to me. I wonder whether Peter has been arrested or if he's gonna come see me, or more likely, if he's taken off, has to stay away from me, pretend he doesn't know me. Finally, late afternoon Friday, a tall, white-haired black man in a thousand-dollar gray pinstripe suit comes to visit me. I know who he is. Alfredo Fridley, the most famous defense attorney in this town. Probably in Iowa. He's considered the best, the Muhammad Ali of defense attorneys. He's got a team of young lawyers who work his cases with him, he has his own private investigator, and he costs a lot of money. Peter may not have bonded me out, probably can't bond me out, but he had to be the one who saw to it that I had the best attorney money could buy. Plus, if you think about it, a jungle-bunny defense lawyer is perfect for a guy accused of attacking a Muslim site.

Fridley and two other young lawyers, one man, one woman, both wearing dark-blue suits, sit in one of the conference rooms. They're both white. The rooms are recorded, I know, but supposedly there's no audio recording of attorney visits.

Alfredo has a surprisingly soft voice. "Mr. Desmond," he says, "I'm—"

"I know who you are."

"I've been retained to represent you. But just because someone has offered to post my retainer does not mean you have to use me as your lawyer. You have a right to choose—"

I laugh.

"What's so funny?" he asks.

He is so slick, so (what's the word?) sophisticated, so worldly, shit wouldn't stick to him if a chimpanzee threw it on him at the zoo.

"The idea that I wouldn't want you. How much were you paid?" I asked.

"Doesn't matter."

"Matters to me."

"I'm not going to be able to discuss that with you. Would you like me to be your attorney?"

"Got a paper for me to sign?"

The young woman pulls three sheets of paper out of her folio. It's paper clipped together because staples aren't allowed in jail.

I turn to page 3. "Pen?" I ask.

She hands me one. She's blond, with high cheekbones and a gorgeous nose and pretty blue eyes, and really ought to be beautiful but she's not. She's sexy, all right, but not beautiful.

I turn to page 3, find the signature block, and start to sign.

"Read it first," Alfredo says.

"Why?" I ask. "I hit the lottery and I ain't gonna turn it down."

"Good," he says. "Can you read?"

"Shithead," I say, but I start reading on page 1 and finish it. "Now," I ask, "can I sign?"

"Any questions?" the woman asks.

"Nah," I say, "I get it." I sign.

"Now," Alfredo says, sitting down across from me finally. "They tell me you're Aryan, a neo-Nazi, and you hate Jews, fags, and us black folk."

I look at him. What's the right answer?

"Ain't far from the truth."

"All right," he says, very politely, "how far?"

"I don't hate African Americans, exactly."

"Could you explain?"

"I think we should be separate."

"So," he says, "let me explain this to my two young friends here, if I can. You're not a white supremacist. You're a white separatist. We should both go our own ways."

"Something like that."

"Jews?"

"They ain't my favorites."

"Homosexuals?"

"Don't much care, but they don't seem right."

"Bryan here, Mr. Desmond," he says, pointing at the young man in the navy suit, "Bryan here is gay."

"Good for him."

"Muslims."

"Don't know any."

"You better start telling me the truth soon, or we're walking out of here."

"They should go away. Sharia law is gonna ruin this country. This is a Christian nation."

"Mr. Desmond," he says.

"Ya."

"I don't care."

I wait. There has to be more.

Alfredo continues, "In the vernacular, sir, I don't give a shit. I'm going to represent you if you still wish it, and all I care about is getting you acquitted. Do you understand me?"

This is one African I do like.

"I want to be clear about this. I don't like you. I don't have to like you. I do like being paid and I have been paid. I do like winning and I intend to win."

"Good," I say, "'cause I don't like jail."

"Well," he said, "I will be asking for a lower bond, but in all honesty, I think you're going to be in jail for a while. What I don't want you doing is going to prison."

I wait.

"Any questions?"

"Nah," I say, "except who paid you and how much?"

"I am not free to tell you."

"OK."

"And you are going to disavow, to the extent you're asked or to the extent we're asked, any knowledge of or support of white supremacy in any of its forms."

"Does that—"

"You are going to do that," he says, a bit more forcefully.

"I'm listening."

"We will be going to your room, your apartment. Someone has access?"

"Jenny."

"Peter Thurgood's daughter?"

"That's right."

"Jenny is going to help us remove any material, signs, posters, or any other paraphernalia that shows you're neo-Nazi. OK?"

"Fine with me."

"After we get you acquitted, I don't care at all what you think or what you have to say about blacks, Muslims, Jews, or even Italians—" He laughs now, although not very loud. "My mother was Italian, you know. Anyway, afterward, I don't care what you think. I just want to get you off now."

"OK."

"Now," he said, "Let's have a little talk about the truth." And so we did.

I know it was either Peter or one of his many friends in the movement who arranged to hire Fridley and I'm grateful to them. But I also want out and I want to talk to Peter. I remember how he came to see me the last time I was in jail, and I'm wondering why he doesn't again. When I do get a visitor, on the video system they have in this new jail, it's not Peter but Jenny.

"I wasn't expectin' you," I tell her.

"I know. Your friend is trying to lie low."

We both know they record these calls and the recordings end up being played in court if you say the wrong thing. By friend, she means Peter.

"I get that. But I'm stuck in here."

"They're tryin'."

"They spent a lot of money on Fridley."

"Maybe," she says.

"How are you?" I ask. "How's the little one?"

"Changin' every day. She misses you."

"Ya," I say, "me too."

"I know," she says. "We all miss you."

"How's Antonio?"

"I think he got in trouble again. Not sure what's going to happen to him, they may be sending him back to Newton." The penitentiary.

"You know any men who aren't in trouble all the time?" I ask.

She smiles. "That's a good question."

I wait.

"Do you like Fridley?"

"I don't like him and he don't like me," I answer truthfully, "but I don't think that matters. He's dead set on winning, and that's what I need."

"That's good," she says. "But we got a problem. We didn't figure it out for a while—that is, your friend didn't. Your lawyer knows about it. Ask him."

"OK."

"Your preliminary hearing is tomorrow."

"That's what they say."

"So you'll be at the courthouse."

"Up to Fridley, I guess. He said they might waive it."

"I didn't know they could do that."

"Guess so."

"Anything you need?" she asked.

"If you guys put some money on the books, I can get what I can. Also, get Coke from the commissary. I'm dying for a Coke."

"OK," she says, "we will. Anything else?"

"How about bail?" I ask.

"I hear you," she says.

Fridley warns me that you never win a preliminary hearing, but even if you could, I wouldn't because a judge would be afraid to dismiss these charges in such a high-profile case. High-profile—that's what he called it.

I sit next to Fridley at the table in a small courtroom on the second floor of the Polk County Courthouse. We passed a bond issue a couple of years ago, and we are going to end up with three new courthouses in downtown, but for the moment, this old one is still where you go to court.

The county attorney calls a Des Moines detective as a witness.

"What's the point of this?" I ask Fridley.

"To get information," he tells me, plain and simple.

He is in a gray pinstripe suit, white shirt, red tie, and looks great. Smells great too. Compared to jail, my god, it's nice to be around him.

They put Detective Robert Harper on the stand, the guy who picked me up and stuck me in a room and asked me to talk to him even after I asked for a lawyer. I asked Fridley if that was allowed. He said no, but it didn't matter if I didn't admit anything. And, Fridley said, it was good I didn't.

Harper gives his name and then the county attorney asks if he was the chief investigator on the Islamic center bombing.

He says ya, and they walk him quickly through what happened that night.

"Do you recognize the defendant in this matter?"

"Yes."

"Can you point him out?"

"He's at counsel table in an orange jumpsuit," the detective, the dick, says.

"Let the record indicate that the witness has identified the defendant," the guy says.

"It shall," the lady judge says.

"How is it that you determined that the defendant was involved in this bombing?" the county attorney asks.

"We have a confidential informant who identifies him as the man who broke into the center and placed the bomb in the lobby."

We've seen the police reports. This wasn't in them. When Fridley gets a chance to ask questions, he pounces on this. "Who is this informant?" he asks.

"Objection," the prosecutor says.

"Sustained," the judge says.

"Your honor," Fridley begins, "how can we prepare a defense against the statement of an unknown person?"

"This is a preliminary hearing," she says. "Testimony that there is a confidential informant creates probable cause. His or her identity is not necessary. If this person is listed as a witness, he or she will be listed in the minutes of testimony."

I whisper to Fridley that we got to know who it is. But I have my suspicions.

He also asks the detective about DNA. Was there any forensic evidence found at the scene?

"The fire wiped out any fingerprints," he says.

"Anything else, detective?"

"There was foreign DNA found."

"Did you run a match with the defendant?"

"We checked."

"And?"

"We did not find DNA that matches the defendant at the scene."

Score one for the guys in the white hats. Even the leading African attorney in this town. Things are lookin' up. Not that it lasts long.

Two

SOMETHING INTERESTING HAPPENS in jail, not that I figure it out at first. I can be a little slow on the uptake. First, one of the white guys is transferred out of the pod one morning. Then, another white guy gets out on bond. We now have two white guys in a pod of sixteen. The other white guy is a thin, older guy who's losing his hair. He takes the bunk underneath me. At that, I grow just a bit suspicious.

"How you doin'?" he asks just before lights out, when we're both in bed.

"Fine."

Then we talk some bullshit. Women. Weather. How long we been in. How long we gonna be in. How bad the food is. Usual bullshit. This is clever, but he finally gets to it.

"I hear you lit that fuse on Douglas. Nice work."

There are black guys all around us. There are two guys whom I know have copies of the Koran in here. One of the guys gets visits from that sheik who's always on TV, Abdul something, in his long colored robes. *This ain't right.*

"Don't know what you're talkin' about," I tell him.

"C'mon," he says, "that was righteous." *Righteous. Righteous. Who talks like that?*

"Don't know nothin' about it."

"Ya, I hear that's what you're charged with. Arson and shit."

"How do you know that?"

"Just what I hear."

"Ya," I say, "from who? The cops? I hear you're a snitch."

There are two black guys right by us, one in each bunk. I don't know if they were payin' attention before, but they sure as hell are now. I hear one of them grunt, something you can just make out, *snitch*.

I turn my face to the wall, just as the lights go out. Sleep doesn't come. I'm waitin' for somethin', maybe an attack, maybe not. I don't have anything to fight with, a shiv or knuckles or anything, but I'm gonna see what I can do. I hear my bunkie get up, maybe just to pee. I listen though and he doesn't come back. When I do fall asleep, it's for the night, and when I wake up to the sound of early morning activity in the pod, my *buddy* is gone. For good, I figure. There's a Mexican in the bed below me.

I don't see Fridley for a while, but those two kid lawyers come just about every day. I figure they're making sure they can bill and eat up whoever's money they're getting to represent me. First, they both come. They want to know my background, who my parents were, where I grew up. I tell 'em the whole fuckin' story, not that they quite believe it. They're going to do some checkin' on my DHS workers. I sign something releasing the information to them.

The next day it's just blondie (Andrea is her name), and she talks to me about strategy.

"Look," she says, "Alfredo is going to want to go over this with you again, probably before the end of the week, but I want to talk to you about something that's important. It's our trial strategy. The three of us have talked, and we've included Mark Miller. Mark used to be with the AG and he's retired, but he consults with us. He's had about forty years prosecuting, so we like to hear what he'd do if our roles were reversed. He'll probably be in to see you one of these days."

"OK."

"You see," she says, "we have to wait now for them to file a trial information and minutes of testimony."

"I don't know what those are," I tell her.

"No reason you should. They're the charging documents, the ones that really tell us what you're charged with, the level of crime, etc. But also, they list the witnesses. They'll probably list this informant. Right now, we just have no idea who this informant is."

She is just so sexy I can't think straight. I mean it. Her face is just enough off that she couldn't be a professional model or something, and it's a face you could tire of, but her teeth hang over just a little and her blue eyes wow me and of course her tits are outstanding and I just want to bend her over the little table.

She waits while I'm havin' my little fantasy.

"I think I do," I say finally.

"You do? You know who their informant is?"

"Ya," I say, "I'm pretty sure they're usin' Nick Spencer, one of the guys on my sidin' crew."

She writes it down. I give her the contact information too. And I tell her about Jenny, the one person I trust to help and not want to hurt me. Jenny will know where Spencer is.

"Keeping in mind what we don't know and don't want to know," she says, this goin' back to my talkin' with Alfredo about the things he didn't want to know (you see, he can't put me on the stand if he knows I'll lie), "is there any good reason to think that Spencer is the confidential informant?"

"Well," I say, "he could be lookin' for immunization."

"Immunity," she corrects me.

"Ya."

"Anything else?"

"Well, he knows where there's some cash. I expect if I'm in jail, he'll be able to get that cash, eventually anyway."

"Ya, is that it?"

"I read people pretty damn good."

"And you read this Spencer guy as—"

"As somebody who'd tell the cops what they wanted to hear."

She explains that the prosecutor has to file the charges within forty-five days of my arrest and by the arraignment date, which was set by the court. But it's four weeks away.

"Nothin' we can do about that?" I ask.

"We'll try. We'll ask for expedited arraignment, but the prosecutor isn't going to like that. I don't think he's in a hurry to file the trial information."

"Why's that?"

"Because," she explains, "once he files that, your speedy trial rights kick in."

I have ninety days from the date they file that charging document, she explains. The state must bring me to trial in ninety days. Now, she goes on, we can waive that and the trial will be put off for six or nine months.

"Is that good?"

"Delay is almost always good for the defense," she says, "but it appears you'll be in the jail until then."

"Ya," I say, "and I ain't exactly safe here." I tell her how the jailers have made it a segregated pod, all except me. She writes it down.

"Never heard anything like that before," she tells me.

"Guess I'm special." I smile at her.

She smiles back. Her teeth show just a little gum below. What a killer smile. Got to get my head back in the game. Quit thinking about sex with this young woman attorney.

"Look," she says, "here's the deal. We still hope to get you out. Either way though, we think they are going to have a hard time getting their case ready in the ninety days they have to bring it."

"Why's that?"

"They need lots of forensic information, and we already know they didn't find your DNA. So that makes the case rushed a little for us too, but—"

"But?"

"We think it might be to our advantage. We think they'll have to rush. They have to present a bunch of witnesses and a bunch of forensic evidence and we just think . . . but here's the thing: usually, we like to take depositions. You know what that is?"

"Nah."

"Where we bring the witness into a room and we have a court reporter and we put them under oath. Then we know what they are going to testify to. If they try to change their mind, we nail them with that. And Alfredo is good. He will nail someone who tries to change their mind. So it's usually really useful to us."

"But—"

"But we don't have time to do that if we make them bring you to trial right away."

"Which we do if we don't what, waive?"

"Ya, waive speedy trial."

"I think that's OK," I say, "but I do want to talk to Alfredo about that again. When he comes again, I'll probably know what's going on in here."

I'm in the shower. There are three other guys from my pod in the showers, all black guys, except I just hear water running, nothing else. No chatter. No sound of men soaping up. When I turn the water off and step out, they are all standing there, still dressed, looking menacing.

"Let's see that tat?" a tall enormous black guy asks.

"None of your business," I say, toweling off. I really hardly dry myself at all. I'm busy bunching the towel together into the only possible weapon I could have.

"C'mon," the guy says again. "Let's see that Irish Nazi thing. I hear you are one of Thurgood's boys."

I consider attacking. Probably wouldn't work but I could get one of the three disabled before I have to fight the other two. Instead, I turn so they can see the green Irish four-leaf clover against the gray swastika.

"Pretty cool," one of the boys says, looking away just before he turns to belt me. I have turned too, so the fist misses my side by inches. I grab hold, covering his arm with mine, clamping down and then bending it. Even though it doesn't break, it still bends in a way it's not designed to. He falls to his knees, and I let him have it on the back of his head. As I do so, someone hits me in the ribs. It hurts, but I don't go down. I face the other two.

"That was not smart," the big Afro says. "Not smart at all. We was just supposed to rough you up a little. Now I'm thinking we might as well put you in the hospital."

But neither one is a fighter. They're just big. And slow. And they don't realize that I have the right position. The first throws a long loping roundhouse punch that I easily avoid. The wall doesn't. He lands it on the concrete and immediately yelps in pain. As I punch him again, the other boy delivers a blow to my lower hip. I hit him while he's still admiring his punch. It's a good straight right to his nose, and while it doesn't put him down, it surprises him. Then the blood flows. The boy with the broken hand on the cement holds it and yelps in pain. I knee the third guy in the groin, and he goes down to his knees. The Afro with the broken hand stands up but moves out of the way and lets me walk back into the pod, which I do, strutting almost, naked, showing absolutely no fear. They may still come with more boys and they may beat me to death, but I ain't goin' down to these Africans without a fight, no how. And they know it now.

Three

ALFREDO AND MARK Miller show up to see me. I am disappointed that Andrea is not with them, but about ten minutes later, she walks in.

Before she arrives, Alfredo and Mark talk to me about Spencer. They found his army record and his criminal history, but none of it is that bad and they tell us some of it can't come into the trial anyway. They do not find current charges for him. They are wondering how I'm so sure, but they are careful not to ask. I say I'm not sure sure, but I think if they have someone, it's probably him. I also tell them about the white guy who was asking me questions.

"That's too bad," Alfredo says, "because we don't know what he told the county attorney. He may still say you admitted to being the bomber."

When Andrea knocks on the door and they let her in, she surprises them by interrupting.

"I understand you were in a fight here in the jail."

"What?" Alfredo asks.

"Don't know if I'd call it a fight. Three of your people jumped me in the shower," I answer.

"Your people!" Alfredo looks offended. Then he laughs. "Three African Americans, huh? Get hurt?"

"I got a bruise or two," I say.

"Two of them ended up in the emergency room," Andrea explains. "The deputy who told me the story doesn't think there will be any charges."

There seems to be some appreciation, or at least admiration, on the faces of the two male lawyers.

"Christ," Miller says, "we got to do something about this. I'm going to ask to see the sheriff."

"Ya," Alfredo says, "do that. Johnny, show us the bruises, will you?"

I'm never embarrassed to show my six-pack. I lift my shirt. There on the upper part of my rib cage is one nice fist-sized red, blue, and purple bruise.

Andrea surprises me. She reaches out and touches it lightly. "Does it hurt?" she asks.

I am afraid to answer. She apparently has no idea the effect she has on me.

"Andrea," Alfredo says.

I lower my shirt.

"The other bruise?"

"Kidney shot," I say, "kinda low."

He uses his fingers to direct me to turn around. I lower my pants just a tad so the bruise on my hip shows. I can't really see this one, but it still hurts like hell, so I'm guessing it looks tough too.

"Christ," Miller says, "I'm going to see McCarthy right now."

"Wait, wait, wait," I say.

He had already stood up and turned to the door, but he faces me again. "Ya?"

"You know what protective custody is like?"

"Johnny's right," Alfedo says. "He'll be in the stir for the next hundred days. Like to drive him mad."

"So what?" Miller asks.

"We use it another way. We write it up in our bond request. And we file it so it can be seen. Might influence a judge, but even if it doesn't, it should get some newspaper coverage going our way."

They move me to a different pod. The new one seems regular now, maybe six, seven black guys, three Mexicans, and the rest white guys. Most of 'em are charged with drug possession, some of 'em with distribution. The war on drugs fills our jails—that's for sure.

Andrea comes to see me. She explains again what the strategy is.

The next morning, they take me to the courthouse. You ride a bus with a bunch of other inmates who need to go to the courthouse. I'm not sure why some things can be taken care of at jail court and some can't, but we're ridin' the bus. You go early.

Then they herd us into this little room, and when your time comes, the deputies take you, orange jumpsuit, shackles and all, to a courtroom.

Alfredo is there waiting for me. He walks over. "I'm not sure how this will go. I'll do my best. You made the paper though—that can't hurt."

"What about?" I asked.

"About how they had three black guys jump you, of course."

He and Andrea and two prosecutors go into chambers without me. I hear some loud talk, then one of the prosecutors comes out and tells the deputy to bring me in.

When I sit down across from the judge, he addresses me.

"Mr. Desmond," he says, "do you have a place to live?"

"Ya," I say, and Alfredo corrects me, "It's 'Yes, Your Honor.'"

"Yes, Your Honor. I've still got my apartment."

"And work?"

"I'm a siding subcontractor," I tell him. "There's work now if the weather holds. But I've lost several jobs sitting in jail."

"All right. All right. You must be doing well to afford Mr. Fridley, here," he says.

Nobody says anything. I can see a smirk on one of the prosecutors' faces, but nobody laughs or anything.

"Anyway," the judge says, "I want you to know that if I change your bail to surety, from cash only, that I'm going to ask you to wear an electronic ankle monitor. Are you agreeable to that?"

"Yes, sir," I say, with the program now. It looks like I might get out.

"Well, OK," he said, "that's good to know. Do you have a landline in your apartment?"

"Huh?"

"A telephone in the apartment that's not a cell phone, connected by the telephone or cable company?"

"I don't."

"We'll have it installed before he posts bond," Alfredo says.

"Well," one of the prosecutors says, "that'll be in the order. If he doesn't have a landline when they try to fit him with the ankle bracelet, he won't get out."

Fridley reacts instantly. "We know how this works. I just told you that we would have it installed. That won't be a problem. We'll have it taken care of."

Andrea is writing down notes.

"All right, gentlemen," the judge says. "I'm going to order that bond be reduced to fifty thousand—that it be cash or surety. Got it?"

Both Alfredo and the prosecutor say yes simultaneously.

"And Mr. Desmond here will be on an ankle electronic monitor if and when bond is posted. That's required. If pretrial release doesn't have one, he'll have to wait until they get one. Understood?" We agree. I'm elated.

Days go by. Andrea comes to see me. She tells me the phone is installed. They're waiting on pretrial release. They're supposed to come see me.

"We have someone to post the bond?" I asked.

"Yes," she says, "Jenny Thurgood is putting up ten grand to Lederman. We're just waiting for the ankle bracelet."

I nod.

"What's Jenny Thurgood to you?"

I wait. I want to do this right. Is there any chance she's asking me if I'm available? "She's just a friend," I say finally. "Her dad is my . . ."

"Mentor?" Andrea says.

"Sure."

"Not a romantic interest?"

"She just had a baby. Somebody else's."

"Well," Andrea told me, "if you're not out by tomorrow afternoon, we'll go back to court."

I'm on the bus the next morning. Everybody wakes up early, of course, and then you get an early cold breakfast. Then they chain you and walk you to a bus and drive you to the courthouse.

Andrea is the only attorney there for us. She complains. The county attorney, somebody new, throws us a curve.

"They've found an ankle bracelet for you at the jail," he says. "Mr. Desmond would be out already if he weren't here at the courthouse."

"How convenient," Andrea says.

"What are you suggesting?" the judge asks.

So I sit in the little room and we all get on the bus at noon, ride back to the jail, where I'm walked back to my pod. I sit on my bed and wait. And wait. And wait. And wait. Andrea and Alfredo have made it clear they think that the jail staff is doing everything in their power to delay things. I usually figure it's just incompetence. Nothin' I've seen at the jail convinces me otherwise.

I missed lunch, and just as they start servin' dinner, I'm summoned. I go outside the pod, where they cuff and shackle me again and a deputy walks me down the corridor to pretrial release.

"Been waiting for you all day," a young woman tells me.

I smile. "Me too," I say.

She looks surprised but goes ahead, takes off my cuff and shackles, and then shows me the ankle bracelet. She explains it to me and makes sure I understand that when they call my telephone, which she says they will do most evenings at nine or so, I answer or I'm in trouble.

She has my clothes. It's a little embarrassing, but she has me take my pants off and sit in my underwear while she attaches the ankle bracelet. I'm trying hard to remain flaccid while this rather pretty young woman works on my ankle. Then it's on, I'm dressed in my own street clothes, dirty as they are, and she tells me how the bracelet works. Again.

Jenny picks me up. The baby is in the backseat, in her car seat, and I sit in back next to her. She's pretty little still and isn't too impressed by me, but I like being with her. I take her finger, and she latches on, squeezing it.

"You two having fun?" Jenny asks.

"Ya," I say, "this is way better than showering with a bunch of inmates."

She laughs, but the joke is on me and she knows it. We talk weather and work and the baby all the way to my apartment.

When we get there, the two of them go up with me. She sits the baby seat on the kitchen table, and she puts on the kettle for instant. "I really need a shower," I say.

"No shit," is her response, which I find amusing, if not enlightening.

When I get out of the shower, I slip on underwear, gym shorts, and a T-shirt and sit at the kitchen table with the girls.

"So," she said, "what do you want to know?"

"Where'd you get the bail money?"

"Isn't mine. Isn't Peter's. I think that's all you need to know."

Couldn't disagree with that. But I do. "Come on."

"Look, Johnny," she says, "I don't really know."

"OK," I say, after waiting a beat, hopin' to coax an answer out of her, "OK. Where's Peter?"

"Not here, that's all I know for sure. I know he's workin' this thing. That's all I know."

"OK."

I am silent.

"What else?"

"Who decided to hire Alfredo Fridley?"

She smiles. "That was a twist, huh? Stroke of genius, I'd say."

"Ya, kind of," I say, "it kinda was. Like hiring a woman attorney if you're accused of rape."

"I don't really like that comparison," Jenny says.

"Nah," I say, "I get it. Still . . . I'm kind of surprised, but I like him."

"Him or that blonde that comes to see you all the time?"

I smile. "She is cute," I say finally. "I'm sure she's out of my league."

"Well," Jenny says, straight-faced, "I'm sure she's used to pasty-faced, short lawyers with guts hanging over their belt. She might be interested in you."

She laughs, showing she's not really mad.

"Look," she says, "I got lasagne on in the oven at our place. You coming over?"

"You shittin' me," I say. "I've been so waitin' for a good meal. Let's go." I wrap the blankets around the little one, put on my boots and parka, and we three walk down the wooden steps, across the yard, and into Peter's house. The smell is wonderful. Jenny opens a bottle of red wine, and I eat three helpings of that wonderful pasta creation of hers. In truth, she's not the best cook in the world, but who gives a shit? She's the only one who'll cook for me, and you cannot believe how much I appreciate it.

"So," she says when we finish, then she picks up little Maria, pulls down the neckline of her blouse, opens the front of her bra, and moves the little babe to her breast. The baby takes to it greedily.

"She's doin' good," I say. I don't know whether to look away or not. It seems natural, but it's not really my child or my woman, so I just don't know what I should do.

"It was a bit of a struggle," Jenny tells me. "Honestly, she couldn't attach at first then she couldn't suck, and swallowing—that was a challenge too. But now, here we are. My little sweetie."

I figure out what to do. I get up, pick up both of our dishes, take them to the sink and rinse them off, load them into the dishwasher.

"You don't have to—" Jenny begins, but I shush her.

"You're handling something a lot more important," I say. Funny thing is, it wasn't just a line. I meant it.

"Look," Jenny says, then while Marie Petra still laps up mother's milk, "I don't like staying here alone. I think we need a security system."

"Good idea," I say, "I think I could do that."

"Really?" she says. "By yourself?"

"Ya," I say, smiling, "I don't think that would be a problem. I'm pretty damned handy."

"So I hear," she says, smiling herself.

"OK," I say, "I have to meet with the lawyers right away in the morning, but after, I'll go to Home Depot and see what I need for supplies."

"In the meantime," she says, still looking down at that baby and not saying anything else.

"Ya? In the meantime?"

"In the meantime," she says, finally, "go get your things. You can stay in Peter's room. I'm scared being here alone."

"Ya," I say. "Ya, I could do that."

"I'll change the sheets," she says. And I put my parka back on and go back to my apartment to get my crap.

Four

ONCE I'M SITUATED and the baby is down for the night, Jenny and I sit in our pajamas in the front room, listening for Maria and talking. We don't talk about the case. She tells me about Antonio going back into the clink, and she tells me about her friend Abby and what's been happening in town. They went to the community playhouse, but she didn't think much of the play. They tried out a new bar in West Glen but kept getting hit on. I like this normal stuff; it's so far removed from the jail and courts and all that crap. Then she tells me about the courses she's taking at the community college. "If I get through this chemistry and the biology class," she says, "I'll enroll next fall in the surgical tech program. Then I can get a real job and take care of Maria and me."

"That's great," I tell her, "good for you. But who watches Maria when you're in class?"

"Abby sometimes," she says. "Usually, I take her to the day care at the college. But I was kind of hoping—"

"Ya," I say, "I'd like that."

"How about your siding work?"

"We'll work that out," I say.

It's after eleven; the baby is sound asleep, so we both go to our rooms. I smoke one last one in bed—in Peter's bed, which feels more than a little bit weird—and I'm putting it out, when Jenny walks in. I don't say nothin'. I'm just lookin' at her. Even in the meager light, this is a sweet thing to see. She has baby-doll pajamas on and—well, she's not as sexy as Andrea or as good-lookin' as some other women I've been with before, to tell you the truth, but standing there I think she's just beautiful. Her legs are lovely. She has a few extra pounds now, but she's getting her figure back. And her breasts, of course, are swollen with milk. She pulls off her top, approaches the bed. I don't move. I am not gonna ruin this.

She lies down by me, then pulls herself so she's mostly on top of me, rubbing her breasts on my chest. I moan with pleasure. She softly touches my bruised rib cage. "Oh," she says, "that must hurt."

"Not too bad," I say. It's all I can say.

"Listen," she says, "this is going to disappoint you."

"OK."

"We aren't going to fuck."

I really don't know what to say.

"You're what I want, Johnny Desmond," she says. "There is no doubt in my mind. I want you. I want you to be my lover. I want you to raise Maria. I want you, but you may go to prison, right?"

It's hard to think. Those breasts are hanging down, and they turn me on like nothing else I've ever seen. I'm so turned on I must be prodding her legs, but she hasn't seemed to notice.

"Ya," I say, "there's a good chance. "We may have the best goddamn lawyer in town, but they have two pretty damn fine witnesses. And they want somebody to hang for that bombing."

"The janitor, right?" she asks. "He's their best witness."

"Ya."

"Who else?"

"I think Nick is their informant. I think he ratted me out."

"Nicholas Spencer?"

"He likes to be called Nick."

She laughs. "Really," she says, and then she reaches down and inside the front entrance of my PJ pants and takes hold of my pecker. "You sure it's him?"

"No," I say, "but my lawyers—" I stop. "Jesus, Jenny." I can't think.

She doesn't move her hand. "Your lawyers?"

"They say the prosecutor will have to list their witnesses on the documents they have to file next week. Either that or they can't use 'em."

"Good," she says. "Good. I think I'm more hopeful than you, but I mean it, we aren't going to be lovers unless and until I know you're going free."

"Ya," I say. "I get that."

"You want release?" she says. Or maybe she asked if I wanted *relief.* Either way, I wasn't going to say no.

I am startled awake. I don't know what time it is. I'm not in a jail cell, but actually, I'm not in my bed either. Then, I see the fiery red end of a cigarette being smoked by a man in the chair opposite the bed.

"You snore," he says.

"Hey, Peter," I say, sitting up on the edge of the bed, "sorry."

"About being here? In my bed? I'm not using it. I suppose Jenny asked you to stay."

"OK," I say, "I'm going to pee."

"There's a bathroom right here. You don't have to go into the hallway."

I get up, walk to the little bathroom attached to his bedroom, leave the door open, lower my trousers, and let her go. Feels great. It's a long stream, probably because I was drinking wine. I scratch myself and walk back in. Peter is in a chair at the base of the bed, so I sit on that end of the bed.

"You're around, hey," I say. "I kinda thought you'd be out of town. Are you sure this place isn't being watched?"

"You'd think so, wouldn't you?" he says. "Guess Des Moines PD doesn't have the manpower. Ol' Bobby Harper goes home every night. I hear his wife has cancer."

"That's too bad," I say.

"You know," he says, "I never saw this side of you. We're in a war, you know. You can't be sentimental about the soldiers on the other side."

"You talking about Detective Harper?"

"I'm talking about that Afro janitor. Why the fuck would you go back for him?"

"I really don't know."

"C'mon, try," Peter says, "I got to figure this out before we waste any more resources on your ass."

"Never asked you to."

"That's true. But tell me, really, what part of 'get out of there' didn't you understand?"

"What part of 'nobody gets hurt' didn't you mean?"

"He wasn't supposed to be there."

"That wasn't gonna keep him alive."

"So that's it," Peter says, after a moment of silence. "You just didn't want anyone to get hurt."

"Ya, I guess."

Then he drops the subject. He speaks in low tones. Apparently, neither one of us wants to wake Jenny. "Nobody saw me come in and nobody's gonna see me go out. I need to know everything you know."

"I'm pretty sure I'm going to prison. That's all I really know."

"C'mon."

"They got an informant. It's gotta be Nick."

"That's how we figure it too," Peter says. "Why is it you think so?"

"Who else would know? I don't know who the bomber is, and he doesn't know who I am. That's how you planned it. The only other person who knows for sure is you. And I know Nick."

"Don't make any assumptions. Don't trust anyone."

"OK, fine," I say. "But they are sure as hell wanting me to turn on you, and I know they're lookin' for you. So that means it isn't you who's rattin' me out."

"Ya," he says, "that makes sense. Besides, it isn't me. Anyone goes down, I go down, and they really want me."

We don't say anything. I tell him, not for the first time, that I will not give him up. He dismisses that idea with a wave of his hand.

"Say," he says, as he lights another cigarette, "what's going on between you and my daughter?"

"Nothin'," I say, "not yet. Might happen but she's made it clear she needs a man who can stay out of the clink."

"Smart girl," he says, and we both smoke quietly.

"OK," he says, "I'll be around. I have a pretty good source in the law firm and I have a source at Des Moines PD and I've got someone in the sheriff's department."

"Goddamn," I say.

"Ya," Peter says. "True believers. So there's always gonna be stuff I know. If and when I need you to know it, I'll get ahold of either you or Jenny. You still trust her, right?"

"Hell, ya."

"Well, when I told you not to trust anybody, I didn't mean her. She's one person I really do trust."

"Ya," I say, "me too."

"Fallen for her, have you?"

"You know my story," I say. "I always hold somethin' back."

"Self-knowledge is power, my son," he says. He produces a flip phone out of his pocket. "Take this burner. There's one number programmed in. If you call it, break the phone after we talk. If I call it, I'll let you know whether it's used up or not." He puts it on the bureau, along with a charger. He puts out his ciggy and walks into the living room. He waits by the door a minute, I can tell, looking out and then slips out the door, which closes silently behind him. I wait for a siren or light, but nothing happens. Moments later, a car starts and drives off.

"How is he?" Jenny asks from the doorway.

"I think he's OK," I say, "seems to still be in charge."

"Peter?" she says, "Always. Or at least he always thinks he's in charge, I never know for sure."

"Ya," I lie, because I have no idea what she means.

"We're different people, you know," she says.

I don't know what to say. I want to sleep. I get in bed.

"Don't be with me because I'm Peter's daughter. That ain't going to work," she says.

"OK," I answer. I hold the sheets up. "You comin' in?"

"Not tonight," she answers. "Not tonight. We need to talk more."

"OK," I say and she turns away.

"Hey, Jenny?" I ask.

She turns back. "Ya?" she says.

"Did you hear us?"

"You and my dad?" she says. "No."

But I wonder. "Love you," I say. I think I mean it too. Life is messy. I'm never sure.

Jenny doesn't respond, but walks back down the hallway to her and Maria's room.

Five

WE'RE BACK IN court a couple of days later. I realize after just a few minutes that Alfredo does not get along with the prosecutors. They seem to dislike each other. There is practically nothing they say to each other that doesn't result in one of them complaining to the other.

We're just supposed to be there for the arraignment. Andrea has told me that that is simple: you stand up, you say that your name is correct and that you're not guilty. Beforehand, Alfredo walks me into the clerks' office and we get a long document. They charge me with the same shit: arson, attempted murder, terrorism, criminal trespass, criminal mischief, and burglary.

"Burglary?" I ask Andrea.

"We'll explain it later," she says.

The lawyers are more interested in the second document. It's called the minutes of testimony, and it's supposed to list all the witnesses against me, which it doesn't. It listed several cops: first one is that Bobby Harper guy, and then someone named Confidential Informant.

We are waiting in the courtroom. There are two television cameras there. I'm sitting between Andrea and Alfredo. Across the aisle, there are three prosecutors, two men and a woman.

The judge walks in, we stand and he stops, looks at his monitor, and then plays with his computer for a while. "Hold on," he says.

When he's ready, he nods to the guys who are behind the TV cameras, and they light up.

"This is Judge Hanson," he says. "Is this Mr. Desmond?"

Alfredo stands. I stand next to him. "This is John Desmond, your honor. We have received a copy of the trial information, but Mr. Desmond would like to be arraigned in person and would like to enter his own plea."

"Has your client waived speedy trial?" the judge asked.

"No," is all that Alfredo said.

"He's not going to?" the judge asked.

"No, Your Honor," Alfredo says, "he's not."

"All right. Trial will be scheduled within ninety days."

Then the woman across the aisle is on her feet. "Your Honor," she says, "I ask that the court enter a waiver of speedy trial for good cause."

"And that is?" the judge asked.

"This is a difficult and complicated case, and we will need more time to prepare it."

Alfredo stands and starts to say something, but the judge waves his hand and continues himself: "It is and has always been the public policy of the State of Iowa that a defendant has a right to a trial within ninety days. I am not going to change that, and I think in asking for that, the State is risking dismissal. That request is denied. Anything else?"

She's back on her feet, but so is Alfredo.

"Ms. Horgan?" the judge asks.

"Judge, we ask you to stay these proceedings so that we might file an interlocutory appeal."

Alfredo is on his feet immediately again, but the judge waves him to his seat.

"That request is denied. Ms. Horgan, I know that you have done this for many, many years and you know what you are doing, but honestly, I don't understand the state's position. Specifically, I find that both of your requests if granted would violate the Iowa Rule of Criminal Procedure 2.33 subparagraph b. And honestly, if I granted either of those requests, I would end up with this case being dismissed. Now, anything else?"

The prosecutor sits. Alfredo is back on his feet. "Judge, the minutes of testimony in this case are wholly inadequate and do not allow us to prepare for trial."

"How so?" the judge asks.

"The State has listed a confidential informant. As they well know, if they are going to list a witness, we have a right to talk to that witness and prepare for that person to testify. We ask for that name now or otherwise that the Court dismiss these minutes of testimony and ask that this case be dismissed or the State required to refile the minutes of testimony."

Horgan is on her feet. "This is ludicrous, Your Honor," she says, and now the judge waves her to stop.

"All right," the judge says, "let me review these minutes for myself. He gets up and we all stand, and he goes back into chambers. Five minutes later, we're summoned in. His chambers are big enough, but there's five lawyers and me sitting there.

"Well, I've reviewed these minutes, and I think we have a problem."

"Of course we have a problem," Alfredo says. "These minutes need to be dismissed."

"We really don't have any problem at all," the male prosecutor says, taking over from Horgan. "As the court knows, we can file witnesses up to ten days before trial."

Alfredo begins to respond, but the judge stops him. "That's not the problem," the judge says. "You can amend your witness list until ten days before trial—hell, I've seen witnesses added at trial. But you do have a problem. The State does not have probable cause for the charges in this trial information without this confidential witness. I know, I know" —he waves at both attorneys to wait—"that I approved the TI, but I did so on the basis of that confidential witness. I should have informed the State that they didn't have probable cause without that witness. So I'm ordering the State to divulge this witness now, name and contact information, or I will dismiss this TI and the minutes."

The three prosecutors leave the room to talk. They're in a hallway, and the exchange is a bit heated. Alfredo leans over to me. "Dismissal," he whispers, "won't necessarily be the best thing for us. They can still charge you later, make you go to jail again, post bail again."

"Is that what they're going to do?"

"They might," he whispers. "I've seen Nan do it before. But in this case, I doubt it because of the publicity."

We sit, waiting. "Judge," Alfredo asks, quietly, "would you like the room."

"No," the judge tells him, "if they don't make the call soon, I'll make the call myself and they won't like it." He smiles. I realize that the prosecutors may hate my lawyer, but the judge treats him with respect.

We wait another five minutes, and then the judge calls out to his court attendant. "Tell that group that we need their call now, get them back in here."

Moments later, the three walk back in. Horgan speaks: "Judge, we'll file amended minutes today. I think we can get this done today, no later than tomorrow."

"So what do we do now, going to continue the arraignment?" the judge asks.

"Instead," she says, "we propose giving them the information on the CI right now, verbally. I'll get the actual filing amended today."

"That's fine with me, Your Honor," Alfredo says.

One of the young men next to Horgan looks down at his legal pad and tells us, "Our confidential informant is named Nicholas Spencer," then gives his address and cell phone number. Not that we need them, I've already provided the info to Andrea.

"Is the defense familiar with this individual?" the judge asks.

"My understanding," Alfredo tells him, "is that this person works on the defendant's construction crew."

"Oh," the judge says. There's a pause. "I've ruled with you, today, sir. You've found out this name based on my ruling. But now, I want to warn you. Nothing better happen to Mr. Spencer. He better be all right and he better be still ready come to the trial in this matter. You don't have to keep him on your crew—" There is laughter.

"I don't know, Judge," I say. "He's a pretty good sider." More laughter.

Then we walk back in the courtroom, the cameras are turned on, and I stand in front of the world and I plead not guilty. Normally, the lawyer does all the talking at an arraignment. But I want to do it.

"Is this your true and correct name?" the judge asks me.

"It is, Your Honor," I say out loud and for all the world to hear.

"Are you entering a plea today?"

"I am not guilty," I say.

Outside the courtroom, Alfredo does the talking to the press. "My client wanted to enter his own not-guilty plea so you'd all know it wasn't a formality. We intend to take this to trial, and we intend to get a verdict of acquittal.

"No, Dustin," he tells a reporter from the *Des Moines Register*, "we will not be waiving speedy trial. We want this done and over with within ninety days.

"My client and I haven't discussed a change of venue," he answers the next question. "We're going to have to take a look at things and decide that on the basis of some research. But right now, I'm thinking we can get just as fair a trial in Des Moines as anywhere else."

Des Moines is kind of a liberal city. Votes Democratic. Voted for Hillary. But it's mainly white, with lots of mainstream Protestants, Catholics, and evangelicals. Not the kind of jury you'd want if you wanted them to like Muslims. We haven't discussed it, but no, I'm thinking, we want this trial right here.

Then they ask Alfredo for his defense. "Our defense plain and simple is that Mr. Desmond is not the man that did this heinous act. It's actual innocence. Of course, as you know, we don't have to prove anything. We don't have to put on a defense. The State has the obligation, we call it the burden in the law, and they have to prove that Mr. Desmond is guilty beyond a reasonable doubt."

He sounds so certain. Funny thing is, he hasn't even asked me whether or not I did the bombing.

Six

ANOTHER FUNNY THING, Nick comes to work the next Monday. We've been busy since I got out of jail working on some new houses for Kudro Construction in the far western end of Clive.

"Johnny," he says, "we need to talk."

"Talk is one thing we ain't gonna do," I tell him. "Look, I don't care if you work on this project, just not with me. And we ain't talkin'. Hell, you may be wearin' a wire."

He gives me a sad, sheepish look.

"Johnny," he starts.

"You know what witness tampering is?"

He starts to speak. "Kudro has some houses in Waukee. Call 'em, find out where they are. Then I don't have to check on those wetback crews."

Nick leaves. In the words of Forrest Gump's mother, *stupid is as stupid does*. I ain't quite that stupid.

On Tuesday and Thursday mornings, I babysit Maria. It's a joy. Jenny leaves some of her milk in bottles in the fridge, and I use the bottle warmer. She usually naps about eleven and then Jenny's home shortly after noon. When she's up, Maria is either lying at her baby jungle gym or sitting laying on her pack 'n' play. I expect that she is oblivious to things around her, but I'm wrong. She bats one of the toys on her gym and it could have been an accident, but I don't think so. She smiles at me. Ain't sure it's a smile, but by God, that's what I think and that's what I'm gonna believe. I am getting an education, 'cause I never really been around a baby before. While she's nappin', I make some sandwiches up for Jenny and me. After lunch, I drive to the law firm. They have one of the old mansions on Grand, converted now to law offices. Alfredo has the big office on the first floor that used to be the dining room. But Andrea and Steve have second-floor offices. Not that I usually go to them, they have our stuff out in the conference room.

On that Thursday afternoon, Andrea and Steve and I read and talk about the fire marshal's report. It's not the final one and everything is tentative, but it's useful, they say. They are especially excited because of the DNA results. "Why did they give us that?" I ask.

"They had to," Andrea explains, and tells me about some case from the Supreme Court that requires they tell us good news, not just bad.

About four, Alfredo walks in.

"This is one fucking dangerous strategy," he says and puts a piece of paper on the table. "If we lose, you end up in prison all the sooner. In fact, if we lose this trial, you probably have your bond pulled and you go back to jail right then from the courtroom."

I don't say nothin'.

"Well, what do you think?" he asks. "Here's a waiver of speedy trial. Sign it and Andrea will get it on file yet today."

"And then," I say, "how long before we get a trial?"

"You sure you want a trial?" he asks. "If I know Horgan, she'll make us a real nice offer sometime before trial, one that will be hard to turn down."

"One that has me going to prison?"

"Probably." He stops, thinks, then says, "No, almost for sure. This has gotten so much publicity, I don't know how she offers us anything in which you don't do time."

"Then she can save her breath," I answer. "I ain't takin' any deal that means I go to the pen. So I guess I want my day in court. How long will we wait for a trial if I do sign that paper?"

"Best guess, we try this case in six months. Could go nine months, not much past that. People will have forgotten a little. The heat will be off a little. Delay is good for the defense."

I think about all this a minute. If I'm going to prison anyway, it would give me six or nine months to watch Maria grow, to play a part in her and Jenny's life. But then, I'd be off to prison anyway and they'd be gone. The only way I see myself ending up with them is to beat this thing at trial. I'm just not sure how we're gonna do that.

"Let me ask you something else," I say. "I take it Nan Horgan is the chief prosecutor in this case."

"Ya," Alfredo says. "John, the elected county attorney, often jumps in on these prominent cases, but he's on the Gwinn murder, so it's Nan running this show." The Gwinn case is an even more famous case, a murder that went on in town. A teenager died of starvation and her parents are charged.

Mark Miller walks in. He's obviously talked about this with Alfredo. "What's he think?" he asks Alfredo, nodding to me.

"So," I continue, "how many cases does she have right now?"

"Shit," Alfredo says, "several. Mark?"

"At least six, probably nine, maybe a dozen."

"So who's going to be more ready for trial if we just make them do it within ninety days?"

"I see your point," Alfredo says. "Still—"

Miller interrupts him. "She'll be ready. She'll jettison every other case if she has to. This is the case she'll care about. She'll spend the weekend before trial in her office, interviewing police officers if she has to."

I turn to Andrea. "You are the one person who seems to care whether I hang or walk out the door," I tell her. "What do you think I should do?"

She gives me a look of well, probably, sympathy, but I can also see she's scared. I've put her on the spot. She hesitates. I get it. She's the junior attorney here. She can't afford a mistake. And she shouldn't advise something that her boss hasn't.

"Go on," Alfredo says. "I want to hear this as well."

"Don't waive speedy," she says. "Make them try it right away. We'll be ready. Horgan may be ready but not as ready as she would be in six to nine months. And with no depositions, there's at least an opportunity that somebody says something useful to us that she's not ready for." Then she hesitates. "Look," she says, "I don't have that much experience, you know, compared to Mr. Fridley or Mr. Miller. I'm not sure you should rely on me."

"He's relying on you because you care about what happens to him. That's not illogical. And ya," Alfredo says, "we can be ready. And we'll get plenty of discovery, like the interview recordings, etc., and the final fire marshal's report. But there's no way we're going to get to depose all the witnesses."

"There aren't that many," Andrea points out, "just two cops, the fire marshal, actually the deputy, Paul something or other, and Nick Spencer."

"Wait a second," Alfredo says, seems excited. "Where's the minutes?"

She opens the file, gives them to him. He reads, quickly.

"Did anyone else notice what's missing?"

"I was gonna ask you," I say, "why they don't have the janitor listed as a witness."

"Bingo," Alfredo says and looks around. No one responds. "Honest to God, I'm old," he says. "Nobody else here remembers bingo. Anyway, Johnny here is so right. Johnny, when we are all done, I want you to think about law school. We need you around here."

"Maybe I could be an investigator," I said. "I got my GED, but I ain't had no college."

"Never mind," Alfredo says, excited. "You may have hit a home run, though. Look, I'm going to drive over to see that janitor. Andrea, you coming?"

She stands. He's almost out the door, then he turns around so that she almost bumps into his back. "And," he says, "we aren't waiving speedy trial. Let this trial commence!"

I put up siding all day Saturday. We're having good weather for December in Iowa, and even though we have to wear coats and we can see our breath, we're getting some houses finished. But Sunday is a day of rest, even for us heathen neo-Nazi fascists. I sleep in and wake to the odor of freshly ground, freshly brewed coffee. There's just no way that a Keurig can deliver that. I put on my bathrobe, walk out, and find Maria in Jenny's lap, sucking away at her breakfast.

"Want some French toast?" I ask.

"You can cook?" she asks.

"Had to learn. If I wanted to eat, I had to cook." It was closer to the truth than I could tell her, but I've always been somewhat grateful to that Madison County bastard for making me cook.

I find the eggs, bread, and vanilla, start a pan heating, pour eggs and milk into a bowl, mix them, then add the vanilla. My mouth is salivating at the mere thought of French toast. God, I hate jail meals. The thought has occurred to me that I couldn't stand prison and had to plan another way out of this. Don't think I could live in Mexico, wonder whether Canada would work? Probably I'd need to go to Central America. Once I get the griddle hot, I slice the bread into halves and dunk two slices into the egg batter and throw it on the griddle.

"Jenny," I say, "I can't tell you how much I appreciate getting these lawyers and posting bail."

"Wasn't really me," she says.

"Never mind. I know you helped. And living here with the two of you has been, well, I'm not that good with words."

"We like having you too."

"See," I tell her, "I never really had a family life."

"I know what you mean," she says, which surprises me. I turn the French toast. Maria finishes and she buttons up.

"Really?" I ask. "It seems like you and Peter——"

"Ya," she said, "we're close. But the movement always came first. Always. That's why now, he's gone and the man I want is facing prison time."

I check the toast. Not quite ready. I don't know what to say.

"Look," I say, "I don't think I can face prison."

"What's the alternative?"

"I was thinking I could relocate."

"Jesus," she says, "I didn't think you were that dumb. In this day and age? Credit cards, the Internet, I don't think that's still possible."

"I'm resourceful," I say, "but it would have to be carefully planned out."

"Look," she says, "I've made it clear how I feel about you, but there's something else you should know."

I bring her two slices of French toast in four pieces, butter and syrup from the fridge. She uses her fork to cut a small piece, tastes it, chews and swallows, and tells me, "That's delicious."

"Thanks."

She eats her breakfast while I make two more slices on the griddle.

"As I was saying," she starts, "I think it might be time to take responsibility."

I turn the toast. I'm not quite sure what she means.

"I don't mean you should plead guilty. Defend yourself, but if they find you guilty, I think you should man up and do your time."

"It could be a lot of time. Attempted murder is one of my charges."

"You saved that man, didn't you?"

We shouldn't be talking freely like this, but it's Jenny and I want to. Still, instead of admitting this, I nod to tell her that I did.

"That's when I realized you were as good a man as I had been thinking you could be."

I couldn't help it. This made me smile. "Your dad wasn't very happy about it."

"See," she says, "I told you we were different people."

When I was seventeen, I saw my mom one last time. I can't remember why. She was in prison, her first stint. Don't know if it was her last.

She was really thin, she'd lost a couple of teeth, and she seemed so fidgety I've always kind of pretended it wasn't really her. I imagined that it was somebody else and my real mom was still out there waiting for me.

It was visiting day at Mitchellville, the state's only women's prison, which is located in the far eastern part of Polk County, only about a twenty-minute drive from downtown Des Moines. I can't remember who took me. It was a social worker or a lawyer. I can remember that she sat with me in the waiting area. It was kind of an enclosed picnic area, with big circular plastic tables and vending machines. Mom ran in and gave me a hug, but I just sat there. Didn't hug her back. Mom asked me if I had any change—she'd love a Coke. I got her one and a bag of Fritos, her favorite.

"Jesus," she said, "these are good."

Nobody said anything. Finally, she asked, "How you doing, sweetheart?"

Not sure what I answered. I knew she was an addict. I knew she was never going to take care of me. I knew she wanted to be my mother but couldn't, wasn't really able to take care of me or anyone else, not even herself. So I told her I was doing good. I had a nice foster family. Told her I was doin' well in school. I just flat out lied.

"But you're still my son, right? Huh, honey?"

"Yes, Momma," I said, "I ain't changed my name and I ain't been adopted. I'm still your son."

She told me Grandma was dead. I already figured as much and I wasn't sure when, but I knew somehow that if she had still been around and healthy, she would have walked to Des Moines if need be to take me back home. If only my ma had left me there. So I asked.

"Ma," I said, "why didn't you leave me at Grandma's?"

"Oh, baby," she said, leaning over her bag of Fritos and cupping the back of my head, "you're my boy. You aren't her boy. You're mine."

I didn't say anything. What would be the point? What I wanted to say, of course, was, *If I was your boy, why didn't you take care of me? Grandma was takin' care of me. Life was good with her. I had enough to eat, no one hurt me, and I walked to school.* But I didn't see the point. I could have hurt her feelings, I guess, but I didn't see the point. So I just told her not to worry about me anymore. I was going to be fine without any parents. She said she wouldn't be in the pen forever. She hoped when she got out, we could see each other. From time to time, I put money on her books but she got out within the next couple of years, and by that time, I was in so much trouble myself, and we lost touch.

Seven

A WEEK PASSES, another; domestic life is simple, quiet, and sweet. I buy a baby toy for Maria for Christmas and a book on anatomy for Jenny. Don't know if she really liked it, but she pretends it's just what she wanted. That pretty much sums her up. She buys me a blue dress shirt and red tie. "For court," she says. She picks up a turkey for Christmas dinner and it's way too big, but I get it thawed, wake up early, and put it in the oven so we can eat about midafternoon. I bought a bottle of champagne, most of which we drank with the dinner, and afterward when Maria goes down in her crib. I sprawl out on the sofa.

"We should do the dishes," Jenny says, but I tell her they can wait. She lies down next to me, her head on my shoulder. I love having her body pressed to mine. I want to reach down and kiss her, but I don't think it would be allowed. We both start to nap. I'm awakened by a cell ringing. It's the burner.

"Merry Christmas," I tell Peter.

"Ya," he says, seemingly annoyed. "I hear you're going to trial."

"That's the way it works."

"That's the way it works, sometimes," he says. "We need to meet."

"OK."

"You know the Popeye's on Merle Hay?"

"Ya."

"Tomorrow morning, six sharp."

It ain't really gonna be the Popeye's chicken. It's code. The meeting is for the Dunkin Donut's across Meredith from the Popeye's. And it ain't exactly there, either. It's in the parking lot down by the closed car dealer. First though, I'm driving in, getting coffee by going through the drive-up and then surveying the area to see whether there's any police activity. If there is, once I park, I'll just sit there in the car, not moving. If I don't see anything, I get out, stand next to my car, and sip my coffee while I wait for Peter.

"I'll be there."

"How is my granddaughter, and Jenny?"

"Both good," I say, "wanna talk to her?"

"Nah," he says, "wish 'em a happy Christmas."

"You mean merry?" I say, without thinking, stupidly.

"Huh," Peter says, "Mary? What?"

"See you whenever," I say, then I hang up, break the phone into two pieces, remove the SIM card, which I put in my pants pocket, and I throw half the phone in the kitchen garbage. The other half I keep in another pocket. When I can, I need to drive to a QuikTrip or Kum & Go and toss the phone parts in garbage cans.

I think about starting on the dishes, but Jenny is lying on the couch still, and I join her, our legs crossing, and now I do reach down and kiss her. Our lips touch, softly, sweetly. "Nice," she says, and kisses me again. This goes on for a couple of minutes, then she looks into my eyes and I know what she's sayin' without her sayin' it. I ain't sayin' it's hard not to keep goin', but I stop. I like lyin' with her on the couch.

I set my alarm for five, comb my hair and brush my teeth, throw on jeans and a sweatshirt, get my parka from the hall closet, and I'm creeping out of the house by five thirty. "What's up?" I hear Jenny ask from her room.

"Just gotta do something," I say, "I'll be back soon."

"Tell my father hello," she says, then I see her turn toward the wall in an effort to go back to sleep.

I don't see any surveillance, no cop cars, nothing. I take at least fifteen minutes before I enter the drive-through for the Dunkin' Donuts, which opens right at six, but I'm not the first car. I get two coffees and three donuts and drive out toward the north, then swing west into the old auto dealer parking lot, parking just next to the abandoned building. I get out, coffee in hand, and stand next to my car. It's cold, and the hot coffee tastes awfully good.

It's ten minutes before Peter drives up. He's in the passenger seat. He gets out, and the other man drives away. We both get in my car and he tells me where to go. We head west down Meredith, out of Des Moines, although I don't trust the Urbandale cops any more than the ones in Des Moines. The theory, of course, is that they are less likely to be tailing either one of us. We park in the Fareway lot.

"OK," he says, "I hear you are going to go to trial right away."

"That's what we're figurin' right now," I say.

"You like your Afro lawyer?"

I hesitate. There's no correct answer. I should hate him. But he has impressed me. And I love Andrea. "Seems to know what he's doin'. Lord knows, the prosecutors don't like him."

"And he thinks you should go to trial soon instead of waiting?"

"Don't think he's sure, either," I say. "But I don't think I can sit around and wait to see what happens."

"Well," Peter says, "I think it's stupid. Delay is good for a defendant. Didn't anyone tell you that?" I'm going to answer, but he doesn't give me a chance. "You really think you'll all be ready for a trial?"

"I guess."

"Well, there's a strong statement, isn't it? Look, Johnny, I want to know if you're thinking about another way out of this."

"Ya?"

"Well, how do you feel about goin' somewhere tropical?"

"Won't pretend I haven't given that some thought. Can a guy really run away like that anymore?"

He looks out the window. I don't think he's gonna answer, then he says, "It's iffy. There's risk. And the FBI will be lookin' for you.

But in Belize or Honduras, well, Costa Rica. Well, if we can get you there OK, you'll probably be OK."

"Jenny told me to man up and do the time."

"She tell you she'd wait for you too?"

"She did not."

"Thought so." He hands me two new burners. One of 'em has a piece of tape on the back. "Same rules for burner one. Two, the one with the tape, that's if you decide you want to leave. But you better give us at least a week's notice. And even then, I ain't sure we can arrange it for you. We'll try though, my friend, we'll try."

Something about it reeks of fraud. It just seems to me that he's givin' me false hope. I can't say for sure, but I have my doubts.

"OK," I say, straight-faced, "what else?"

"I want you to know," he says, then sips his coffee, "that this ain't our only effort. We got something else in mind."

"I think you've done enough," I say.

"Ya, well," he says, "my ass is on the line too. I'm sure they are interested in knowing who planned this." Now, I get worried. If Peter isn't sure I'll stay quiet about him, how long before they just take me out?

"And," Peter goes on, "I think we can do something else that helps us both."

I hesitate, but then I say it. "Don't hurt Nick."

"He deserves anything that happens to him," Peter says, "but that ain't the idea. Not that we haven't considered *moving*."

So this is what bothers me afterward. I no longer believe what Peter tells me. He has somehow gotten me one of the best defense lawyers available and gotten somebody to bond me out, but also, I'm pretty sure that he is more interested in protecting himself than me.

I work four days a week, including Saturday, spend two mornings with Maria while Jenny goes to school. I go to the law office when they want me, but that is rare these days. They are getting ready, Andrea tells me, and when they need me, they'll tell me. Actually, Alfredo and Mark are trying another case in federal court and Steve is there with them, so I'm pretty sure Andrea is the only one who is still working on my case.

Trial is scheduled for February 21, a Tuesday morning, at the Polk County Courthouse, a four-story granite building on the south side of downtown. It's old and it's been cut up over the years into various small courtrooms, but we're scheduled for one of the big ones, in front of Judge William Blank, a person who's old enough to retire, but hasn't. I met him for the first time at a pretrial hearing in January. He dresses impeccably, wears a salt-and-pepper beard, horn-rimmed glasses, and always has a stern disposition.

We're here for a pretrial hearing, and as I understand, that's when you often get an offer from the prosecutor. But we didn't. And it's not like we're the only ones here. There are lawyers all over, five different prosecutors on one end of the long table and more like twelve defense lawyers on the other. Alfredo, though, sits on the bench next to me, waiting his turn. There are also lots of other defendants, although most of 'em, I admit, are in orange jumpsuits, sitting in the jury box. As a result, there are three deputies in the room as well.

"Mr. Fridley," the judge announces. "You are here for Mr. Desmond?"

"Yes, Your Honor," Alfredo says after standing.

"Is your client here?"

"He is seated next to me."

"Very good. Where is Ms. Horgan?"

One of the young guys who is with the county attorney's office stands and announces that she is in another courtroom and will be coming shortly. Typical. They love to make me wait, especially when we're paying Alfredo $400 an hour.

We wait, ten, then twenty minutes. The judge looks up from what else he's been doin' and calls Alfredo up. "Mr. Desmond, you too," he says.

"Has your client waived?" he asks Alfredo.

"He has not, Your Honor."

"Going to?"

"We will not be waiving, Your Honor, "Alfredo tells him.

"Then I don't think we should even think about changing the trial date, do you?"

"No, Your Honor, we are fine with February 21."

"All right, Shannon," the judge says to his court attendant. "Since Ms. Horgan can't grace us with her presence, could you prepare an order setting this down for trial? Any defenses, Mr. Fridley?"

"Innocence," Alfredo says.

"Any defense to be noticed, beyond innocence?"

"No, Your Honor."

"Any motions to be filed?"

"Only limine," Fridley says, and we're done. He waves us back to our seats, and within a couple of minutes, the court attendant walks back to us and hands me a copy of the order. As we're walking out, Nan Horgan is walking fast into the courtroom, files under her arm.

"Where are you going?" she asks Fridley.

"Order's done," he says.

"Wait, wait, wait," she says. "I'm going to need a continuance."

We walk back in the courtroom, and she and Fridley approach the bench. The judge looks up, and I can hear them talking. "Mr. Desmond," the judge says, "please come up here."

I do. Horgan is talking.

"Judge," she says, "we're going to need more time. I'm asking you to find good cause in that the Polk County attorney's office, the Des Moines police, and the fire marshal all need more time to investigate."

"Then you should have waited before charging my client," Alfredo says loudly, forcefully.

"In the interest of justice," she begins.

"I don't want to hear it, Nan," the judge says. "That's not how speedy trial works. Surely you've read the appellate cases."

No one says anything.

"As I see it," Judge Blank says, "you have two options. Get ready to try this case on February 21 or dismiss. You can do it without prejudice, bide your time, and then when you get your investigation fully taken care of, charge this defendant again, or not. But we are not—"

"Judge," she says, "even if I could have a week. Speedy doesn't run until March 2."

"Then you should have set the date later to begin with," the judge says. "I'll see you both on the nineteenth. I'm looking forward to it."

Eight

MARIA DOESN'T WANT to go down this Tuesday morning. She takes a bottle and plays in jungle gym a bit, then tries to roll over. She is able to move on to one side, but not back again. I lie down by her and help her move back. She rolls right back onto her side. I roll her all the way to her stomach, but this just annoys her. She gets fussy. I roll her back. She's on her side again in a jiffy. I help her to her stomach, again. This time, after a moment, she rolls back over to her side, and then her back.

When her mom walks in, we are both still on the floor, Maria rolling back and forth. "Mom," I say, "Mom, you have to see this!"

Jenny stands there and watches the performance. There is a smile, then she picks her daughter up. "Have you given her a bottle?"

I confess I haven't.

"Who's the kid, huh?" she asks, but she has a smile on her face. She sits down and begins to feed Maria. I just lie there, happy. I had no idea how a child can make you feel like you're something. And it isn't even my child.

Jenny must be able to read my mind. "I want to have your baby," she says.

"Put that kid down," I say, with fake enthusiasm in my voice, "and watch me make her a sister!"

"I'm not kidding," she says, "but not right this moment. I need a little more of a break. We just have to figure out how to do this before you go away."

"Geez," I say, "you're really turnin' into a glass-half-empty girl."

She leans back, lets Maria suckle, and says, "Scoot. You're due at the law firm."

Andrea is going over my testimony for the third time. She tells me to be serious, quit kidding, answer the way I'm supposed to. The testimony is planned out from start to finish, but they continue to make little changes; plus, they tell me it may change because of what happens at trial. In the end, they also make it clear it's my decision whether to testify or not.

"We'll make a recommendation to you," Alfredo tells me, "a very clear one. But it's still your decision. Most everything else at trial is attorney strategy, not that—that's your call."

"Don't you think a jury wants you to say you're not guilty?" I ask.

Of course, he says, but "the minute you say something they don't believe, they just figure you're guilty. They forget that everybody on the stand has prejudice, if it's just that they are self-aggrandizing, or just trying to make themselves look good. That works for most witnesses, not the defendant. They'll hold any misstep against you, even if it's not really a misstep."

He tells me the story of a guy who wanted to take the stand. He did pretty well. He denied the crime. He had a plausible story about why he didn't do it. He even had a sort of alibi: although the witness said the crime had occurred at noon, he had been at the garage where he worked until almost twelve thirty.

"That was all true, as a matter of fact," Alfredo said. "The reason it was true was that the witness had the time wrong. The crime actually occurred shortly after one. The witness just screwed up the timing."

"Didn't that help your client?"

"Would have," Alfredo said, "except that he had admitted to the cops that he'd been there, even though he told them he hadn't committed the crime. The jury held his own alibi against him because the cops said he was there. And the alibi was based on wrong information to being with."

"Fake news?" I asked.

Alfredo scowled at me. He's not a fan of our new president. I like Trump. A lot. But I'm mindful of what Petticourt said, that having him get elected will put a dent in the movement instead of helping it along, and maybe prevent the revolution we so desperately need. So I guess . . . I don't know any more.

But here's another thing about testifying: they tell me, don't be too pat. If you sound like you rehearsed the testimony, the jury will hold that against you too.

"Shit, shit, shit," I say. "Is there any way to get this right?"

"It can be a zero-sum game," she says. I know what she means, but I also wonder if she's just trying to sound smart.

She begins again.

"Sir," she says, in her best lawyer voice, like we were in court, "what is your full name? And spell your last name for the court reporter."

"You know," I tell her, "Desmond isn't really my name."

"What? What? Now you tell us?"

"It is, I guess," I tell her, "but I wasn't born with it. It was O'Connor."

"Why did you change it?" I asked.

"I didn't," I said. "Someone at child services did."

"OK," she says, "let's get back to this. Please spell your last name."

"O-C-o-n-n-o-r," I say.

"C'mon, Johnny," she says, hitting me off the shoulder with her notes, but I can tell she thought it was funny. I spell Desmond.

"Now," she says, "you are the defendant in this matter?"

"What if I say I'm not?" I ask. "Do you think they would just let me leave?"

"Do I have to hit you again?"

It's kind of funny. We spend two hours pretending to testify, when best guess is I won't actually testify at all. But I really enjoy spending time with Andrea. And I have the idea, true or not, that she likes me too.

Then, after we've worked way too long, had dinner brought in from Jimmy John's, after Andrea has loosened up, taken off her shoes, and we have got this testimony down, maybe too pat, she puts her papers down on the desk, rubs her eyes, and then looks at me.

"Johnny," she says, "is there something between us?"

It takes me by surprise. I'd been leaning back in my chair, hardly even thinking about anything, almost ready to doze off. "Are you asking—" I start.

The space between us is gone. Andrea is standing right by me. I put the chair back down on the ground, and she puts her hand on the back of my head and looks down into my eyes. "I think you might like me," she says.

"Andrea," I say.

"My family and friends call me Drew."

"Drew, I adore you. You don't know how much time I've been thinkin' about you. I just don't—"

"Shhh. Shhh. Just listen to me," she says, then her lips graze mine. It's such a chaste kiss. I reach up to kiss her back.

"Stop it," she says. "You have to know something. OK? Listen to me." All the time, she's still holding my head and gently rubbing the back of my neck. It's driving me wild.

"OK," I say meekly.

"There are rules. The Iowa State disciplinary rules say that I can't have sex with you or I lose my license. My law license. I don't want to lose it."

I say something lame. I know it's lame when I say it. That's how I realize just how stupid it is, but I say it: "Who's gonna know?"

"Oh, Johnny," she says, "it always comes out. The minute you're unhappy with me."

I wave my arms at the papers on the table. "Jesus, Andrea," I say, "doesn't all this show you that I can keep quiet about stuff?"

"I know," she says, "I know, but you have to understand how this would work for me. It's a direct red-line rule, no intimate relations with a client."

Then all of a sudden, out of nowhere, she's on me. She's sitting in my lap, facing me, her skirt pulled up and she's kissing me. It's wonderful. She is just so alluring. But I'm the one who pulls back.

"Look," I say.

"Oh, Jesus, no," she says.

"Look. We can wait. You don't know how much I have wanted you. I still, oh Christ, I think you can feel what I'm tryin' to say, I want to fuck you so bad. But we can wait. Can't we?"

She stands, straightens her skirt. She touches the back of my head again, just for a moment. She looks down at me, her lower lip being held between her teeth, and one tear runnin' down a cheek. "Ya," she says, almost sobbing. "Oh God, you're right. When this is done, I'm going to get a suite for us at the Marriott."

What a mess. I finally have a woman . . . I finally have two women who want me. I'm no prude and no virgin. I've been with women. I had my first one when I was only fifteen, and that was probably statutory rape, of me. But I never was with a woman before who turned me on as much as Andrea. And I've never felt about a woman like I feel about Jenny. And I can't have either. And if I lose this trial, I probably won't have either one ever. Life can be shit.

Things are in an uneasy truce. I side three days a week, except for really cold and wintry days, but then I often work drywall. It's not my best thing, but I can do it competently enough to get by. I take care of Marie two mornings a week, but Jenny is in a new semester and she's changed to Monday and Thursday afternoons. I go to the law firm those mornings by nine, and usually, Andrea works with me, sometimes Steve, sometimes Alfredo.

Maria is changing fast. I had no idea. I really thought babies didn't do anything but suck and cry, eat and poop for the first six months. But she's got a real personality. She's holdin' her head up, she smiles at us and I think it's clear she knows us. Well, hell, she's probably always known her mom, but now she seems to really know me. I get such a big kick out of her. I had no idea. Had I known, I would have had kids long ago.

The week before trial, Jimmy Kudro called me at my job site. We were having exceptionally warm weather, 70s in Iowa in February, and I had the siding crew going big time. We had about thirty houses that were almost ready, so we were working every hour we could. I was a little worried when Jimmy got me that he had found someone else to take over the job. But that wasn't it at all.

"Johnny," he says, "you still going to be gone next week?"

"Ya, you know why," I tell him. "My lawyers say it will probably spill over into the next week as well."

"All right," he says, "we'll send one of our contractors out to make sure your crew knows what it's doing. Spics." It seemed like he spit that last word out.

"Ya," I acknowledge, "they need somebody watchin' over 'em."

"Not why I'm calling, though," he says. "Nick Spencer hasn't been at work for the last three days."

I don't know what to say. I feel a shudder go through me. My gut churns. I feel like a chill is coming up my leg. *Shit, shit, shit,* is what I think.

"Did you get ahold of him?"

"Haven't been able to," he says. "We been tryin'."

"Jimmy," I say, "I can't call him."

"Jesus, Johnny, we just want to figure out why he hasn't shown up for work."

"I know," I say, "I know, but I can't call him. But I'll ask somebody else to go look for him."

"Good, thanks," he says, and we hang up. I call Jenny. The baby's down but she agrees to call Nick and if she can't reach him to go, by his place once Maria wakes up. I check my crew, tell 'em I'll be back, and then drive to Peter's house. Jenny is in her room, probably getting dressed. I get my burner out of the bureau and tell her I'm leaving again.

I drive a block away, don't see anyone following me, and use the burner. Peter answers.

"Nick Spencer is gone."

"Good for you," Peter says.

"What did you do, Peter?"

"Shut the fuck up you dumb shit," he says. "I'm losing faith in you."

"Don't hurt him."

"Asshole, break this phone. If we need you, we'll call the other one. 'Course, I don't see why we'd need you anymore. You've gone soft, Johnny. It's sad."

And he's gone.

I drive to the Fridley mansion. I find Andrea in her office, meeting with somebody, apparently a client. She excuses herself and closes the door behind her and takes me by the elbow.

"What is it?" she says.

"Something important," I tell her.

She walks me into Steve's darkened office. She closes the door behind me. Then she steps up to me, puts her hand between my T-shirt and my belly, and starts to move it up to my chest.

"Stop it," I say. "This is important."

She gives me that look, amused but pulls her hand away. "What?" she whispers.

"Nick Spencer is gone. Can't find him."

"Crap. You didn't call him, did you?"

"No. He works for the same home builder I do."

"Thanks," she says, and turns away. "I've got to tell Alfredo." She goes to the door, opens it, then turns back. "Johnny, you didn't have anything to do with this?" she asks.

"Christ," I say, "I thought you knew me."

Nine

T HE TRIAL IS starting on a Tuesday, but the judge is calling the jury in the Friday before, to go over a few things with them, eliminate some of the folks with surgeries or plane tickets they can't get back. Then he'll also hand out questionnaires. Monday is President's Day, but we will pick up the questionnaires Monday morning at eight thirty and take them back to the office. So it's all hands on deck at the law firm on February 20. When I get to the office, the secretaries are making copies of the questionnaires. I get one stack, Alfredo his own, Miller his own, and Andrea and Steve share one.

"I'm going to my office," Alfredo says, "as is Mark. You three go through them right here. We'll meet here in ninety minutes and review them."

When they've left, I turn to Andrea. "We can choose who we want?"

"Not that simple," Steve answers.

"Ya," Andrea says, "at least in Iowa, jury selection doesn't really mean you pick a jury. It just means you get to take some people off."

"Oh," I say, "you can't choose anybody?"

"Nope," she says, "but there's a certain number we can take off the jury. And there's always some we can take off for cause . . . well, uh, ask the court to remove for some good reason. That's called a challenge for cause. The ones we take off just to take them off are *strikes*. We have eight of those, but believe me, it won't be enough."

She and I start through the list. To my surprise, there are four cops, three from Des Moines on the panel, plus three women who identify their husbands as either cops or sheriff's deputies and one whose husband is with the DCI. "Shit," I go, "that's unlucky."

"Happens time after time," she says. "Never seen a jury panel without a cop. Last year we had a panel on a sex abuse case, and the investigating officer was on the panel!"

"Couldn't be on the jury, could he?" I ask.

"No," she says, "for once, we got him off without having to strike him."

She also finds two attorneys, one of whom is a public defender and one who works for the state of Iowa. "They will be worth talking to," she says. "Alfredo is outstanding at jury selection. After the first day and a half, they'll really like him."

"Good," I say, thinking about what happens if he runs out of money. Guess I owe him at that point, not that I can figure out how I'd ever pay him.

We go through the list of names, one by one. I recognize one name, from the construction company I subcontract for. Andrea says there are two other names who have been represented by the Fridley firm. These three will all be struck, I'm told.

Then we start writing down what everyone does, who has kids, who doesn't, how much education they had. Then we start down the jury questionnaire.

About a third say they hadn't heard about the bombing. "That's suspicious," she says, but I'm not sure I agree. That's the way the public is sometimes. That's how Obama happened.

Of the other two-thirds, most, nearly four out of five, say it won't affect their ability to give me a fair trial. "This is our worry," she says.

"Why's that?"

"Some of them are flat-out lying. Like every jury, there's going to be a bunch of people who don't want to serve. A bigger problem for us is the ones who want to be on the jury so bad they'll lie."

I am silent, thinking. Steve chimes in, "This case is a little different. There are probably a few out there who like what you did—sorry,"—he quickly corrects himself—"what they say you did. There's enough anti-Muslim fervor in this country right now that a few people will want to serve on the jury because they liked the bombing."

There's a bigger problem though, and we all know it. There are some of these jurors who want to be on the jury so they can make me pay. And those people will by lying about it too.

We go on and on, reading their answers to questions. Steve has a computer program in which the answers are inputted, when we're about halfway through the questionnaire, a secretary brings us the results. I know Des Moines is a Democrat city and I know the county voted for Clinton, but I'm just a little taken back by some of the things most of the jury agreed with:

People should try to all get along.

Everyone has a right to practice their own religion, no matter which religion.

Prejudice and racism have no place in the judicial system.

"Why'd we have these questions in here?" I ask.

"We didn't," Steve says. "These are all from the prosecutor."

But there is another question which gives me a little hope. About 40 percent of the jury panel says that Islam is a religion at armed struggle with the American government. "That question is going to prompt some questioning during *voire dire*," he says. "Nan is going to look at ways to take someone off if they're prejudiced against Islam."

"Good luck with that," Andrea says.

When Alfredo and Mark join us, the consensus is that the jury is pretty typical of Des Moines. Alfredo sits at the head of the table.

"So who's our ideal juror? Throw it out, people."

"Women," Steve says.

"Almost always the right answer," Alfredo says, "but I'm unconvinced in this case. What do you think, Mark?"

"Take a good look at our defendant," Miller says. "The young women are going to eat him up. Am I right, Andrea?"

"I think so," she answers. "Why are you hesitant, Alfredo?"

He sits quietly for a moment. Then he starts, "Women are usually good for the defense. They are more sympathetic. And that might be the case here. Here's our conundrum. Are we looking for people who don't believe Mr. Desmond here bombed the center? Or are we looking for people who believed Mr. Desmond went back and saved the janitor? As a result, will they give him a pass? And who are those people?"

"Either way," Miller says, "I like women over men."

There is polite laughter.

"You know, Mr. Miller," Alfredo says, "this is an equal opportunity employer. If you want to announce a different sexual orientation, we will accept that." Now the laughter is a bit louder, but still, I'm thinkin', its because they want to give the boss the laughs he's lookin' for.

Miller, a grating, mustached, short but somehow stuffy man in his sixties just gives Alfredo a look that one could read as *C'mon now.* There are a couple of giggles.

"I mean it, though," Miller says. "Whether we're scrounging for jurors to not believe he's guilty or believe he went back to save the janitor, either way I think women are just more empathetic. We want women on this jury."

"Of any age?" Alfredo asks next.

"Younger women for sure," Andrea says.

Alfredo looks over his glasses, which, I've noticed over the months, are for reading only. He seems to be trying to communicate something to her, but I'm not sure what.

"How about younger men?" Steve asks.

"That may be our *hell no* group," Miller says.

"Well," Andrea chimes in again, "first we need to get all the cops and their relatives off the jury, then we can think about the rest."

"I don't think she's seen you work a jury," Miller says.

"Maybe not," Alfredo says, "but as usual, we have lots of cops and they need off this jury."

The conversation goes on for another hour, and to me, a lot of it is pointless. You don't get to pick a jury, maybe, but getting the right people off seems important to us.

Then we start on the list. They've all marked which jury members they want rid of, which ones they want to challenge, which ones they like, and which ones they need to have Alfredo ask questions of. When they've talked through the whole list and agreed to most of them, Alfredo tells Steve and Andrea to work up the list, marking it "the usual way." Copies all around at court tomorrow.

He and Miller leave.

I walk out of the office, drive to Gateway, and buy a Margherita pizza and a six-pack of Fat Tire. When I get back to the law firm, I bake the pizza in the first-floor oven. When it's done, I walk plates and beer into the conference room where Steve and Andrea are working.

"Break time," I say.

"I told you I liked this client," Steve said.

Andrea said nothing. We all dug in on the pizza.

"What's Alfredo saying about Spencer?" I asked them.

"We knew exactly what he'd say," Steve answered, "right?"

Andrea nodded. "Ya," she says, "hope he's gone for good, get ready as if he's going to testify. We'll probably know when Horgan gives her opening statement."

Ten

I WEAR THE shirt and tie that Jenny gave me the first day
of trial. She knew that one day while I was at the law firm,
Steve took me over to the Men's Wearhouse and bought me a blue
blazer, a dark-blue woolen sport coat like a professor might wear,
three dress shirts, four ties, three pairs of slacks, a belt, socks, and
shoes. Trial clothes.

"Geez," I say, "thanks."

"Don't thank us," Steve answers. "It came out of the retainer."

"Ya," I say, "I been worried about that."

"I wouldn't," he says. "Whoever is bankrolling you is bankrolling
you."

I must have looked like I didn't know what he was saying.

"She gave us some more money," he told me.

"Cool." I know that was weak, but what else was I going to say?

Even though the stuff from the law firm was pretty good stuff, I
wore the shirt and tie from Jenny because, well, because they were
from Jenny. And I liked it all right. The shirts Steve picked out were
light-colored, blue, white, and patterned. Jenny brought me a dark-
blue shirt that I wasn't sure went with the tie she chose, but to hell
with that, I wore them. And as it turned out, Jenny was the only one
in the world who came to the trial on my behalf.

We are all seated at counsel table when the jury walks in. There
are so many people that they fill the jury box, then the next five rows

of pews. Jenny is sitting alone in the back row, and there are two other brown people I don't know. There are sixty-four jurors in all. Alfredo had asked for more, but the judge seemed to think it was enough. On Friday, I'm told, the judge let eight people off the jury.

The judge begins talking to the jury. He introduces the lawyers and me and reads off the names of the witnesses. One member of the jury admits that he was a Fridley client sometime and he's taken off. Another is married to an assistant county attorney and she's allowed off. A couple of them have questions, but nothing that gets them off the jury.

When the judge is done, Nan Horgan stands and walks to a small lectern the judge has set up between him and where we are sitting.

"Good morning," she tells them, then introduces herself and the other lawyer who is with her, a really young, thin bald guy named Kevin. He stands and makes it a point of turning so they can all see him.

Then she starts talking about the case, about what happened and then she starts asking them questions. She spends a long time on reasonable doubt. To hear her talk about it, it's kind of a guideline, a nice thing, but not somethin' they need to worry about. And mainly, reasonable doubt doesn't mean all doubt, right? She asks some individuals about that.

Then something she talks about surprises me.

She turns to one of the men in the jury box and asks, "Mr. Coughlin, let's say there's a car accident. Driver A is at fault. He is speeding. He changes lanes too fast and he hits Driver B's car and forces it into a streetlight."

"OK," the middle-aged man says.

"Now, the car starts to be on fire. Driver B is going to die if someone doesn't get him out, but it's dangerous. Driver A goes up to the car, opens the car door, and drags Driver B out of the car. Got that?"

"Ya, I understand."

"Of course you do," she says. "Now, Driver A saves Driver B. Is he still at fault for the accident that damaged Driver B's car and for harming Driver B?"

"Of course."

"But he saved him."

"He saved him from something he caused to happen."

Then she talks to ten, twelve more of these folks with the same scenario. Driver A may have saved the other driver, but the accident was still his fault.

One lady has a problem with the scenario. "Shouldn't he be rewarded for saving the other driver? He risked his life, didn't he?"

"That's not the question, though, is it?" Horgan says. "You're being asked whether to convict him of speeding and driving recklessly, let's say. The fact that he saved the other driver, does that change anything about whether you'd convict him?"

"I don't know. It was a good thing."

"You don't sound convinced," Horgan says. It's a light touch, but a good one. The woman shakes her head. In front of me, Andrea writes on my legal pad: *She'll take this juror off.* Then Horgan says to her, "But remember, you don't have anything to do with sentencing. Don't you think the judge might take that into consideration on sentencing?"

"I suppose," the woman says.

She changes her story as she gets to the jurors on the hard wooden benches behind me.

"So," she says "what if I have a different case? A father is watching his infant child. He puts him to bed in his crib, then goes out for a beer."

The jurors nod. "When he comes back, his house is on fire. Heroically, he enters the burning house and runs upstairs and—"

Alfredo is on his feet. "Objection, Your Honor," he says. The judge waves him and Horgan up to his bench. After a little whispering, all the lawyers and I go into his office along with the court reporter.

"All right, Mr. Fridley," the judge says, "what's the objection?"

"Your Honor, Ms. Horgan is perilously close to trying this case in *voire dire*." The judge moans. I don't think that's a good sign. Alfredo either doesn't notice or ignores it.

"Before there's any testimony, before there's any evidence, before opening arguments, Ms. Horgan is trying the case."

"Don't try the case, Nan," the judge says.

"So," she says, "can I continue to use that scenario or not?"

"I believe the operative term from Mr. Fridley," the judge says, "is close. Close. Not that you've crossed the line. I'd appreciate it if you don't use an example that is exactly parallel to the alleged events in this case. Mr. Fridley, your objection is overruled. I am not going to step into *voire dire* unless there's something egregious."

"Judge—" Alfredo begins.

"And," the judge intervenes, "it seems to me that Ms. Horgan has opened the door and given you an opportunity." Which I didn't understand, but Alfredo did.

Nan continues, talking to juror after juror for two solid hours, until the judge takes a break. The jurors walk back to their room; we grab some lunch at Zombie Burger. Alfredo does not join us.

"Does he even eat?" I ask Steve and Andrea. Alfredo is seriously thin. It makes him look great in a suit.

After lunch, Nan continues, talking about reasonable doubt, about the fact that the court will hand out the sentence, the jury doesn't have to worry about that, and then talking a little about police officer testimony and the fire marshal. Finally, she walks through with each of the people in the courtroom a very simple question.

"If we prove beyond a reasonable doubt that this person right here"—she points at me—"this man, Johnny Desmond, committed this horrific act, bombed this building, tried to kill anyone inside, a hate crime, an arson, an act of terrorism, that he damaged private property for which he had no right to damage, if we have proved that, are you willing to find him guilty?"

Eventually, every juror says yes, they would find me guilty if that was proven.

We take another break, and Alfredo gets on just before three thirty in the afternoon. He introduces himself, Steve, and Andrea and then has me stand. "And," he says, "it is my honor to represent Johnny Desmond."

Then he turns Nan's dog-and-pony show on its head.

"You heard Ms. Horgan ask, ask each of you, one by one, if they would convict Mr. Desmond if . . ." He raises his voice now. "If . . ." Again he raises his voice. "If, if, if his guilt is proven beyond a reasonable doubt.

"But you know, I think it's important that you remember that he is in this courtroom an innocent man. He has stood in front of a judge and God and said that he's not guilty. He has done so, and he has gained what all of us citizens of this United States also have, the presumption of innocence. He is innocent today as he sits there. He is innocent in the eyes of the law. He is innocent until . . ." Again he raises his voice. "Until and *if* the state proves his guilt beyond a reasonable doubt."

Then by memory, he starts on the jury and takes each of them, one by one, through this: *Is this man innocent? Today as he sits here, is he innocent?*

And if the state doesn't prove his guilt beyond a reasonable doubt, will you find him not guilty? Will it bother you to find him not guilty?

He finished with all sixty-four by four twenty, and the judge sent us all home for the day.

"I see what you mean," I whispered to Andrea.

"I want everyone in the conference room at seven," Alfredo says. His request is apparently our command.

"I need something," he begins when we're all gathered. He's in a polo shirt and jeans. I've changed into jeans and a T-shirt. Only Andrea is still in her trial clothes. I'm pretty sure she's been at the office since we left the courthouse.

Miller starts, "I assume you're talking about Nan's car accident scenario. It was pretty smart."

"Yes, it was," Alfredo says. "So tell me, if she opened the door, how am I going to walk through it?" Nobody says anything.

"Anybody?" Alfredo asks.

"OK," Steve says, and stops. "What if we say this, we say there's a car wreck. Somebody pulls the hurt man out. That doesn't make him the person who caused the wreck, does it?"

Hmmm. Seems like we all said that at once.

"I'm worried about that," Alfredo says, "because I don't think that's what we'll argue at trial."

The room is quiet.

"I'm sure this burst of creative expertise is really giving Johnny here some confidence," Alfredo says finally.

"OK," I say, "why don't you ask it different? You notice anything about the two examples she used? In neither one did she say that the guy meant to cause the accident or the fire. But in this case, that's what I'm charged with. I supposedly wanted to bomb that center. Ask them if they believe the kind of person who would intentionally bomb a building is the same kind of person who would go back to save someone."

Andrea drops her pen. Steve stares at me. "Yes," Miller says.

"It's good to know someone on this team is thinking," Alfredo says, "but I can't use that either. For a good reason, a reason I hope you'll understand by the time this trial is over. Still, it's really a good point that she didn't use an example with intent. I might be able to use that." And he walks out.

The next morning, he continues to talk to the jurors about the case, about themselves, and he concludes by talking about Nan's examples. And how, in both examples, the persons didn't intend to hurt anyone. And in this case, Nan has to prove intent.

The judge will give you the law, Alfredo tells them. But that will tell you that to commit arson, I had to intend to commit arson, to commit a hate crime, I had to intend to do so, and to commit attempted murder, I had to intend a murder. And again, each one tells him that they won't convict me if Nan doesn't prove that Johnny

Desmond intended any such thing. "And so," he says, his voice rising, "I ask you to remember, that each of you: Mr. Johnson, Mrs. Barnes, Mr. Williams, Miss Eberney, Mr. Wallace—" For a moment, I think he knows all fifty-nine of them by heart, but then he stops. "That each of you, each and every one of you gave me your commitment that you would require the State to prove its charges beyond a reasonable doubt and that if they didn't, you would find my client not guilty."

The actual selection goes fast. Andrea and Steve and Tom have all given Alfredo a list of who he should take off the jury. Each time Alfredo gets a strike, he marks a name with a little red dot and then turns to me.

"Agree?" There is one person I like that he doesn't. I decide he probably knows better than me.

The first four names we take off are cops or cops' relatives. Then we get down to nitty-gritty. We take off both black men; we leave the one black woman on the panel.

Nan takes off most of the people I like. There is a college professor on the list and another man with a master's degree. She strikes them both. She strikes a man who kind of skirted around the issue of what he thought of Muslims. She strikes the woman who doubted her car-crash story.

We are left with eight women, five young, three older, and four men, all middle-aged or older. One is retired, the rest work, with the exception of a young mother who stays home with her children. We get to the three alternates, and there he is, one strikingly young car mechanic with a Fu Manchu, whom nobody wanted on the jury, but we could only take one person off and the one we did has a brother who is a Des Moines cop. So Mr. Fu Manchu is our alternate.

This is our jury, God help me.

Eleven

"HATE IS ON the rise in our city. Hate is on the rise in this state. Hate is on the rise in this country, in the world. But you, ladies and gentlemen, you have a chance to do something about it. You have the chance to tell the city, the state, and the nation that we won't tolerate hate. You can do that by convicting this man, Johnny Desmond, of arson, of attempted murder, of terrorism, of hate."

That's how Nan Horgan starts her opening statement. She's fiery, passionate. It's something I haven't seen from her before. It's hard to sit here and take it too. I'm supposed to not react, show no emotion, regardless of what is said. That ain't easy. An opening statement, the lawyers tell me, is supposed to be the road map to what the witnesses will say. But neither lawyer sticks to that. Nan hardly ever mentions witnesses. Instead, she tells a story, from beginning to end: how a white supremacist group decided to blow up an Islamic center, how someone we don't know built a bomb, how two men were in an old car they later abandoned, they opened the locked door at the Islamic center, one of them put a bomb inside and they then hurried across the street to see their handiwork. Then when they realized that a janitor was there, they hurried back and got him out. They saved him yes, but only from what they themselves had caused.

The police went looking for the persons who did this, Nan told the jury. The police knew pretty early on that a hate organization in this town, the Posse Comitatus, was behind the bombing. They knew it had been orchestrated by a man named Peter Thurgood. They figured out with good detective work that it could have been two young men, Johnny Desmond and Nicholas Spencer. Then they tried to talk to those two men. One of them told the story. Nicholas Spencer told them what happened.

Andrea looked at me. Steve whispered something to Alfredo, who leaned, wrote a note on his legal pad. *Guess we know what happened to your friend.*

"And," Horgan continued, "he's going to take that witness stand later this week and he's going to tell you that it was Johnny Desmond who put that bomb inside the building and watched to see that the Islamic center blew up. It was also Johnny Desmond who went back to get the janitor. That doesn't mean a thing, because he was only preventing a tragedy of his own making. He is a bomber. He is a white supremacist and he is a thug. And when you've heard the evidence, you'll agree and you'll have no problem convicting him of all these crimes."

It took her almost forty minutes to do all that. Then, Alfredo got to his feet. He looks at us, he acknowledges the judge and Horgan and me, and then he starts in, slowly. He thanks them for being there. He reminds them of reasonable doubt.

"You heard Ms. Horgan. She wants to make this a case of community revenge and punishment, retribution, shall we say? There's only one problem with that. She hasn't proved any of this. Pay attention at trial, will you, to see if she can. You already know and the judge will instruct you that she must prove her case beyond a reasonable doubt, the most difficult standard under our law."

Then he went right after Nick. Why was Nick saying it was Johnny Desmond? Because they asked him to? Because he got a sweet deal? What was his role? Was he going to end up going to prison? If he admitted that he went there to bomb the Islamic center, was the State of Iowa as intent on sending him to prison as they were with my client?

Then he talks about the presumption of innocence and the responsibility of the state to find me guilty beyond a reasonable doubt. The defense need do nothing, he says. Mr. Desmond doesn't have to testify, doesn't have to put on witnesses; everything is up to the state. And they can't meet that burden. And as a result, "you will not have a problem bringing in a not-guilty verdict." All in all, this day, Horgan had the better of it.

The judge takes a break. When we're all back in the courtroom, he says, "You've heard the opening statements of counsel. Now the State of Iowa will introduce its evidence. Ms. Horgan, you may call your first witness."

They bring on that cop, the guy who arrested me. The skinny bald lawyer, Kevin, asks him questions. He asks three questions when one would do, but it's all pretty effective. The cop talks about how he saw the center that night, how badly it was damaged, what the fire marshal said. He introduces some twenty photographs of the damage. Then he talks about how they looked for someone who broke into houses with an Allen wrench and finally how they found Nicholas Spencer and he told them the truth—that he and Johnny Desmond had bombed the Islamic Center.

It took more than an hour, but when Horgan finished, Alfredo was on his feet.

"What did you promise Mr. Spencer to get him to testify?"

They object. Alfredo and the bald skinny kid go to the bench, and after a couple of minutes, the judge announces that he'll allow the question.

"I didn't offer him nothing."

We already know the deal that Spencer got. Alfredo bores in.

"Who did?"

"Pardon me," the cop says.

"There was a plea deal on the table before Nick Spencer gave you a statement, wasn't there?"

"There was. It wasn't from me."

"Who was it from?"

"The Polk County Attorney's Office."

"OK. What was that plea deal?"

Harper says he's not sure he remembers it all.

"Do you remember if Spencer is going to do time?"

"Yes, he is, ninety days in jail."

"Ninety days," Alfredo says. "Ninety days in jail. Not prison?"

"No."

"Will he plead to a felony?"

"Misdemeanors."

"If he didn't have the deal, would you have charged him with misdemeanors?"

"No, sir."

"Felonies?"

"Yes, sir," the cop says.

"How many, perhaps five?"

"Perhaps."

"Arson?"

"Yes."

"Attempted murder?"

"Maybe."

"Terrorism?"

"Yes."

"Damage to property?"

"Yes," the cop says, "criminal mischief."

"All felonies?"

"Probably."

"And how much time could Mr. Spencer have served if he was convicted of all those crimes?"

Horgan is on her feet. "Objection," she bellows.

The jury is sent out for a break. When they're gone and we sit back down, the judge begins, "Ms. Horgan, this was Mr. Bell's witness. Am I correct?"

"Yes, Your Honor."

"Then he, and only he, has a right to object. Mr. Bell, do you object?"

'Course he does. He claims we're trying to get into the jury's mind what the possible sentence could be for my crimes if I'm convicted, which, of course, we are trying to do. But more importantly, we want them to know what a sweetheart deal Nick is getting, which Alfredo says more carefully and more lawyerlike than that and the judge agrees.

"If you are going to use Mr. Spencer as a witness," the judge says, "and you have cut a plea agreement with him in advance, the jury is going to be told what that deal is," he says. "Your objection is overruled."

The cop tries not to answer. "How long he served might not be the same as the time he's sentenced to."

"How long could he be sentenced to if convicted of all those charges?"

"That depends," the cop says, "on whether or not the sentences are consecutive or concurrent." Alfredo has him explain the difference.

"Now, Mr. Harper, if Mr. Spencer was convicted of all these charges, what's the least amount of time he could be sentenced for?"

"Twenty-five years," the cop says. I hear a quiet murmur from the jury box.

"And the most amount of time he could be sentenced to?"

"One hundred and twenty-five years." The murmur is there again, louder.

"One hundred and twenty-five years," Alfredo says. "Seems like ninety days is a little bit better, right, officer?"

The young bald lawyer objects, and Alfredo withdraws the question. He goes through another twenty minutes with the officer, how there's no direct proof, no DNA or other evidence that links me to the crime. Then we're done for the day.

On Thursday, the state brings in the rest of its witnesses. A cop who worked with Harper, who says the same thing. The assistant fire marshal, who talks for more than an hour about the bomb, how it was rigged with a cheap watch and how much damage it was supposed to do and how much damage it did do. He has some more photographs and the results from lab tests. Alfredo objects to none of the exhibits, which worries me, but Steve and Andrea already told me he wouldn't.

Alfredo asks him about any evidence linking me to the crime scene.

"None that I know of."

"Who else would know?"

"Des Moines PD, I suppose."

"And if they don't have any?"

He walks him through a few more of the things he testified about, then turns away from the witness, then turns back.

"Oh, Mr. Bishop," he asks.

"Did you look for foreign DNA at the scene?"

"We did."

"Find any?"

"Yes, sir, we found seven deposits of DNA of persons other than those known to work there or spend time there regularly."

"Seven foreign DNA specimens?"

"Yes, sir, that's what we call them."

"Did you try to match them, any or all of them, with Mr. Desmond, here?" Alfredo points back at me.

"We did."

"Any of his DNA found at the scene?"

"No, sir."

When Alfredo is done, Nan gets some questions in: how people don't always leave DNA, that its absence isn't conclusive, that a fire might help destroy any DNA that would have been left behind. After that, Alfredo asks him one more question:

"Any forensic evidence at the scene you can link to Johnny Desmond?"

"No, sir."

Then they bring on the sheik. I know that's not what he's called. But he looks like a sheik, in long, colorful, loose African clothes. He talks about the damage done to the building, how the janitor almost lost his hearing, and then Nan Horgan starts in on how he feels that Islam is under threat in Des Moines.

Andrea looks up, Steve too. Alfredo waves them off. He lets the man talk. *Not sure what he sees here, but I'm beginning to trust his judgment, at least in the courtroom.* The man talks about Islam, a religion of peace, or so he says, for another forty-five minutes. When Alfredo gets a turn, he's quick.

"Know Mr. Desmond?"

"I do not, sir."

"Know whether he was at the center that night?"

"No, sir."

"Know whether he was the bomber?"

"No, sir."

"You do know something about the criminal justice system, though, don't you?"

"Sir?"

Horgan objects.

Before Alfredo can say anything, the judge announces, "My ruling on your motion in limine stands."

"You may answer," Alfredo says.

"I do know a little."

"Because you were once convicted of a felony, correct?"

"I was."

"And you went to prison."

They object again and the judge rules with the state, *but it seems to me that you can't unring the bell.*

Twelve

LATE THAT AFTERNOON, Horgan calls two waitresses from the IHOP. Neither one can identify me, but the first one tells the jury that an older car came across from the U-Haul place to park in the mall parking lot, parked facing Douglas so the two men in it could look out across the street. Then, the other one recounts how that same car sped over to the U-Haul, going through a red light, how the driver got out and ran and then as they saw him come back with another man over his shoulders. Then, she says, there was an explosion, the Islamic center blew up and burst into flames.

Alfredo asks each of them the same question. "Can you identify that driver?"

Neither one can.

Friday morning is the big day. When I arrive in the courthouse with Andrea, Nick is outside the courtroom, sitting next to the cop who testified first. He looks up at me, but I can take direction. I don't acknowledge him and walk right into the courtroom.

Horgan calls him immediately. Nicholas Spencer, member of the Posse Comitatus. Horgan is really into that. We never called ourselves that. We were Thurgood's boys.

Spencer tells it pretty much like it was. Except he forgets the part where he asked me not to go back and just let the janitor die. But otherwise, he tells how he and I met, how we work together, and how

I came to him with this project. He can't say it was Peter who put me up to it, "but who else?" he asks.

Then to my surprise, Horgan takes him through his plea deal. He'll plead to one serious misdemeanor and get probation. If he doesn't follow probation, he could go to prison for a year. He'll plead to three simple misdemeanors and get ninety days in jail total.

Finally, she asks him if he can identify the man who put the bomb in the Islamic center.

He says he can and points to me.

"What's he wearing?"

"A blue coat, white shirt, red tie, gray slacks," Nick says. "That's Johnny Desmond. I'd know him anywhere and whatever he was wearing."

Alfredo bores in. He spends at least a half hour on the plea deal. He talks about what a simple criminal mischief means—that it's for damage of less than $200.

"Do you think this bomb caused less than $200 damage?"

"I don't know, sir."

Then what simple criminal mischief means. What a sweet deal he's getting. It's all pretty effective.

"Why should we believe you?"

"Because I'm telling the truth."

"But if you aren't, if you're making it all up, it's exactly what the police wanted to hear, isn't it?"

Objection, speculation. The judge agrees.

"Before you gave this evidence to the police, you had an attorney, right?"

"Yes."

"And that attorney demanded that you didn't get a felony charge, didn't he?"

"I guess."

"When you named Johnny Desmond, true or not, you knew that was why you were there and you were going to get a sweetheart deal, right?"

Objection, speculation.

"He may answer if he knows."

Which means, I guess, he should say he doesn't know, but good old Nick answers yes, he knew he was getting a good deal. Then Alfredo bores in on Posse Comitatus. Did Nick sign up for this group? Were there meetings? Minutes of those meetings? Did Peter Thurgood or Johnny Desmond have a calling card or any proof of membership? What is there to show that he's actually a member?

To this day, I don't know if Alfredo got the answer he wanted or the answer he didn't want. He's a devious old shit, that's for sure, and I put nothin' by him. But, well, I still don't know.

"Ya," Nick says, "we all had the tattoo."

"Tattoo?"

"Yup. It's the Nazi thing, the four-sided thing, you know, with a green shamrock kitty-corner on it. If you've got that tattoo, you're in."

"All members have it?"

"Far as I know."

Alfredo has a few more questions, about how Spencer himself was guilty, Spencer was there, he knew they were going to bomb the center, he was willing to do it. If someone had died, they would have died. Spencer did nothing to save anyone. Spencer just went along with the plan. When Nan gets back up, she asks him if he'll show his tattoo.

"Ya," he says, and stands.

Alfredo objects, tells the judge they had no notice of this.

"It's demonstrative only," Horgan tells the judge, "but it was elicited by Mr. Fridley here. He's opened the door."

The judge agrees. Nick shows the tattoo. It's one I am quite familiar with.

Horgan then asks the judge to direct the defendant to reveal any tattoos on his chest.

Alfredo stands as does Andrea. Alfredo objects, wants a conference in chambers.

But I am standing too, unbuttoning my shirt. When I pull my shirt out of my pants, everyone goes quiet.

"Wait a minute," Alfredo says to me, but I pull the dress shirt apart, pull my undershirt up, and reveal for all the teal tattoo on my lower chest, which reads, in script, *MARIA*.

From that distance, I can't tell if any of them can see that it obscures another tattoo that was underneath. I don't think so; it's not easy to see.

Horgan objects now.

"To what?" Alfredo says, "You asked him to do it."

Moments later, the jury has left, and the lawyers are talking. Horgan wants to examine my tattoo, to have an expert examine it.

Alfredo has other ideas. All of that would, he says, would violate my right against self-incrimination.

They go back and forth. It's heated. Finally, the judge puts up his hands.

"Ms. Horgan," he says, "you asked him to show his tattoo. He did so. You opened the door, and he walked through it. I don't believe he has any obligation to show any more, to answer any questions about it, or to have any examination unless he testifies. On the other hand, if you can find the person who gave him the Maria tattoo, I would probably allow his or her testimony."

And so, the prosecution rests. Next, Alfredo will call his witnesses. He says he has one, but he hasn't talked to me about the witness. We'll start Monday morning. When we walk out of the courthouse, he grabs my shoulder. He's older. He's fit, but not as fit as I am, and I could knock him on his ass, but I let him spin me around. "What the fuck do you think you were doing?" he asks.

Then he laughs, puts both hands on my shoulders, shakes his head slightly, and says, "Do you think they could see that it has another tattoo underneath it?"

Andrea winks at me. She found me the tattoo parlor in Kansas City. Took us all day to get there and back home. We also found a nice barbecue place near downtown. We both ate until we were about ready to burst. We don't think Nan Horgan will find the tattoo parlor.

Friday morning breaks cool and overcast. I am thinkin' about what if I never ever again wake up in Jenny's house. If I'm convicted, Alfredo has told me, Horgan will move to cancel my bond and send me to jail until sentencing. And this is the day, one witness from us and then closing arguments. Although everything will probably come down Monday, I lie in bed, thinking about what I should do.

Jenny's in the doorway. "Want breakfast? I've got coffee brewing."

"Ya to the coffee," I say, "but I'm not sure I can eat."

"Worried about today?"

"Ya, sure," I say. "I'm worried about everything. Honest to God, if it wasn't for you, I might just head south on I-35 and see how far I could get."

She laughs then. "Me," she asks, "little old me?" She walks to me, gets on the bed, astride me, and kisses me. It's not a chaste kiss. I reach up for more. We kiss for a while like two high school kids in heat, then when I reach for her boob, she stops me.

"You have to get to court."

I grab that coffee, hurry into the shower, and head downtown. As soon as Maria's sitter shows, Jenny will join us in the courtroom.

Then it happens. Alfredo calls Lester Kelvin, the janitor at the Islamic Center. Alfredo starts by getting his story. Lester works full-time cleaning the offices at one of the financial companies downtown. He puts in some extra hours at the center, for which he doesn't get paid, because he's trying to repay Abdul for something he did for one of their kids. He owes the man. He was at the center the night of the bombing because they'd had a kids' event that day and made quite a mess.

"As far as I can tell, nobody knew I was coming. Usually, at night, like that, there's no one in the building." *Strike the attempted murder,* I think.

He walks him through the events of that night as if he were the prosecutor. Horgan objects. Not relevant, she claims. The judge asks Alfredo, "What is the relevance of this, Mr. Fridley?" It kind of seems like he'd like to stop this testimony and have the trial over. But the two lawyers meet at the bench and talk and whisper some more and then the judge says the testimony can go ahead.

Lester tells how he showed up late, unlocked the back door, went to the janitor's closet. He tells how he started to fill the janitor's tub next to the wall with warm water and suds. Then, a young white guy comes running in the back door, shouting, sayin' they got to get out. When Lester doesn't move, the guy hits him, grabs him, and drags him out of the building. Lester awakes to find the man putting him on his shoulders. Then the man drags him to the next building, the U-Haul dealerships, brings them around the corner, and puts him on the ground. Soon after, they hear a big explosion. They can see fire over the top of the U-Haul building. The white man gets in the car and backs out of the lot, into Douglas Avenue, and speeds away.

"Do you know who the men were in the car?" Alfredo asks him.

"One of 'em was that Nicholas Spencer guy," Kelvin says. "The cops had him come by and I identified him."

"And the other man, the man who dragged you out of the building. Do you know who that was?"

"No, sir, I don't."

"Would you recognize him if you saw him?"

"I hope so, I think so."

"Is he in the courtroom?"

"Don't think so."

"I'm going to ask the defendant to stand." I do. "Is that the man who came into the back of the building and got you out?"

"I sure don't recognize him." Lester lowers his glasses, looks at me for a moment. "No, that ain't the man."

Horgan tries hard on cross-examination. "You like the man who saved your life, don't you? You told the police that you wouldn't identify him, didn't you?" Objection, hearsay. But for some reason it's allowed.

"I don't really remember what I said that night. I was shook up."

"You are grateful to the man who saved your life? You'd lie for him, wouldn't you?"

"Ma'am," Kelvin says finally, exasperated with the questions. "I think I'm the victim here, not the criminal." I see the jury nodding to him. They agree with him that she's not treatin' him right.

She continues. "Sir, regardless of what this man did for you, he blew up the building where you were working, didn't he?"

He stops her again. "Ma'am," he says, "I don't know what you know and what you don't. I don't know what you think. I know this." He leans over and points at me. "That ain't the man who pulled me out of that building. It ain't. I wish it was. I'd go over right now and hug him and kiss him, and my wife would like to thank him and my kids would like to thank him."

"No more questions—" she starts.

"I ain't done," Kelvin says. "The kind of man—"

Horgan stops him. "I don't have any more questions," she tells the judge.

"Maybe so," the judge says, "but I'd like to hear this. Go on, Mr. Kelvin."

"Well," Kelvin says, "I was trying to say that the kind of man who would bomb an Islamic center, the kind of man who would hate that much, that ain't, it just ain't the kind of man who would save my black butt by risking his own life. So no, I don't care what you're tryin' to imply, I am grateful to that man and I always will be and I tell you something else. This man at the table, he ain't the same man."

Thirteen

I T'S ALL OVER but the shouting. That afternoon, the lawyers and the judge work on jury instructions. There's lots of disagreement, and the court reporter comes in. Andrea complains about three or four instructions, asking for an extra one on somethin' or other. I kind of zoned out. Horgan disagrees with everything Andrea wants. It takes a couple of hours, and the jurors are sent home. In the end, far as I can tell, the judge uses the instructions exactly as Horgan asked for them.

The next morning, both lawyers give closing arguments. Horgan can hardly contain herself. The passionate, excited, and belligerent woman I saw that day at opening—she's back. "Do not let this man get away with this. What a stunt. Relying on the sympathy of a janitor whose life he saved to tell you he wasn't the bomber. But you know he was the bomber. Nicholas Spencer told us so. The police told us so. They are both members of the Posse Comitatus, followers of Peter Thurgood and his evil, hateful agenda.

"And that tattoo stunt! Knowing that it could come up, knowing that he needed to cover up the Nazi swastika, he did it. But did you notice anything? The Maria tattoo he showed you was in exactly the same place as Nicholas Spencer's swastika. Did you notice that?

Don't let hate continue. Stop it. Convict this man and show the world we won't put up with bombing Islamic centers. It's up to you. You can show the world who we truly are.

She takes forty to forty-five minutes, and it's nothin' new. She finishes with "Show the world, show the country, show Iowa that we do not tolerate this hate, we do not tolerate bombings, we do not tolerate arson. Convict Johnny Desmond on all counts."

Alfredo is known for long closings and this one is at least an hour. But it's quite simple really.

"The police think they know, but they quit investigating. What would we know if they'd kept investigating instead of deciding that Johnny Desmond was the bomber? What do we know? We know there is no physical evidence linking him to the crime. They only have Nicholas Spencer, a man who is getting one of the greatest breaks in criminal history, only going to serve ninety days for blowing up a building and causing a fire. One-year probation and ninety days when he could have been sentenced to one hundred and twenty-five years in prison.

"But most importantly, he has a reason to lie.

"Who is it that has no reason to lie? It's Lester Kelvin. Yes, ladies and gentlemen, one man, one slight, older man who works the Islamic center without pay, who mops the floors and empties the trash bins to pay back a good that had been done him—he is the man who had no reason to lie. And he told you straight out that this is not the man he saw that night. This is not the bomber.

"Kelvin came here of his own free will to tell you Johnny Desmond wasn't there that night. He had no axe to grind. He had no offer of leniency from the state. In fact, did you notice that the State of Iowa didn't call him? The one man who was an eyewitness, they don't use as a witness. Why is that? But we called him and he just came and told you what he knew. That Johnny Desmond wasn't the bomber. Enough said. That's reasonable doubt in a nutshell."

Horgan gets one more chance, supposedly to react to what Alfredo says. And she does point out that Kelvin said I wasn't the man who saved him but couldn't say I didn't do the bombing. Then she goes off completely on a new tangent. "There is an atmosphere of hate in this country, in this state, in this city. Hate hate hate. You can stop it. You can at least prevent Johnny Desmond from hurting anyone else."

She goes through each crime, each element, lawyers call them, to show how I'm guilty of each one. "If you believe Nicholas Spencer, Desmond is guilty. And Spencer knows. He went there for the same reason. He works with Desmond. He knows him. He knows what they did.

"What about Lester Kelvin? Kelvin told you that Johnny Desmond did not save him that night. He also told you that the man who would hate enough to bomb wasn't the man who saved him. So whatever Lester Kelvin said or didn't say, Johnny Desmond was the man who bombed the Islamic center, an act of terrorism, an act of arson, an act of attempted murder, an act of hate.

"Convict him of arson, attempted murder, of criminal mischief, of assault, of everything under the sun."

It kind of shakes me. She's so strong again it's hard not to agree with her.

Just before noon, the jury goes out. As they do, I see Horgan and the skinny bald kid shake hands with Alfredo and Steve and Andrea, and everybody tells everybody what a good job they did. Nobody shakes my hand.

The judge tells me to stay in the courthouse. The lawyers and I can have an unused courtroom on the same floor. Alfredo and Andrea and I go in it, Steve runs across the street to the Hy-Vee, the new downtown grocery store, to get sandwiches.

"What do you think?" I ask.

"I never tell anybody anything at this stage," Alfredo says, "because I've been surprised so often. I thought yesterday went well for us. That's all I can say."

Andrea gives me a wink; Alfredo can't see it.

"How long will they be out?" I ask.

"First," she says, "they'll order lunch. After lunch, they'll start by picking a foreman, then who knows."

"Quicker the better," I say, but Angela and Alfredo are both shaking their heads to tell me I'm wrong.

"Quick verdicts are usually good for the prosecution," Andrea says.

"Oh," is all I can get out.

We sit there, quiet, maybe ten minutes. Steve is at the door. No sandwiches.

"We should have given them someone else's cell phone number," he says. "We have a verdict."

"Jesus Christ," Alfredo says.

I'm supposed to see whether they look at me when they come in, but I'm too nervous. I feel like I'm gonna fall down at the table. I don't think anyone else knows how this feels. Unless you've been charged with a crime and gone through a trial and are facing prison, how would you know? The jurors all kind of walk to the jury box in a hurry, and no one seems to look at anyone else.

When the jurors are in the box, the judge asks if they have a verdict. Fu Manchu stands up. "We do," he says.

He hands the verdict to the attendant. She hands it to the judge,

"As to count I, arson in the first degree," the judge says, "we the jury find the defendant Johnny Desmond not guilty."

Oh my God. I almost drop down on my knees. Andrea holds on to my arm.

"As to count II, attempted murder, we the jury find the defendant not guilty."

And so it goes, five times in all, five verdicts of not guilty.

It's over, just like that, in no time at all. I sit down. I can't help myself. Tears are falling down my cheeks. I turn. Jenny is there, reaching over the bench to me. I wrap my arms around her in glee. I lift her up, almost over the bench. Then it's Andrea, we are hugging. She holds on, won't let go of me. I can hear her crying. And then Alfredo and Steve shake my hands.

The judge asks if anyone wants the jury polled. Not sure what that means, but Horgan says yes. The judge asks each juror whether this is their verdict. They all say yes.

He thanks them, tells them they're relieved, but their lunch is waiting for them in the jury room. He tells them to wait because he wants to talk to them.

Then after they've left, the judge looks at me. "Mr. Desmond," he says, "you have been acquitted by a jury of your peers. Congratulations, sir, you are free to go. Your bond is canceled. And thank you to counsel for a well-tried case. The Court will issue a verdict of not guilty yet this afternoon."

We try to leave but at the bottom of the courthouse steps, there's a crowd of reporters. Three television cameras are on. Alfredo says he'll do the talking. We wait because Horgan is giving them a statement first.

She says we respect the jury's decision, but they got it wrong.

When Alfredo gets to the bottom of the stairs, Jenny and Andrea and I slip out the opposite way, and we're outside the courthouse before anyone can catch us.

"We're all going to the Brewhouse," Andrea says. "Come on, you two."

"I really need to get back to Maria," Jenny says. She hugs me again. "Enjoy it," she tells me. Andrea and I see her to her car, and when she pulls away, we start walking east. It's just two blocks from the courthouse, and we are on our second glass when Alfredo and Steve arrive.

"Congratulations, Johnny," Alfredo says. He orders beers for Steven and him. It is a big day.

"Mr. Fridley," I say, "I cannot tell you how much—"

"Then don't," he says, "don't. Besides, I think the person you really have to thank is Lester Kelvin."

We all swig a beer and then I ask, "What did he tell you beforehand?"

"You have to understand," he says, "that if I knew he was going to lie, I couldn't let him testify."

"Right, right," I say, "you told me that before."

"So the only thing he told me beforehand was that he was never going to remember it was you, not in a thousand years."

We all drink again. Then Alfredo stands. "Great win, guys. See you all tomorrow. Except you, Mr. Desmond. I never want to see you again."

My face burns. Then I get it. He knows. He knows why I did it. He knows who I am. And he still got me off.

Steve has one more beer. When it's finished, he turns to me. "You should know something," he says. I turn to him.

"We've been telling you something, going along, let's say, that may have given you a false impression that someone was bankrolling you."

"Ya," I answer.

"That was partially true. Some money did come in."

"OK," I say.

"But it wasn't . . . well, listen, what impression did you have about the money?"

"I figure Peter or one of the other people in the movement got it."

"Kind of what we figured. Remember, we never told you that."

"OK."

"The little money we got was from an eighty-year-old black woman who moved to Florida a few years ago when she hit big on a lawsuit here in Des Moines. Her brother is the Rev. Willis Garry of the First Universal Baptist Church of Des Moines."

"Christway Cathedral? Up on MLK?"

"That's the one."

"The black church?"

"African American, predominantly."

"I don't see—"

"Ask yourself who the deacons of that church might be."

"I assume you are going to tell me Lester Kelvin."

"Really close. No cigar. Actually, the deacon is Deanna Kelvin, his wife, who appreciated more than anyone that you saved Lester's ass that night."

"And they gave you fifty thousand?"

"Not even close," Andrea said, "we did it as a favor to Willis and Deanna. Millicent gave us enough money to cover expenses and to pay a little of the associates' time—that would be Steve and me."

"No money from Peter or anyone else in the movement?"

"Never heard from any of them."

I got up. I walked to the john and let her loose. I walked to the back patio, which was closed because it's winter, even though warm as hell, and stood there for a few minutes. The stuff going through my mind was just so disturbing I couldn't deal with it and didn't want to. When I walked back in the bar, Steve had left.

Andrea sits close to me. "He doesn't know you," she says. "Alfredo doesn't know who you are. Neither does Steve."

"Maybe," I say, "or maybe they know me better than you do."

She leans in to me, close like a lover, puts a hand on my face, pecks my cheek.

"Look," she says, "let's blow this joint. Come to my place." She moves her hand onto my leg, high up on my leg. I look at her. She is just so sexy. I am already responding physically. It's been so long. *What's wrong with an afternoon between the sheets with a woman who looks this fine?* At the moment, I can't think of one.

Fourteen

I EXPECTED AN apartment, but Andrea's place is more a townhouse. It's right downtown within a block of the Civic Center, and it's a two-story, furnished in modern millennial, if you get my drift. We sit in her living room, lookin' out on Grand Avenue, and she pours us each a glass of wine. A California cab that she claimed cost $100 a bottle. When you get past ten bucks, I can't tell the difference.

She swirled her wine, I sipped it. It was pretty good.

"Kind of wondering," I say, "what's next? Will Horgan appeal?"

"She can't," Andrea told me. "That the beauty of a jury's acquittal in a criminal case. It's the one big advantage the defense has. If we can get someone found not guilty, the state cannot appeal."

"Wow." But still, I waited for the other shoe to drop. Andrea said nothin'.

"Can they charge me with something else?"

"Never seen that happen, except if there was some other kind of incident. Basically, they get one chance to bring you down."

"Did you know all along where the money came from?"

"Not really. I'm an associate, not a partner. I get my salary either way."

She gets up, moves over to sit by me. She puts her wine down on the table, moves her hips to touch mine, and then brings her mouth to mine. We kiss lightly, then more urgently. I stand up.

"You know I want this, huh?" I said.

"Then come over here," she says, and then does the one thing I hoped she wouldn't. She unbuttons her blouse.

"Wait a moment," I say.

"Why?"

"Why?" I say, and I couldn't figure out why I was saying it either. *I mean, Christ, why wouldn't I sleep with this woman?* "Listen, I know what I'm gettin'," I say, "but what the hell are you gettin'? A guy who narrowly avoids prison. A guy who barely finishes high school and does it finally at reform school. A guy who puts siding on houses for a livin'. Have you thought about this?"

She smiles. It's a killer smile. God, those teeth hangin' over her lips. "Johnny," she says, with those gorgeous eyes, that blonde hair, over those gorgeous pointed boobs, "I'm not asking you to marry me. I just thought we might have some fun."

"It would be fun," I say. I mean, Christ, how could I deny it? I moved back to the sofa, where her blouse was open to her waist. I could see her white frilly bra and, better yet, what it held back. But it was her belly button, an innie, and that flat stomach that I had never seen before. We kissed softly. Then again, urgently and for a while. And even though I figure it's a mistake, that I shouldn't be here, I am here and this woman is offering me something I'd wanted for a very long time.

Jenny and Maria were both asleep when I walked in the house, just after one. I turn on the kitchen lights to reveal the remains of a pan of lasagne, one of my favorites, and something Jenny, who was not that good of a cook, claimed she couldn't make. There was an open bottle of red wine, too, probably bought from Sam's Club for five bucks, and a note from Jenny. "Congratulations, wish you'd been here," scrawled on a piece of legal pad paper.

I leave my clothes on and crawl on top of the covers on Peter's bed and fell asleep. I wake in the morning to Jenny's pushing on my right shoulder. "Get up, asshole," she says. The tone of her voice is clearly not affectionate. I groan.

"Look," she says, "I've got to go to class. I need you to take care of Maria. When I get back, we can make other arrangements."

Like that, she's gone. I nearly fall back to sleep, but then I hear Maria. Not so much a cry as a groan, her fussy sound. I stand up, go into the living room, and find her in her chair. I walk back to the bathroom, pee for just about forever, wash up, brush my teeth, and go in and get Maria. Her bottle is due in thirty minutes, but I pick her up and start rocking her. She isn't one for just rocking with you, but today she seems to take to it just fine.

I like it, too, just rocking back and forth, trying to get rid of this wine hangover that I wasn't used to. I almost fall asleep again, then think that I better put her down so I won't. But when I do that, she wails, so I pick her up and start rocking again. She quiets down, and we go on like that for a while. It finally comes time for her bottle and I warm it up and she takes it greedily. I then change her pants and put her down in the crib, then go to my room. When I wake up, I find Jenny and Maria in the living room.

"He lives," Jenny says.

"Look—" I say.

"Never mind," she said, "I don't need an explanation. She's a gorgeous girl."

"That ain't it," I say.

"What ain't it? You slept with her, didn't you?"

I ain't proud that I done it, but I done it. I lie to her. I just couldn't let go right then, not like I should have been able to. "No," I say. "Guess we might have, but I don't know. I just didn't know what to do to tell you the truth."

"Good," she says, walkin' over and kissin' the top of my head. "Now, you smell like a brewery. I can't believe I left my baby with you. Go get a shower."

I get up, start off toward my bedroom, and then turn to her. She nods. "I know," she says, "I know. Go get your shower."

BOOK FOUR

People are crazy and times are strange
I'm locked in tight, I'm out of range
I used to care, but things have changed

Bob Dylan, "Things Have Changed"

One

I T'S JENNY WHO convinces me to go. I don't know that I would have. A lot of water had passed under the bridge, as they say, and I thought maybe I should let good enough be. I had finally turned my life around, had a life, a family, and a business. Wasn't that enough?

"You know better," Jenny told me. I don't know that I did, but when Jenny speaks, I try to listen. It's like she's my Jiminy Cricket. So I told her I'd go see her. That's all. I didn't even promise that I'd talk to her, didn't promise that I'd tell her who I was. I wore my black SF Giants hat to hide my face just a little. But let's back up a moment.

But first, two days after I came home, I invite Andrea to coffee. She meets me on the Caribou on Ingersoll. Her office has a couple of new high-profile cases. They represent the high school kids accused of burning down one of the wooden bridges in Madison County. They also have the guy from the Bachelor TV show who ran into the back of a farmer and killed him. She starts to tell me about the new cases, then reaches across and puts her hand over mine.

"That was nice," she says.

"No shit," I say. "Probably the finest night in bed I ever had."

"But we won't have another, huh?"

How the hell do women know these things? How did Jenny know? How does Andrea know?

"It's just . . ." I don't know what to say.

"You don't have to say anything. Really. There's something I've known all along. Jenny's nice, she's sweet. You're a family. Still, I figured I could compete with Jenny, you know, on looks, on everything. But I knew I couldn't compete with that baby."

Deanna Kelvin calls Jenny the next week. They want the three of us for dinner Friday night. She says yes. She don't even ask me what I think, but what the hell could I say? The man saved my life. It's weird though. They have this little place on the east side, not exactly the ghetto, but a pretty poor area. Lot of little clapboard houses, and what's weird is, some of 'em are really well taken care of, others are let go. Kelvin's got this nice little yard out front, and although the driveway is coming apart, the house itself looks OK. You might call it a ranch; it's a one-story for sure, green in color. Deanna greets us at the door with hugs and kisses me on the cheek. She's about sixty, a big busty mulatto woman, kind of a ginger color, with an enormous white-toothed smile that, well, makes you feel OK. Seems like she'd crush Lester if they got romantic, but then I wonder if people that age still do have sex.

Lester ain't the next one at the door, though there are three other young women, all in various shades of black skin, two of 'em holdin' babies in their arms. They are chattering to Jenny and Maria and finally, me. Maria is excited, looking all around, taking it all in, as she does. She's too young to be scared of strangers, but she's sure interested in everything goin' on around her. Then there are three young men, all about the same build, all the same colorin', and they are introduced to me as Lester's sons. Not Deanna's, Lester's. Then from the other room, where the television set is still blarin', I'm introduced to Deanna's son and daughter. There are kids runnin' all over.

"My grandbabies," Deanna says, and there's this huge table laid out for dinner.

I'm introduced all over to so many kids, grandkids, friends, neighbors, and others I don't know who's who within a few minutes. Honestly, it's the most black people I've seen since jail. Most of 'em seem polite, courteous, but not like they really want to shake my hand. Deanna introduces me to Frederick—Frederick Milton Kelvin, Lester's oldest son. "This is the man who saved your daddy," she says, and Frederick stands in front of me, looking me over. He's probably five years older than me and taller, but he's not in that great of shape. I could take him if I had to. And for a moment, I think he may try something.

"Also the man who almost blew him up, right?" Frederick says.

"Milton!" Lester says. "This is a celebration. This is a night to enjoy each other and know what we done for each other, right, Mr. Desmond?"

"Johnny," I say. "It's Johnny."

"Am I right, Johnny?"

"I hope so, sir," I tell him, and I mean it.

"'Course it is," Deanna says.

And then we're all sitting around this table that underneath the cover must be a ping pong or pool table. There's a huge glazed ham, a whole turkey, and roast beef as well as all sorts of vegetables laid out in bowls, bowls that don't go together, some green, some white, some blue or red, in various shapes and sizes. I don't honestly recognize all the vegetables.

Lester says grace. We all bow our heads. There are three kids in high chairs, and only the youngest one doesn't comply. "Dear Lord," Lester begins, and says something lovely about how we ain't friends, so far we're just people that helped each other, but we hope to be friends someday.

Then the food is passed around and people eat fast and conversation goes on around me like I'm at a basketball game surrounded by fans from the other team. There's talk of March Madness, the NBA, the latest music on the radio, about the Muslim ban, and for some reason, about whether the Des Moines waterworks should be split up with the suburbs. I'm lost about half the time.

"You have a favorite NBA team?" Fred asks me.

"Don't have much time to watch," I say, "but I really like that Steph Curry."

Frederick bangs on the table. "I knew it! He's half white, right?"

It's Deanna who stands now and stares the young man down. And he backs down to her stare. Nothing is said, nothing has to be. "Sorry," he says.

"No," I say, "I see what you mean. But I don't think that's why he can hit a three-pointer from downtown."

"Well," he begins, "there is something else I want to ask you."

It's Lester now, who intervenes. "Silence," he says and there is.

He stands. He holds up a glass, and because there's been absolutely no alcohol tonight, I figure it's just water. "To Johnny Desmond," he says, "who risked his life to save mine."

The toast seems universal. If anyone else withholds the incantation, I don't know it. We drink our water.

It's an hour before most of the guests have left, except their daughter Chantelle, who, along with her two little girls, apparently live with the Kelvins.

Deanna asks Jenny if she wants to help her with the dishes. I know she doesn't mean it. Jenny has Maria in her arms, and there's no sign that she's expected to put her down. She's been in the arms of at least seven black women tonight, of all ages and times of their lives, but she finds her way back to Jenny for her nighttime feeding.

Lester and I walk into the screened-in porch, which is way too cold, but he doesn't seem to notice. "Want a beer?" he asks. I'm surprised but take a Bud Light from him as he opens his own.

"Son," he begins, "there's something I don't understand."

I sit down. I wait. Guess you know I ain't a big talker and now I just can't imagine I'll know the right thing to say.

"I take it from your quietness that you don't want to talk to me about it," he says.

"You may be the only person whom I owe an explanation to," I say. "Go on."

"How could you?"

"How could I blow up that center?"

"That's the question, son. How could you be that man? And how could the same man with the guts and goodness to go back and get me be the same man who'd blow up a building just 'cause it ain't his religion? I mean, what's the matter with you?"

I was still tryin' to figure out what to say when he just continued.

"Son," he says, "are you so full of hate? It's a hard thing for me to understand, seein' all I seen in this world till now, but I know there's still some of that—well, hell, there's a lot of that out there anymore. Still, I'm not sure I know what I'm tryin' to say. I guess I need Deanna to tell me what I mean. Do you know what I mean?"

"I don't think I'm filled with hate," I start.

"But then, son, how could you do it? A bomb! My God, that was dangerous to you too, wasn't it?"

"Yes, sir, it was," I say. And then it strikes me, why am I being like this to this old, bent -over, gray hairs-haired, thin little African? I once woulda used the n-word for him so easily and now that seems wrong. This old, little, bent -over black man? Why am I listenin' to him like this, takin' this shit from him? And I am. I don't even feel mad at him, just a little, well, uncomfortable, I guess. I've been lookin' down at brown people so long, it's hard to look up. But this man kept me out of prison. Ssimple as that. And I find, when I think about it, that I do care what he thinks about me.

"Listen—" I say.

"No." He stops me. "You listen. 'Cause you don't have to tell me anything. You saved my life and I done a good turn back to you, but it ain't the same and I ain't sayin' it is. So if you don't want to talk to me about it, I understand. It just don't seem . . . I don't know . . . right, somehow. So I guess I'd like to know."

Lester has this way of working his way around to what he's saying. No point in saying something with three words when ten will do. At first, I found it annoying. Now I kinda enjoy it.

"OK," I say, "I want to tell you. I'm not sure I understand things either and I'm not sure I know what I'm going to be thinkin' goin' forward, but it ain't the same as I was thinkin' goin' into this, I'll tell you that much.

"I lost my whole family when I was a boy. Social workers took me away from my mom. I never had a dad. I lost my grandma who really did take care of me. When I got out of reform school, well, the people in the movement, they were the ones who helped me, cared for me. They were my family. But I just don't know anymore."

"And you fell in with Peter Thurgood? He's a hater, son, pure and simple."

"Maybe," I said, "but he was the only one I ever had who believed in me. So I followed his lead."

Lester just nodded. It seemed like it meant that he understood, whether he did or not.

"I had nothin'. I didn't have school. I didn't have a trade. He helped me. Gave me a place to live. Gave me hope. Got me in the sidin' trade. And you should know, Jenny is his daughter—"

He looked like he was not only surprised but angry.

"But she's nothin' like her dad. In fact, she's the person who's really tryin' to get me to change how I think."

Again, nothing. I'm sittin' there and he's standin' there and sometimes walkin' back and forth in the room. And I think again, *what do I care?* But I do. It's a funny feelin'.

Deanna walks in the room.

"What's going on here?" she asks.

"I'm just trying to figure things out for myself," Lester says. "I mean you and I both know what we owe this boy, but what kind of a person bombs an educational center? I mean really, how much hate is in this boy to do something like that?" I don't know how long he would have continued, but Deanna put out a hand and shushed him.

"Lester Kelvin," she said.

"Yes, ma'am."

"Is this the man here who saved your life?"

"You know it is."

"Is this the man who risked his own life to save your skinny old black ass?"

Lester smiles. "Yes, ma'am."

"So what's the point?"

"The point is," I say, just a little afraid to get in between those two, "that there was somethin' wrong with me to do that, and I didn't really know it at the time. And I owe you two a lot. I could be in prison overalls right now, spending most of the rest of my life that way. Instead, I get to be here with Jenny and that baby and get to know you folks, and I guess I'm trying—" Now Deanna's hand is up for me.

"None of that, now," she says.

"Lester," she says, turning to him, "this man saved your life and that's why we called him over and don't forget it."

Two

I KEPT SLEEPING in Peter's bed and Jenny kept not joining me there. We hugged, kissed a little, but like two young kids, never went further. Without knowin' for sure, I assume that this is all some kind of payback for my sleeping with Andrea, which was fine, except, of course, that I wasn't sleeping with either of them.

One night, I hear Jenny up and about with the baby. I take it Maria wouldn't sleep, but neither did she want to feed or rock or anything else that Jenny offered. I got up, wearing only my pajama bottoms, sandals, and a T-shirt, picked up the baby, grabbed my car keys off the counter, and went into the garage. By the time I had Maria belted in the car seat in the back of my car (a car seat which I had paid dearly for and had only been used twice), Jenny was in the front seat.

"Why don't you try to get some rest?" I said.

"I have to see how this works out," she answered. We backed out, worked south to Hickman, and then turned south to the freeway. By the time I hit the western edge of the freeway and turned on to 35/80 heading north, Maria was sound asleep. By the time I got to the East Mixmaster, Jenny was asleep too. I drove around to the Thirty-first Street exit, worked back to the house, and found that the baby was sleeping so soundly I could get her down in her crib.

Then I walked back, fell onto Peter's bed, and prepared to renew my own night's rest. But moments later, Jenny was beside me. I reached for her, threw a hand over her back, and she snuggled in. I turned to kiss her, which I did, on her forehead, and soon after I heard the sounds of her dozing off again.

After that, we slept together. That was all. Like an old married man and wife, we shared a bed, in our pajamas, hugging and kissin' sometimes, but mainly just spoonin'. Was it enough? Seemed like it for a bit.

Two nights later, just after we get to bed, we hear somebody poundin' on the front door. I walk out in my undies, go to the door, look out the curtains, and there's at least eight Des Moines cops there. I figure it was in for me then, no doubt. I open the door and tell them that the baby's asleep and what do they need?

It's that cop Thill. I don't see the other one. "Jenny Thurgood," he asks. She walks up behind me, rubbing her eyes, wearing her baby-doll PJs and an open pink robe. "Ya," she says.

"We have a warrant to search the home of Peter Theodore Thurgood, signed by the Honorable Robert Blank, District Court Judge, District 5C, Polk County District Court."

"Wait, wait, wait," I say, but he pushes the search warrant into my chest and tells me to sit down on the couch and shut up. Jenny tells him about the baby bein' asleep, and one of the other cops takes her by the elbow and walks her into the baby's room. They go in and then he comes out and shuts the door behind them. I pop open my cell and call Andrea's private number.

"This is Andrea," she says, and I think she's still at work.

"Listen," I say and tell her about the search warrant.

"Instruct Officer Thill to await my presence," she says and she's off. I ain't even sure she knows where we live. Thill, upon hearing this, laughs and they start pulling open all the cabinets and tossing everything out. "Where's Thurgood's desk?" he asks, and since there really ain't any such thing, I tell him that and show him where Peter's bedroom is. They tear all the covers off our bed, pull the mattress off the box spring, then pull up the box spring and lean it against a wall. They open the closets and remove everything (though most of it is my clothes), take everything off every shelf then remove all four shelves and pound on the back wall, punching in two or three holes.

Then they go through the chest of drawers (again mostly my shit) and tear everything out and toss it on the floor. I've got $400 in a pocket and they take it. All the wooden drawers in the living room are taken out and the contents dumped. Nothin' is left alone, nothin' in the kitchen, nothin' in the bedrooms, including the spare one, which is more like storage space. They find a safe. I knew it was there but never knew how to get in it, much less what was in it. They take it. They take everything out of the bathroom medicine cabinets, take everything out of all the drawers by the sinks, throw everything out of the cabinet below the sink, throwing various soaps, cleansers, and the like on the kitchen floor, then take everything out of the refrigerator and the freezer, piling it on the kitchen table. That's when Andrea walks in the front door in a dress and overcoat, her work clothes.

"What the hell is going on here?" she asks at nearly the top of her voice.

Thill brings her the warrant.

She reads it. As we hear things breaking and crashing in the basement, she reads aloud, "'Various papers of Peter Thurgood related to Nordic USA Warriors.' What the hell are you doing taking stuff out of the refrigerator?"

There's two of 'em in the garage too, going through Jenny's car.

"You know he hasn't been here since you arrested my client, right?" she asks Thill.

"The warrant is valid. It's for this address. Shut up, counselor, before I arrest you." Andrea sits next to me on the couch, continues to read the warrant, and whispers to me that they have a right to the search. The last thing they do is roust Maria's room, taking everything out of all the drawers and the closets, though it's mainly stuff for the baby. Jenny picks up Maria and they pull up her bedding, but this they do put back.

They take Jenny's laptop, but it's really hers and there's nothing on it. I have no idea if they found anything, but it didn't seem like it, unless there's something in the safe. In the spare room, there was some Nordic USA literature, but they didn't seem interested. I know Jenny is clean, and I don't do drugs anymore and Peter was very anti-drug, so I didn't expect them to find anything like that and I don't think they did. They ignore the liquor bottles. Peter kept nothing regarding the movement here. He was just too smart for that. I didn't know what was in the safe, but I guess it would be personal papers, tax returns, maybe a will—nothing about the movement.

When they're done, Maria is awake and Jenny sits in the recliner in the living room and feeds her. Andrea and I try to put things back, but it's pretty much useless. They have made a great hash of the property, even pouring out some powders and lotions into the bathtub. Jenny has a crying Maria in her arms and asks if she can use my car to take her to a friend's. I throw her the keys. Andrea and I work a little longer, at least trying to save any perishables, picking up stuff and putting it in cabinets and drawers, so you can at least walk in the house. Some stuff is ruined. They opened white packaged items in the freezer. They poured cereal out on the counter, poured the coffee beans out of the plastic canister, and atop that, the flour from its white canister. It's just after two when I tell her she should get some sleep. "We can do the rest of this tomorrow."

"You're right," she says. She walks into my bedroom. We lift the box spring back on, take the mattress off the floor, put it back on and then she starts pulling a sheet on top of it. When she's got the bottom sheet on, she sits down on it and pulls off her shoes. Her stockings are next. I get just a quick look at her upper leg as she removes her left stocking. She starts unbuttoning her dress.

She lifts her face and looks directly at me: "Should I keep going?" I'm on top of her, on the bed, pulling her dress up to her waist, and then, well, you know. We kiss. And again. Tongues come out. She pulls her dress off, I unfasten her bra in back and I can't look away. I don't even turn down the lights.

Jenny's bright. She knows. She has to. I spend time trying to work. I had all the work I wanted before I was charged, but it dropped off after that. My old contractors, the ones who liked me, no longer are interested. I'm thinking about a different trade or going back to school. I spend time watching the baby while Jenny goes to school. But I also spend afternoons and early evenings at Andrea's. She's a willing, daring lover, and we have found a joy in the physical act that's beyond anything I'd ever had before. But every night, I'm back in Peter's bed, and Jenny lies next to me, spooning sometimes, rolling away sometimes, never asking, not wanting to know or knowing without asking, but waiting, waiting to see if Andrea and I are a thing or a just a quick fix like a dose of meth.

A week later, she comes home from school and I see the resolve on her that I know well. "What the fuck is going on?" she asks, as if she doesn't know.

"I don't know what to say—"

"Johnny, you never know what to say."

Touché, I guess. Who am I to argue with that? She has Maria in her arms and walks off, into the kitchen. I go to my room, lie down on the bed, and think, as much as I can. It's easy to say I want Jenny. But I want Andrea too, no doubt about it. And the sex . . .

I go out after a little while, but Jenny is in Maria's room and I hear nothin' from her. Finally, I get in my car and go out. I hit a Coney Island place on southeast Fourteenth and put away more grease than any human being needs, in three sittings. I drive down the street, past the Capitol building, and then loop downtown. Just after nine, I come back into the house, happy that my keys still work.

The house is quiet. I'm pretty sure that Jenny and Maria are home, but there's little sign of it. I peek through the door of Maria's room. She's cooing and I open the door a little more. Jenny's there in the rocking chair and she shushes me. I close the door, pee, brush my teeth, and take off my clothes. I usually sleep in my underwear, but since Jenny has been coming in, I've taken to wearing my gym shorts. I turn off the light and try to sleep, but I keep thinkin' and nothin' seems clear. I want a home and a family and I've got one with Jenny. But it ain't my home and it ain't my baby. Is it real love? I mean, we haven't even made it and I'm sure enjoyin' Andrea. I make up my mind. I get up, grab some fresh socks out of my drawer, put them on my feet, take off my shorts, and look for my jeans. It's time I spent the night with Andrea.

I hear the baby cry and Jenny calls out. "Honcho," she says, "could you get a bottle ready?"

We're tryin' not to feed her at night, but Jenny is the mom and she's decided to make an exception. I get to the kitchen, find one of Jenny's bottles in the fridge, and put on a pan of water to warm it. Within minutes, I'm bringing her the bottle.

"Go ahead," she says, so I stand there like a doofus, in my underwear, holding Maria and feeding her. I look down and I know. Finally, I know. Or think I do.

"Jenny," I say as Maria is finishing up, "come to bed with me."

Minutes later, she's standing by my bed. I pull off her shirt, unbutton her jeans, and then pull them down. I remove my own underwear, lie down, and Jenny is beside me. We kiss. I undo her bra. They tumble out. I move my hand down to her panties and begin sliding them down her hip.

"You sure?" I ask.

"Are you?"

I lie again. I have no idea what I'm sure of. Just a moment ago, I was headed to Andrea's. I don't tell her that what I want to do is try this out, which, I am, somewhat. I want to see if the sexual act is as good as it has been with that blonde with overbite who will do virtually anything in bed. I want to see if the natural affection I have with this woman, with Jenny, will translate into good sex.

There is somethin' there, somethin' I don't have with Andrea. It's hard for me to say what. Jenny will never do all the things Andrea does, or let me do all the things to her that I do to Andrea. But it's nice. Better than nice. I enter her and we finish and then we hold each other and play with each other and I respond again, and this time, we do things as Jenny would like them. When we finish, when I am lying beside her, spooning, and I am lightly rubbing her shoulder, I feel . . . I am not quite sure, but I guess the closest thing to what I feel is contentment. There is no disappointment. There is no feeling of "I wish I were with Andrea."

This is what I want.

Three

THEY CAUGHT PETER in Kentucky. I thought he was holed up in Georgia, but he was driving a rented SUV when he got stopped just outside Lexington. They seized several thousand dollars and two guns, a handgun and a shotgun, both of which were illegal for him to possess, because he's a felon. Alfredo told me the first day I met him that Iowa had warrants out for Peter right after my arrest. The lawyers were worried that if they caught Peter, he'd sing, and that might be the nail in the coffin for my case. I didn't think he'd tell anybody anything. But honestly, I don't know anymore whether I really know him.

Andrea and I met him in one of the lawyer rooms of the jail, the morning after he had returned. Technically, he was represented by the public defender. Alfredo's firm couldn't represent him. And I don't know how Andrea sneaked me into a lawyer room. I didn't want to Skype with Peter because that's all recorded by the jail. The lawyer rooms are small, with circular tables and four plastic chairs, but the conversations there are supposedly not recorded. I think the whole thing was tricky, 'cause Andrea isn't his lawyer and I ain't even that.

Peter looks older, thinner. His hair is unkempt, he has a three-day beard, and of course, the usually well-dressed fifty-five-year-old is sitting in a smelly orange jumpsuit. Reminds me of when he came to see me.

"I'm Johnny's lawyer," Andrea tells him, "not yours. But I have to keep his confidences."

"And I've told her this is all privileged," I say.

"A third party destroys the privilege," Peter answered, and Andrea nodded in agreement. Once again, it's a mistake to underestimate Peter Thurgood.

"If somebody wants to tell," she said, "but that's up to you, Mr. Thurgood. And you're the one in jail, not Johnny. He was acquitted, so it would be pretty difficult for the State of Iowa to prosecute him again."

"Worked out pretty good for you, huh, kid?" he said.

"Not with any help from you," I answered him.

I looked at him. This little man was the one who had given me most of the things I had, but also had encouraged me to hate, to join the movement and had caused me to face prison time. That ain't to say I wasn't responsible for my actions, just that it was at Peter's behest that I did a lot of 'em. He's also Jenny's father and Maria's grandfather. And he helped me over and over, including givin' me the place over his garage, even if it was to get my help with the movement. Like just about everything else in my life, I'm just flat-out confused about how I feel.

"So this is what, an intervention? Are you here to tell me how you've been hurt by me and I didn't do enough?"

"Forget that," I said. "I know how I feel and I don't think you care."

There was a look on his face of what, surprise? Maybe it was acceptance.

"I really thought you were helping me. I thought you were bankrolling me, supporting me, tryin' to keep me out of prison."

"Didn't need to, though, did I?" Peter asked. "I figured it was a great ploy, a Afro lawyer."

Andrea groans in disgust.

"Look," he says, "I need to know one thing and only one thing. You helping them?"

"I ain't said anything to anyone," I tell Peter. "And I won't."

He sits back, apparently in relief. "I suppose they got Spencer?"

I want to tell him what I know. That Spencer's deal was just for me, didn't include Peter, and Nick, whom Peter might run into in jail one of these days, had no real incentive to turn on Peter. What's more, as we both know, Nick never dealt with Thurgood directly. I gave him all the instructions. They came from Thurgood, but Spencer would only know that from me. Classic hearsay. But Andrea has warned me, don't say a thing. She's pretty sure it isn't recorded, but she doesn't want me to admit any crime to Peter, whom she believes could still try to help himself by ratting me out.

"Nick is in jail. You haven't seen him?"

"Pretty sure they're keepin' us apart," he says.

And we're at an impasse. I want to tell him I love his daughter, love his granddaughter, but not in front of Andrea. And I don't want to know any more about how he helped me or didn't help me. Andrea has told me that my acquittal will make it tougher for the State to prosecute Peter. That's probably all the help I can give him.

"All right, Peter," I say, "is there anything you need?"

"Son," he says to me, after a minute, "you were a good soldier."

That's the thing. Andrea gives me the sign, the one that says shut up. But I want to answer him. I want to say, *That's the problem. You made me think I was a soldier. But all I ever did was hurt people. I didn't do anything to make things better. I just thought I was. I wasn't a soldier at all, just a kid with ready fists and lots of guts who was willing to lose my life if need be to blow up a stupid educational center because it was for Muslims. And the man who led me into all this, that man that I once loved—that man almost cost me my freedom. And it was a black man, in Peter's words, a Afro, who kept me from going to prison and let me have a life again.*

'Course, I don't say any of that. I just tell him goodbye, and I hand him a picture of Maria.

I take Andrea to lunch. Remarkably, she tells me it's over.

"Look, Johnny, I really enjoyed it. It was great. You're good in bed and it was lots of fun. But what else have we got in common?"

I stand, lean over the table, kiss her forehead. I'm glad she doesn't back up to avoid it.

"You, Andrea," I say, "are one classy woman. I'm always goin' to miss you."

"I'm not goin' anywhere," she says. "And you are just so interesting. So we're going to be friends." Which makes me smile.

I've been tryin' to figure out what to do next about Lester Kelvin. I'm inclined just to let it go. We're different people, and I'm pretty sure we aren't gonna be friends any time soon. Plus, I still got that white supremacist stuff going around in my head. I almost want to call it crap, but I ain't sure yet. It's what I believed a long time, and for all I know, if I really thought about it, I still do, to some degree. All I'm really sure about is that I don't know anything for sure.

Jenny takes hold of things. She comes home from school one afternoon and tells me that Lester and Deanna are comin' over for dinner.

"What?" I ask. "Geez."

"You're cooking," she says.

I run to Fareway. I ask for a bread-and-butter roast, the Dahl's special, but since Dahl's closed, Fareway gives me the closest thing to it. I get a bag of potatoes, onions, and carrots, and I have everything in the oven by three.

Lester and Deanna come in about six. She's sportin' a bottle of white wine. I put it on the table, alongside the salads, and I never say a word. I ain't exactly a wine expert, just what Andrea has taught me, and I know better than to bring that up.

Maria is in her high chair. It's almost a first for her. She doesn't eat table food yet, but she does like being part of the party. Lester and Deanna dig in and they both, almost at the same moment, tell Jenny how good everything is.

"Johnny's the cook," she says.

They both act surprised. I tell them I learned it from a farmer who was my foster parent for almost a year. "It's just about the only thing I got out of being in foster care for so many years," I say.

We eat up, drinkin' the wine, talkin' about next to nothin'. They seem afraid to bring up anything about the law, crime, Trump, or any of what's goin' on in town. They tell us about the grandkids, about their kids, and about the warm weather we've been havin'.

After we finish, we pile the dishes in the sink, and Jenny and Deanna start in on 'em. Lester and I go into the living room, but you got to know that it's within five feet of the dinky kitchen. I get Maria out of the high chair and bring her in with me, put her down on the floor under the play gym, and we both watch her, smiling all the time.

"Still livin' in Thurgood's house, I see," Lester says.

"He's deeded it to Jenny," I tell him. "She's decided to sell and if we can find something different . . . Maybe in Clive. Windsor Heights. I don't know."

"Guess I'm goin' to have to accept that, if we are going to be friends." He laughs, just a little. Then I can see he is serious. "Are we going to be friends?"

I look at Lester Kelvin. I am not sure what to say. Truth is, I still think he's a lesser man, a lesser person, 'cause he's brown. I think this country was made by the white race, and the changes it's been undergoin' aren't for the best. All these Mexicans, havin' to speak Spanish, takin' jobs away from white people, all the crime in the inner city, all the poor women tryin' to raise families without any men around. At the same time, I don't know how to say this, but I kind of love this man. I have more natural affection for him than for Peter Thurgood or virtually anyone 'ceptin' maybe Jenny and Maria. And Andrea, but I'd never say that out loud. And truth is, I think maybe Deanna is one of the best people I know.

"I'd like that," I say.

Four, The Last Chapter

I T'S NOW SIX months since I was found not guilty. I feel no remorse over conning the jury, but I think back now and can't believe I was willing to put a bomb anywhere. And I have a little pride in knowin' that once I realized there was someone there, I made sure that person didn't die in a catastrophe of my makin'.

Nick got out of jail and moved away. Don't know where. I never talked to him again. Rumor is he's part of the movement, but I've found that movement rumors are not exactly, well, reliable. Peter Thurgood got bailed out, then got new charges in federal court, and they came to arrest him again. They came just after six in the morning. Jenny and I had just gotten up because Maria still doesn't sleep through the night. We told the deputies we hadn't seen him since he got out, which was the truth. They searched our house and the car, and that's the last we saw of Peter. Someday they'll catch up to him, I'm sure. When they do, Andrea tells me, he'll go away for a while.

Andrea's got a new boyfriend, a lawyer for one of the downtown firms. He comes over with her sometimes, and then sometimes Andrea sits for Maria so Jenny and I can go out. He tells me he's a transactional lawyer, whatever the hell that means. Andrea says it means he's never in a courtroom. They seem good together, and I'm OK with it, even though I miss bein' able to run over to her townhouse on Saturday afternoons for a blow job. The nicest thing is that she and I are still friends, and you have to give Jenny the credit for that.

Maria's bio-father, as Jenny calls him, is still serving time. He got transferred from Newton to Fort Dodge. Andrea did some legal work for us, result of which is that we're terminating his rights to Maria. I had to give an affidavit sayin' I was goin' to adopt her, which is a no-brainer, even though Jenny and I have not yet decided to get married. It'll be a first for both of us. But that seems funny. Seems like we're already married. We've slipped into an easy way of bein' together: we sleep together, raise Maria together, I put any money I get in her checking account, and most nights, when she comes into bed, I reach for her. That part is damn fine, but it's not what I had with Andrea. It's less and it's more. Jenny once told me we were not having sex, but making love. I like to think that's true.

Jenny took a job at the Blue Sky Diner. I was runnin' out of cash and having a hard time findin' work. Then Lester took me to see Abdul Mohammed, the same man whose center I once bombed. He wasn't exactly friendly with me, although Lester told me he'd never seen the man be anything but courteous to any one in existence. "You," Lester said later, slapping me on the shoulder, "are the exception to the rule." Finally, Abdul told Lester that we should start up a business. There's investment money for minority businesses and lots of houses in the poor areas of this town need fixin' up and lots of government money is available for that. And so the Capital City Remodeling, Repair, and Refurbishment Co. was born. Andrea did the paperwork, filed us with the state and the feds, and Lester and I filled out the minority business part, allowing us to get a federal loan at a low interest rate. He has to own 40 percent, and he does, but he doesn't really get any profits. I'm employing two of his kids, and as a result, there ain't much profit. But business is growin' and I think we're goin' to have somethin' here. And since I'm out of the money I got from that robbery, I am finally able to help with our family's finances.

Plus, Jenny convinced me to take a class with her at the community college. The suburban campus has a day care and we take Introduction to Western Civilization on Tuesday and Thursday nights. It's mind-blowin'. And I don't mean just those Greeks and Romans and all that. I mean that I enjoy going to school. That's a first. I talk in class, I read the assignments and then google the topics and read some more. Jenny claims I'm showin' her up, which ain't good, but she takes it well. If it's true, honest to God, I think it's the only time I show her up.

And I love her. I know I should be able to say somethin' more about that, but I can't. I love her. When she walks in the house, I feel happy. When I see her with Maria, it makes me feel, well, like life ain't that bad. When she comes to bed with me, I feel like I finally have what I want in this world, and I ain't lettin' go.

And then Jenny tells me. She's the one who convinced me to go. I don't know that I would have. A lot of water had passed under the bridge, as they say, and I thought maybe I should let good enough be. I had finally turned my life around, had a life, a family, and a business. Wasn't that enough?

"You know better," Jenny told me. I don't know that I did, but when Jenny speaks, I try to listen. It's like she's my Jiminy Cricket. So I told her I'd go see her. That's all. I didn't even promise that I'd talk to her, didn't promise that I'd tell her who I was. I wore my black SF Giants hat to hide my face just a little.

I go in right after work one night. It's a bit of a drive to the west side, 'cause we're workin' near the fairgrounds, but I go in, still a bit dirty, still wearin' sunglasses and the dark Giants hat, tryin' to hide my face and I sit in a booth by myself. She comes to me. "What can I get you?"

I order iced tea, scrambled eggs and hash browns and toast. She smiles. "Pot roast on special tonight?" she says. I stick with the breakfast. It's a favorite of mine.

I sit and watch. I drink my iced tea, and when my meal comes, I pick at my eggs but wolf down the greasy hash browns, because a day of putting up new drywall in an old house has given me an appetite. I just keep lookin' at her and watchin'. I don't want to give away that that's all I'm there for. And she's busy, which helps. She don't have time to pay attention to what I'm doin'. She's still thin, but not the thin of bein' on drugs. She's still kind of pretty. I always thought she was. I can tell she's had a hard life, but her hair is still blonde, it's curly now, and she's wearing pretty blue glasses. She's friendly and courteous to everyone and seems to do a good job as a waitress. She brings me tea without my askin'.

"Like workin' here?" I ask.

She smiles. "Better than my day job," she says. I get that. It's tough to make it these days. So far, Trump hasn't fixed that.

"Oh, what else do you do?"

"Honey," she says, "is there anything else you need?"

It's been so long. I don't know how to read her any more. I really don't. Is she pissed or just . . . what?

"It's flattering, honey," she says, "but I could be your mother."

I snicker, just a little. I hesitate, but still. It's just too much in a way.

"The check," I say. And she writes it out right there standin' by my table.

I leave her the exact amount, then pull out two one-hundred-dollar bills and put them underneath the check. She's the only waitress, so I'm pretty sure she'll get 'em.

I walk out, to my new truck, the one our business bought with the government's minority loan money. I still can't get over that.

I open the door, start to get in.

She's come out of the door of the diner.

"Honey," she says, "I think you made a mistake."

"Nope," I say, "just my good deed for the day."

"It's too much," she says.

"It ain't, though." And I get in my front seat.

"Well, thank you," she says, "it'll mean a lot to me and my little girl."

And there it is. I'm getting ready to walk away, and I'm pulled back in, like nothin' else would. 'Cause I think, I guess that that little girl is OK, but can I just leave things as they are without bein' sure? I remember it all, my life before, how I suffered, even the things I want to forget. I don't know what to do, so I decide I got to go back and ask Jenny. She'll know what to do.

Which means, of course, that this isn't the last time I'll see my mother.